THE GERMAN PLOT

Heinrich Himmler replaced his glasses. "This is a war, among other things, of terror and counterterror. This weapon would be far more decisive than gas. Can you imagine London uninhabitable for a decade? The British will make peace to preserve their cities! They're too decadent to accept the losses that the German people will. That's why retaliation won't work for them. We can hold them to ransom, because we are willing to give everything! And when peace comes, Dr. Siegner will have time to prepare the last argument—the bomb! Good night, gentlemen."

We will send you a free catalog on request. Any titles not in your local book store can be purchased by mail. Send the price of the book plus 50¢ shipping charge to Tower Books, P.O. Box 270, Norwalk, Connecticut 06852.

Titles currently in print are available for industrial and sales promotion at reduced rates. Address inquiries to Tower Publications, Inc., Two Park Avenue, New York, New York 10016, Attention: Premium Sales Department.

THE
FENRIS OPTION

R. D. Jones

TOWER BOOKS **NEW YORK CITY**

A TOWER BOOK

Published by

Tower Publications, Inc.
Two Park Avenue
New York, N.Y. 10016

PROLOGUE

Kharkov-Berlin

May 30–31, 1942

The major climbed the dugout steps into the daylight and gulped a breath of the spring air. After the fug of the underground command post it felt alive; it carried, for a change, only the slightest stink of burning and high explosives.

He unfolded the rough map the Wehrmacht colonel had drawn for him, and studied it. It was several kilometers from the command post to his destination, a wood surrounding a ravine to the east. It would be a slow journey, what with the smashed-up terrain and the danger of mines. He glanced at the sky with irritation. It was getting late in the day.

He tramped across the soft earth to the waiting halftrack. The driver was dozing behind the wheel, and the replacement gunner they had brought was looking more nervous than ever.

As the major clambered into the vehicle the driver snapped awake and looked at him expectantly. The major gestured at a muddy track angling off to the left.

"Go along that for two and a half kilometers. There's a fork just short of a village; turn right there and I'll give you more directions."

The halftrack slued forward, lurching. The driver cursed. "Sorry, Major. We haven't had any clutch spares for these things for weeks. This one's just about had it."

The major didn't answer. He pulled a photograph from his tunic pocket and studied it closely. The face in the picture was young, almost unformed. There's something there, though, he thought, something they want badly. He put the photograph away.

The heavy vehicle clattered over the harrowed Russian landscape. This area had been savagely fought over as little as a week ago and there was a lot of wreckage about. From the city of Kharkov to the north, columns of greasy smoke still rose thousands of meters in the dusty air. The Russian counteroffensive had come within a hair of recapturing the city, but had finally been driven back after suffering frightful casualties.

And plenty of losses for us, too, the major reminded himself. He glanced down at the map on his knee. A streak of mud disfigured the Wehrmacht field-gray of his trousers. He flicked at it with a distaste that was directed not entirely at the mud. I'll be glad to get back into SS black again, he thought; this cloak-and-dagger business isn't what I bargained for when Weil asked me to help.

"There's the fork. Go along it for a kilometer. Then start looking for some unit signposts." He peered at the sun. "Go faster. We're a long distance away yet."

The halftrack's engine protested as the vehicle accelerated. The three men began to bounce on the hard seats like peas on a drum. The driver glanced sideways at the major whenever they struck a particularly rough stretch.

The major ignored the glances; the rough ride was the least of his concerns at the moment. He badly wanted to find the man in the photograph and get him onto the plane

6

before dawn. The trouble was that this part of the front was still disorganized, with widely separated units trying to regroup after the fighting. It might take hours to find the right tank platoon. I hope to Christ he hasn't been killed, worried the major.

What did Berlin want him for, anyway? They wanted him in a hurry, there was no doubt about that. And the security on the operation was unusually tight. The major, as a crosscheck on the man's identity, had a question to ask him, and a memorized list of answers to expect; but he himself had no idea what either the question or the answers meant. He had overheard one phrase, dropped in an unguarded moment, but it was quite opaque.

Physics, Weil had said. It had something to do with physics.

The stream was so noisy that Siegner barely heard the popping of the first shots from the trees on the east rim of the ravine. Then, simultaneously, three small fountains rose in the water a rifle's length ahead of him, and the jerrycan he was filling was jerked from his grasp.

A large boulder jutted from the streambed a meter to his left. He threw himself behind it as more bullets splintered the stones where he had been kneeling. He caught his elbow painfully on an underwater obstruction and swore. The water was six inches deep and icy but he was sweating.

They must be green, he thought. Shooting downhill like that threw them off, veterans wouldn't have missed. How the devil am I going to get out of here?

He was protected by the boulder but even a poor marksman would kill him before he got back up the bank to the trees. They were obviously stragglers, though; the main Russian resistance had ended in this area several days previously. They might very well melt eastwards into the woods as soon as they realized they had missed.

Cautiously he raised his head. Rock splinters zipped through the air.

They obviously don't know about the tanks up above, he thought. Bloody hell. Why didn't Hoffman detail someone to cover me? Or why didn't I ask? We've both been in Russia long enough to know better. He resigned himself to wait until someone noticed how long he was taking to fetch the water. He'd have to keep an eye peeled to warn them when they came, though.

The late sun fell on his uniform without warming him. His sweat dried and turned as cold as the water in which he lay. There was no more firing from the east bank. Five minutes passed.

He heard a faint hullo from above.

"Snipers!" he shouted, as loud as he could. "Keep down!"

The calling ceased. Still no shots from the woods. Hoffman's voice trickled down the bank. "D'you know where they are?"

"I'm not sure. There's a dead tree straight across from me. It might have been from there."

"Just a minute."

Siegner waited. Then a tank engine started up; he could hear it faintly over the rush of the stream. The roar grew louder and was punctuated by the squeak and clatter of treads. The long 75-millimeter gun of a Mark IV tank poked over the edge of the ravine and stopped. Siegner covered his ears.

The gun banged twice, violently. Branches, mixed with smoke and dust, flew from the trees on the east bank of the ravine. The tank's machine gun hosed the woods for a few seconds.

8

"Shake a leg," called Hoffman after everything had fallen back to earth.

Siegner put his head out, cautiously, from behind his boulder. Nothing. He stood up, half-expecting a fusillade from the trees. The woods were silent. He sighed and picked up the jerrycan. It had been holed but was still usable.

"Thanks," he called upward.

"Don't mention it." Hoffman scrambled down the bank. "Do you want a hand with the water?"

"It's a bit steep to haul both cans up at once."

"By the way," Lieutenant Hoffman asked him as they labored up the slope, "what've you been up to while my back was turned? Regiment radioed that somebody was coming out to the line to see you. More or less told us not to let you get killed before whoever-it-is arrives."

Siegner halted, partly to catch his breath. "I haven't any idea what anybody wants to see me for. Anyway, I haven't been out of your sight since March."

"It's been an interesting three months, hasn't it? One damned thing after another."

They arrived at the tank line hidden among the trees. Hoffman slouched off in the direction of the latrine; Siegner gave the water to the cooking detail and squelched away to the command tank to find his other pair of socks. While he pulled off his wet boots and dried his feet he wondered about the signal from Regiment. Could they possibly be scouring the Wehrmacht for scientists to do weapons research? He felt a hint of excitement at the idea of getting out of Russia but clamped down on it immediately. No use raising too much hope.

Still . . . since he had arrived in Russia he had worked out, in his head, several possible uranium pile configurations, and had thought rather hard about the military applications of such a device. There was no way that anyone

9

back in Germany could know that, though, and in any case no one in authority had ever seemed very interested in such experiments. Their minds were too fixed on the conventional.

He shrugged mentally and put his boots on over the dry socks. It was damp, but bearable. He would find out why they wanted him before he did any more speculating.

By the time it was dark they had eaten and had posted sentries. Siegner was washing out his mess kit when the radio operator of the second tank of the platoon popped his head out of the hatch, and called softly, "Regiment's just radioed again. They want to know whether our visitors've turned up yet. Should I tell them we'll call back when they do?"

Hoffman looked up and was about to answer when, on a vagary of the evening wind, they heard the clatter and squeak of a tracked vehicle grinding up the slope to their rear.

"Ask them if there've been any loose Russian tanks reported around."

The radioman's head disappeared and reappeared a moment later. "They say no, Lieutenant, and have we got one?"

Hoffman kept his head cocked a moment longer and then relaxed. "It doesn't sound like a tank, I think it's a half-track. Tell Regiment our visitors just got here, whoever they are."

A couple of minutes later they heard the machine squeak to a stop, the slamming of doors, a challenge from their own sentry, and an irritable response. The men around the fire drifted away to find bedrolls. Hoffman and Siegner waited in the flickering glow.

Out of the dark woods, into the small circle of light

among the trees, stepped three men. The first, by his uniform, was a tank crewman—new to Russia by his apprehensive look—and behind him was the halftrack driver. The third wore a clean, pressed uniform with a major's insignia on it.

Everybody saluted. The major said:

"Lieutenant Hoffman? Sixth Regiment, Third Panzer?"

"Yes, sir."

"I'm late and in a hurry. I want to see your gunner, Peter Siegner."

"This is Siegner."

The major turned and looked him up and down, and then compared him to a photograph which he drew from his tunic. He appeared satisfied.

"I'd like to speak to him for a moment, alone."

"There's nobody around behind the end tank, sir."

When they had got well away from the others, the major said, "Tell me about graphite."

It is the uranium pile, Siegner thought. I'm getting out of here. To what? He was so tired that neither staying nor going seemed especially preferable.

"The other calculations were too small by half. Or more."

The major regarded him thoughtfully, as if waiting for him to add something. Then he said, "Good. You're the one I'm looking for. Get your kit."

"Now? But—"

"Your kit."

When Siegner got back to the fire with his gear the fresh-faced tank crewman was looking more apprehensive than ever, the driver was poker-faced, the major disinterested, and Hoffman was furious but too outranked to say anything.

He turned to Siegner and said quietly, "I can't believe you're behind this."

"I swear I'm not, Lieutenant. I haven't any idea what's going on."

"Good-bye."

"Good-bye, Lieutenant."

"I hope babyface here is as good a gunner as you were."

"I hope so too, sir." They both saluted.

The major, the driver, and Siegner went off down the hill. It was beginning to rain.

He was awakened two hours later by the rasp of heavy aircraft engines being run up not far away. He had fallen asleep in the lurching cab of the halftrack a few minutes after leaving the frontline position. The anonymous major had volunteered no information and Siegner had asked for none.

The halftrack ground to a halt. Siegner could make out little through the mudstreaked windows but supposed they were at some kind of an airfield checkpoint.

"Papers?"

A sentry had materialized from the darkness and was standing by the driver's door. The major, without speaking, handed a small booklet to the driver, who gave it to the sentry. There was the gleam of a hooded flashlight.

The sentry's voice was noticeably respectful when he handed the papers back. "Sir. The runway is about two hundred meters ahead, on your right. Please stay on the road. There are some unexploded shells about."

As they clattered along the track Siegner noticed that the aircraft engines had settled down to a steady pulse, as if it were about to take off. The halftrack slowed. The light of a distant flare glimmered on the squat outline of a Junkers 52 transport.

The halftrack stopped. "Get your kit and yourself onto the plane," instructed the major, "and don't get out until you're in Berlin. There will be a stop at the Brest-Litovsk airfield but you are not to be seen. The plane's crew will remain on the flight deck. There's food, water, and a pee-can under one of the benches. Someone will meet you at Tempelhof airport. D'you understand?"

"Yes, sir." Siegner saluted. The major touched his cap and disappeared into the waiting halftrack. As it clanked away Siegner tried to see the divisional insignia, but it was too dark. He turned and heaved himself and his kitbag up the ladder into the Junkers. From somewhere a ground crewman appeared, pushed the ladder in after him, and slammed the door. After a moment a dim light came on. He was alone in the cabin.

Stowing his kit under a bench, he searched until he found a belt with which to strap himself down. The Junkers was already in motion; it had turned slightly and was bumping over the rough grass of the airstrip. As it gained speed the corrugated fuselage sides banged and drummed until he thought the rivets would pull loose, and then quietened as the old transport hauled itself into the air and settled down to a sedate 160 miles an hour.

The drumming of the engines and the vibration were soporific. He fell asleep almost immediately, despite the hard bench and the chill of the unheated aircraft.

It was the first time he had ever flown. Originally he had wanted to join the Luftwaffe, but because of his studies he had left off trying for it until it was too late, and at the end of it all, the army had got him.

Siegner's father had always been bemused by the ease with which his son had grasped mathematics and physics. A clever but not well-educated man himself, he had done

13

well, after 1933, as a small tool-and-die manufacturer. Peter was very good with machine tools himself; an only child, he had spent most of his school holidays building models in his father's workshops.

He grew up in a good, solid, middle-class neighborhood on the outskirts of Brandenberg, and had done all his pre-university schooling there. When asked by friends whether his son would carry on in the family business after graduation, the elder Siegner would squint, as if looking into the sun, and say, "Well! I'm afraid I'm going to have to leave that to Peter."

Some of the friends found this mildly shocking.

Peter's mother was a resigned woman, who kept house well and did her best to keep up with her energetic husband and son. After three miscarriages, she had accepted the fact that there would be no more children, and came to look upon her only child as the center of her life.

Both she and her husband would have been politely incredulous had they been told that their son was a genius. It had never occurred to Peter to wonder about his ability, either. It was something he accepted, like the weather.

When he won a scholarship to Heidelberg in 1937, his mother could hardly bear it. Her only consolation was that, when the war erupted in September 1939, he was exempted from the services because of the importance of physical scientists to the Reich's war effort.

That consolation had disappeared in the aftermath of the fight with the department head, the departure from the university, and the induction into the army. Peter suspected still that the induction had been so remarkably fast because the head had spoken to some cronies of his in the Party about the affair. What had happened was quite simple. Peter had had the nerve to suggest that Bothe's measurement of the diffusion length of thermal neutrons in carbon might be

14

wrong; that the incorrect results had arisen because of impurities in the test medium caused by exposure to atmospheric nitrogen; and that if he were allowed to repeat the experiment and prove it wrong, this would show that graphite could indeed be used to moderate an atomic fission pile.

The department head had refused to allow the experiment. Peter, angry, had persisted. The disagreement culminated in a shouting match in the head's office, and the precipitate departure from the university. In a subsequent meeting which was intended to smooth things over, the department head had informed Peter that students at his level were supposed to learn, not instruct and criticize. Peter accused the head of pigheaded narrowmindedness, and that was that. Three weeks later, on April 17, 1941, he reported to the Berlin military district induction center.

Because of his technical background, he was trained as a tank gunner and sent to Second Panzer Division as a replacement. After that came the grueling, failed attack on Moscow, in the snow; the bitter winter retreat and Hitler's stand-fast order as the fresh Siberian divisions came roaring in from the vast spaces of Asian Russia; and finally the transfer to Third Panzer and the vicious battle in front of Kharkov.

In the middle of all this, in February 1942, his parents had been killed—or more precisely, disintegrated—by a stray RAF bomb meant for the Alkett tank factory in Berlin. He did not receive the news until late March, when the front had stabilized. There seemed no point in applying for special leave to go home, since there was no longer one to go to. He remained where he was.

And now, at 5500 feet over Russia, he was retracing in hours the weary route he had traveled for the ten months before.

The Junkers landed at the Brest-Litovsk airfield just as

15

it was growing light. He drank some of the water and ate part of the bread and sausage from the bag he had found under the bench. He felt rested, but dirty and unshaven. There was a clanking from the wings as the aircraft was refueled, and then a growing rumble as it turned and lumbered off down the runway into the air. Siegner could imagine the crew's opinion of him.

They landed at Tempelhof a few minutes before eight in the morning. As far as he could tell from the air, there wasn't very much damage in Berlin. It would take an awful lot of high explosives to make a hole in a city the size of this one, he thought. He remembered that he had been told that the great terminal building had been red before the war; whatever it had been, it showed only dirty camouflage now.

As the Junkers rolled to a stop, a nondescript gray Citroën (looted from the French, no doubt) pulled up by the exit door and halted. Siegner opened the door and jumped to the ground with his kit. He stood blinking in the morning sunshine. It was warmer here than in Russia and he felt disoriented by the abrupt change in his surroundings.

The man who climbed out of the rear of the Citroën wore the uniform of a major in the SS. That shook Siegner. Until now he had assumed he was still in the hands of the Wehrmacht, the regular army, which was jealous of its soldiers. He couldn't imagine how the SS could have extracted him from his unit without some remarkable contortions.

The SS officer said, "Heil Hitler," and flung out his arm. Siegner hesitated momentarily, thought better of giving the Army salute, and repeated the SS man's. The officer noticed the hesitation and smiled faintly. They shook hands.

"I am SS-Major Weil. You're Peter Siegner?"

"Yes, sir."

"Get into the car. We'll arrange a bath and something

16

decent to eat. Then you'll find out why you're here.''

Two hours later, fed and clean, dressed (to his consternation) in a freshly pressed SS lieutenant's uniform, he stood at attention in a green-walled office in the HQ block of the SS barracks at Lichterfeld. Behind him hovered Weil, who had brought him in, and at a plain pine desk sat a thin, spectacled man in the uniform of an SS colonel.

When the man spoke his voice was very clear and soft.

"I am Colonel Kruger. Please sit down, both of you." He centered a photograph on the desk, looked at it, studied Siegner, and put it away.

"Weil, you are already aware of part of what I am going to say. Siegner, I must ask you to open your mind fully to it. After you have heard it, you will not have the choice of cooperating or not. So I will put one question to you, now, this once only. Would you prefer to stay in Germany, and work on a project which will make full use of your, ah, rather remarkable abilities, or would you rather return to your unit?''

That's a lot of choice, Siegner thought. Aloud he said: "I'll stay here.''

"Good. I thought you likely would, hearing it put that way,'' said Kruger dryly. "Needless to say, unauthorized disclosure of the nature of the project carries the death penalty. Understood so far?''

Siegner nodded. Kruger steepled his fingers and went on.

"A group of civilian scientists is attempting to produce a machine, I believe it is called an atomic pile, which will make possible the construction of a very powerful bomb. Siegner, you have studied under some of these people. The work is secret, but not so secret that the British and the Americans are likely to be unaware of it.

"It is the intention of some very important men that a

17

more carefully hidden project be established. These are the people for whom I work, and I report directly to them. A mass of equipment and materials has been assembled in the southern Reich, and a well-protected place established for the work. You are to be placed in charge of the scientific activity of the project. Staff has already been selected—without their knowing it, of course—and I can assure you that they are all competent people. You will be able to refuse any of them, however, if you think they won't be suitable. The team is quite small, for security reasons. Workers and technicians will be allocated as the physical requirements of the work dictate. It will be your responsibility to identify those requirements.

"Do you have any questions?"

Siegner felt the same detached, odd light-headedness he had experienced in his first combat, when he had seen the work done on a Russian cavalry unit by machine guns and an artillery barrage. Stop, he thought, concentrate on the technical questions. Concentrate on those, you understand them. There's a lot of politics here, dangerous politics.

Aloud he only said:

"Why have I been selected?"

"We interviewed several of the scientists on the current project, the one the Allies likely know of, about possible candidates for this operation." Kruger gazed out the window for a moment. "Under a pretext, of course. Your name kept surfacing, normally in tones of regret over the loss to German science. You may not be aware of it, but you are acquiring quite a reputation. The deciding factor was that you could be quietly removed from your military duties without anyone noticing very much. By the way, I should add that you'll have access to reports on all progress made by the other teams—although we hope you'll surpass them fairly soon. No one on the other teams is cleared for this

18

project, so you won't be able to contact them directly." Kruger smiled faintly. "A couple of them were quite distressed to hear that you were missing at Kharkov, several weeks ago."

For the first time, Siegner experienced real fright. Already missing on paper, there would be no one to protest if he were to become so in fact. He was utterly in the hands of the SS. Through a dry throat he managed to say, "The technical problems are very great. I will need a lot of heavy water, shielding, control mechanisms . . . a great deal of chemical processing and handling equipment, with staff who know how to use it." He licked his lips. "I hope you realize that it's not the same as designing and building, say, a new tank. The uranium-238 lattice configuration is well defined but we don't know how . . . ." A thought struck him. "It would have to be the element-94* alternative, we can't build a uranium bomb, too difficult to separate out the explosive isotopes . . ." He realized he had begun to think out loud. Kruger was gazing at him with amusement. Siegner flushed, thinking, they knew I wouldn't be able to resist this chance. But can I carry it off?

Rather sharply, he said, "It can be done, given enough time and resources. But I'll need other knowledgeable people, to reflect my ideas and help shape them. If I could see—"

"No! Absolutely not!" Kruger's voice was no longer soft, and he slapped the desk for emphasis. "Any information you need from other groups will be obtained for you by Major Weil. Their reports will go to you as a matter of course, as I said before. But there must be absolutely no suspicion on their part that any of this is going on. That is final." He stood up. "Weil will be taking care of you from

---

*Plutonium. The Germans never named it during the war.

here on. Go to the south. Inspect what has already been done. Set up a timetable, ask for whatever else is needed, go to work. Reports will be submitted every two weeks at the minimum. You can look over the dossiers of the proposed staff before you go. That's all. Heil Hitler.''

"Heil Hitler.''

When they had gone, Kruger picked up his telephone and dialed a number. There was an answer after the third buzz. He said into the mouthpiece, ''Kruger here, Herr Reichsführer. Dr. Siegner has accepted. *Fenris* is activated.''

I

London

January 23–February 22, 1944

Gordon Mclennand, Lieutenant (RNVR) winced as ice blew in lumps from the wings of the B-24 Liberator and hammered on the fuselage. The racket, added to the bellow of the four engines, was deafening. He hauled himself out of his seat and lurched forward to the navigator's station.

"Hey!" He had picked up the expression at Oak Ridge, but the navigator didn't respond, American though he was. It was very noisy in the aircraft.

"Hey!" he shouted more loudly, and tapped the crewman on the shoulder. The navigator turned, raised his eyebrows, and gestured to an intercom headset on the bulkhead. Mclennand put it on. The racket subsided a little.

"What can I do for you, sir?" The voice was thin in his ears.

"When will we be landing?"

"Croydon is in twenty minutes. But the weather's filthy, so we might have to divert. We'll see when we drop out of this; the weather forecast says it should be clear below two thousand feet. It'd be nice if it were."

"I hope the altimeter's bloody well right."

"So do I, sir."

Mclennand left the headset at the navigator's station and

21

poked his head up between the pilot and the flight engineer, who were both staring tensely through the windscreen. Beyond it there was nothing but gray, wet cloud and wads of snow. The pilot spotted him out of the corner of his eye and said something Mclennand couldn't hear. The flight engineer turned around and bawled; "You'd better strap in. We're about to come out of the overcast."

As he turned away, Mclennand saw the gray begin to shred into wisps of vapor. Through the rents a gray-brown landscape, streaked with white, became visible. England.

The B-24 bucked and pitched all the way down to the runway; then they were rumbling along the tarmac, sluing a bit as the tires walloped ridges of slush. At length the aircraft turned onto the perimeter track and grumbled down a taxiway to the dispersal area. A gray Austin was waiting in the drab afternoon light.

Mclennand peeled off the flight gear he had been given and stacked it neatly in his seat. Then he went back to the flight deck.

"All the best in England. My compliments on your flying and navigation. Up the Yanks."

The pilot looked pleased. "Up the Limeys," he answered, and began unbluckling his harness.

Mclennand found his suitcase and scrambled out of the aircraft. At the bottom of the ladder he looked up to see Varley tramping over to him through the slush. The triangular face of the driver was pinched and gray, the effect of too many years of war showing, in a way it didn't on the other side of the Atlantic. Mclennand felt guilty.

"Take your bag, sir?"

"That's all right. I'll just take it into the back with me."

They climbed into the Austin and the car slithered away from the dispersal area. After a few moments Mclennand asked, "Any specific orders as to where I'm to go at the moment?"

"No, sir. Except that I'm to take you home and ask that you call in as soon as you're rested."

"Fine. Take me around to the flat, then. D'you remember where it is?"

"Certainly, sir."

As the Austin scurried through the London streets Mclennand was content to relax in his seat and think about Jean. He should have called her from Croydon, he realized. She might very well be at work; God knew how her shifts at the hospital might have been changed in the six weeks he had been away . . . the United States, Oak Ridge, Los Alamos. What he had seen there both chilled him and left him in awe. The vast factories, the confidence of the Americans that the atomic bomb was only months away. What's that going to do to Hitler's Reich once we have it, he wondered. Since the failure of the German attack at Kursk the summer before, they'd been retreating all along the eastern front. There couldn't be too much longer before the Anglo-American invasion of France, either. Plenty of time to get killed several times over, though, he reminded himself. Especially if the Germans manage to build a bomb of their own. That looked improbable, fortunately. They seemed to have made little progress since 1942, about the time he had been seconded to Pierce's section to keep track of developments in German physics.

If only I could tell Devereaux all I've seen, he mused. But the Manhattan Project has the tightest security I've ever encountered, anywhere. They really should have sent us both, though.

He was getting drowsy; it was a long flight from Halifax to London. Near home he fell asleep, so that when the

23

Austin stopped outside the block of flats in Bedford Place, Varley had to shake him twice to waken him.

At the flat door he rang twice but there was no answer. She must still be at work. He let himself in, and, without bothering even to carry the suitcase to the bedroom, collapsed into the armchair, took his shoes off, and instantly fell alseep.

He was awakened by the rattle of a key in the lock. Before he could get out of the chair the door swung open and his wife struggled through it, encumbered by a parcel. She saw him and dropped the parcel.

"You're home!"

They cannoned into each other's arms in the middle of the living room. A minute or two later she asked, "Why didn't you ring me?"

"I should have. The driver was waiting, though, and I was too tired from the flight to think straight . . . is there any tea?"

"Better than that. Whiskey. I managed to find some blouse fabric." She gestured at the parcel, still on the floor. "I was going to surprise you."

"Better early back and unsurprised than late and surprised."

"I love you," she said, and then, "I'll make some tea."

Mclennand rang Devereaux while the kettle boiled. "Alan, it's Gordon. I just got back. Anything new?"

"You made it, eh? DESPITE WIND AND SNOWY WEATHER. No. it's been the usual. I tried to reroute as much of it as I could, or take care of it myself, but there's still rather a pile on your desk."

"A big pile?"

"Well, not yet, but on the way there. When do you think you'll be in? Pierce was getting a bit worried about some of the backlog."

Mclennand sighed. "I'll be there at eight sharp tomorrow morning."

"Right. See you tomorrow, then."

As he rang off, Jean returned from the tiny kitchen. "Work?"

"Yes. I rang Alan."

"D'you think he'd like to come for supper this week?"

"Seriously? What would we feed him? Or have you been at the black market?"

"No, of course not. But with you away, I've managed to build up a bit of a stock . . . we have so few friends since we left Cambridge."

Mclennand thought for a moment. Intimate though his working relationship was with Devereaux, he had never contracted any social ties with the man other than the occasional drink at the pub in Northumberland Avenue, near the War Office. The idea of anything closer hadn't occurred to him.

"Let me think about it."

"All right. I'll call you from the hospital tomorrow. If it won't go, then just say no. Otherwise bring the poor man along tomorrow evening. He doesn't have any family nearby, does he?"

"No, I believe they're all in Sussex." He emptied his cup. "May I please have some whiskey? After that I'm going to take a bath and go to bed."

"Me too, except the bath." She paused and said, "After that we can go to sleep."

Mclennand grinned at her as she filled both their glasses.

Devereaux was in a foul mood. He had intended to get to the War Office cubicle he shared with Mclennand by seven-thirty, but his landlady had kept him awake until two in the morning by clattering pots and pans in the kitchen directly below his bedroom. As a result he had overslept. On top of that, nearly the fag end of his month's pay had been spent on a cab to get him to work by eight. Pierce didn't appreciate lateness.

He stamped irritably down the corridor to the tiny office at the rear of the building. As he opened the door and entered, Mclennand looked up from a pile of message flimsies and said, "Top of the morning, flyboy."

"Good morning. To start off with, you're not Irish, and what the devil is 'flyboy'?"

Mclennand grinned, exposing large white teeth. "It's American for 'airman'. Which you are, Flight Lieutenant, poor chap. How's it been going here?"

"How has what been going? I hope to Christ I'm not going to have to suffer through a barrage of American slang until Hitler decides to pack it in. That would be entirely too much. Well." He struggled out of his greatcoat, slung it on the hook beside the door, and sat on his desk. "Not much new, I'm afraid. Their team at Berlin-Dahlem is still diddling along with its calculations, as far as we can tell. Thanks to your sojourn among the colonials, you'll probably be able to assess that better than I. It's in the file marked Dormouse. Oh, my God. I've a report to do for Pierce by lunchtime. Talk to you later."

Mclennand opened the file. It contained the last six weeks' worth of intelligence on the development of the German fission pile. It was pretty sketchy, but it appeared that they had made next to no practical advances in the past month and a half. That seemed to be their main difficulty; they were very good on the theoretical aspects of the problem, but were poor at translating the theory into practice. They weren't experimentally oriented in the same way the Americans were. And lucky for us, too, thought Mclennand. He studied the file until noon, comparing its contents with the information he had acquired in the States, while Devereaux fumed away at his report.

A few minutes after twelve Devereaux, his good humor partly restored by the completion of his task, unfolded his lanky frame from behind his desk, and suggested, "Lunch? Or are you too busy?"

Mclennand's head ached slightly from the close air in the office and the intense concentration he always put into his work.

"Glad to stop. Down the street?"

"Good enough."

It had begun to sleet. They raced around the corner to the pub in Northumberland Avenue and managed to jam themselves up to a table next to two Guards officers, who looked irritated at the intrusion.

"Shepherd's pie?"

"I suppose so." Mclennand reflected gloomily on the difference between wartime food in Britain and the United States. "I'm afraid I was spoiled in America."

They ate. After swallowing the last starchy bite, Devereaux muttered, "The sleet's stopped. Can we go for a stroll on the way back?"

They emerged into a dribble of sunlight which quickly disappeared, leaving the streets their usual wartime winter gray. After walking for a minute or two in silence up toward Whitehall, Devereaux asked, "How much can you tell me?"

They walked a few yards while Mclennand thought. Technically he was senior to Devereaux, having gone straight out of Physics at Cambridge into Intelligence during the Munich crisis in 1938; his naval rank, however, was not precisely equitable to Devereaux's RAF position. Besides, Devereaux had been in combat, while he had not. It was a gray area defined on a day-to-day basis by Mclennand's longer and wider experience in Intelligence.

Devereaux, though, was a brilliant improviser in that field. While Mclennand arrived at his goal by deduction, the other often preempted him by a flair for thinking as a German would in a given set of circumstances. His degrees in German and economics helped, but served really as a support for this trick of putting himself behind an enemy's desk.

There was a limit, though, on what Devereaux should be allowed to know about American advances in atomic physics. It had been difficult enough for Pierce to obtain permission to send Mclennand to the United States, and it had finally been given on condition that he pass only enough information to Devereaux to allow the latter to make his appraisals of German progress. It was an infuriating, hand-tying stipulation, but there was no way out of it in the present circumstances.

"For Christ's sake, slow down."

"Sorry." Mclennand's walk tended to speed up when he was concentrating. He looked up at the low cloud, beyond which a faint drone betrayed the presence of an air-craft. "Do you ever have an urge to do another tour on Lancasters?"

A silence. Then Devereaux answered quietly, "I've sometimes felt guilty about being in Intelligence rather than doing the second tour. I'd be lying, though, if I told you I was anxious to go back for another thirty missions."

They walked on a little. It was beginning to sleet again. Finally Devereaux said, "I suppose I can guess why you asked that particular question."

"It's pretty simple," the other answered. "If you know

28

as much as I know you'll never get back onto combat duty. We couldn't risk your being captured."

"I see."

They had turned left and were some yards down Whitehall when Devereaux spoke again. "It's not going to be long before the Americans have a bomb, though, is it?"

"No. But it won't be this year."

"We'd better get back to work, I suppose."

Mclennand spent most of the afternoon being debriefed in Pierce's office, and was instructed to prepare a report for forwarding to the Joint Intelligence Committee. At the end, Pierce said, "As you know, we're receiving information as a matter of routine from our American liaison, but we need your eyewitness report as well; it'll help put the whole matter into our perspective. The Americans were quite open, I suppose?"

"Very. There were some things I wasn't let in on, but they were quite complete about the rest."

Pierce filled his pipe and puffed energetically. Rubbing his short square fingers to remove the tobacco crumbs, he asked, "D'you believe there is any chance at all of the Germans stealing a march on us?"

"Given what we have on their facilities, I'd say no. The plant the Americans built to extract the fissionable uranium from the inert stuff covers acres and acres and needs unbelievable quantities of electricity. The Germans couldn't hide an installation that large, to start with, and diverting enough electricity to run one would play the devil with their conventional weapons production. There's been no sign of either situation."

"There's an alternative to using uranium, though, isn't there?"

"Yes. You can build a bomb out of plutonium, which

is a byproduct of an operating fission pile. But nobody knows yet how much plutonium would be needed to produce an explosion. It's thought that the Germans have too little time left to make any amount of it at all, even if they had an operating fission pile. You need a lot of heavy water for a pile, too. The air raid on their heavy-water plant in Norway—and the sabotage before that—must have set them back months.''

Pierce stretched back in his chair and swiveled to gaze out the window across the Embankment to the sullen gray Thames. "I just can't fathom it," he mused. "They were doing so well before the war, and even until 1942. Why haven't they put more effort into it? It would seem the natural thing for a crew like that, what with Hitler's unalterable resolves and thousand-year empire and all the rest. Can you imagine one of those things going off over there," he asked, jabbing his pipestem at the misty outlines of Waterloo Bridge, "wiping out most of central London? What would we do if they threatened to pop a second one on us?" He swung back from the window and glared at Mclennand. "Doesn't it seem peculiar to you?"

"I've had the odd nightmare about it."

Pierce sighed. "Well, we can only go on the information we have. I don't know where a lot of it comes from, but it's well-vouched for. That'll be all for now; have your report to me by four o'clock Wednesday."

When Mclennand got back to the office Devereaux said absent-mindedly, without looking up from the file on his desk, "Your wife called about three."

Mclennand looked at his watch. Five o'clock. Too late to inflict a supper guest on her. He telephoned the flat.

"Sorry I wasn't here. Meeting with the powers that be."

She sounded gloomy. "It's all right, anyway. I've been called back to the hospital for an extra shift tonight. I was just leaving. D'you want to ask Alan around for tomorrow evening?''

Mclennand found he had already decided. ''Yes, just a minute.'' He cupped the receiver. ''Alan. Can you come to supper with Jean and myself tomorrow evening?''

The other looked up, plainly delighted. ''Of course. I'd like to very much.''

Mclennand felt slightly guilty about not having asked before. ''Yes,'' he said into the telephone, ''we'll be there about six. Barring emergencies.''

''Good. See you in the morning.''

He rang off, cleared his desk, and locked the files in the safe. Devereaux looked up again as he was putting on his uniform cap and overcoat.

''Thanks very much. I hope it won't be too much trouble.''

''None at all. Burning the midnight oil tonight?''

''Till this is read. Then home, such as it is.''

''Good night, then.''

''Good night.''

Devereaux was already in the office when Mclennand arrived next morning, a little late and out of breath. The RAF man possessed a thick mop of reddish-brown hair, and had buried the fingers of both hands in it. Both his elbows were on the desk and he was staring fixedly at a single message flimsy lying on the blotter in front of him. He looked perplexed.

''What've you got there?''

''Oh. Good morning. Didn't hear you come in. Pierce brought this down about ten minutes ago. He wants us to evaluate it and meet him in his office after lunch.''

''Pierce brought it down?'' Normally internal messengers delivered the day's crop of new material.

''Yes. He said it was an odd one. I must say I agree.''

"Let's have a look."

The text was a brief one: "REQUIRE 200 KG P-9. URGENT. FENRIS." The addressee code was TRISTAN.

"That *is* odd. P-9. They've been using that as the heavy water reference for years. They've never been able to get enough for a pile. But they've never been short by as little as two hundred kilograms."

"That was bothering me, too. Pierce was also concerned about this *Fenris* and *Tristan* business. Those codes've never cropped up anywhere else, apparently."

"Where did it come from?"

"Southern Germany. That's all Pierce would tell me."

"Not the Berlin-Dahlem group, then. Somebody else. Somebody we don't know about, dammit."

Devereaux was fishing around in the bottom drawer of his desk; eventually he surfaced with a tattered copy of Bullfinch's *Mythology*. "I was about to look *Fenris* up when you came in. *Tristan's* easy enough, fair-haired hero type."

They had always been perplexed by the German tendency to use code words that could give a hint as to the nature of an operation. Allied codes were different; you wouldn't be surprised to find yourself participating in something called *Rutabaga*.

"Here's *Fenris*," said Devereaux. " 'The Fenrir or Fenris-Wolf. A monster in wolf form, chained by the dwarves, who breaks loose on the day of Ragnarök, the great battle between the gods and the powers of evil, and helps to defeat the gods. When he yawned, his lower jaw touched earth, and his upper, heaven.' "

"Nasty piece of work, isn't he?"

"It would fit for somebody with a doomsday mentality. They've been big on that in Germany, lately."

"We'd better start cobbling something together for Pierce."

They spent the morning sifting, collating, cross-checking, and rereading stacks of reports and intercepts. Near lunchtime Devereaux became frustrated and went down to the archives to look over prewar material. He returned, dusty, empty-handed, and irritable, at five past one. By the time they left for Pierce's office they had to admit that they had absolutely nothing of significance to add to the message. There was no context for it whatsoever.

All Pierce said when they told him was "I thought as much. But keep trying; there may be other intercepts. I'll make sure you're on the list for anything concerning *Fenris* or *Tristan*. That's all for the moment, then."

Devereaux said in the hallway, "That wasn't very satisfactory. But he's got a bee in his bonnet about something."

"Might not be this. He's got more on his plate than we know about."

"What's for supper, then?"

Mclennand began to laugh, and then stopped. From somewhere in the depths of his mind an equation had surfaced. He immediately wished he hadn't thought of it.

"What's the matter?"

"One plane plus one bomb equals one city."

It kept them pretty quiet for the rest of the afternoon, and after that, all the way to Mclennand's flat in Bedford Place.

Devereaux was not a particularly emotional man, but he hated the war with a passion. From the moment he had started operational flying on Wellingtons in 1941, the carnage and waste on both sides had sickened him. His wife had been killed in an air raid on London in March of that year, and he had thought at first that dropping bombs on German cities would redress the balance in some way, or make him feel as though it did. It hadn't happened. The

33

back- and mind-breaking work of putting a heavily laden bomber over a target in the face of nightfighters, flak, searchlights, bad weather, dead and injured crewmen, and God knows what else, drove any sensation of revenge as far away as the moon. Little by little the wound had healed, and by the time his squadron converted to Lancasters he had, against the odds, survived twenty-three missions. When the thirtieth was done, and he was posted to an Operational Training Unit as an instructor, he found, rather to his surprise, that the pain had faded to a wistful sorrow. She was gone, and he had dealt with it.

He had been at the OTU for barely six weeks before being given the opportunity to join Pierce's staff. (Pierce had grumbled, "A degree in economics and German and you hide yourself in Bomber Command for two years. Can't think how we missed you.") Analyzing the German economic situation's effect on weapons research suited him, particularly when they got going on the Reich's progress in nuclear physics. He and Mclennand had been able to add some valuable observations to the mainstream analyses carried out by Dr. R. V. Jones and other high-level scientific advisors to Churchill.

He found the work too intriguing to pursue much of a social life. An occasional weekend's leave he spent at his parents' farm in Sussex, walking the Downs with the farm dogs and practicing the marksmanship of which he had been so proud before the war. The evening at the Mclennands' would be a rare break in his routine.

As they stood outside the flat door they could hear an animated conversation going on inside. Mclennand exclaimed, "Good Lord! That sounds like Catherine," and hurried in. Devereaux closed the door behind them and stood uncertainly, fiddling with his cap. Jean was sitting on the sofa beside an unfamiliar young woman who had the palest blonde hair Devereaux had ever seen.

"Catherine," said Mclennand, and then, "Oh, sorry. Catherine Gavin, I'd like you to meet Flight Lieutenant Devereaux. We share an office in Whitehall. Did you come up today?"

"No. yesterday. Mother had a touch of the flu and it was time I visited her and father in any case. I'm very pleased to meet you, Lieutenant."

Mildly discomfited by her formality, Devereaux answered, "Alan will do just as well. I'm only an airman now by courtesy, anyway."

"I've invited Catherine to stay for supper," Jean told them. "It's been absolutely ages since we've seen you, Cat. Excuse me. I've got to get things on the table. Stay here and talk to these two, will you, Catherine, and keep them from pestering me. There's sherry and whiskey in the cabinet by the door, help yourself."

"How's the farm?" asked Mclennand a minute or two later, as he subsided into an armchair, a large Scotch in his fist. Catherine was drinking whiskey as well, Devereaux noted with approval. With something like disappointment he saw that she wore a plain gold wedding band.

She sighed. "Tony was always more comfortable with it than I think I'll ever be. But the neighbors have all helped and I think my head will stay above water. You remember Jacob, who was there before the war?"

Mclennand nodded.

"He stayed on because of his eyesight, he said, but I think really it was because he's too old. But he's tried to teach me everything he knows about farming. And I've had Land Army girls to help out the last four summers, of course." She turned to Devereaux. "I was an utterly helpless London know-it-all until I married a Sussex farmer. That put the shoe on the other foot, I can tell you. I can hew wood and draw water with the best of them, now.''

Mclennand laughed and said, "She never was as nose-in-the-air as she likes to pretend she was. Jean and I knew Cat before the war—they went to school together. Then she married Tony and it was off to the wilds of Sussex.'' He stopped and looked uncomfortable.

Catherine smoothed over the rought spot. "It's all right, Gordon.'' She turned to Devereaux, her smooth hair like a pale helmet, "My husband was killed in the Blitz in 1941. It's his farm that I run now. He was very much a part of it, and because of that my recovery has been complete.''

"I'm very sorry,'' Devereaux said awkwardly. He didn't like to mention his wife's death in front of Mclennand. "My father farms near Burgess Hill. The name Gavin isn't from around there, is it?''

"No. We're near Winchelsea.''

In the conversation that followed Catherine and Devereaux found that they had much in common; so much, indeed, that Jean had to interrupt them twice to get them to come to the table.

Several hours later, Devereaux looked at his watch and reluctantly accepted that it was time to either leave or miss the last Underground to his lodgings south of the Thames. As he pulled his coat on, Catherine said matter-of-factly, "I'm going to be back at the farm in a few days. If you ever happen to be in the neighborhood, do drop in. I confess I occasionally need to talk to someone other than the local farmers and the clergyman. Very undemocratic, I'm afraid, but there it is.''

He turned slightly pink. "I'll certainly keep it in mind. I don't get out of London much, these days, though.'' He waved to Mclennand. "Thanks for everything.''

"See you tomorrow."

An hour later, with Catherine asleep on a couch in the living room, Jean whispered to her husband, "She doesn't usually take to people that quickly."

"Don't go poking your nose in where it's not needed," muttered Mclennand, and fell asleep.

For the next four days they handled the usual routines of evaluation, commentary, and reporting, and occasionally worried at the question of who (or what) *Fenris* might be. Devereaux spent another evening with the Mclennands (Catherine, to his disappointment, had returned early to Sussex), missed the last Underground to Lambeth station, and slept over. Then, early the following Tuesday afternoon, Pierce summoned them to his office.

"We've got another one," he said without preamble, as soon as the door was closed. "It's making the Joint Committee nervous, I can tell you, but nobody's been able to put any reasonable interpretation on it. There's some suspicion the Germans are trying to feed us false information, but it doesn't have that flavor to me. It's coming too much out of the blue, for one thing. Have a look."

The message was again from *Fenris* to *Tristan*. It read: "ALL STOPPED. AWAITING P-9."

After studying it for a minute or two, Mclennand suggested, "The lack of context makes me think most of the communication is by scrambler telephone or teleprinter, and this was a radio transmission made because the other communications broke down. Maybe because of our bombing?"

"Quite possibly. I can tell you that this is in fact a radio intercept. Air Force Intelligence has told us that one likely area of communications breakdown is between Berlin and the extreme south of the Reich. Not very far from the Swiss border, likely."

37

"Mountainous terrain, then, if it's as far south as Austria." Devereaux jiggled the message flimsy from one hand to the other. "An underground installation?"

"It might be. We haven't had a close look at that area for some time. I'm going to try to persuade Air Force Intelligence to send over a photoreconnaissance Mosquito as soon as we have a better indication of the source. But it'll be like pulling teeth to get them to divert any sorties from France at the moment." Pierce gloomily regarded his fingernails. "Everything's tied up doing reconnaissance for the invasion. Is there anything you can think of that might flush out more information?"

They worked at it for some time, without result. Finally Devereaux offered, "D'you suppose we're going about it from the wrong end? If we were a German research team, where would we be getting our heavy water?"

"Since the sabotage and the air raid they've been able to get next to none at all," Mclennand reminded him. "Although if they're using a combined graphite and heavy-water moderator, there might be nearly enough. But I find it hard to believe they need only two hundred kilograms," he added.

"And that's likely still in Norway, at the Vemork plant."

"Yes," answered Pierce. "As far as we know, it hasn't been moved."

"What about the other fission projects? The ones we know about?"

"They've always been short. Are you suggesting that some of the Norwegian heavy-water inventory was diverted to, ah, another destination?"

"Yes."

"It's possible, I suppose." There was a long silence. Pierce fiddled with his pipe. At length he said:

38

"I should tell you that there is a suspicion that the Germans are intending to move that heavy water out of Norway within the next few weeks. And that measures are being taken to prevent it from reaching Germany."

"Is there enough in the shipment to give them what they need?"

"There might be," Pierce said carefully.

"We could always," Devereaux half-joked, "let them get away with it and see where it goes. Then we'd at least know where *Fenris* was."

Pierce stared at him over the pipe. "Are you out of your mind? There are some people on the JIC who would have you arrested for treason for suggesting that."

"It's a possibility," Devereaux protested, stubborn now. "Suppose it isn't stopped before it reaches Germany? If we could trace it after it got there, we might have better options than if it disappeared completely."

"He's got a point," interjected Mclennand.

Pierce ruminated, staring first at one, then the other. "Well," he said finally, "I'll put the suggestion before the JIC as an alternative in case the Germans get away with it. In the meantime, think about the messages some more. I'll let you know tomorrow if there are any further developments in the Joint Intelligence meeting."

On the way back to their office, Mclennand said, "You're a gung-ho bastard, and no mistake. Pierce nearly had a fit. Were you serious about letting the stuff be trundled happily off to Germany?"

Devereaux looked thoughtful. "No. But I'll tell you what I'd do if I were running the security for *Fenris*. I'd make sure it looked as though that heavy water were destroyed; that way, if there were any suspicion on the enemy's part, it'd disappear in the general round of self-congratulations at having got rid of a dangerous threat. The whole operation would be that much more secure. It only makes sense to allow for that." He paused, and grimaced. "I hope the JIC sees it that way."

"Defeatism's never popular," Mclennand informed him. "Remember I told you, when they stand you up against a wall."

"You should have told me earlier, dammit."

Pierce was gone nearly all the following day. Devereaux, edgy over the *Fenris* situation, fidgeted about the office until Mclennand, somewhat irritated, said, "Either sit down or go home. When did you last take a day off?"

"Mid-January, I think. Went and tramped around the Downs. Bloody cold. Ever been to Chanctonbury Ring?"

"No," said Mclennand. "Old hill fort, isn't it?"

"Yes. It was there before the Romans came. They didn't have much use for it, too high up in the Downs. You have to climb from the road for about half an hour. Ghostly place. There's a meadow sloping up to the hilltop, nothing but grass—in the summer—and cow-slop, and right at the top this stand of trees. The clouds roll right through it on an overcast day, and all the trees are green with lichen. Odd to think it was sort of a town, once."

"Houseman wrote a poem about that kind of thing."

"Did he?" A long silence, while Devereaux stared out the window. Mclennand asked, "Will you be dropping by to see Cat next time you have some leave?"

"I've thought of it."

"You might as well, you know. She asked you to, or as near as I've ever heard her."

"I suppose I ought, then."

Mclennand thought he should stop pushing, but went on anyway. "Living alone in a room in South London isn't good for anybody."

Devereaux began to laugh, then stopped, still looking out the window. "Gordon, don't worry yourself about it." He turned back to the desk. "I got over Nancy's death some time ago. You and Jean needn't worry yourselves over me. Good enough?"

Mclennand was embarrassed. "Sorry."

He was spared further apologies by the whirr of the internal telephone. "Pierce," he mouthed to Devereaux around the receiver. "Yes. We'll be right up."

Their superior was pouring out three mugs of tea when they arrived. "No milk or cream, I'm afraid," he apologized, "and precious little sugar." He settled back in his chair and stirred the tea furiously, as if he could generate more sugar by sheer physical labor. "The Joint Committee," he told Devereaux, "was impressed by your suggestion, although it was indicated that plans have been made for such an, um, unhappy alternative." He sipped his tea, regarded the cup morosely, and set it down. "There's not much we can do from here at the moment. Apparently the contact with the Norwegian sabotage team is very tenuous. Anyway, the Vemork plant will be watched and if the shipment isn't destroyed before it leaves Norway we'll try to follow it to its destination using what contacts we have in Germany."

"Suppose they take it out by air?"

"That'd be tricky. We can probably spot a takeoff from the area but keeping track of it once it's over the Reich will be another matter. We simply have to hope that the worst won't occur." He picked up his tea and blew on it. "If the worst does happen, we have to depend on the unlikelihood of the Germans being as close to a fission pile as the *Fenris-Tristan* exchange suggests. Although," he added unhappily, "if *Fenris* is telling the truth, the cat will most certainly be among the pigeons."

41

"Amen," said Mclennand, with feeling.

Devereaux, silent, stared gloomily at his tea.

Devereaux was finally persuaded to ask Pierce for two days' weekend leave. Pierce agreed, adding only, "Make sure the duty officer knows where you're going, and leave a telephone number if you have one. I want to be able to get in touch with you in short order if something happens."

When he telephoned Catherine Thursday evening she sounded both surprised and pleased.

"How long is your leave?"

"I have to be back in London Sunday evening. I thought I'd go on to Burgess Hill on Saturday evening, after leaving you."

There was a short silence. Then she said, "I'm just thinking about the trains. There are so many troop movements down here nowadays that travel over that way can be difficult. Never mind, we can check on that on Saturday. There's an apartment over the carriage house I can put you up in, if necessary. What time does your train get in?"

"Supposedly at noon."

"Good. I have to drive into Hastings to see about some bills. I can pick you up at the station."

"Thanks very much. See you on Saturday."

Friday passed slowly. Mclennand had caught a cold and was snuffly and irritable. Pierce was away; nobody knew where. Over a stiff whiskey after work, Mclennand asked, "Any plans for your leave?"

Slightly embarrassed, Devereaux answered, "I'm going to spend Saturday afternoon with Catherine and catch a train over to my parents' after supper."

"You might as well call her Cat, everybody else does. Incidentally, you won't get to Burgess Hill that easily. The trains are all stuffed with soldiers."

"She mentioned that."

"Well," said Mclennand as he called for another whiskey, "You'll enjoy yourself. She sets a fine table, even with the rationing. She's a remarkably capable woman."

"I thought that myself."

"It comes out even more as you know her better. When Tony was killed, she went completely to pieces for two days, and then started to pick up the pieces and put them back together. She's much tougher than that porcelain-doll exterior would have you believe. It's heavy work running a farm that size, I suppose, even for a person bred up to it. But she rubs along very well . . . has a gift for bringing out the best in people who work for her. Couldn't do it, otherwise."

Devereaux tipped back the last of his pint. "I must go and get some supper and some sleep. See you Monday."

"Hang on a minute. I'll see you to the Underground."

As Devereaux's train pulled in, Mclennand said awkwardly, in a rush, "Be careful how it goes, Alan, the war's not over. Any of us still might not make it." He hunted for words. "I don't want to see either of you, you know . . ."

Devereaux grinned, walloped his friend on the shoulder, and wormed into the packed carriage.

He caught the eight o'clock train out of Charing Cross the next morning. It was jammed with officers and other ranks of every description and nationality—Poles, Czechs, Free French, British, American—and he had difficulty finding a seat. There were several halts on open countryside while long strings of railway cars rumbled by, loaded with tanks, enigmatic tarpaulined crates, guns, all the lumber of war. At the old Victoria Gothic station in Battle they made an unexplained fifteen-minute halt during which rank upon rank of silver American bombers drummed across the winter-clear blue sky. The noise shook dust from the carriage windows.

"More for the French railways," muttered the American flight sergeant beside him. "Won't be long now before the sons of bitches get invaded."

It was half past twelve before the train rolled into Hastings station. He saw Catherine near the end of the platform as they pulled in; she was standing next to an ancient, prewar shooting brake. Surrendering his ticket to the platform guard, he hurried down the steps in time to see her wheel the old car around the corner. She leaned across the seat and opened the door.

"Hop in. I only just arrived myself."

"Thanks." He shoved his bag into the rear seat and levered himself in beside her. With intermittent snorts and pops, the car puttered away from the station.

"It needs new sparking plugs," she explained, upshifting expertly, "But they're almost impossible to find, except on the black market, or so I'm told. How was the journey down?"

"Good enough, although half the Allied armies must've been going to Hastings this morning."

She laughed and maneuvered the car around an enormous lorry carrying part of a burned-out Lancaster fuselage. "They're everywhere, aren't they? Especially the Americans." She gestured over her shoulder at the receding lorry. "So's that kind of thing. People kept hoping it would be over by next Christmas, but it never was. Everyone looks so tired and gray. Even you." She half turned to look at him. "Being cooped up in a tiny room in the War Office can't have done you a lot of good over the past couple of years."

She herself looked very well indeed. The green kerchief

drawing her smooth hair back was, at a guess, silk; a sad remnant from richer prewar days. Gray eyes in an oval face. Devereaux felt lightheaded for a moment.

To recover himself, he said, "It's not like office work must have been before the war. There's more interest . . . and more tension, that has to be expected, of course."

She looked apologetic. "I shouldn't have said that, nobody likes to be told they look tired, even if they do . . . I'm sorry." To change the subject, she pointed through the windscreen. "They'll be lambing at that farm up ahead in a month or two. We helped out, the spring before the war. It seems so long ago, now."

They drove on in silence for a few miles. Then she said:

"There it is. Sevenoaks. It's been here for three hundred years. One of the oaks died during the Great War, but the name stayed . . . Sixoaks wouldn't sound right, would it?"

At the beginning of a graveled lane there was a stump, which was followed by six ancient oaks whose bare branches overshadowed the bushes—honeysuckle, Devereaux guessed—that lined the other side of the narrow drive. At the end of the lane stood a low stone farmhouse, thatched, with small latticed windows set deep into thick walls. There were flower boxes under the windows. On the left stood a carriage house, separated from the main building by a patch of gravel.

"The barns are out behind the house. The land stretches out that way"—she gestured to the left—"mostly pasture, with some wheat. There's a bit of a wood, too, farther up the hill."

There was a man clambering around on the roof, apparently inspecting the thatch. At the sound of the car he descended slowly to the eaves and started down the ladder leaning against the corner of the house.

"That's Jacob," Catherine said. "I've had a problem

45

with a leak over the pantry. It almost ruined the winter's potatoes; we didn't catch it fast enough and the water got into the root cellar.''

"You mentioned Jacob the other night."

"So I did." As they got out of the car she continued, "He lives in a cottage over the road. His father worked for Tony's father; Jacob's stayed with the farm since 1933. I couldn't keep the place above water without him. There are two other hands about the place in the week; he hires and manages them. Jacob!''—this to the man, now at the foot of the ladder—''What d'you think?''

"It should be all right now, Mrs. Gavin." He trudged over to them, folding up a clasp knife and tucking it into his overalls pocket. "It was that bit where the snow got in a year ago. Rotted out over the summer, most likely."

The two of them conferred rapidly about the winter's damage to the northwest fences. Devereaux was fascinated to hear the depth of farming knowledge her questions and instructions revealed. She had obviously learned a lot in a hurry.

She turned and called him over. "Jacob, this is Flight Lieutenant Devereaux. If he can't catch a train to Burgess Hill this evening he may be staying over. Could you please see that the carriage house rooms haven't anything nesting in them? You can leave the cold frames till next week; there's not enough of the day left to get a good start on them."

Jacob took a careful look at Devereaux. What he saw encouraged him slightly; despite the name, the lad didn't look French.

"Devereaux," he said. "Burgess Hill. Used to be Devereauxes farming over that way."

"That'd be my father," Devereaux told him, surprised. "How did you know?"

46

"My dad's brother worked over t'Hayward Heath before the Great War," he explained. "If he hadn't married my aunt he would have married a Cummings girl from down near your dad's place. But she died in the flu in '18. She worked on the Devereaux farm, as he liked to recall when he'd had a few pints."

"Good Lord." Devereaux turned to Catherine. "That would have been Rose Cummings. She used to help with the spring cleaning. My mother thought a lot of her." He turned back to Jacob. "It's the same Devereaux, all right. My father still has the farm."

"Well, then, Mr. Devereaux, when next you see your father ask him if he remembers Tom Thorpe. Tom used to go down to the farm often enough to see Rose, or so he says." He hitched up his jacket. "I'd best be getting off now to the fences, Mrs. Gavin. I'll see to the carriage house as well and then be off home. Good day to you, Mr. Devereaux."

"Jacob," she murmured, as he stumped away, "He never ceases to surprise me. I was sure he'd disapprove of you here . . . but he doesn't. They're so conservative, as I'm sure you know, and me a Londoner brought here by Tony . . . I've had my ups and downs. Shall we be going in?" She giggled, a surprising sound from her. "I've been picking up the dialect, too."

The kitchen was a beamed, stoneflagged, low-ceilinged room with a huge fireplace. "I do most of my living in here," she told him. "Usually there's enough coal to keep the home fires burning. Most of the rest of the house is closed off, though. There isn't enough reason to keep it all warm. The big fireplace hasn't been used for years; Tony's parents were going to put in an oil stove but they never got around to it."

"Do they live near here?" asked Devereaux, and instantly wished he hadn't, for her face saddened.

"Oh, no. They were killed in a car accident the year before I met Tony." She poured water into a teakettle. "We seem to have a lot of death in our families, don't we?"

"It seems to be the way these last few years."

She put the teakettle carefully on the coal stove. The subject was apparently closed.

"I still have some bacon from the last slaughter at the Pennington farm—it's up the way. And a half-dozen eggs. We'll have some lunch in a moment. You can wash up in the scullery there. The other necessities are out behind the house, I'm afraid."

Fresh eggs and bacon were rare eating for Devereaux. Between the two of them they demolished everything in sight. Afterward he dried the dishes as she washed them; he was amused at how natural it felt. When the last teacup had been put away in the massive oak cupboard next to the kitchen window, she decided:

"It's such good weather, we'll take a walk up Fell Hill."

Later, for Devereaux, that walk became one of those vivid memories in which each incident, each recollected word or gesture has a brightness which keeps it clearly etched when recent events have worn away. The bright day, the delicate bare strands of aspen branches against the sky, the old paths they tramped with the puddle-ice crunching underneath their boots, the vigor of the young woman beside him, all were concentrated into one unforgettable image. At the top of the hill she stopped, and pointing out toward the southwest, said:

"Look. You can just see the house from here. On clear days I'm sure I've been able to see France. I used to come up here often, when the farm was too much for me."

Devereaux was about to raise his arm and put it about

48

her shoulders, and then remembered again, Mclennand on the Underground platform, the two desks in the tiny room in the War Office, Pierce, the tired American sergeant on the train, the ineradicable smell of boiled beef and cabbage in his room in Morley Street. He said, almost brusquely, "Probably a bit too far to see France. Perhaps we'd better be getting back down. Dusk's coming soon."

She looked at him, startled for a moment, and then her expression cleared. "You're quite right. The walk back can be tricky in the dark. I'm afraid I've made you miss your train, if there was one."

He looked miserable. "I'm sorry, it's just that—"

She took his arm and shook it gently. "It's all right. Please don't worry."

They trudged down the slope in the darkening air. Then Devereaux muttered, as though begrudging the words, "This is happening between us rather suddenly, isn't it? Without warning."

Her face in the dusk was opaque, unfathomable. "Yes. But please let's not talk about it today, or tomorrow. Not till we've been apart for a week or two. These days we're all so—expendable. I don't want to be expended again. You don't either, I think."

"Gordon told you?"

"Jean did. I hope you don't mind."

"No."

It was mid-dusk by the time they reached the farmhouse. They prepared and ate supper in an odd atmosphere of comfortable proximity interspersed with moments of nervous distance. When Devereaux yawned for the second time, Catherine put on her coat and said, "For my reputation you must sleep over the carriage house. Come along, Flight Lieutenant."

Jacob had built a coal fire in a massive pot-bellied stove

49

in the corner of the converted loft. Catherine made up an old string bed with a feather mattress and an eiderdown from the house, and said, touching him lightly on the cheek, "Goodnight. The fire will burn till morning if you don't disturb it. What's the matter?"

"Nothing. Only, if your telephone rings, it may be for me. Please wake me up immediately; it may be important."

Her eyebrows lifted. "They have this number?"

"I had to give it to them. They have to know where I am at every bloody moment, almost."

"I see." Her face was remote, thoughtful. "Good night again, Alan. I'll see you in the morning."

"Good night, Cat."

She went away down the stairs, into the dark.

Sunday passed in much the same peaceful, companionable way that Saturday had, with the same edge of tension. But Devereaux noticed in her a faint, but unmistakable reserve.

In the car at Hastings station she kissed him lightly and said, "I'll call you from the Mclennands' or mother's the next time I'm in London. It'll be about two weeks. Are you likely to get leave in that time?"

Thinking of *Fenris*, he said, "Not likely."

"I have to be in London on the twenty-second, in any case. My mother's birthday is the next day. As an only child, I feel compelled. Here's your train."

Mclennand's cold had got worse; so much so, in fact, that he stayed away from work on Tuesday.

Devereaux was given a minor reprimand for failing to lock a file in the safe before going home Wednesday night.

Thursday Mclennand came back to work, sniffling.

Friday nothing happened. Nor Saturday, nor Sunday.

Sunday evening Devereaux tried to telephone Catherine. All the circuits were busy.

The following Tuesday morning they had a brief conversation with Pierce. There had been no attempt yet by the Germans to remove the heavy water from Norway. When the move did come, the Norwegian sabotage team would try to sink the ferry carrying the drums as it crossed Lake Tinnsjö on the way from the Vermork plant. "After the bloody stuff is disposed of," Pierce told them, "you can go back to drawing graphs of German electricity consumption. As long as that isn't reallocated, they've given up trying to build a pile. Or so we hope," he added.

Over lunch Mclennand told Devereaux to cheer up. "The authorities have things well in hand, remember."

"I assume you're being a bit sarcastic. Doesn't this *Tristan-Fenris* problem bother you?"

"Of course. But we're not in a position to do much about it. What d'you think of the whole business?"

Devereaux ruminated for a moment. "All the information we have indicates that they've made no real progress since June 1942. Which is why these radio intercepts make me nervous. You know how false information works; first build up a context, then slip in the information you want the opposition to believe, so that everything fits. There isn't any context in this case. It's as though we really did overhear something we weren't intended to." He circled the rim of his beer mug with an index finger. "Pretty thin beer."

"Unless it's what they intended to happen," suggested Mclennand. "They might want to panic us into doing something rash, to see if we're getting high-grade intelligence from somewhere."

"That could be it," admitted Devereaux. "Does that feel right to you, though?"

"No."

Devereaux looked over his shoulder at the rapidly filling pub. "We shouldn't be talking here."

As they walked back to the War Office in the February drizzle, Mclennand asked, "Have you been in touch with Cat?"

"Not since Sussex. I tried to telephone Sunday night but I couldn't get through."

They skittered out of the splash of a passing car.

"I can't stop worrying about bloody *Fenris*," Devereaux continued after brushing slush off his coat. "Pierce took the words out of my mouth—it's not like them to ignore something as potentially decisive as this. Suppose all the fumbling they've done since 1942 has been a cover for the real project. Something the Dahlem and the other groups aren't even aware of. The reason they can't seem to get enough heavy water."

"That's awfully far-fetched, if you don't mind my saying so."

"I expect you're right. In a week we'll probably be able to forget about the whole business.

Late in the evening of February 21, Pierce was still at work in his chilly, bare office. Or rather waiting, as he had been waiting all evening. At least it was quiet tonight; there had been two sharp German air raids in the last four days—the first heavy ones for years—and they had caused a lot of damage.

The raiders must be suffering ferocious losses, though, he mused. If only we'd had good radar-controlled night fighters during the Blitz. That would have given the buggers a bloody nose, for sure.

He was about to give up and go home when there was a sharp rap at the door.

52

"Yes?"

"Duty officer, sir. Urgent dispatch."

Pierce signed for it, unlocked the dispatch box, and withdrew the envelope it contained. He gave the box back to the duty officer and waited till the door closed. Inside the envelope was a message flimsy: "FERRY SUNK WITH ALL DRUMS OF SHIPMENT ON BOARD. OPERATION CONSIDERED SUCCESSFUL."

Pierce chuckled with satisfaction and burned the flimsy in his ashtray.

He gave Mclennand and Devereaux the gist of the message the next morning. The two of them went through the day in a state of suppressed euphoria; not a great deal of work got done. In mid-afternoon Mclennand received a telephone call from his wife. Catherine had come unexpectedly up from Sussex. Would Devereaux like to come to supper?

Devereaux agreed happily.

Just before they left for the day, Pierce stuck his head into the office. "Alan, Gordon. We've just received word that the Dahlem installation has been evacuated to Tailfingen. So their main effort has been set back even further. Apparently it was the big Berlin raid on the fifteenth that made them leave. Thought you'd like to know." He disappeared.

"Well, we'll have something else to drink to this evening," said Devereaux. "Wish it were a big bottle of red Bordeaux. You don't suppose Himmler would swap a case for a couple of Ministry of Supply officials?"

Mclennand snorted. "The Germans'd be getting the worst of the deal. Let's go."

As they entered the jammed Trafalgar Underground station, Mclennand observed, "They're getting some of their own back for that Berlin raid Pierce mentioned. People haven't been taking shelter like this since '41.''

At their Russell Square stop they had to pick their way among several families camped in the Underground for the night. Babies howled indignantly. Harassed mothers arranged blankets under the Bovril and loose-talk-costs-lives posters. It was like being transported back to the Blitz. They emerged into the street with some relief.

"No sign of a raid so far," observed Devereaux as they climbed the stairs to the flat.

"Too early. They hardly ever used to come over this early, remember?"

The evening didn't start off well. The men were still euphoric over the good news of the morning, which they could not share with the two women; and Jean was depressed because of the new flow of civilian injured into the hospital. The German bomb loads had been mixed incendiaries and high explosive, and a number of children had been savagely burned. Catherine seemed moody and disinclined to conversation. To Devereaux it seemed a long time since the afternoon on Fell Hill.

The Mclennands were in the tiny kitchen, drying dishes, by the time the other two had got onto a more comfortable footing. Devereaux was trying to calculate whether his pay would stretch to taking Catherine to supper when the first sirens began to wail.

"Damn," grumbled Mclennand, wiping his hands on a dishtowel as he put his head out of the kitchen. "Do you want to go down to the Russell Square shelter?"

"They're probably after the docks. We could go down to the cellar if they get nearer than that."

"Makes sense. Anyone for a drink?"

Nobody was, though. A few minutes later the thudding of bombs became distinctly clearer. Mclennand finally said,

"The buggers are off course again. We'd better go downstairs."

As they trooped down to the cellar with a few other residents of the building, Jean giggled. "At least the war has brought the cost of upper flats down. Nobody but us wants to live with only a roof between them and a bomb."

"Don't complain. It's the only way we can afford the place."

Catherine's face was strained and white. At the bottom of the stairs, she said, "Living in the country, I haven't had a chance to get used to air raids."

Mclennand grinned at her. "Living in the city, I haven't either. You don't get used to them; you just get better at pretending you are."

The shelter was a storage area, lit by two dim bulbs, at the rear of the building. The window-to-ground level had been bricked up. A few of the occupants attempted conversations, but these trailed off as the thuds and crashes got steadily nearer.

A series of bangs close by rose to a crescendo, which was suddenly punctuated by one horrendous roar that made the dust fly out of the beams overhead. The lights flickered. A child near the entrance began to cry. They all waited, hunched and breathless, to find out if there was another bomb in the stick.

The next explosions were much fainter.

Devereaux shook dust out of his hair and was surprised to find his hand gripped fiercely in Catherine's. She held on until the all-clear sounded.

Jean muttered as they climbed back upstairs (the lights, remarkably, were still on), "I bet we lost some window glass in that last one."

The telephone was ringing inside the flat. Mclennand

55

hurried in and picked up the receiver while Jean went to look for damage. He listened for a moment, said, "We'll be ready," and replaced the receiver very slowly.

Jean came back from the bedroom. "Just one cracked pane. I can mend it with a bit of tape. What on earth's the matter?"

Mclennand didn't answer her. He and Devereaux were staring at each other with worried faces. Mclennand said, "That was Pierce. He's sending a car for us. We're to come immediately. He said 'the wolf has yawned.' "

"Sweet Jesus Christ," said Devereaux. "They've got it."

II

The Reich

March 13–April 5, 1944

Dr. Anna-Marie Lerner went through the police checkpoint at the exit from the Innsbrück railway station and looked hopefully about for the car which would take her the last few kilometers to the installation in the mountains. The train from Dresden had been twelve hours late and she wasn't optimistic about anyone being there to collect her. Now she would have to bully the stationmaster into letting her use the telephone.

She felt rumpled and gray. Dresden had been unrelievedly depressing; only sporadically bombed, it was quickly filling with refugees from other, more devastated centers. Her parents, particularly her mother, had exuded utter gloom. None of the friends she had gone to see—those who hadn't been scattered to the corners of Europe, Africa, and Asia by the war—had been much more cheerful. Getting through to the end of the war seemed to be the only real goal anybody had; moreover, there were enough unpleasant rumors about the possible consequences of defeatist talk to make people guarded in their conversation, even with old friends.

She really wished she hadn't taken the week's leave. It had been difficult enough to persuade Boehme that her absence would do no harm to the project, and then she ended by returning more depressed than when she had left. She felt a wave of irritation at the recollection of the man's complaints about her departure "at such a critical time," as he had put it in his pompous manner. Although Boehme had no actual authority over her, he had fussed until Siegner had pointed out that her work was complete until the pile was actually running. Then he still grumbled. Like most dyed-in-the-wool National Socialists, Boehme disapproved of female professionals; only her reputation as an excellent analytical chemist had kept him polite to her. That, and the hope of getting her into his bed.

She sighed and turned away from the empty Südtingler-Platz that fronted the station. She ought to have married Kurt when he asked her two years ago. All that remained of him now were slowly blurring memories and a few letters, the last one from Stalingrad, where he had vanished utterly along with the wreck of von Paulus's Sixth Army.

She made her way to the stationmaster's office. The man looked her up and down disapprovingly. She had become used to that on the train journey; anyone who could look well fed in this fifth spring of the war was obviously taking advantage of good Party connections. As she perhaps was, but not in the way that anyone in the cramped, down-at-the-heels train could have imagined. You had at least to credit Boehme with keeping their bellies full.

"I would like to use your telephone, please. It's urgent."

"You're Dr. Lerner?"

She was surprised. "Yes."

"Somebody's been calling every hour since this morning. I told them thirty minutes ago the train was coming in shortly. They said you were to wait, they're sending a car."

She went back out to the front of the station in time to see a dirty gray Tatra pull up. Boehme protruded his spherical head from the driver's window.

"Anna-Marie! Just a minute, I'll get your suitcase."

He stuffed it into the back seat and waved her to the passenger side. She sat as close to her door as she could. Boehme started the car and they rolled up the street toward the Aldrans road. A watery afternoon sun glistened for a moment on the Patscherkofel and the shoulder of the Rastkogel beyond. The beautiful, beautiful mountains, she thought. Only I wish I didn't have to live under them.

Boehme jabbered away for most of the drive up to the complex, his pudgy hands fiddling nervously with the steering wheel. She paid little attention until he mentioned Strasser.

"What?" She could have bitten her tongue off for showing so much interest.

He glanced at her, startled. "Poor girl, you're tired. I was just saying that our energetic security captain has lately taken an unusual interest in Horst Roth, how he came to be chief technical officer, that sort of thing."

She thought quickly. "I was under the impression Strasser was supposed to handle external security only. Isn't he infringing? After all, we were all checked exhaustively when the project was established."

"My dear girl," he fussed, "that's what they *told* us. What's really the case may be another thing entirely. But why are you so concerned?"

There was nothing for it but to cover her slip with flattery.

"I thought you were handling security for scientific personnel. Strasser's getting involved doesn't seem fair to you."

He puffed up visibly as he swung the car onto the Sistrans road. "Well, that's true, but with all the pressure I'm under I'm glad of all the help I can get." He tried to reach over and pat her knee but the car jolted and he missed. "Don't

59

worry about me. Working with the SS has its compensations, you know.''

I'll bet it does, she mused, relaxing against the seat as he began to ramble about his plans for using SS contacts to make large quantities of money once the war was over. She must be more careful in the future; she had headed him off easily this time but other mistakes might be harder to cover.

The SS guard at the installation gate checked their passes and waved them through. The place wasn't very impressive; dingy barracks for the SS guards and the technical staff; a concrete bunker-like affair jammed up against the rock wall of the mountain. Snow and ice everywhere.

The senior scientific staff had originally been billeted in a house outside the compound, but with air raids worsening all over the Reich, Weil had insisted that they move into the underground complex itself. They were much too valuable to lose. So now they led a troglodyte existence, surrounded by harsh electric light, the smell of damp concrete, and the all-pervading hum of ventilation fans.

''Home,'' she muttered gloomily as they got out of the car and tramped across the packed snow to the bunker that hid the tunnel entrance. She immediately wished she hadn't said it; Boehme was certain to pat her arm in sympathy. He did.

They met Strasser coming out of the bunker. He was speaking in quick efficient tones with two SS engineers. Boehme halted in dismay, and exclaimed, ''You don't mean to say you're going through with it?''

Strasser was a square, energetic man with flat green killer's eyes. Anna-Marie, like all the others in the project, knew little about him except that he had been decorated for destroying three Russian tanks in one day, using satchel charges, in the dreadful winter of 1941–42. Slightly

60

wounded at the battle of Kursk, he had been in charge of external security since September 1943.

Now he eyed Boehme with unconcealed dislike. "Orders. The tunnel is to be mined, with one switch in my office, the other in the control room."

"What the devil for? The Russians will never get this far. Suppose there were an accident, and the tunnel were blown? We'd be trapped. I suppose you're mining the emergency exit, too?"

"We are. But there's a five-minute delay between the time the switch is thrown and the mines go off." Strasser's eyes flicked momentarily to Boehme's small paunch. "Time enough for even you to get out. Good day, Dr. Lerner, Dr. Boehme," he said, and stalked off with the two explosives experts in tow.

So much for the compensations of working with the SS, thought Anna-Marie. Much as she disliked Boehme, she felt a small twitch of sympathy for him; his attempt at authoritative questions had been deflated so easily. Of Strasser, she herself was unashamedly frightened; and she suspected that the same was true of Boehme. Of all the senior people in the complex, only Siegner appeared unmoved by the SS captain's menacing presence. But then, Peter had been on the Russian front himself.

They walked down the hundred-meter length of the entrance tunnel. There were cryptic symbols chalked on the stone walls at regular intervals, marking the positions at which the explosives would be laid. Boehme saw them too.

"The Russians will never get this far," he said doubtfully. "It's all a waste of time."

He hadn't been away from the complex for six months. Anna-Marie refrained from describing the devastation she had seen on her way to and from Dresden.

They reached the open blast doors at the entrance to the main installation. Anna-Marie, with distinct relief, went to her quarters, washed, and changed into working clothes: trousers, blouse, a heavy prewar fisherman's sweater. It was invariably chilly in the tunnels, despite all attempts to heat them.

She set out to find Siegner, starting with the pile control room. The corridor leading to it was crowded with empty crates, test equipment, and tools. As she picked her way around a reel of heavy electrical cable, Horst Roth poked his head out of the control room entrance.

"Oh. You're back. Good." Roth gave an impression of offhandedness that completely misrepresented his perfectionist working habits. "Looking for Peter?"

"Have you seen him?"

"He's been in his office—if you can call it that—most of the day. Doing calculations, again. He's likely still there."

No one, witnessing the interchange, could have guessed at the relationship between them.

"Thanks. See you later." She had adopted some of Roth's mannerisms herself. "Are we getting closer to the pile startup?"

"Better ask Peter. I just build them, I don't design them." This was not precisely true; Roth's abilities had been the key to some of the shielding design.

She nodded absentmindedly to the two or three technicians she passed on the way to Siegner's office. With most of the construction completed, there were fewer workers in the installation than there had been. Only a handful knew what it was for; these would remain at the site until the project was completed, while the others were released for employment elsewhere. She imagined that Strasser would have ways of ensuring that they kept their tongues behind their teeth.

When she entered the cubicle that served as an office for the head of the *Fenris* project, Peter Siegner was leaning back in his chair behind the desk, his hands behind his head, staring at the low ceiling. When he saw her he jumped to his feet.

"Anna-Marie. I hoped you'd be back today. It's almost ready to go." He shoved aside a stack of papers that threatened to overflow onto the floor, and fished two shot glasses and a bottle out of his desk. "French brandy. Boehme got hold of some two days ago." He regarded her with a wide grin. "I suppose you'll have some anyway?"

She nodded and smiled back. "Whatever else I feel about Hans, I have to admit he's an expert scrounger."

He sloshed brandy into the two glasses and handed her one. The liquor gleamed a subdued gold in the dim light of the desk lamp. "To *Fenris*. May we confound our enemies."

"To *Fenris*." She sipped the brandy. It was delightful, even in a short glass. Then she asked, "Why did they give us such an overdramatic code name? I've always wondered about that."

"We live in a dramatic age." His voice was ironic. "The name's appropriate, anyway . . . although it's not one I'd have picked."

"What would you have called it?"

"Oh, I don't know," he answered vaguely. "Only it wouldn't give such a good hint as to what we're doing here." He drank some more brandy. "By the way, do you know what that idiot did?"

"Boehme? No, what?"

"Well, it just comes out now. Strasser discovered it while

you were away. Apparently last month Boehme got three radio messages sent to the *Tristan* supply depot outside Berlin, without going through Strasser. It was while we were in a panic about getting the last of the heavy water. One message was about needing two hundred more kilos of it, the second a hurry-up, and the third an overdramatic 'We got it, hooray!' ''

''But all communications are supposed to be by tele-printer or telephone.''

''I know. But they kept failing because of lines cut by bombing. So Hans took it upon himself to hurry things up. It worked, too!'' Siegner's voice was slightly sarcastic.

''We would have received the heavy water sooner or later. Weil would have seen to that.''

''Don't say that to Hans. He's convinced he did it all himself. He's conveniently forgotten that the switch of the heavy water shipment in Norway was planned by somebody else.''

''So that's where it was coming from.''

''I didn't know myself until it arrived. Weil was quite pleased at pulling it out from under the noses of the British, especially as the dummy shipment was sabotaged the next day.''

''Do you think the British know we've got it?''

''Weil says he thinks not. Incidentally, Strasser was livid with rage when he found out about Boehme's fiddling. I could hear him bellowing all the way in here, nearly. He was all for having Hans summarily shot. Weil defused him a bit, but I don't think we've heard the end of it. It had to be reported higher up, of course.''

''Now that you mention the incident, it seemed to me that Strasser was even shorter than usual with Hans this afternoon.''

"Well, that's why. D'you want to go to the mess hall for supper? We can have some food sent up here instead; it'll be cold by the time it gets here but it'll be easier to bring you up to date. We're going to start testing the neutron flux tomorrow."

"I'll stay."

When Siegner awoke at six the next morning, he found himself tingling with an anticipation he had not felt for years. It was the tingle he had felt as a child on Christmas Eve, with the presents still to be opened. He savored the prospect. A self-sustaining nuclear reaction. Hard to believe.

He stretched under the rough blankets. For two years, throughout the intricacies of the construction and the secrecy, he had felt daily more like a scientist and less like a soldier—to his relief. The calculations and design for the graphite reflector structure; the slow amassing of the uranium cubes for the core; the shielding and cooling design; the plutonium extraction alley with its remotely controlled manipulators; all these had driven the war so far away as to be little more than a faint gleam and rumble on his horizon. That Germany would almost certainly lose the war if *Fenris* were a failure rarely troubled him; even the constant pressure from Weil and Kruger to speed the work had only served to intensify the challenge. That *Fenris* would produce a weapon was subsidiary; the morality of it troubled him only occasionally. In any case, according to the projections he had made the previous day, that weapon would not likely be made at all. Once the pile was running he would be able to be certain. Although heads could roll, and his might be one of them, that seemed of small consequence beside the scientific triumph. Because of the political aspect, though, he had tried to keep Anna-Marie well clear of the theoretical and design decisions concerning the element-93 production itself. Her job was the chemical extraction of the substance from the irradiated uranium core, and if there were too little of the explosive in the first place, she could hardly be blamed.

He was in his office by seven and made some coffee. He winced at the bitterness of the first sip. They were putting in even more acorns than previously; he must be about to turn into an oak tree.

He had barely finished the coffee when the office door flew open and admitted Boehme. The man was sputtering with indignation.

"Sit down, Hans. What's the trouble?"

Boehme jiggled uncomfortably from foot to foot. "I haven't got time. But you'd better do something about Roth. He's going to get us all into trouble. You know how Strasser has already been sniffing around him."

"What's he done?"

"He told a joke, that's what. To me, of all people, a Party member. It's a good thing none of the SS heard it. Roth'd be on his way somewhere else by now."

Siegner was irritated. The administrative chief was always fussing about things like this. "That's unlikely. What was the joke?"

Boehme looked discomfited. "I don't want to repeat it."

"Well, you can hardly expect me to give him a scolding if I don't know what he said. Besides, you might have misunderstood him."

Boehme looked glassy eyed. He took a deep breath, as if about to leap into icy water, and blurted, "Berlin. 1950. At a conference at Supreme Headquarters it is debated how best to go about using the new revenge weapons. The conference breaks up without a decision because it cannot be determined whether the two aircraft should fly side by side, or one ahead of the other.''

Siegner dissolved into laughter. After a moment he recovered himself. "All right. I'll have a word with him. But as people working on the revenge weapons ourselves, perhaps we'd better not worry too much over jokes about them.''

Boehme tried to see the logic in that, failed, said a huffy good-bye, and stamped out.

For the rest of the day, Siegner, Roth, and six technicians carried out tests on the pile and its shielding. Around noon Siegner drew Roth aside and told him about Boehme's complaint.

"I thought he'd go running to you like a wet hen. Do you want me to apologize to him for my poor faith in final victory?''

"Not at all. Just tell your jokes to myself or Anna-Marie from now on. I know you can't resist needling him, but he is the senior administrator.''

"He'd like to be in your shoes, get some of the glory for himself.''

"Don't concern yourself about that. We'd better go back to work. I want to get the neutron source into the pile cavity before lunch.''

At six o'clock they were finished. Siegner sent the technical staff back to their barracks, and worked out with Roth some minor adjustments to the shielding distribution. Roth scribbled furiously on a notepad. "We should be able to complete the modifications within three days. After that we can go anytime.''

Siegner initialed the work order and went off down the tunnel. He noted with approval that the cleanup crews had got most of the crating and spare equipment out of the way and into storage.

An SS engineering squad had been drilling holes for the demolition charges in the main tunnel and the blast doors had been closed to keep the noise and dust out of the central complex. As he swung the heavy doors open, Anna-Marie caught up with him.

"Supper?"

"I was on my way to the mess. The food's not much nowadays, is it?"

They fell into step. At the bunker exit, Siegner halted.

"Do you," he began, and stopped.

"Do I what?"

They walked on a little in the gathering dusk.

"I wonder, sometimes," he said. "What we're doing. Should the work be used in the way they're . . . we're going to? It seems a little . . . perverted, somehow. Like some of the rumors. You've heard them, I suppose?"

She nodded. "There was a Jewish family living near my parents' until early last year. They're gone. Nobody wanted to talk about it." She paused. "I don't really, either."

He went on anyway. "I saw a lot of ugly things in Russia. Not just them, either. Us, too. I got numb after a while. Fatigue."

She was taken aback. He had never mentioned Russia to her before.

"They're bombing our country flat," she said angrily. "You haven't been away from here for a year. You don't know how bad it has become. Children. Old people. Nowhere to go." She kicked furiously at a lump of snow. "It would be better if none of it had ever started. But what will happen if the Russians beat us? Can you see them? In Berlin?" A tear ran down the side of her nose and she wiped it on the back of her mitten. "I'm sorry."

"I'm sorry too."

They had reached the mess-hall path when a voice behind them called suddenly:

"Dr. Siegner."

He looked around. Strasser was hurrying toward them from the direction of the headquarters block. The SS captain saved his breath until he was a couple of meters away. His flat green eyes flicked to Anna-Marie's damp cheeks, then to Siegner, expressionless, professional. "Excuse me, Dr. Lerner. There is an urgent message for Dr. Siegner. Could you excuse us, please?"

She gave the most delicate hint of a shrug and went on toward the mess.

"What is it?"

Strasser grimaced. "They want you in Berlin."

"Now? We're almost ready to begin the last tests."

Strasser looked indifferent. "You know how it is, Dr. Siegner. They call, we go." He became slightly more animated. "I think it's because of the security breach that snot Boehme committed. If you'll come to the HQ block I'll give you the message. It doesn't say much."

As they walked, Strasser said, "You know, I haven't any idea what you're doing under that mountain—and I don't want to know—but I hope your superexplosive works. For all our sakes. Especially mine."

"What are you so worried about?"

Strasser favored him with a grin full of teeth. "If the Russians ever catch me, I'm a dead man. How about you?"

"You know very well I was a tank gunner."

Strasser grinned again, without the teeth. His moods, when he showed them, were unpredictable. "The Regular Army, that's right. Third Panzer, wasn't it?"

"Partly."

"A good outfit, Third Panzer." His voice was musing.

69

"Nothing there to be ashamed of. Kharkov and all the rest. Well, we were both in Russia. Not like that prick Boehme. Where did you find him, anyway?"

Siegner allowed his voice to go a little stiff. "He was assigned. He's a reasonably good scientist, and an excellent organizer."

"He's been organizing his secretaries, all right. The poor girls have started wearing their skirts down to their ankles."

Siegner had to laugh. "You're a bit moralistic, all of a sudden."

Strasser said conversationally, but with an edge, "I'm an SS officer. I don't like Boehme, but he's loyal. On the other hand, jokes about 1950 are all right—in 1950. Perhaps you ought to keep that in mind, Dr. Siegner."

He doesn't miss much, thought Siegner as they entered the headquarters building. I wonder who told him? One of the technicians, likely. Or maybe Boehme.

In the office Strasser picked up a message form and handed it to him. It read simply: "PERSONAL FOR SIEGNER VIA STRASSER. REPORT PRINZ ALBRECHT-STRASSE IMMEDIATELY. AIRCRAFT WILL BE AT WEILHEIM AIRSTRIP 2130 HOURS. KRUGER."

Siegner inhaled sharply, then whistled.

"Christ almighty."

"Yes, sir, Dr. Siegner," Strasser said, grinning, this time with the teeth. "Reichsführer Heinrich Himmler wants to see you. In person."

Strasser wouldn't have been so cheerful if he had been the one called to Berlin, reflected Siegner as the Mercedes threaded its way through the rubble. The damage to the city was much worse than he had expected. They had had to land at the great Rechlin base rather than at the Tempelhof airport, which was out of service.

70

How did it get so bad so quickly, he wondered. Fortified in his cavern, paying little attention to the arid news that was all that was offered by Goebbels's press, he had missed the first crumblings of the Reich. Anna-Marie had had reason to be as distressed as she had been.

The SS driver stopped at a mound of rubble and began a violent argument with the Kripo who was stationed there to prevent looting. Siegner tapped the driver on the shoulder.

"Do as he says. Go around the other way."

Cursing, the driver reversed. It was a surprise to Siegner to hear such snarling between the civilian police and the SS. When the driver had calmed down, he asked, "What's the matter, Private? Civilians getting too much for you?"

"Sir. I apologize. There're too many of them, that's all."

And that, thought Siegner, is exactly the reverse of the problem. There are not nearly enough civilians. We should have made sure there were more of us, before ever our military, or whoever it was, started this.

What are you thinking of, he asked himself suddenly. Without this you would be a badly paid laboratory assistant in some pointless organization. You are building what might be the world's first fission pile. Remember that.

Thanks to Heinrich Himmler.

That could give you pause for thought.

There were five of them there in the room in the Prinz Albrechtstrasse, after Siegner arrived. Heinrich Himmler sat motionless behind his great oak desk, his small round spectacles glinting in the pale yellowish light of the single lamp by his blotter. Kruger and Weil were in armchairs on either side of the desk, hardly visible in the shadows.

The last person in the room was a vague form, half-hidden in an armchair, facing one of the tall windows. The blackout drapes had been drawn partially aside to afford a dim view of the battered street beyond. Siegner had barely time for a glance in that direction before the Reichsführer-SS spoke to him.

"You are Dr. Peter Siegner. Of the *Fenris* project." Himmler's voice was high, almost petulant, as if resenting Siegner's authority in a field which he could not command.

"Yes, Herr Reichsführer." His bowels felt liquid. In the single light he could tell that Kruger and Weil were both pale, strained.

"In a report, sent to me from a certain Captain Strasser, I understand that the security of the *Fenris* project has been breached not once, not twice, but three times, by the action of Dr. Hans Boehme. He is under your authority. Do you have an explanation for this?"

Siegner contracted into a pinpoint of concentration. "My authority doesn't extend to radio communications, Herr Reichsführer. All such are supposed to be handled by Captain Strasser." A peculiar concern for the potbellied, near-sighted figure of Boehme awoke in him. "I can say that Dr. Boehme's concern for the success of *Fenris* might have drawn him into a breach of secrecy, however." An inspiration raised itself. "He has been a Party man since 1935. I can't imagine him doing such a thing except out of worry that the results of the project might be too late for the defense of the Reich. After all," and he took a chance, "it is possible that the target date would be set back if he had not urged the delivery of the P-9 in any way available. One can't really expect a soldier, even such a good one as Strasser, to see all the dimensions of such a complex project. One ought to remember that Dr. Boehme is in charge of materials procurement for *Fenris*, and that the heavy water, the P-9, is a major part of his responsibility."

He had given Kruger an opening, he realized with relief. Weil had relaxed slightly.

"Is this the case, Kruger?" Himmler asked.

Kruger took a little time—not too much—before answering. "It's possible, Herr Reichsführer. Because of the difficulties in communication lately, the heavy water might still be delayed had Dr. Boehme not acted. We would have lost valuable days."

"So Strasser's dereliction of duty was fortunate for the project."

He had caught Kruger with one foot off the ground.

"Captain Strasser cannot be everywhere at once," offered Weil, somewhat desperately. "It was set out in the original organization of communications that the senior scientists would have access to radio equipment in the event of an emergency. As perhaps this was. Do you agree, Dr. Siegner?"

"Yes." He was about to add more, but thought better of it. Kruger shot him a grateful look.

There was a long silence. The man in the armchair by the window stirred slightly. Himmler collected himself hurriedly. "The security over communications will be tightened. No radio messages will be transmitted without Strasser's approval, except in the event of total breakdown of landline communications, together with Strasser's incapacitation or absence. There will be no leave for Strasser until the project is completed. You will see to this, Colonel Kruger."

"Yes, Herr Reichsführer."

The leader of the SS turned to Siegner. "Now, Dr. Siegner. Since you are here, perhaps you will tell us how the project is going." He smirked. "As I am a fighting man

73

rather than a scientist, perhaps you could leave out some of the more technical details.''

It's a good thing Himmler can't see that disgusted look on Weil's face, Siegner thought. He collected his wits and began slowly, battling the waves of fatigue. He had not slept for twenty hours.

''The basic idea is that certain metals, if packed together in sufficient quantity, form an explosive of enormous power. Unfortunately—or fortunately—they are very hard to obtain.''

''How much is enough?'' Himmler's eyes looked like small stones behind the thick glasses.

''A few kilos. You could hold the mass in your hands. It would destroy a city.''

The Reichsführer-SS giggled. ''That's what the others told Speer. No one took any notice of it but me.'' His eyes danced toward the armchair by the window. ''Go on.''

''The problem is, as I said, that the metals are very hard to obtain in such quantity. We know there are at least two possible ones. The first is uranium-235. It's present in the naturally occurring, ordinary uranium-238 that we got from Belgium in 1940. However, the 235-isotope is chemically identical to the ordinary uranium, so it's very difficult to extract it. At least, not without great expenditure of electrical energy. Too much for the capacity of Germany at—at this difficult time.''

He paused, wondering if he had made a mistake. No one spoke.

''The other way is with an artificial metal which doesn't exist in nature. It has the number ninety-four. Nobody has got around to naming it yet. It is produced as a byproduct in an operating fission pile. The ordinary uranium actually changes into the new metal, according to the theory. It can be separated from the ordinary uranium surrounding it, by chemical means, and then purified.''

''According to the theory.''

''The theory was verified in experiments done by the Dahlem team, and others elsewhere, both before and since the war began.''

''Continue.''

''Once enough of the element-94 has been isolated, it can be formed into a configuration which will allow it to function as an explosive. It—''

''One moment.'' Himmler raised a pale white hand. ''How long will it take to produce enough of this metal, the explosive? To use against, for example, the Anglo-American invasion if it comes?''

Caught, realized Siegner. To lie or not?

He decided to lie, a little. ''It will not be immediate. I believe—''

A stirring from the armchair. A well-remembered voice asked, ''Less than a year?''

Oh, my God. It was the man himself. Siegner's tongue tied itself into knots.

Himmler, surprisingly, came to his rescue. ''Less than a year, Dr. Siegner?''

''Yes. Less than that. But the byproducts containing the explosive are likely to be extremely dangerous. Worse than any chemicals or compounds known. The separation must be done with extreme caution.''

A sigh from the armchair, hardly audible. The voice asked again, ''How much more dangerous?''

Siegner glanced at the Reichsführer-SS. Himmler nodded slightly.

''A few kilos of it, properly distributed, might make a city uninhabitable for months,'' Siegner told the dim figure.

75

"Perhaps years. It doesn't dissipate like a gas, you see. It stays with and goes on contaminating everything it touches."

"Not like a gas?" The voice was stronger.

"No. Much worse."

"How could it be distributed?"

Sweat trickled from Siegner's armpits. The faceless conversation was destroying his concentration. He thought desperately.

"An aerosol would work. The byproducts of the reaction could be put into liquid suspension and sprayed from an aircraft. Across the prevailing wind."

"A rain of death."

"Something like that." He waited. Himmler stared into space. Weil and Kruger sat motionless.

The voice began again, this time inflexible, iron. "It has always been my resolve to destroy the enemies of the Reich by any means available. This man has given us the power to devastate cities. Reichsführer Himmler,"—Himmler stared fixedly at his hands on the green blotter before him—"you will see that two things are done. First, that Dr. Siegner's work is in no way interfered with. Second, that if it is impossible to construct the explosive device in time for the invasion, then work will be carried out to employ these . . . byproducts, to inflict such disaster on the anglo-Americans as will make them ask for peace. There is no more to be said."

Adolf Hitler, Chancellor and Führer of the Greater German Reich, stood up in the gloom and stared at them. They all shot out of their chairs and stood at attention while he shuffled out of the room.

There was a long silence after the door closed.

Finally, Kruger ventured, "What about reprisals? It's not possible that the Americans are incapable of this themselves."

Himmler took his glasses off and fiddled with them. "You heard what he told us to do. Do it."

Kruger was reluctant. "We've never used poisons. Although we could. There are the Sarin and Tabun gas stockpiles. Why this and not those?"

Himmler replaced his glasses. "This is a war, among other things, of terror and counterterror. This weapon would be far more decisive than gas. Can you imagine London uninhabitable for a decade? The British will make peace to preserve their cities. They're too decadent to accept the losses that the German people will. That's why retaliation won't work for them. We can hold them to ransom, because we are willing to give everything, while they are not. And when peace comes, Dr. Siegner will have time to prepare the last argument, the bomb. Good night, gentlemen."

In the corridor outside, Weil muttered, "What about Berlin uninhabitable for decades? Or the Ruhr?"

"Shut up, you idiot," hissed Kruger, and bundled Siegner and Weil downstairs into the waiting Mercedes. As the car door closed on them he said, "Get Siegner onto the plane and back to the complex. We'll discuss the situation later."

"Heil Hitler," said Siegner.

Neither Weil nor Kruger replied.

He awoke in his quarters at three that afternoon, dry-mouthed and stiff. He had tried to sleep on the aircraft, but it had proved impossible. He was tense; his body felt tight and hot. He wondered if he were catching a cold. Not much wonder if he were, living in the damp chill of the pile complex.

He rolled over and switched on the light, staring at the calendar on the roughly paneled wall. March 16. A day behind, nearly. He stumbled out of bed and used the chemical toilet in the tiny bathroom partitioned off from the—bedroom? No, the cave he slept in. Like Roth, Anna-Marie, Boehme, and a few of the other key scientists. Strasser was unimportant enough to live like a human being, under the sky.

If you really think about it, mused Siegner, we're not really much better off than convicts. Almost never seeing daylight, a toilet nearly in the same room where you sleep. And try to find another job, ha. Not much different from the Russian front, that way.

He heated some water on the hot plate and shaved. He really ought to go to the compound for a shower, he thought. Himmler's face seemed to stare at him from the gloom behind his shoulder as he stroked the lather from his chin. Damn.

He finished shaving and combed his hair. The oily feel decided him. Off to the bathhouse for a shower.

He was halfway down the access tunnel, a bundle of clean clothes under one arm, when he spotted Boehme, head down, hurrying toward him.

"Hello, Hans."

Startled, Boehme looked up from his shoes. "Hello. I didn't think you'd be up yet. I was on my way to the pile room." He was agitated, shifting from one foot to the other.

"Well, I'm up. What's the matter? Some equipment gone astray?"

"Yes. Well, no, not really." He jiggled his hands in his coat pockets for a moment, indecisive. "That's not what's bothering me. It's Strasser."

"What's he done?"

"I saw him for a couple of minutes after lunch today. He as much as told me I was going to be shot for breaking security. He said you had gone to Berlin. To see Himmler. About me."

78

Siegner frowned. "He's breaching security himself, if he told you that. Nobody's going to shoot you, Hans. At least, not before the rest of us. Stop worrying."

"You saw Himmler, though?"

Siegner exhaled resignedly. "Yes, since you know about it already. He wanted to know how the work was progressing. We have a very high priority." He didn't mention Hitler's presence; there was no use frightening Boehme out of his wits entirely.

"It went well, then. For the project, I mean."

"Yes. Very well." He decided not to mention the alternative to the bomb.

Boehme emitted a noise of relief. "Thank you. I was rather worried."

"It's all taken care of now."

As he started down the passage, Siegner couldn't resist adding, "Hans."

The other looked back with a worried smile.

"No more radio messages, Hans. Or Strasser might get his wish."

Boehme hurried away up the tunnel without answering. Dammit, thought Siegner, there was no need for me to rub it in, too. I suppose I'd better go and have it out with Strasser. After a shower.

It was past four when he arrived at the headquarters block. Some SS privates were swabbing out the gun barrel of a Kfz-234 armored car parked near the steps. They watched him curiously as he went up the path to the shabby building.

Strasser was in his office, feet on the desk, smoking a cigar. A teletype cricketed on the other side of the thin partition.

"Good afternoon, Dr. Siegner. I thought it likely I'd see you today. Have a chair."

79

Siegner lowered himself gingerly onto the battered wicker seat. "I'm going to have to ask you to leave Boehme alone."

Strasser sniggered. "I wouldn't touch him with that old barge pole." His face went expressionless. "I hear the bastard's cost me my leave for the indefinite future. I just heard from Weil." He gestured toward the teletype room.

Siegner tried to mollify him a little. "It would have happened to all of us soon, anyway. We're so close to the, ah, result."

"No doubt." Strasser glowered out the window. "Did you see what I've got out there?" He jabbed his thumb in the general direction of the front of the building.

"An armored car. Adequate for shooting Boehme with, I should think."

Strasser grinned, with the teeth showing. "I don't think I'll need to. You've already put the fear of God, or the SS, whichever comes first, into him. Haven't you?"

"Yes, if you want to put it that way."

"All right, then. I was getting tired of teasing him, anyway. But that kind of man asks for it, don't you think?"

Siegner's temper was fraying rapidly. "Captain Strasser. Please confine yourself to overseeing the physical security of this installation. Boehme will make no more radio transmissions unless you authorize them. Nor will anyone else of my staff use the radio without your permission. But if I hear of any of them complaining of you again to this degree, I'll complain myself. But not to you. Higher. Clear enough?"

Strasser appeared unconcerned, even disinterested. "Clear enough." With a sudden change of subject, he asked, "D'you know why I've got that clapped-out wreck of an armored car outside my door?"

"No. Why?"

"Security. They think in Berlin that if I've got a middle-sized gun on this wonderful mountain, then everything's secure. The thing's so old I wouldn't dare fire it myself. You were in Russia, you know how it goes. Give the soldiers a little, get them to do a lot with it. Or die trying. Bugger it. Anything else?"

"No."

"Then I'll get on with my job, you get on with yours. I'll leave Dr. Boehme alone. You keep him away from the radio. He can't be trusted."

The armored car crewmen were gazing disconsolately at their vehicle when Siegner left. He waved, but they only stared at him.

Anna-Marie and Roth were waiting outside his office when he arrived there. The glare of the electric lighting picked out lines of strain on the chief technical officer's face. "There's a problem."

"I gathered that from your woebegone expression. Let's talk about it in the office."

They sat on the hard chairs. Roth lit a cigarette. "Six of the cube casings are improperly sealed. If the heavy water gets into them and contacts the uranium we'll have a fire like the other people did several years ago."

The casings prevented the U-238 cubes of the core from reacting chemically with the heavy water in which they were suspended. They had been almost impossible to obtain, because of the purity required of the metal; no more would be forthcoming.

"Can they be repaired?"

"Five of them, Pickert thinks. The sixth, no."

Pickert was the staff metallurgist.

"Then we'll have to run the pile one cube short. How long till repairs are done?"

"Ten days to two weeks. It's a slow job."

Siegner groaned. "We're under a lot of pressure to start. Can it possibly be done any faster?"

"You'll have to talk to Pickert."

Anna-Marie asked, "What happened in Berlin?"

Siegner reflected for a moment. They would have to know. "If this goes any further at all," he told them carefully, "we will all be in very serious trouble. Particularly me. Please keep it strictly to yourselves."

He described the strange meeting in Himmler's office, leaving nothing out. At the end, when he had fallen silent, they looked at him as though he himself had gone mad. Finally, Anna-Marie breathed, "But have they taken leave of their senses? What about retaliation?"

"That's the question Weil asked before Kruger kicked us both downstaris. The two of them can't do anything about it, not if Himmler's breathing down their necks. They'd be relieved of their posts, or worse, if they tried. We've all heard rumors about Himmler's displeasure."

"Not to mention Hitler's," added Roth.

"What about us, then," Anna-Marie wanted to know. "Should we try to slow the work down?"

"Not wise. I wonder sometimes whether Boehme might not have instructions to report anything like that to Weil."

They mulled this over while Siegner laced and unlaced his fingers in the dim light of the desk lamp. Finally he said, "They might be partly right, of course. I was in Russia. When—if—the Russians arrive in Germany, it will be as bad as anything you can imagine. They'll never leave, either. The only hope of the men in Berlin, apart from our succeeding in constructing a bomb, is to get the Western

Allies to accept something less than the unconditional surrender they've demanded. Hitler will never agree to a surrender, and the Allies strengthened his position by insisting on one before any negotiations can take place. I think he sees in this . . . alternative to the bomb a way of negotiating from a position of some strength. The bomb is better for Germany's reputation, but this will do if it has to."

"What about retaliation, though? They haven't thought that through. They can't have."

"I'm afraid they may have done so, partly, anyway. Weapons with this kind of portability and destructiveness favor the weaker side. If one aircraft can devastate a city, you don't need a bomber fleet to strike back at an attacker."

"We'll run out of cities before they do."

"Yes. But the gentlemen in Berlin may feel we have nothing to lose, anyway. The Allies have a good deal to lose; they're winning, after all."

"Don't say that in Strasser's hearing."

"I won't. But that's what I meant by a position of some strength. A trapped rat bites hardest."

"What about the moral question? We've never used gases yet."

"You haven't forgotten the RAF raid on Hamburg, surely? A hundred thousand, so it's said, burned to death in two nights? I'd rather be gassed than fried. If I have to choose."

"This isn't a gas," Anna-Marie reminded them. "It may be far worse."

"We don't know that yet," interposed Roth.

Siegner steepled his fingers and stared past them in the dim light. "He who pays the piper calls the tune, as they say. We've been allowed to do the kind of research and development work here we'd never have been able to in peacetime. We knew that weapons were the purpose when we started. We never *have* had any authority, and don't now, as to how the results of our work will be used. The fact is, we have to go on. They'd never let us stop.''

''We could blow it up,'' said Anna-Marie, without thinking. ''We could use the mines Strasser's putting in.''

They all sat in appalled silence, as though there were a fourth person in the group who had said it.

Siegner reacted first. ''This place may be the last chance there is of keeping the Russians out of Germany. As long as there's that, I can't accept the idea that was just mentioned. Let's forget it was ever said. Anyway, Weil said at the airport as I was leaving Berlin that the explosives won't be laid until the invasion situation clarifies. The Russians are still a long way away.''

''Then we go on.''

''Yes. We go on.''

It was in fact exactly two weeks before Pickert managed to get the cube casings repaired. Anna-Marie and Sommer, the remote-control specialist, made some final adjustments in the extraction alley, whose machinery would grind the irradiated uranium cubes to grit and dissolve the grit in acid. The separation of the various fission products would go on from there. Siegner fussed with his slide rule and pages upon pages of calculations, but told no one what he was trying to find out.

After a week of this enforced delay, punctuated by rumblings from Weil in Berlin about their lack of progress, Siegner browbeat Hans Boehme into obtaining two sets of skis and poles. He and Anna-Marie spent hours slithering about the slopes above the caverns where they worked. Boehme grumbled about what would happen if they broke their necks and tried to persuade Strasser to stop them.

Strasser merely instructed them to stay inside the SS patrol perimeter that ran up the mountain past the emergency exit to the pile ventilation shaft, and back down to the barracks area.

They had grown so used to their cramped underground existence that their own exhilaration at being out on the glittering slopes surprised them. One late afternoon, shortly before the repairs were complete, Siegner told her as they were taking their skis off by the entrance bunker, "You know, much as I'm frightened at what may come of the work we've done here, I have to admit I'm glad we're going ahead. A working fission pile. It's like a Christmas present. I never though I'd even get a chance to see one, much less be responsible for helping build one myself. I've been obsessed by the idea for years. Even in Russia."

She had been bubbly all the way down the last slope, but now her face turned serious. "I felt that way myself, until you came back from Berlin a couple of weeks ago. But now . . . if we could just start it up, see that it runs, and then turn it off and go back to living in peacetime, that would be a Christmas present indeed. The one I'd like." She kicked moodily at a lump of snow. "I'm not going to get it, am I?"

"I'm afraid it's very unlikely."

She leaned on a ski pole and looked up toward the heights of the Patscherkofel, blue and rose in the deepening dusk. "Were you ever married?"

He was very surprised. She had hardly ever asked a personal question in the two years they had been working together. When they first met he had noticed that she was an attractive woman, with her wide mouth and glossy dark hair, but in the pressure of work she had become so familiar to him that he had almost ceased to notice.

"No. Nor you?" He already knew, of course. He had

seen the SS dossiers on all the installation staff.

"No I might have been by now, if he hadn't been killed in Russia. At Stalingrad. But you knew that."

"Yes. I'm sorry."

She shivered.

"Cold? We'd better go in."

"I felt for a moment as though someone walked over my grave. I'm getting depressed." She jabbed her skipole angrily into the snowbank. "Yes, we'd better go in."

Two days later they were able to begin the core reassembly. Anna-Marie had been preoccupied and distant since the conversation outside the entrance bunker, and Siegner hadn't pressed her to go out on the slopes again.

At 3:00 in the afternoon of April 4 they had completed the reassembly. The glittering cubes of the core hung on their fine alloy wires, each cube six and a half centimeters on a side; the whole mass was suspended from a remotely controlled crane that could move along an overhead track into the extraction alley. Beneath the U-238 lattice gaped the core cavity, with control and instrumentation cabling snaking from panels and connectors set in the concrete that surrounded the graphite-and-powdered-uranium reflector. Several cadmium-plated control rods, operated by hydraulic rams, jutted from strategic points in the mass. The mathematics for those had cost Siegner many a long hour with a slide rule; he was still not sure that their design was as it should be. In the event of a runaway, there was a dump drain in the bottom of the cavity that would allow the heavy water to be removed by high speed pumps in under thirty seconds.

Outside the pile room itself, and separated from it by a massive concrete and lead partition, was the control room.

It was entered from a cross-corridor through a heavy steel door. Racks of instruments lined the wall on either side of the lead-glass observation port that gave on the pile chamber. In front of the port was a monitoring console. To get into the pile room you went through a thick, pluglike door in the left front wall of the control room. There was a secondary access from the extraction alley which in its turn could be reached from the laboratory chambers.

Siegner sat down at the console and stared through the greenish port at the concrete bulk of the pile, the core glinting in the floodlights above it. They were so close. Suppose it didn't work? Suppose it worked too well and the damned thing melted?

He shook his head and stopped supposing. Turning to the others in the room, he announced, "We'll run through the checklist now and then leave it for today. At six A.M. tomorrow we'll start the live runup. The blast doors to the main entrance and the emergency exit will be closed, so I want only those staff members here who are required for the operation. This is in case of the unexpected. We don't want unnecessary casualties."

Boehme appeared relieved. Most of the technicians looked disappointed.

"I want all instrumentation gone over after the checklist is complete," he went on. "Dr. Roth, would you please see to that? Let's begin."

It took an hour to run through the checklist. Not for the first time, Siegner wished for a machine that would simulate all the variables in the operation of the pile. Unfortunately, none such existed; they would simply have to start the pile and see what happened.

"All done. We'd better eat supper and have an early

night. We don't want any bleary eyes in here tomorrow morning.''

Nobody smiled at his forced attempt at humor; they were all much too tense. There was little conversation in the mess hall, and they picked at their food. Even Boehme was less self-important than usual.

The six of them who had to live underground with the pile trailed silently up to the bunker entrance a few minutes after seven. Above them the mountain hulked obsidian in the night, outlined by glittering stars. The blacked-out barracks were rectangular shadows against the snow. It had turned very cold. Somewhere off in the distance toward Sistrans a dog barked.

Inside the complex they spoke a desultory good night. A few minutes later the passageway lights were dimmed. In the pile room the core gleamed cold under the worklights.

At a few minutes after twelve, in the accommodation corridor, a door opened silently. Roth's head edged around the rough wooden frame; he glanced quickly up and down the passage. No one. He slipped out of his room, closed the door carefully behind him, and padded noiselessly on bare feet along the concrete to Anna-Marie's door. He scratched on it softly, the sound almost lost in the hum of ventilation fans.

Nothing happened. He shifted nervously on the balls of his feet, peering up and down the dim corridor. He scratched again, this time more loudly.

The door opened a crack and an eye peered at him out of the blackness. Anna-Marie gasped, opened the door, and pulled him into the room. She closed the door and fumbled for the light switch.

"I thought it was Boehme," she hissed. "What in God's name are you doing here? If there's any suspicion of us . . .''

"We've got to talk about this insanity. I haven't been able to get to you for days. Boehme keeps sniffing around."

"I know. I don't know if he's suspicious or whether he's trying to get up nerve to proposition me." A thought struck her and she whitened in the dim light. "They haven't got onto us, have they? Ever since the SD branch of the SS took over the Abwehr—"

"Not yet. A lot of the counterespionage section officers have been leaving since the SD got rid of Canaris. But there haven't been any arrests at our level, as far as I know. Unfortunately we haven't much time before this section of the network starts falling apart. Then there'll be no way of letting anyone know what's going on here."

"Who would we let know, anyway?" she whispered furiously. "With the SD in control of the Abwehr, with Canaris gone, there isn't any resistance left. That I know of."

Roth ruminated on this. German military intelligence, the Abwehr, had been controlled by Admiral Canaris, an officer of the old school, until February 1944. Then the security section of the SS, the SD, had persuaded Hitler to unify all intelligence operations under their control. Canaris had been forcibly retired and was now rumored to be under house arrest. Neither Canaris nor the Abwehr had ever had much use for SS and SD methods and there were hints that their commitment to a Nazi victory was less than total.

Eventually Roth said, "There's still some. I don't want to tell you any more."

Anna-Marie took a deep breath. "There's still one alternative we haven't discussed."

They sat side by side on the cot for a full minute before he muttered, "Go on."

"How many Germans want the Nazis in control of Germany? That might happen if they forced a negotiated peace.''

"Not many of us. But you're thinking of—"

"Treason. We might as well use the word. There's no one in Germany who can and will stop this project, is there?''

"I don't know. No, there isn't.''

"Could we get information to the Allies? The Western Allies?''

Roth scrubbed his hands through his wiry black hair. "They'd never believe us.''

"What about with documents?''

"Plants. They'd think they were plants. To frighten them. The kind of thing we did before the war. They're wary.''

"They'd believe Peter.''

"Peter's under this mountain with us, not in England. Do you think he'd go, anyway?''

Her wistful, brief hope of leaving, with Peter and Roth, the blood-drenched rubble of the Third Reich, faded. "No. I thought he might, two days ago. When we came in from skiing I was going to sound him out on slowing the project down somehow. But he started to talk about the pile before I could say anything. He's obsessed with it. He said so himself. He wouldn't go; he wants to see if it'll work.''

"Suppose Hitler's right? Suppose they do blackmail the Allies into negotiations?''

"Are you as mad as all that? Germany's going to be smashed no matter what we do. If we don't go down like mad dogs there may be something left. If we use this . . . thing they may wipe us off the face of the earth. If we stop now, we'll have said there's at least one line we won't cross.''

"I can't understand why Peter won't see it.''

"He dreads the Russians. Anyway, he wants to see if he can build the frightful thing, the bomb, I mean. He has to make the fission poisons to do that. He doesn't want to acknowledge what's going to be done with them. They're a problem in physics, not a reality."

"You've become rather attached to him, haven't you?"

She picked at the rough cloth of her nightdress as it lay on her knee. The two of them had shared the dangers of being Abwehr operatives in an SS organization ever since they had been inserted into the project, right at the beginning. "Yes," she admitted finally.

"It could be done," muttered Roth. "But we'd need some backup, some proof. Peter's never let either of us get near the critical information, except verbally. We've got to have something more convincing than that."

"The work I've done on the extraction procedures might do it. I could give some of that."

"It would probably do." He leaned down and massaged his feet; they were freezing. "When were you recruited?"

"Nineteen-forty. I was finishing my degree. The Abwehr wanted contacts in science, chemistry particularly, to keep track of things. It was mostly for counterespionage, then, of course." Her whisper was bitter. "What about you?"

"I went in about the same time. They eventually found me a job at Degussa, where the uranium was refined."

The air was thick with memories. Eventually, Roth whispered, "We can always hope the damned thing won't work. Then the problem will be over for good."

"Yes."

The springs of the cot creaked. Then she said, "But if it does, can you contact the Allies?"

"There's a man in Innsbrück I might be able to use."

"To contact the Allies?"

"No. But," and he hesitated, "there was a rumor. In 1941. That Oster had a line to them."

"*Oster?*"

"It was only a rumor. It said that he leaked to the Norwegians that we were going to invade them. That part of the network might still be active. For the moment, anyhow. I could try it. There was a code word for getting to him or his people. I know it."

She eyed him speculatively in the dimness. "You're higher up in the Abwehr than I thought."

"Yes. But my name isn't in any files. Oster recruited me himself, and got me into the Degussa plant. I think he was afraid something like this might happen." He frowned. "Oster's been under house arrest for almost a year. But there might be something left of the channel. Suppose we wait to see if the pile runs. If it does, I'll try to get word out."

"If they find out, we're dead."

She had spoken aloud.

Outside, in the corridor, Siegner stood frozen, his knuckles about to fall on the paneling of the door. Slowly he let his arm drop to his side. He had not heard Anna-Marie's words plainly, but Roth's voice was clear enough in response.

"Not so loud, for God's sake. I'll see you tomorrow."

Siegner flung himself down the corridor to the door of his own cubicle and shot through it. The click of Anna-Marie's doorlatch was hidden in that of his own. A moment later a faint creak told him that Roth's door had closed as well.

So much for unburdening himself to Anna-Marie, he thought ruefully. I've paid no attention to her for two years, I shouldn't be surprised if she's picked up with somebody.

Better Roth than anybody else. But it's odd I never noticed any hint of it.

He was disappointed, just the same.

Siegner, Roth, Anna-Marie, two instrument technicians, and Sommer had assembled in the control room by a quarter to six the next morning. Siegner noted, with mixed emotions, that Roth and Anna-Marie were hollow eyed and tired-looking. He supposed that he looked much the same; he hadn't slept well. His dreams, which he could not remember clearly, revolved around Russia, the battle at Kharkov, the face of the unknown major in the firelight. Anna-Marie had been somewhere there too; he couldn't remember how.

They ran through the checklist one last time. At the end of it Siegner told them.

"If we can't damp down the reaction with the control rods after it starts to run by itself—if it does—we'll dump the heavy water. I don't think there is much chance of it getting out of hand. But watch the core water temperature; if it edges past the red lines, we'll go to the emergency procedure. I'm more worried about steam generation than anything else at the moment. Let's begin."

They took their places, Siegner at the monitor console, Sommer at the core manipulators, Anna-Marie at the control rod panel. The technicians hovered over their gauges.

The main feature of the monitor console was one that Siegner had designed and built himself. It was a plotter that compared the neutron generation from the trigger in the center of the core cavity with that at the outer edge of the reflector. The vertical scale on the plot paper ran from one hundred to one hundred and twenty. He had calibrated the machine so that when the line plotted across the unreeling graph paper reached the one hundred level, the pile would

93

be critical and the self-sustaining fission reaction would be running. There were other instruments to measure the neutron density at the moderator perimeter and points inside it, but he would use these readings later for accurate analysis of the processes within the core. The plotter was the control point for the startup.

"Check blast doors closed, main and emergency tunnels."

"All closed." The green lights glittered above Sommer's panel.

"Extraction fans on."

"Check. Building to speed." Above the pile chamber the great cooling fans began pulling air from the inlet tunnel past the pile assembly, driving it up the long exhaust shaft to the stack on the slopes of the mountain six hundred feet above.

"Fans at speed."

"Lower the core."

It took six minutes for the two and a half tons of uranium cubes to descend to the stops in the cavity. They inserted the beryllium neutron source. The plot rose slightly. About five.

"Turn on the pumps. Slow speed. Stop at the halfway mark."

The floor of the control room began to vibrate slightly. Unseen, the heavy water began to ascend the walls of the cavity around the uranium cubes.

"Halfway."

The plotter lodged at ten.

"Take it up to three-quarters," Siegner ordered.

At three-quarters the plotter reading was twenty.

"Let's go the rest of the way. Be ready with the dump."

When the cavity was full, the plotter stood at thirty-five.

"All right. Let's have some readings."

They checked internal neutron density and temperatures. Siegner worked his slide rule. After two hours, at ten o'clock in the morning, he was satisfied.

"We'll start pulling the control rods now. First level."

The hydraulic rams withdrew the rods a few centimeters. The plotter gave fifty. Siegner rubbed his chin. It was working.

"Second level. Then we'll stop again."

Sixty-eight on the plotter.

"Temperature?"

"Sixteen."

"Let's take some more readings."

It was noon before he was satisfied. There was no mention of eating.

"Next level."

The plotter rolled. Eight-five. Anna-Marie and Roth exchanged glances.

"Next level. Watch it carefully this time. I think it's going to go."

The rams hauled the rods out again. The temperature stayed at sixteen degrees. The plotter hummed.

"Ninety on the plot."

"Ninety-five."

"Ninety-eight."

"One-oh-one. Temperature?"

"Rising. Twenty degrees."

"Be ready to run the rods in again. Ready with the dump."

"Temperature is forty. Leveling off. Forty-two."

They waited.

"Still forty-two."

They waited some more. The cooling fans rumbled.

"Still forty-two."

Siegner leaned back in the console chair. "That's it, then. We've got three levels yet on the rods. We won't pull them any farther for now; we'll get the pile up to full efficiency later.

"But we've done it. It runs."

Above his head, Anna-Marie's and Roth's eyes met.

III

England—The Reich

April 25–May 19, 1944

As they descended toward the Sussex coast, at five thousand feet, the starboard Merlin began to stumble and smoke. Flying Officer Colin Patterson craned his neck to look past his navigator at the offending engine.

"Bloody hell. We must have caught some flak on the last pass." Patterson studied the gauges low down by his left knee. Oil temperature was passing 120 degrees and the pressure was sliding down below safe limits.

"We'd better feather the starboard. Get ready with the fire extinguishers in case she burns."

Brian Mackenzie pressed the right-hand feathering button and held it until the solenoid engaged. He flipped up the cover on the starboard extinguisher button and was about to press it when Patterson interrupted.

"Hold on a minute. It might run again if we have to have it."

The starboard propeller of the photographic reconnaissance Mosquito jerked to a stop. Patterson closed the throttle and radiator flap and switched off the ignition. The engine showed no sign of fire.

"Good enough. How long to Tilford Bridge?"

"Twenty minutes."

"Might as well go there. No use diverting."

For a few minutes they watched the patchwork of southern England slide past beneath the stationary propeller. Patterson kept a good deal of power on the port engine, slanting the Mosquito down toward the early evening landscape below.

"Port engine's getting a bit warm," observed Mackenzie.

"I hope we haven't got a chunk of iron in that one too. Maybe we should have diverted."

"It won't be long now, anyway," Mackenzie told him. "We're only a few minutes out."

The radio crackled. "Tango ground calling," it said. "Aircraft on southeast approach. Please identify."

"That's us. Better tell them who we are."

"Tango ground," said Patterson into his microphone, "this is A-Able. We are the aircraft on your southwest approach. We have one engine out. We're about ten minutes from you. Over."

"Roger, A-Able. We were expecting you. Reception committee will be waiting. Out."

Patterson kept plenty of height. The Mosquito still had 2000 feet at five minutes from the airfield. Patterson backed off the port throttle until the aircraft was traveling at 180 knots.

"Let's see if the flaps are working."

"Fifteen degrees of flap." Mackenzie reached down and moved the control. The Mosquito slowed and lifted. Patterson advanced the throttle slightly. He decided against starting the starboard engine; if it failed on landing they would almost certainly crash.

"Flaps are good."

"Try the undercarriage."

The aircraft slowed rapidly and began to sink as the

98

wheels came down. Patterson worked the trim wheel to counteract the sudden tail heaviness. The airfield was in sight a couple of miles ahead. They were at a thousand feet and traveling quite fast; patches of snow and brownish-gray trees whipped under the wings.

"Undercarriage down and locked."

"Could be worse. We'll shut down the port engine about five hundred yards out. I don't think we'll have to go around again."

Ahead they could just make out the blocky forms of the emergency vehicles at the edge of the runway. A group of children on the boundary road waved at them as they shot over it. Mackenzie waved back.

Patterson reduced the port throttle. The Mosquito sank faster. He opened the engine up a little, then backed it off again.

"We've got a fire in the starboard," said Mackenzie. "Buggeration."

A tiny slip of flame was peeping out at the seam between the engine cowling and the wing. Mackenzie pressed the extinguisher button. Nothing happened.

"A few seconds to go." Patterson's voice was unhurried. "Jettison the hatch as soon as we stop."

The Mosquito flared down to the end of the runway, shot across the boundary marker, and touched the paving. Patterson worked the brakes. More flames ripped from the starboard engine. Emergency vehicles clanged along the runway toward them. As the Mosquito slued to a stop Mackenzie and Patterson were already unbuckling their harness. The heat from the fire in the starboard engine was intense; it tightened the skin over the cheekbones.

Mackenzie released the escape hatch in the canopy roof and pushed it aside. He hauled himself through it, shielding

99

his face from the flames with his arm, slid onto the port wing roof and dropped heavily to the ground. Patterson followed as the fire trucks pulled up, bells clanging. A squad of men dropped off the trucks and began spraying the engine with foam. Mackenzie and Patterson backed away.

They were staring disconsolately at the crippled aircraft when the Austin that had been following the emergency vehicles drew up. The squadron intelligence officer got out and hurried over to them.

"You chaps all right? No injuries?"

"Only the crate. It was a bloody good one too, dammit."

The intelligence officer favoured A-Able with a professional glance. "The cameras are likely all right, anyway."

"That's the main thing." Mackenzie's voice was slightly sour.

"Sorry. How long did you have Able?"

"Three months."

"Cheer up. We'll get you another one. It looks as though this one's a write-off, I'm afraid. Can I get you back for debriefing now?" he asked, apologetically. "There's an awful lot to be done."

Pierce cradled his chin in his hands and stared at the thin file lying on the blotter before him. It was stamped TOP SECRET; a small sticker in one corner bore the single word *Fenris*. There were only four sheets of paper in the file: three message flimsies and an appraisal written by Devereaux and Mclennand. The appreciation was not very long.

Devereaux shifted uncomfortably in his chair. He had reversed it and his arms lay one atop the other along the back. Mclennand stared out the window at the April rain. Over the smoky reaches of the Thames it was growing dark.

100

At last Pierce grumbled, "There isn't really anything else to go on, is there?"

Neither of the other two answered. Mclennand uncrossed his legs and recrossed them the other way.

Pierce uncradled his chin and said wryly, "I suppose, looking back, that there wasn't that much reason to, almost, panic." He opened the file and extracted the bottom flimsy. "'Fenris yawns,' it says. What was that you found out about the Fenris wolf, Alan?"

Devereaux tipped the chair forward onto two legs. "The myth said that when Fenris yawned, his lower jaw touched earth, and his upper, heaven."

"The message doesn't actually refer to heavy water, though, does it? Was the assumption that it means they have the stuff too great a one?"

"I don't think so," said Mclennand, and went on staring out the window.

Pierce seemed nonplussed. "What makes you so, ah, adamant?"

Mclennand frowned. "I can't really tell you. It's not rational, it's what you might call a . . . conviction. The last six weeks of silence bothers me more than additional intelligence would. I feel we ought to do something, but I have no idea what."

"Alan?"

"I'm not as sure as Gordon but I can't bring myself to disregard the situation. The possibility of some clever Germans starting up a pile we don't know about is too much of a risk for us to take, no matter how low its probability. If we had more information on where the heavy water got to, it might be worth sending a reconnaissance flight. But we can't ask the PRU people to start a full-scale search of southern Germany for a target that small. Remember the trouble we had locating the Würtzburg radar stations? And they were on our own doorstep, practically."

"Every recon machine is tied up photographing invasion targets in France, anyway."

"There was that unlikely triangulation," offered Mclennand. Purely by chance, it had been possible to make a rough calculation from about the direction from which the third message had come.

"That puts it on a line somewhere between here and, approximately, Munich· or Innsbrück. That's better than southern Germany but still not nearly good enough to ask for an overflight," answered Pierce. "Not with the current demand on the photorecon units. It wouldn't be a very big target, would it?"

"They could hide most of it under a mountain, if they were willing to make the effort. Not very comfortable living conditions, so there'd likely be barracks for workers and security troops. But the whole thing could look like an ordinary military installation."

Pierce closed the file and stood up. "I've asked for a special meeting of some of the scientific advisory staff. I wanted to get your last word on the subject before I see them this evening. They aren't going to be easy to convince, I'm afraid." He put on his coat. "I'd like you to know, though, that I share your gloomy outlook. The damned thing stinks to high heaven. I'm going to try to get some pressure exerted on some of the other intelligence-gathering organizations to look harder, or at least see if there's something tucked away in a file somewhere that would help. But don't get your hopes up."

Devereaux and Mclennand returned to their office and locked up. Rain streamed down the windows behind the blackout curtains.

"It's another dirty night."

"D'you think he'll get anywhere?"

"No. We don't have enough information."

"Just a feeling."

"Feelings won't convince the Air Staff."

"No, they won't, will they?"

The next morning was clear and bright. Devereaux spun his hat at the coatrack as he came through the office door. The hat narrowly missed Mclennand's head.

"Bloody RAF," Mclennand observed. "Can't hit anything."

A note lay on Devereaux's blotter. Mclennand gestured at it. "Pierce wants to see us as soon as we're both in. He must have left the note here last night after his meeting."

"It's either very bad news or very good."

"More likely the former."

It was. Pierce was still wearing his coat and was looking angry.

"Get your coats on. We're going for a drive. We'll be gone all day, so lock everything up."

"They wouldn't listen?"

"I'll tell you in the car."

A staff car was waiting outside the front door. To Devereaux's and Mclennand's surprise, the driver got out and went into the building. Pierce slipped behind the wheel and the other two followed him into the car. Still silent, Pierce gunned the vehicle away. They crossed Westminster Bridge and headed south toward Reigate. There was no conversation for a good half-hour.

Eventually Devereaux ventured, "Where are we going?"

"To Tilford Bridge Photographic Reconnaissance base. To see a friend of mine, Group Captain Patrick Gilford. Commands 37 PR wing. You've probably heard of him, Alan."

"He was involved with Bomber Command PR a few years ago."

"That's the man."

They digested this in silence for a few miles. Pierce seemed disinclined to talk. At length Mclennand said diffidently, "I take it the meeting last night didn't . . . "

"Come to much?" Pierce snorted, then blew out his cheeks. "No. There's a conviction among the powers that be that the whole *Fenris* situation is either (a), a red herring, a deception that didn't get off the ground, or (b), the real thing. If (a) is true, then there's no problem. If (b) is true, there's still no problem, because there's no chance the Germans can do anything with the heavy water in time to affect the war." Pierce grinned at Devereaux in the rearview mirror. "Didn't know I'd studied logic, did you, Alan?"

"It sounds like pretty poor logic, if you don't mind my saying so."

"No dissenting opinions?" asked Mclennand.

"A couple. The trouble is, none of the really big guns—Jones, for instance—were there. Nobody much wanted to rock the boat. The best that the dissenters offered was that the matter would be taken up with the Joint Intelligence Committee—again. And the JIC has more than enough on its collective plate already. So the dissenters were outweighed. A note of the meeting will be submitted, that's all."

"So now we're off to Tilford Bridge."

"We are. If I can get round this bloody convoy."

Ahead of the Austin a column of lorries, tanks on transporters, huge American trucks, and all the paraphernalia of the supply war was proceeding southward at a docile twenty miles an hour. Pierce swore and gestured to Mclennand. "There's a map in the glove box. We'll have to go around this lot or we won't be there till noon. See if there's a way to leapfrog them."

Mclennand studied the map. "There's a secondary road, next right. It'll put us back on this one about twenty miles farther on. But you'll have to be quick or the column will be at the intersection before we are."

For the next thirty minutes they careered along the country lanes, Devereaux expecting to become part of a hedgerow at every turn of the road. Mclennand looked longingly at a pub called *The Dog and Pheasant* as they regained the main road.

"That did it, then," said Pierce with satisfaction as he accelerated away south. "Another hour. Then lunch and a chat with Patrick."

They rolled up to the gates of the airfield at a few minutes past twelve, and were waved straight through. Obviously they were expected. At the operations block a short, chunky officer came down the steps as the car drew to a halt. The man had a stiff brush of wiry black hair, thinning at the temples. His uniform cap sat precariously, as if about to fling itself to the winds at the first excuse. As they got out of the Austin the officer bawled:

"Ian. Glad to see you. Just in time for a drink."

Pierce waved his two assistants forward. "Flight Lieutenant Alan Devereaux. Lieutenant Gordon Mclennand. This is Group Captain Gilford. I'm glad you mentioned the drink, Patrick. We could all use one. And some other help, too, if you've a way to give it."

"Come into the office. We can talk there, won't be able to if we use the Mess. I'll have some lunch sent over."

They installed themselves in Gilford's narrow office, whose walls were plastered with low- and high-level reconnaissance photographs of every description. A large-scale map of Germany was tacked to the wall behind the desk. Taped to one corner of it was a three-view plan of a Heinkel 219 nightfighter. Red, green, and purple crayon-tracks disfigured the paper face of the Third Reich.

Gilford caught Devereaux studying the silhouettes of the Heinkel. "Nasty piece of work, that one," he said. "Was it around when you were on operations?"

"No. Mostly Messerschmitt 110s and Junkers 88s. The odd single-seater."

"It's a good thing there aren't more of them about. They give some of our Mosquitos trouble from time to time. Very fast; a bit faster than a photorecon Mossie under the right conditions. Maneuverable, too. They pack an awful wallop in the gun department, unfortunately." Gilford turned to Pierce and waved an arm at the photograph-laden walls. "I'd show you my picture museum if you had time, but I don't suppose you have, do you?" His voice was slightly wistful.

"What's that one up there?" asked Pierce. "The one just under the waterstain next to the window. I've been wondering about it ever since Alan started worrying about your Heinkel."

Mclennand and Devereaux exchanged glances. Pierce was rarely so transparently transparent.

A knock on the door interrupted Gilford's reply. A batman carried in a large plate of sandwiches and a pot of tea. He left, and reappeared a moment later with a tray of glasses, cups, and saucers. Among the glasses and porcelain was a large bottle of whiskey.

They stared at the photograph while the batman opened the whiskey. When the door had closed behind the man, Gilford poured four drinks and said, "What do you think it is, Lieutenant Mclennand?"

"I couldn't hazard a guess."

"Lieutenant Devereaux?"

"I could guess, but I'd rather not."

"It's a high-level photograph of a radar mast, taken at sunrise so there'd be enough shadow to provide an indication of its height. You can see the shadow falling across the bunker, that whitish rectangle on the right. It also gives an indication of the height of the bunker. Wonderful thing, trignometry."

"Things show up well at sunrise or sunset, then," observed Pierce.

Gilford finished his whiskey and picked up a sandwich. "You already know that, Ian. What is it you want me to do?"

Pierce stared at his thumb resting on the rim of the whiskey glass. "I can't tell you why we're . . . concerned. But there may be an installation of some kind, near Munich or Innsbrück, that could hide something frightfully dangerous. But all we have at the moment on it is the skimpiest of information."

"Is 'we' the collective Intelligence establishment, or you three gentlemen?"

"We three."

"Ah."

Pierce set his glass down and picked up a sandwich. He bit into it fiercely. "Corned beef," he complained.

"Sorry."

"There might be something visible in the area that would give us an indication of whether we're on the right track," Pierce continued between bites. "Or whether the thing's operational or not."

"But you don't know what it looks like, or precisely where it is. How big an area are you talking about?"

"Alan?"

Devereaux answered, slowly. "If it does exist, I believe it's under a mountain somewhere near Innsbrück. Munich is on the right radio bearing, but it's too far from the Alpine foothills to be likely. Furthermore, there are no major rail lines going toward the mountains on that bearing except those leading to Innsbrück. They'd need nearby railways to handle the kind of heavy equipment they'd have to have. The most likely area covers about two hundred square miles."

Gilford ate the rest of his sandwich. Then he asked, "Are you requesting low-level photography of two hundred square miles?"

Pierce bit his lip. "Not possible, is it?"

"I'm afraid not. If you had a pinpoint target, perhaps. The kind of thing we're looking for is hard to see even at low level, right?"

"We think so."

"I might be able to handle one, or even two, trips to the spot, if you knew where it was. Slip them in between the major reconnaissance operations for the invasion. But the kind of coverage you've suggested isn't possible. It's all being used up in France." He fiddled with another sandwich. "I'm sorry, Ian, I just can't do it."

They listened for a moment to the rasp of an aircraft engine being tested far off by one of the hangars. Mclennand set his glass down and asked, "What would the conditions be for a flight?"

"H'm. Good weather over the target area, obviously. Knowledge of the position of the target to within a couple of miles. Early morning or late afternoon, if you need to see shadows. That would mean a flight from here starting at night, high level, timed to reach the target at dawn. You

108

wouldn't want to come back in daylight, much, but you could go on to a base in Italy. The photography would be done in a highspeed, low-level pass, coming down from the transit altitude. Easy enough, if you know where to go to find what you're looking for.''

"Suppose you had that," suggested Devereaux.

Gilford shrugged. "We could do it. There might be a row about doing it without authorization, afterwards, but if you're so convinced there's danger, we really ought to have a look, oughtn't we?''

"Thank you, Patrick," said Pierce.

Gilford picked up the whiskey bottle. "Another drop? I can't myself, I've a meeting this afternoon. But feel free.''

They refused, and made their departure a quarter of an hour later. Back in the car, once outside the airfield gates, Devereaux suggested that the journey hadn't achieved much.

Pierce looked irritated. "You don't know Patrick. The chat we had will be like a flea in his drawers. He won't be able to forget it until we get him some information on the target. Then he'll send a plane without any prompting. We—I—won't have to go through channels.''

"Are you sure he'll do it?''

Pierce laughed. "If there's any unusual danger to his crews he'll say no. But if he thinks his people can do it, and if we can give him the location, and if it's slightly unbureaucratic, he'll go ahead. By the way, did you notice the coincidence of his name and the airfield's?''

"Gilford-Tilford," Mclennand said. "Neat.''

"Patrick thinks so," Pierce smiled. "Says it makes him feel at home.''

In his office several miles behind them, Gilford finally

took his eyes from the map of Germany and began to search in a desk drawer. Out came a length of cord marked off in tens of miles. Standing before the map, Gilford began to measure off distances from Tilford Bridge.

When he stretched the cord for his last measurement, his right thumb hovered directly over Innsbrück.

"Isn't there anything you can tell me?" She shifted beside him, looking over his head at the tape-mended windowpane. "You and Alan have been acting oddly ever since March, looking as though . . . I don't know. As though something were about to go wrong."

Mclennand rubbed his bare chest and watched the late afternoon clouds sidle by beyond the strip of tape masking the crack in the glass.

"I know you can't talk to me about what you do, much," she told him. "But you haven't behaved like this since Dunkirk. It can't be as bad as that. Can it?"

"I can't tell you, Jean." It embarrassed him to say it.

"I know. God damn it." She rolled over and sat up on the edge of the bed. "But when my husband and his friend go about looking like the Saturday end of a wet week for three months on end, you can hardly blame me for being upset. What about Catherine," she went on, "stuck down there in Sussex, wishing Alan would go and see her again? How do you think she feels?"

"Cat?" asked Mclennand. "I didn't think that had gone very far. With Alan, I mean."

"Of course it hasn't. How could it, when they don't see each other from one week's end to the next? She's been here twice lately and you've both been off at the War Office, worrying about whatever it is you're worrying about."

Mclennand beat a hasty retreat from the subject. "Cat'll be here soon. Alan should arrive about seven."

110

His wife looked at him disconsolately. "I'm sorry. I do want this evening to be pleasant. But you've been so withdrawn lately, it's getting on my nerves."

"I'm sorry, too," he answered. "I can't do anything about it."

They dressed in silence.

Catherine arrived at the flat at half past five, carrying a bottle of Bordeaux. "It's the last of the prewar stock Tony had laid in," she explained. "I thought we should celebrate the beginning of spring. Is Alan coming?"

"About seven," she said. "We invited him for supper but he said he couldn't come."

Jean relieved Catherine of the wine and went into the kitchen. "Gordon thinks he's concerned about the rationing, using up our meager wherewithal. But the one thing I won't do is to let the war prevent us from entertaining our friends."

Devereaux arrived shortly after they had finished eating. After a slightly strained beginning he and Catherine fell into an animated and detailed discussion of the spring planting. Devereaux was plainly a little homesick for the country. When he could finally get a word in edgeways, Mclennand suggested bridge. They played for some time. Finally Devereaux looked at his watch and exclaimed, "Good Lord. I'm going to miss the last Underground home. I'd better be off."

Catherine rose hurriedly to her feet. "I didn't realize it was so late. I'd better go as well."

Mclennand began to suggest that she was welcome to stay over, but his wife silenced him with a look. As Devereaux and Catherine put on their coats, she said, "Cat, try to telephone before you go back to Sevenoaks. Alan, make sure she gets on the right Underground line."

Catherine laughed. "I haven't been away from London that long."

"All the same. Good night."

"Good night."

The night air was soft, with a light, warm mist. An aircraft droned faintly somewhere far overhead. With the blackout and the mist it was exceedingly dark. Devereaux felt for Catherine's hand and found it. Her fingers tightened around his.

"We'd better hop it. The last trains will be running soon."

They found the entrance to Russell Square station after a couple of false tries and, still hand in hand, clattered down the stairs. A few more timorous souls had encamped on the platform for the night. As they waited for the train, Catherine said, "At least the air raids have stopped."

"There're rumors of other things to come, though. The Germans aren't finished yet, no matter what we'd like to believe."

She shivered slightly in the damp air. "I know. You're involved in that a little bit, aren't you?"

"A little."

They stood comfortably side by side. The approaching train drove a gust of air laden with odors of ancient soot, ozone, damp bricks, and mortar around them and made them turn their heads aside. As they boarded the carriage Catherine disengaged her hand and slipped her arm through his.

"Where do you get off?" asked Devereaux.

"Bond Street."

"Oh." He was disappointed. She would have to change trains at the next stop. "Never mind, I'll come with you and see you on your way."

"Thank you." She turned to him on the hard seat. "Alan, I have to stay in Sussex for the next few weeks, because of the farm. Is there any possibility you could come down for a little while? I'm sorry to be so forward." She smiled faintly. "It's the war, you see."

He squeezed her arm against his side, very conscious of the contact through the heavy wool of his RAF greatcoat.

"Absolutely." He leaned over and surprised her by lightly kissing the end of her nose. She turned rather pink. "I'll try to get some leave within the next couple of weeks. As soon as I know when, I'll telephone you."

She pressed closer to him. They rode that way until the train pulled into Holborn Station.

She met him at the Hastings railway terminal on a windy, bright, Saturday afternoon. The train was two hours late, and more crowded, if possible, than it had been on his previous journey. Devereaux had had to stand for most of the way, having reached Charing Cross only a minute before the train was due to leave. Large numbers of servicemen had stepped on his toes. He was irritable.

The irritation dissolved as he went through the waiting room and saw Catherine hurry in from the street. As before, her pale hair was confined under a kerchief. She wore a light suede jacket that could have been found in more expensive London shops before the war. Devereaux hadn't seen such fine leather since 1940.

"I'm sorry I'm late." He grinned. "It's the war, you see."

She flushed a little and straightened the jacket self-consciously. Several women in the waiting room looked at her garb with a mixture of envy and disapproval. It was too far into the war for luxury to be fashionable.

"It's all right, I'm late myself. The car wouldn't start. Jacob said it got too damp last night for the poor old thing."

They got into the shooting brake. As they left the station, she asked, "Did you see how some of them looked at me? Back there in the station?"

"I suppose it was the jacket."

She shifted gears viciously, slowing for a hedge-hidden turn. "Yes. There's a certain class, pardon me, category, of people who would like everyone else to be as miserable as they are."

"I admit you look very well. But expensive for this part of the country so far along in the war."

"I did it because you were coming. Normally I try to blend in."

He was touched; she had made herself vulnerable because of him. "I thought you might have. I'm very . . . flattered. No, that's not the word."

"The word isn't surprised?"

"No. Not really."

"Good. I wouldn't have wanted you to be surprised."

"Catherine," he said, and stopped.

She glanced at him sidelong. "We should talk about this later. When I can concentrate on something besides this bloody road."

A couple of small tree branches had blown across the paving. She twisted the wheel expertly and swerved the car around them. "Before the war I would have gone over them. The tires are nearly worn through, though, and you can't get more. It makes for careful driving. By the way, why didn't you write? It's been two weeks."

"What about?" Then, because that was too brusque, he added, "There's nothing much to write; work, eat, sleep. The odd evening with Jean and Gordon. Doesn't make for very interesting reading."

"I'd be interested. Do you ever see any of the men you flew with?"

"Not really." He thought of explaining that some of them were dead, and that the others were scattered throughout the Royal Air Force by now. "Not really," he repeated, and fell silent. He suddenly remembered the smell of oil, petrol, hot metal, explosives; the indefinable scent that was the characteristic odor of the flight deck of a Lancaster bomber. He closed his eyes for a moment, and it went away.

She had noticed, and said quietly, "I'm talking too much." She speeded up a little.

They rode along the spring lanes until Devereaux said, "We must be nearly there. Wasn't that the milestone we passed last time?"

"You've an eye for detail. Yes. The lane is just around the curve."

It might have been a repetition of his last arrival, except that there were blossoms starting on the apple tree by the corner of the farmhouse. Jacob came out of the carriage house, waved, and went back inside.

As Devereaux unloaded his bag from the car, she told him, "You must have passed muster last time. Jacob doesn't feel he needs to check again, I guess."

"You're well protected from infamy."

As they entered the cool gloom of the farmhouse she said, "I thought there might have been a small scandal from having had you stay last time. I suppose the war has changed that kind of thing, or Jacob decided not to mention it to anyone. Probably the latter. It would have been a nine days' wonder, before the war, wouldn't it?"

"I should think so."

After lunch they decided, in the immemorial fashion of lovers, to revisit the place where they had first sensed the

115

necessity between them. Catherine advised, after a slight hesitation, "It won't be so cold as last time, but you'd better wear something warm. No, your greatcoat's too heavy. Would you be uncomfortable in something of Tony's?"

He could hardly refuse. It was an exquisitely crafted sweater of finespun wool; when he put it on it fit perfectly. She took him by the arms and said softly, "I should tell you that I'm not trying to turn you into Tony. He would have liked you to wear this. He told me, once, that if he were killed he'd want me to keep the farm going. But he said that it would be hard for me to do it myself. Tony's gone. I'm still here. That's all I'd like to say about it."

He nodded and they went out into the day.

They followed the same lanes as before, up the slopes of Fell Hill. Where previously there had lain snow-tufted grass and tinkling ice in the puddles, there was now fresh green on the southern hill faces and in the ruts of the lane. In the more sheltered hollows there were occasional violets. At the summit of the hill they found a sun-warmed stone and sat on it to talk. Eventually it grew colder in the westering sun.

They were about to leave the hilltop when she asked:

"What's going to happen to us, do you think?"

He was as much at a loss as she. "I don't know. Twice up here I've almost muttered something about marrying you, but . . . "

"I know. It seems too soon because of, oh, everything." She looked far out into the gathering dusk toward the unseen enemy coast of France. "But because of the war, one's caught. You hesitate to go ahead, because the future's so uncertain, and you're afraid to delay, because there might not be another chance . . . " She gestured helplessly. "It's an impossible situation, isn't it?"

116

He laughed, but it was not really a laugh. "I suppose it'd be better to put off a decision until the war's over. It shouldn't be all that many more months, one way or the other."

"One way or the other." She studied him intently, but could read nothing from his face. "Do you mean there's still a chance for the Germans?" She stopped, appalled.

"Damn." He rubbed his cold cheek miserably. "I should keep my mouth shut. Please don't let it go any further. Wait, I'm sorry, I know it won't."

She was visibly upset. "I knew there was a problem between Gordon and Jean, now I know why. You've both been in a daze since February. There's nothing more you can tell me?"

He shook his head. After a silence she said, "We'd better go back. It's getting colder."

They talked little on the way down Fell Hill. She was preoccupied, and little wonder, thought Devereaux. Why couldn't I have stayed silent? Things were difficult enough already.

But as they walked over the flagstones to the farmhouse door, she looked up at him and said decisively, "Jacob will be off the farm until tomorrow noon. There's no need for you to sleep in the carriage house tonight."

They ate breakfast the next morning ("Sausage, toast and tea," apologized Catherine. "The hens haven't been laying well.") in a curious atmosphere of shyness and intimacy. Devereaux was consuming the next-to-last sausage when the telephone rang. Catherine disappeared into the hall.

"It's for you. Gordon."

He went to the hall and picked up the receiver with foreboding. Mclennand's voice came faintly over the line.

"Can you get back as soon as possible? Something's come up."

"Old Norse myths?"

"I'm afraid so. If you can't get a train by noon, call Pierce. He'll send a car for you."

"All right. See you later."

Back in the kitchen, Catherine was pouring more tea. "We'll just have time for this. Then I'll take you to the station. There's a train to London at nine forty-five. I take it that's what the call was about?"

"I'm afraid so," he said, echoing Mclennand's words.

She sighed. "The milking will be late, but I can get Jacob over before we go. You'd better pack. I'll see to the car." A pause. "I know I'm being very brisk, but I need to be. Please understand."

Devereaux nodded and went to pack his gear.

There were six of them around the long, polished conference table. Devereaux and Mclennand sat down near one end, nearest the door ("Below the salt," Devereaux said later). Darlington, Pierce's immediate superior, presided in a leather armchair before the window, Pierce on his right. The other two were anonymous men whom neither Mclennand nor Devereaux had ever seen before. They wore pinstriped suits and were quite expressionless.

Darlington introduced them as Cooper and Smith, and opened the file which lay on the table before him. Without looking at it, he intoned, "The signal I am about to read to you exists in two copies only, of which this is one. A transcript of the pertinent facts will be supplied to Commander Pierce for evaluation by his staff. The second full copy remains with the Joint Intelligence Committee. There will be no verbal or written communication outside this group as to the source or content of this document, without

118

previous written approval from myself.''

"The signal was intercepted one day ago. It was sent—by accident or intent—in an obsolete Abwehr code that hasn't been used since the outbreak of war. It is this fact that makes the evaluators think that either it is a plant, or a genuine attempt by an unknown party to inform us of certain events inside Germany. There is some precedent for this last possibility, as you may be aware. Not all the German intelligence organizations are completely loyal, at least not to Hitler.''

"The curious thing is that it was addressed to an Abwehr agent in Lisbon. This agent we doubled in 1942 and he has been feeding doctored information to the Germans for us ever since. Needless to say, he has been, h'm, residing in England for the last two years under the care of Mr. Cooper and Mr. Smith. We were all most surprised that he should receive a message such as this one. The code wasn't one he had been given.'' Darlington picked up a single sheet of paper from the file and read:

" 'To Blackbird. Attempt to determine any concern in your circles as to the installation at Sistrans. Situation is critical. You have very little time. Wolf.' ''

He replaced the sheet of paper in the file and gazed around the table. "Any observations?''

I take it,'' said Pierce, "that 'Wolf' is not the name of Blackbird's controller.''

"That's right.'' Darlington looked directly at Mclennand and Devereaux. "Gentlemen?''

" 'Wolf' looks like an intentional connection to *Fenris*,'' observed Mclennand. "Very obvious, though. Were there any peculiarities about the German text?''

Pierce looked startled and then emitted a snort of laughter. Darlington appeared puzzled. "I was going to mention that in a moment. The word 'critical' was in English, not Ger-

119

man, when the original text was decoded. Ah, the more scientific types haven't been got together on the message yet—I take it this could be significant to them?''

Mclennand had to remind himself that both Darlington and Pierce were far removed from the details and vocabulary of nuclear science. '' 'Critical' is a jargon word used to describe the point at which a nuclear reaction becomes self-sustaining,'' he explained. ''In other words, when an atomic pile's begun to operate.''

''Where is Sistrans?'' asked Devereaux.

Cooper answered. ''It's a small village a little way outside Innsbrück. South of the river Inn, on the side of a mountain called the Patscherkofel.''

''It's the right place, isn't it?'' said Pierce.

''What do you make of the message?'' broke in Cooper. ''It's blatantly obvious if one has any idea at all of the background. Perhaps suspiciously so.''

Pierce fumbled for his pipe, inspected it carefully, and laid it on the table. ''Yes, it is. But it has a tone of desperation that makes me think we're dealing with an intentional message from some distressed Germans, probably connected with the Abwehr. Or what's left of it since the SD took it over last winter. Likely Canaris's old guard has a finger in it somewhere. To me the inclusion of the English word is a dead giveaway. It was sent specifically for us to receive.''

Smith spoke for the first time. His face had become red with indignation. ''Are you saying that for the last two years we've been operating a double agent that the Germans know about? That he's a triple?''

''We wouldn't know about that,'' said Darlington smoothly. ''Your committee has never had any reason to suppose Blackbird a triple, though, has it?''

''Never.''

120

"Then he probably isn't," offered Pierce. "I would guess that someone high up in the Abwehr, some time ago, suspected that Blackbird had been doubled, but pretended ignorance in case Blackbird were needed for just this sort of thing."

"It might be disinformation," argued Cooper. "Planted to give us a fit of nerves."

"You said yourself it was blatant. Disinformation is normally more subtle than this."

Darlington turned to Pierce. "Your advice is to accept the information as both accurate and true?"

"I don't see how we dare do anything else."

Smith still looked angry. "There will have to be very careful planning about any response to 'Wolf'. We can't assume that Blackbird's real case officer and 'Wolf' are the same individual. If we do, and they aren't, the real case officer over there is going to start asking awkward questions. It could blow both your informant, and Blackbird. We can't take that risk."

"Commander Pierce," said Darlington, "you're the officer in charge of this particular chunk of the investigation. Could you please see that such planning takes place, if need be? It's in no one's interest to blow a double agent."

Pierce nodded. "I don't think that it will be necessary to respond as yet. It might be preferable not to, actually. If 'Wolf' becomes more desperate, because we're apparently ignoring him, he may send us more detail on this—project of theirs. To persuade us to act."

"He must be pretty desperate already," mused Cooper, "to take such a frightful risk as that message. He might already be under arrest, in fact."

"We'd better hope he isn't," Smith put in sharply, "or they'll know about Blackbird soon enough."

"Turning to more mundane matters," interrupted Darlington, "how are we going to verify this item of information, if we're not going to be able to go directly back to 'Wolf'?"

"If you would be so good as to excuse us, sir," said Cooper. "I believe this part of the discussion to be out of our territory."

"By all means. Thank you, gentlemen. Commander Pierce will be in touch."

Pierce lit his pipe as they closed the door behind them. When the pipe was drawing well, he suggested, "We could use photographic reconnaissance, now that we have pretty much a pinpoint target."

"Would it be wise to alert the Germans to our suspicions?" Darlington wanted to know. "Most of our PR units are being used in France at the moment, like the bombers. Germany's hardly being touched until the invasion's ashore. A stray Mosquito hanging about near Innsbrück might be suspect."

"Not if it appears to be photographing something else. Like railway yards in Munich, for example."

"In any case," said Mclennand, unasked, "They could hardly move the installation without losing months of work, if they could move it at all. Although they could put a bloody lot of antiaircraft guns around it."

Darlington leaned back in the leather chair. "You think bombing is a possibility, then?"

"If *Fenris* is under that mountain, bombing won't do much to it," said Devereaux. "I suppose we could hope to seal up the access tunnels, if we could be sure of getting them all. There's probably more than one way in or out."

"How about destroying power lines?"

"They'd have generators for a project that important."

122

"So they would. Bombing's iffy, then, Flight Lieutenant Devereaux?"

"In my opinion, it's not a sure thing."

"Furthermore," added Pierce, "we can hardly ask for a thousand-bomber raid on the basis of four radio intercepts. Why don't I have a chat with Patrick Gilford? He's commander of 37 PRU Group at Tilford Bridge. He'd likely have an idea or two about getting a close look at the area, at least."

The old devil, thought Devereaux. He exchanged a glance with Mclennand, who smiled faintly.

Darlington studied Pierce for a moment or two. "Very well. Let me know by this time tomorrow what he has to offer. I'll try to explore some other avenues with the Air Staff. Although they won't be very receptive at the moment, I'm afraid. Nobody's got any bombers to spare these days, or anything else, for that matter. Good day, gentlemen."

They collected their documents and left. Outside, Pierce favored them with a slow wink. Devereaux thought it quite out of character.

Gilford put his feet on his desk and said, "I thought I'd see you lot again before very long. Got a little more detail, have you?"

"A little." Pierce felt around in his jacket for matches and found none. Gilford tossed him a box from the desk. Mclennand and Devereaux stared at the wall map of Germany.

"What is it, Ian? Leave off your pipe and let me in on it. Stop enjoying yourself so much."

"It's precious little I've got to enjoy these days," grumbled Pierce, jabbing the smoking pipe bowl with his thumb. "Anyway, there's a mountain outside Innsbrück, called the

Patscherkofel. Under it is something we need to know about, we think.''

"We think.''

"Yes.''

"How do you expect me to acquire photographs of something that's under a mountain?''

"I don't know." Pierce sucked on his pipe, which had gone out. "Your chaps are able to fly down mine shafts, aren't they?''

"Only on the sixth Sunday of each month. Stop hedging, Ian.''

"Tell him, Gordon.''

Mclennand cleared his throat. "This installation was likely planned with a lot of care and thoroughness. There wouldn't be much to see. A few barrackslike structures, a road, probably a small-gauge rail line that goes to an entrance and disappears. Or they might have removed the railway once all the heavy equipment was installed. There may be power lines going in, but they could be buried. Also, much higher up, some sort of shafthead for cooling or ventilation. There would have to be cooling if the device were to operate at efficient temperatures. However, it might also be cooled by water pumped from the river Inn. In that case there ought to be a pumping station somewhere near the river. The cooling pipes might run above ground; if they did, they'd be easy to spot.''

"Rather vulnerable, though.''

"Rather. My money's on buried water pipes or air cooling.''

Gilford unloaded his feet from the desk and pulled a large map case from behind his chair. "Prewar maps of the area around Innsbrück," he explained. "I borrowed them from our files after you were here last. Let's have a look at the Patscherkofel district.''

124

He spread the map on the table and they clustered around it.

"Beautiful skiing country," observed Mclennand.

Gilvord smoothed a crease in the paper. "Been there yourself?"

"No. A cousin was. I was on a student exchange from Cambridge in 1936 but I never got over that way."

"Cambridge, eh? I was at Oxford. What were you reading?"

"Physics," answered Mclennand, and immediately could have bitten his tongue off.

"In any other circumstances that would be called a security breach," said Pierce dryly. "Let's get on with it, if we may."

"H'm." Gilford traced the mountain's contour lines with his finger. "A few villages. Not much else."

"Sistrans was mentioned."

"That's the location you want, then."

"Yes."

"Tricky getting vertical coverage, at high speed, in half light, in that terrain. Would oblique photos do?"

Mclennand sounded disappointed. "Both would be best."

"It would also be best to do the photography in one pass, though," Pierce pointed out. "We don't want them to know we're onto them if we can help it. Two passes couldn't be considered an accident."

Gilford whistled through his teeth. "You're making it difficult. How far up the slope do you expect the cooling vents to be?"

"Several hundred feet, vertical, at least."

"Can't do it in one pass, oblique. Have to be vertical, to get what you need."

Pierce left the desk and sat down in his chair. "Patrick,

I'm sorry we've been so pushy. We'll tell you what we'd like to have, and ask you to get as much of it as you can.''

Gilford looked relieved. Mclennand and Devereaux resumed their seats.

''Go ahead.''

Pierce ticked off the items with gestures of his pipe stem. ''We're wondering how many of the following things are near Sistrans. One, barracks or living area suitable for one or two hundred workers. There may be the remains of more living quarters, from previous construction activity. Two, an entranceway into a tunnel complex under the mountain, likely with a rail line or an old railbed leading to it. Last, any sign of towers or chimneys higher on the slope. This isn't a bomber target at the moment. It's simply a confirmation of a certain type of activity going on in an out-of-the way area of the Reich.''

Gilford pulled a notepad from his desk drawer, planted it on the map, and made several notes. He referred to the map, and made several more. ''I'll work it out with the intelligence officer. I'll call you tomorrow and let you know what I think. If it's yes, then all we have to wait for is good weather.''

''I hope we don't have to wait too long,'' said Pierce. ''A week at the outside.''

In fact it was eleven days.

''There's a mountain,'' said the intelligence officer, ''just southeast of Innsbrück.''

''There're a lot of mountains southeast of Inssbrück,'' Patterson told him.

''Sorry?''

''Which one?'' elaborated Mackenzie.

''It's called the Patscherkofel. They want—''

He broke off as Gilford entered the briefing room.

126

"Sorry, Keith. Go ahead."

"They want photographs of the north slope, low down. Vertical," the intelligence officer continued.

"What's the slope like?"

They went on through the briefing. Patterson and Mackenzie would leave Tilford Bridge at quarter to four in the morning and be over the target area as the sun rose. Cruising altitude would be 38,000 feet, enough to keep them out of the reach of most German night fighters. The final approach would be a feint over Munich, as if to photograph the rail yards there, and then a steep dive and turn for the final low-level run to Innsbrück, sixty miles south. A smoke generator had been rigged under the Mosquito's port engine nacelle. When the generator was running, it would seem to observers on the ground that the aircraft was damaged and flying low to avoid interception, rather than to make a photography run. Well out of sight of Innsbrück they would gain height and fly over the Alps to the Allied air base at Foggia in Italy.

Finally, the intelligence officer put down his pointer and stepped away from the map. "Weather next, chaps."

The meteorological officer gave them a forecast of light cloud and some undercast as far as Karlsruhe. After that it would be clear with occasional cumulus banks. Mclennand appeared satisfied.

"Any questions?" asked the intelligence officer.

Mackenzie and Patterson remained silent. It was the longest flight they had made yet.

Gilford nodded. The two briefing officers shuffled their papers together and left the room. Then Gilford repeated, "Any questions?"

After consideration, Patterson said, "We've been very busy in France. Why this, all of a sudden.?"

"Come back," answered Gilford, "and one day I may

127

be able to tell you. All I can say at the moment is that it's very important indeed.''

"There's no known flak around the target," said Patterson. "That's the only thing that would be uncomfortable. The mountains are no problem as long as we don't have to dodge anything.''

"Good enough. Have a good time in Italy. Drink a bottle of wine for me. Better yet, bring me one back.''

They were driven to the dispersal bay at three that morning. The ground crew had already pulled the tarpaulins off the Mosquito, and were standing around it, blowing on their hands. It was quite cold and a little misty.

D-Dog was an older machine, a pale blue Mark IX photoreconnaissance Mosquito. There was a 36-inch camera in the bomb bay, and two F24 cameras behind the pilot's position. They had taken the oblique F24 out of the bomb bay to save weight, and auxiliary fuel tanks had been fitted; the aircraft could fly comfortably to Hungary and back, if need be.

Patterson and Mackenzie lugged their parachutes and other gear to the ladder which led up to the door in the lower flank of the plane's nose. Patterson asked a few questions about the engines; the length of the flight had made him a bit more nervous than he usually was before a sortie.

"They're in good shape, sir," the crew chief assured him. "Pop you along at four hundred and twenty, sweet as can be. No problems with night-roaming Huns.''

"Thanks." Patterson hauled himself up the ladder and wormed into the pilot's seat. Mackenzie, following, squirmed about looking for his map case, which had jammed between his buttocks and his own seat on the right of Patterson's. This was one of the few things they both disliked about the

Mosquito; it was a difficult aircraft from which to escape in an emergency. However, they flew so high and so fast that interception was extremely rare. There were no guns or warning radar on the plane; it was the price paid for the speed and altitude and the weight of the cameras and fuel.

Patterson waved and a ground crewman began priming the starboard engine. At a touch of the starter button, the propeller turned, kicked, and the engine fired. Patterson ran it up to warming speed and then started the port Merlin. The dimmed dispersal lights glimmered in the disks of the propeller arcs.

They went through the flight checks while the engines warmed. The ground crew had scuttled out of the way of the slipstream. At three-forty Patterson asked for permission to move out.

"D-Dog cleared to taxi."

They rolled onto the runway. The mist was evident, but not thick. Patterson lined the Mosquito up with the flare-path, a stretch of dim lights in the darkness.

A green flare arched into the sky. Patterson advanced the throttles, waited until the Merlins were at takeoff power, and released the brakes. D-Dog shot down the flarepath and lifted off into the misty darkness within a few hundred yards.

The crew chief looked after the pale shape as it glimmered off into the night.

"Too bloody easy to see, if you ask me," he said to the AC2 at his elbow. "Pale blue Mosquitos were never meant for night flying. Must be a bit of a panic on."

"There's been bugger-all gossip on this one, though," said the other. "Must be a real flap, no mistake."

The visibility of the pale aircraft against the night sky didn't worry Patterson very much. He took a leisurely twenty minutes to climb to 34,000 feet; there was plenty of fuel but he always liked to allow for emergencies. Mackenzie gave him a course far out to the west-southwest, calculated to later swing them over the coast of France not far from St. Malo. This would keep them well clear of any Allied night bombing and the possibility of enemy nightfighters. D-Dog settled down to an economical and comfortable 300 knots.

They turned toward the land at a quarter to five. Patterson increased speed slightly. The French coast remained dark as they crossed it; either they hadn't been tracked on radar, or there were no heavy antiaircraft guns near them, or the Germans were all asleep. Most likely, though, was that a single aircraft wasn't worth shooting at.

Mackenzie commented on this.

"Doesn't mean they don't know we're here. Keep your eyes skinned."

Mackenzie returned to scouring the night sky, as he had been doing ever since they left England. "Pity the kite's so pale and the night's so dark," he grumbled.

"Their nightfighters can't catch us, anyway. Maybe in a pass from the front one could get a shot at us, but he'd have to be lucky to get into position in time."

"What about that beast the skipper has taped on his map? Rumors say it's awfully fast."

"The 219? Not many around. Fortunately."

"H'm."

"I'll watch. You better do some navigating. Give me some kind of ETA for Munich."

Far below them a wispy cloud cover obscured the dark countryside of France. Northward a vague flicker or two of light diffused on the horizon.

"French railways catching it again."

"Looks like." Mackenzie swiveled his protractor and gave Patterson the new course.

"The winds weren't supposed to change, were they?"

"No, but it'd be a first if they didn't."

Patterson thought for a moment. "We could use Lake Constance for a navigational check."

"I think we'd better. I don't fancy hanging about in the dark, looking for Munich, if the winds aren't what they're supposed to be."

Patterson corkscrewed the Mosquito gently across France to the intersection of the Swiss and German borders. The motion, designed to disturb the aim of any undetected night-fighter that might be creeping up on them, was vaguely nauseating. Both men were stiff-necked and irritable by the time Mackenzie said, "I see the lake. A bit to port. We're too far south. Head port three degrees till I can work out the final approach."

Six miles below, the lake was a pale glimmer in the dark. Mackenzie gave the course for Munich and Patterson pushed the throttles forward until D-Dog was traveling at 400 knots. The run into Munich would take twenty minutes. He cork-screwed the aircraft more violently.

Six miles from their projected turning point over Munich, Mackenzie thought he saw something in the darkness above the Mosquito's fin.

"Fighter! Turn port, go!"

Patterson rammed the control column to the left, turning toward the unseen attacker. He held the turn until they were heading back the way they had come, and then climbed slightly and reversed course again. The Mosquito bounced violently around the night sky, never keeping the same course or altitude for more than a few seconds running.

Nothing.

"Either it's gone, or there wasn't one."

"Where the hell are we?"

"Not too far off, I think. Keep the same heading. The turning point can be varied a bit."

The Oberleutnant at the controls of the Heinkel 219 was puzzled. He was certain he had caught a glimpse of the intruder aircraft before it vanished from his sight and the radar display alike. The enemy plane had been remarkably easy to see, as though it were a full moonlight night, or as if the intruder had been a light color. He glanced nervously over his shoulder at the night sky above and behind. These nights there were Mosquito nightfighters all over the place, although you wouldn't expect to find one this far south in Germany. Their activity seemed to have dropped with the intensity of the bombing raids, anyway.

"Any sign of it?"

The radar operator behind him said, in a preoccupied tone, "No. Try going starboard a bit. He probably turned toward us."

As if to contradict the operator's words, the ground controller's voice cracked in the earphones. "Drache One. The intruder is now heading for Munich. Steer 080 degrees, same height."

"Shit," said the observer. "We'll never catch him now."

"Not unless he turns and we can cut the corner."

They had crossed the course of D-Dog at nearly right angles, and had then turned starboard. By the time Patterson had swung back on course for Munich the Heinkel was eight miles off and still receding. The Oberleutnant yanked the big nightfighter into a tight turn and steadied it on the course of the intruder.

"What d'you think it was?"

"Must have been some kind of Mosquito. That's the only thing that's that fast. I thought it was white."

"Wasn't a nightfighter, then."

"Might have been a daylight reconnaissance machine," piped up the radar operator. "They paint them a sort of light blue."

"What in God's name would a daylight recon plane be doing over here at this time of the morning? Even if it will be light soon?"

"Don't know," said the Oberleutnant, and pushed the throttles forward, all the way.

The approach to Munich was straightforward. A few antiaircraft batteries obligingly loosed off a dozen or so rounds, as if to confirm that the darkish blot in the paling countryside was indeed the city.

"Turn starboard to 195 degrees."

They were to fly a straight line, descending at high speed all the way, until they saw the trace of the river Inn. A sharp turn to starboard would put them over Innsbrück at 3500 feet. Another turn, this time to the left up the valley under the Patscherkofel, would place them over the target area for the camera run. Then on to Italy, provided there really was no flak and they didn't hit the mountains. The sun was nudging the horizon.

"Are we on time?"

"Dead on."

"Going down. Floors, please."

Mackenzie watched the sky behind them. They were dropping so fast that Patterson had to reduce power to keep the dive at safe speed.

A faint glint in the northeast caught Mackenzie's eye. It

was well off, behind them and to starboard.

"There's something pissing about up there on our right. Behind us."

"How far away?"

"Maybe five or six miles."

"Probably Focke-Wulf 190s. Can't catch us."

Mackenzie studied the spark. "It's getting bigger."

"Damn. You must have seen something back there, all right. It's that bloody nightfighter."

"A 219?"

"Has to be, if he's catching us up."

"Buggeration."

"There's the river."

The Mosquito tipped into its turn and shot off down the course of the Inn toward the city. Thirty seconds later the outskirts slid under the nose.

"Camera run beginning. Start the smoke."

Mackenzie turned reluctantly from the dot in the sky behind and glued his eyes to the windscreen. He flipped the makeshift switch that started the smoke generator.

"It should be dead ahead, up the valley." He started the cameras.

"There!"

They roared over the far edge of the city, banking left, then right as the lower reaches of the Patscherkofel swung under the aircraft. They were a little too low; Patterson raised the nose. The slopes fled by underneath the wings. In the bomb bay the cameras clicked. A rank of huts and a heavy, blockhouse affair disappeared sternward. As they gained height, Mackenzie exclaimed, "Look! Down there. In the trees, dead port."

Patterson spared a glance. It was a massive concrete block, higher than wide. Specks of men stood around it. It had to be several hundred feet higher on the mountain than the buildings they had just photographed.

"Never mind it. We probably got it on the film. Where's that bloody Heinkel?"

"Jesus." Mackenzie looked behind. The dark speck astern on the right had become a black blot, sparkling underneath.

"Turn right, go!"

Patterson snatched D-Dog around in a 180-degree turn, heading straight back underneath the Heinkel. Tracer and 30 millimeter cannon shells streamed ten feet over the Mosquito's canopy, followed by the huge shadow of the night fighter. The Heinkel pulled around barely in time to miss the knees of the mountain. "Christalmighty," breathed Patterson, and gave Dog all the throttle there was. "Where is he?"

"Where is he?" snapped the Oberleutnant.

"Can't see him." The observer's voice was strained; the near miss with the ground had shaken all of them. In daylight, against the varied colors of the terrain, the Mosquito was hard to detect.

"How much fuel?" asked the Oberleutnant.

"Not much. Enough to get back, no more."

"Did you see the smoke from his engine?"

"Yes. The right engine."

The Oberleutnant considered. Fighting at low altitude, in this terrain, with a heavy aircraft, was exceedingly dangerous even against a damaged enemy. Especially when fuel was so low. He made his decision.

"He won't get home with a burning engine. Can you see him yet?"

"I see the smoke. He's heading south. For the Brenner Pass."

The Oberleutnant shrugged. "He won't get over the

135

mountains. We must have hit him with the first burst, before he turned. Let's go home."

The observer, who had seen Dog smoking before they opened fire, was content to remain silent. After all, the Mosquito might have been hit by flak. They would get some credit, at least.

Thirty-six hours later, the photographs were in London.

IV

The Reich

May 20–July 8, 1944

The upper slopes of the mountains bulked gold, rose, and blue in the westering sun. Roth, looking up at the peaks, slipped on the duckboarded path and planted one foot squarely in a puddle. The cold water squelched around his toes. Isn't it the way, he thought. Eyes on the mountain peaks and one foot in a mudhole.

What had happend to that British aircraft of the day before, he wondered, looking southwest toward the Brenner. It had obviously been in trouble, pouring smoke from one engine that way. And the Luftwaffe fighter that was after it damned nearly spread itself all over the mountain, too. Somebody had told him the English machine was a Mosquito. Well, the mountains surely have swatted that one, he told himself.

He had been going for breakfast when the Allied aircraft had roared over the compound, bringing the guards tumbling out of their barracks in various stages of undress, but too late to do anything except stare after it as it dragged its plume of smoke down the valley. He had hoped, for a wild moment, that it was the target-marking airplane for a bombing raid that would put an end to *Fenris* once and for all.

Instead, it had disappeared and life had gone on more or less as usual. Strasser had been nonchalant about it.

"Probably sizing up Munich for an attack and got caught," the security captain had told him later, outside the mess hall. "Trying for Italy on one engine. Won't get there." He had eyed Roth. "What do you think it was here for?"

"No idea. Haven't spoken to RAF command for years."

He had suddenly been afraid he had gone too far, for Strasser had fixed him with cold green eyes and said nothing. After a moment the SS captain had laughed. "Roth, you're a joker. Always joking. Keep our *Fenris*—whatever it is—going. Win the war for us, Roth. You and the rest of the trolls under the mountain."

He had laughed again and marched away toward the HQ block. Roth had had to suppress an almost ungovernable urge to kick the man off the duckboards into the mud.

Fenris. Keep it going, you trolls.

Roth had begun to hate the reactor. It sat there in the cavern, its cooling fans humming, a squat concrete presence that dominated their days and nights. Siegner worked like a man possessed, testing, calculating. Anna-Marie and Sommer adjusted their extraction equipment again and again. Boehme fussed; the other scientists waited and bit their nails.

And it had taken Anna-Marie and himself three weeks after their eyes had locked in the pile room that day, *three weeks*, he reminded himself with something approaching fury, to decide to get a message out. First they had hoped that the reaction would fade, that the pile design was wrong. It wasn't. Then there was the possibility that Peter would see what he was doing. He didn't. Lastly there was a week and a half of delay trying to think of a reasonable excuse for Roth to leave the installation for a few hours.

138

Finally Roth, at wit's end, had told Boehme that he was sick of being stuck on a mountainside for week after week and that he was going into Innsbrück to relax for a few hours. Strasser hadn't said anything, only watched him as he drove out the gate. The old man in the bookshop had been guarded, but had said that he would try to move the message up the line, somehow. Roth had expected arrest at any moment since then, but apparently the Abwehr net was still secure. Oster must have planned it well.

And then, nothing. He had given up hope. Finally the Mosquito, and nothing again. He hated to think about the situation; he had hoped that the message would bring some action, but all there was to show for it was a shot-down aircraft, if that in fact had anything to do with the message at all.

He had also had to gamble on the possibility that other leaks from the complex, or from its unavoidable contacts with Berlin, might give the British a context for his information. He and Anna-Marie had originally wanted to include technical details of the pile in the message, but the old man had told him that it was far too much text for safe transmission. On the spot, Roth had furiously concocted the modified communication. The inclusion of the English word—which he had learned, by accident, from Siegner—had been a momentary inspiration, one which made his blood run cold later, when he thought about the risk. The old man had accepted the English, but that was likely because he had no idea of what it meant.

How many of us are working for Germany, Hitler, the Allies, or one, all, or none? Roth wondered. Strasser was working for Hitler, and his own skin; that was plain enough. Siegner, for himself and his child, the fission pile. Anna-Marie? Germany, perhaps.

Roth merely wanted the whole thing over with, and a peaceful existence in Bavaria.

Not likely to get that, are you, he thought viciously, and knelt down to untie his soaking shoe.

A rumble on the duckboards made him look up. Siegner was trotting down the path, his face preoccupied. He almost tripped over Roth.

"Sorry! I was thinking about something else. What's the matter?"

"Stepped off the duckboards and soaked my foot."

"Oh. Sorry," he said again. "Listen. There'll be a meeting tomorrow morning, at nine, in my office. Bring the papers on the modifications we were talking about, could you? Weil will be there, maybe Kruger. Have you seen Strasser?"

"What for? Is he invited?"

"Yes. First time. Something's come up. They want him in on it, for some reason. You didn't twist your ankle or anything?"

Roth was wringing his sock out over the puddle. "No. I saw Strasser near the mess hall a few minutes ago. I think he was going to his office."

"Thanks. See you later. Or tomorrow, whichever."

He trundled away down the duckboarded path.

"Or whichever," muttered Roth, staring after the retreating vulnerable, slender back. He dragged on the wet sock and shoe and went on up the mountain to look at *Fenris*.

The control room was warm after the chill of the evening. Roth peered through the massive port at the concrete bulk of the pile and then turned away and asked Anna-Marie, "How's it going?"

"It's going . . . well."

He heard the pause in her voice and glanced at the technical staff grouped around the instrument consoles. Nobody seemed interested in him; he was a constant presence, after all.

"See you later, then." He flicked his eyes toward the entry, caught her answering glance, and left.

He was puttering about in the deserted drafting office when she came in. He glanced at his watch. Half an hour had passed.

"Sorry," she apologized. "I didn't want to be obvious. I didn't know exactly where you'd be, either."

"Doesn't matter. Did Peter tell you about the meeting?"

"Yes." She put her fingertips to her mouth, looked at them, and laughed shortly. "I've been biting my nails again. I thought I'd got over it."

"Did you know Strasser's going to attend?"

She fidgeted, and then sat on a stool. "Yes. It means that the SS is taking more control."

There was a noise in the corridor. Roth shuffled desperately in a pile of blueprints, pulled one out, and said, pointing to the white tracings, "The alley access is here. If you move the cores to the grinding unit here—yes? What is it?"

The technician, who had his head in the room before he noticed them, turned red and then white. He palmed his cigarette quickly.

"I'm sorry, Dr. Lerner, Dr. Roth. I had no idea—"

Discretion overcame confusion and he disappeared.

"Wanted a smoke. Just a minute." Roth put his head out the door and bawled, "If you want to smoke, do it in the safe areas. Don't do it in here, for God's sake."

"Yes, sir" floated back down the corridor.

Roth returned to the table. "They're always doing that.

141

It's the one thing that gives me hope for Germany. What did I pull out of the mess, anyway?"

She giggled. "Plans for the Turkish bath we never had nerve to build."

"Jesus Christ. We'd better burn that as soon as we can. Anyway," he went on, "Strasser. Where were we?"

"SS control."

"Right. They're going to try for the bomb. Peter will go along with that. But the other option is more likely, or I'm very mistaken. Peter might have to swallow that, too. Suppose that's the one they choose?"

"We can't let it be done," she said quietly.

"We've had this conversation before."

"I know. But the pile wasn't running then. Peter may go on, simply to find out what can be done with the thing. It's producing odd things every day. He's fascinated."

"These 'odd things' are dangerous, aren't they?"

"Nobody knows how dangerous, yet."

"At least they haven't taken any away for . . . experiments."

"No." She laughed a bit wildly. "But every day I expect to see a few ragged people shipped in to see what would happen."

"They've done it already, haven't they, other places?"

"I wouldn't be surprised. With gas, though, not with what we've got here, obviously."

"Rumors get around."

"Yes, they do."

They looked at the plan of the Turkish bath for a few moments.

"What would change Peter's mind?" asked Roth.

"I don't know," answered Anna-Marie Lerner. "I haven't been able to think of anything."

Strasser, fixed rigidly at attention, his jackboots spotless, the Iron Cross and his combat badges glowing on his tunic, watched as the muddy Horch staff car rolled into the compound. He had taken care to have the area laid with sawdust to soak up the mud; no splashing through puddles here, if he could help it.

Two men in sloppy civilian clothes got out of the rear seat of the Horch. Nobody held the door for them. Security, thought Strasser. "Heil Hitler," he said, and saluted.

The two men were Weil and Kruger. They returned the salute as though it tired them to do so. "Where's the meeting?" asked Kruger.

"Up there inside the complex, sir."

"Inside. Well, I suppose since I issued the security order, I'll have to put up with it. Take us there, Captain Strasser."

Two rough deal benches had been jammed into Siegner's office to produce a kind of conference table. Kruger sat at one end, Siegner at the other. Weil, Boehme, Strasser, Roth, Pickert, Anna-Marie, and Sommer distributed themselves along the sides. The scientists, Kruger noted, had bunched themselves at Siegner's end of the table. It was only to be expected.

Kruger was quite worried. He himself had serious doubts about the use proposed for *Fenris*, particularly in the light of the current Allied military advantage, but—apart from the influence of his SS loyalty oath—he was kept from protesting by the fact that such a protest would mean a swift posting away from the project, most likely to a penal battalion on the Russian front, where his lifespan would be measured in days. He had debated contacting the fragmentary German resistance movement but that was at least as dangerous as disagreeing with *Fenris*. He had no option but to carry out his orders. Besides, you never knew; the project

143

might just possibly still win them the war, or allow a peace negotiated from strength. The scientists might refuse, though. If they didn't do so outright—realizing that refusal could mean their lives—they might still contrive to slow the project down. It would be up to Strasser and Boehme to see that they didn't. Boehme's secret reports had shown no delays so far, however.

Kruger tapped his pen on the table. "Let's begin. There will be no notes taken of this meeting, nor any transcripts prepared later. Nothing of this discussion is to be committed to paper.

"It has been proposed that, if it is not possible to make the fission explosive by the end of the year, the raw materials—you call them wastes, I believe—will be used as the weapon themselves."

Sommer, Boehme, and Pickert looked shocked. Siegner didn't; that was to be expected, but Kruger noted that Doctors Lerner and Roth merely appeared worried. Siegner has told only these two, he reflected. There could be the makings of a conspiracy here.

Strasser merely appeared mystified. "I don't understand, Colonel."

"Be so good as to inform us all, Dr. Siegner."

Siegner cleared his throat. "*Fenris,* Captain Strasser, is a nuclear fission pile. It splits the basic parts of matter and reorganizes it. One particular metal which is made in this reorganization is an explosive so powerful that a grapefruit-sized mass of it could destroy a large city. It, as well as the other substances produced, is deadly in other ways we don't entirely understand. The proposal is to use these substances, if we can't make enough of the explosive in the time allowed, as a kind of poison gas. Except that they are far more lethal than chemicals because they last far longer.

They could make a city uninhabitable for months.''

Strasser was thunderstruck.

"Clearly put." Kruger leaned forward. "This meeting has been arranged to decide which alternative will be selected, and to establish a schedule for its execution. It is also to inform Captain Strasser about the critical nature of the whole exercise, and help him determine possible sources of security breakdown. Dr. Boehme is therefore relieved of all security concerns regarding the scientific staff." Except the reports, Kruger reminded himself. I'll have to get Strasser to inform him of that exception.

Boehme turned red, began to speak, and then thought better of it as Kruger's cold eyes swiveled toward him. The light, clear voice went on.

"Dr. Siegner. What is the earliest date enough of the explosive will be available? If it's to be more than a year, the question becomes unimportant."

"It is unimportant under that constraint." Siegner spoke as precisely as the SS colonel.

Kruger exhaled a long, slow breath. It was going to have to be the aerosol, then. Damnation.

"Then how long until enough of the other material will be available?"

"To be effective over how large an area?"

"Several square miles. A beachhead, for example."

"Or a city?"

"Or a city." One might as well be blunt. None of them could retreat now.

Siegner looked torn. Kruger knew he was trying to decide whether to lie or not. A look of defeat passed across the physicist's face.

"The end of June. The extraction and concentration will require more or less time after that, depending on the concentration required. We can assume an aerosol distribution, by aircraft?"

"Yes."

"A week in the extraction alley should be enough, Dr. Lerner?"

"I concur."

They are very formal, Kruger thought. They do not like this very much. But they will obey.

Siegner spoke again. "No doubt you realize that this will halt the fission process until further uranium for the lattice is available. And that by the end of June there will likely be only enough material for one or two . . . treatments of an area."

"The Allies won't know that. Also, further uranium can be made available." Or so I hope, thought Kruger. It might be possible as long as the Lancasters and Fortresses were pounding targets in France, to smooth the way for the Allied invasion; but as soon as that assault had come all the bombers would be rededicated to destroying the industrial power of the Reich. This whole thing bears rather the air of a bluff, he reflected.

"Given what has been said so far, then," Kruger went on, "the target date for beginning the extraction procedures is June thirtieth. By June fifth the aerosol equipment will be shipped here, together with an expert in its design and use."

"I haven't dealt with this kind of equipment before," Roth told him. "I expect that modifications will have to be made to the aerosol containers. Particularly for shielding. And the waste products will have to remain in liquid suspension for aerosol use."

"Is this a problem?"

"No. The extraction procedures use liquid solvents,"

146

said Anna-Marie. "But we will have to discuss with your expert whether the solvents we use are suitable for an aerosol. If they are not, we will have to isolate the wastes and then introduce them into a proper liquid medium. The extraction process is flexible enough to handle that."

Kruger looked at her. A pretty woman, French-looking. Her dossier noted that her ancestors had been Huguenots who fled the religious persecutions in France nearly three centuries ago. Evidently the strain had bred true. She was, Kruger thought, too pretty to be so calmly describing the preparation of a weapon that could devastate cities.

He reprimanded himself for sentimentality and said, "The time between the fifth of June and the readying of the aerosol for use is intended to allow such modifications and adjustments. Captain Strasser."

Strasser looked up from his folded arms.

"The delay on the laying of the explosives in the tunnels has been extended indefinitely. You are to carry it out on direct orders from myself or Captain Weil, and from no one else."

Another possibility gone, thought Anna-Marie. She dared not look at Roth.

The conference continued until nearly noon. They went over details of security, additional staff for the work on the aerosol system, and a general updating for Weil and Kruger on the more technical aspects of their progress. At the end of it the two men from Berlin refused lunch and left hurriedly for the Weilheim airstrip.

"They must be in a rush, to take a chance on going by air in daylight these days," observed Strasser as he and Siegner watched the Horch slither down the muddy road. "You've really got a nasty piece of machinery in there, haven't you?"

147

"It's all in how you use it."

Strasser snorted. "In times like these, you use whatever you've got. I never doubted we'd win eventually," he went on (quite seriously, Siegner was surprised to realize), "but it cheers me up to know we've got something like that under there." He jerked his thumb over his shoulder at the mountain behind them.

"It's a great relief to all of us," responded Siegner, dryly.

Boehme, angry and upset, collared Anna-Marie in the main corridor and virtually dragged her into the extraction lab. A couple of technicians diplomatically left for an early lunch.

"You and Peter. And Roth. You knew, and didn't tell me."

She gestured helplessly. "It was a technical matter, not a scientific one. You weren't involved. We needed to know. You didn't."

"I very much did need to know. I'm in charge of staff security. I mean, I was." he deflated suddenly. "I was at the time."

She decided that he had better be mollified. "Hans, I'm sorry. I'm sure that if Peter had known you'd be so upset, he would have told you." In a pig's eye, he would have, she thought. She patted his arm, noticing suddenly how like a pudgy, disappointed ten year old he looked. She immediately felt sorry for him. "You're the best possible administrative head for the project, you should know that by now. We've never gone short of any equipment or materials, ever. Or food. We'd all be as unhealthy as those people I saw on the train weeks ago, if you didn't feed us so well. And the work would be far behind if it weren't for your ability to find the things we need."

He thought about this for a moment, and brightened. "I suppose there is that. But that damned Roth always acts as though I'm a complete incompetent."

"Is he still teasing you?"

"Not so much. I suppose Peter told him to stop it. He's an arrogant bastard. Roth, not Peter."

"Yes, he is, a little."

Boehme moodily tapped a glass condenser with his fingernail. The sound was a tiny, clear ring against the subterranean hum of the cooling fans in their shafts. "I never was a very good scientist," he admitted. "I was always better at the paperwork and organization than theories and experiments. I suppose that's why Roth doesn't think much of me."

"He's a little arrogant, as you say. Do you want to go for lunch?"

"I suppose so. Just don't let Roth get in my way."

"I won't. Cheer up, we'll be finished in a few weeks."

I'd like to string Roth up by the balls, he thought, as she led him out of the lab. One of these days I'm going to. One way or another.

Anna-Marie and Roth spent the next few days in a state of suppressed despair. The evening before the aerosol spray equipment was due to arrive, they managed to walk back from the mess hall to the pile complex without the company of any of the others. It was a perfect early summer evening, warm, but with a fresh odor of mountain snow and meltwater. The ground had dried and there was green everywhere.

"Do we send another message?"

Roth kicked at a pebble. "I can't make up my mind. There was absolutely no response to the other one; nothing at all came back down the line, as far as I know. I can't even be sure if it was sent, or if it was, whether the British paid any attention to it. I don't know if I dare another trip into Innsbrück. Strasser thought a lot about me even before he had full security control. Now that he's got authority over the scientific staff as well, he's making it difficult to get out of the area. He'll watch me particularly. And remember what Peter said about Hans. He may be reporting on us himself, direct to Weil or Kruger.''

She nodded. Strasser had tightened regulations on leaving the compound, especially for the scientists, as they were the valuable individuals.

"If we're going to do anything, it'll have to be soon."

"I know."

Above them, a hawk searched vainly for updrafts in the cooling air. They watched it silently for a moment or two.

"What about Switzerland?" she asked.

"Neither of us would make it there. We're too closely watched. Peter might be able to get away; they're sure of him and I don't think they pay so much attention to his movements. But he won't go."

"Not even now? When he knows the other alternative has been chosen?"

"Maybe he has something planned that he's not telling us."

"Maybe," she said, without conviction.

They were nearing the complex entrance. "The man in Innsbrück you told me about," she said. "He's the contact for the network, isn't he?"

"What's left of it since the SD has been in charge. I think likely the message went from him eventually to a case officer running one of our agents on the other side. A few of them are thought to be doubled. The case officer would have to be in on it, but it would be a perfect way to get information to the British. Pass the message to a doubled agent. It's neat."

"It might let the British know that we know he's doubled."

"It might be worth the risk. I was given a high priority when they placed me here. I expect the text was checked with another Abwehr higher-up before it went out, anyway.."

"If it went out."

"Yes. If it did." Roth hunched over as if to gather strength. "I'll try again. I'll try to get into Innsbrück as soon as I can. I may have to wait, though . . . the aerosol equipment's coming tomorrow. I have to work on that."

"I could go."

"My contact doesn't know you. It has to be me," said Roth, and they walked into the bowels of the complex.

Strasser, from the window of his office, watched them disappear into the entrance bunker. He crossed to his desk, sat down, and picked up the telephone.

"Get me Weil, in Berlin," he told the switchboard operator. "Put it on the scrambler circuit."

It took a couple of minutes to get the call through. Eventually Weil's voice, distorted by static, said in his ear: "Weil here."

"It's Strasser, Major Weil. There was a message for me to call you. I'm sorry I wasn't here when you rang; I was out checking the guard perimeter."

"No matter. My . . . immediate superior has been concerned about something ever since our visit. He wished me to discuss it with you. Is this line secure?"

"Yes, sir."

"Good. It concerns the technical head and the woman chemist. It bothered Colonel Kruger that they weren't as surprised as they ought to have been over the nature of the project."

151

"I presume Dr. Siegner told them. Was that a security breach? I wasn't in charge in that area at the time, of course."

"I'm aware of that. No, technically it wasn't a breach. What's bothering us is why he told only those two. Do you have any ideas?"

"Well, I see Dr. Siegner more with Roth and Lerner than with any of the others. I don't know whether that's from necessity or choice. I didn't know until a few days ago what *Fenris* was, so it's hard for me to tell whether they always meet because of work. Lerner, there's no funny business about her. Or about Siegner. They both seem loyal, and neither has been out of the compound for the last couple of months. Roth has, though."

"Was there anything peculiar about that?"

"Not especially. But he's never taken Germany's struggle seriously enough, jokes about the war effort, the High Command, that sort of thing. Boehme used to complain about it until Siegner put a flea in Roth's ear."

"How's Boehme doing, by the way? Is he cooperating more?"

"I've made some use of him from time to time, mostly to tell me what our friend Roth is saying. He doesn't like me much, but he dislikes Roth even more. Boehme's a good National Socialist."

"Essentially, then, you have no reason to suspect . . . conspiracy among any of the scientific staff."

"Not so far."

"Where did Roth go?"

"He said he had to get out of the place to relax. They were having some delay with something, I don't know what. I don't know where he went. There was no provision at the time for checking the movements of senior staff."

"Is there now?"

"Yes."

"Good. I wish I knew where Roth went. There are some people who are not . . . wholeheartedly for the war effort, if you take my meaning. Some in very high places, too."

"Yes, sir."

"Try to watch anyone who leaves the compound. In fact, I'd suggest that all junior staff be confined to the area until the project is complete. Senior people cannot be subject to the same constraints as the rank and file, of course. But perhaps you could strongly suggest that they should check with you before they leave the complex. At that point you can decide whether or not to have them followed, depending on how you read the situation."

"Yes, Major Weil."

"Telephone me if anything unusual comes up. Otherwise, the normal channels. Oh, and remind Dr. Boehme to continue his reports to me. After the meeting the other day he may believe that they are no longer required. They are. Good-bye."

"Good-bye, Major Weil."

Far away in the office in Berlin, Weil replaced the receiver in its cradle. Kruger said:

"So?"

"I think there's a potential leak. The chief technical officer. Remember, the Abwehr was recruiting vigorously in the scientific area, a few years ago. And there are a few fragments of the Abwehr counterespionage operations still about, that Kaltenbrunner and the SD haven't got their hands on. I'd bet that if Roth is breaching security, he's doing it for one of those. And the Army could know what's going on here, perhaps. There's been no sign of that, though. What d'you think we should do."

"Nothing, for now. I'm still trying to talk Himmler into slowing down the project, even if he can't stop it. I'm not making much progress, I'm sorry to say. We might be able to use this situation, although I'm not sure how. It might give us some freedom of movement if we have to decide whether or not to go ahead with the wastes option. Unearth a leak, have to delay the project while a full investigation is carried out, that sort of thing . . . let's just watch the situation, for the moment."

The aerosol equipment was delivered the next day, in a large truck escorted by a staff car and a section of SS troopers on motorcycles.

"Good God," exclaimed Roth to Siegner as they watched the cavalcade draw up to the main gate. The two of them had just come from breakfast and had been about to walk back up to the complex when the rumble of vehicles had turned them around. "They might as well be waving banners saying, 'Here we come! We're very important!' "

"Following orders, no doubt," observed Siegner in a dry voice. "We'd better go back and meet the man in charge. What was his name?"

"Saur. Joachim Saur. He worked on something hush-hush before the war. Gas, I believe."

"That would fit with the equipment he's bringing."

They trudged back to the headquarters block and watched while Strasser flipped through a sheaf of papers handed to him from the cab of the truck. Satisfied, the security captain waved the truck and the staff car through the gate. The motorcycle escort pulled up in a neat rank and turned off their engines. The rear door of the staff car creaked open in the sudden quiet and a rotund, balding little man with a cheerful red face got out. He looked around, blinked for

154

a moment, and then trundled toward the only two civilians in sight.

"Dr. Siegner?" he looked swiftly from Roth to Siegner, trying to guess which was which. His voice was light and pleasant. Siegner nodded, to spare him embarrassment. "Dr. Saur? I'm Siegner. Very pleased to meet you."

I wish I could say the same, thought Roth.

"Likewise, likewise. This must be Dr. Lerner . . . ?"

"I'm Dr. Roth. Dr. Lerner has longer hair."

Nonplussed, the little gas expert glanced quickly from one to the other, not sure of what offense he had offered, if any.

Siegner gave a short laugh. "Dr. Lerner is a woman. My colleague here has a joking manner; you'll get used to it."

"Oh. I beg your pardon. Where do you want me to have the truck unloaded?"

"Captain Strasser will have that taken care of. Oh, by the way, this is Captain Strasser, our security chief."

Strasser gave a curt nod. "Put it in the storage cavern across from the extraction lab?"

"Yes, please. As we arranged yesterday."

"Parts of it are rather fragile," worried Saur, "especially the valves."

"Don't worry. There won't be any damage." Strasser walked away and began to detail men to unload the truck.

"We're all rather tense and short-tempered," apologized Siegner. "We're very near completion; that's causing it, I think."

They began to walk up the hill. "What *is Fenris*, exactly?" queried Saur. "They were all very vague about it in Berlin when I was told to start getting the equipment together, a couple of weeks ago."

"They were that sure we'd go along with it," muttered Roth involuntarily.

"What?"

"Sorry. Thinking out loud."

Siegner momentarily looked at Roth out of the corner of his eye, and then asked Saur, "Were you told anything at all?"

"Hardly anything," the little man told him apologetically. "I'm more of an engineer than a scientist, really. They did say you'd brief me as necessary."

Siegner had in fact received a document from Kruger the day before, specifying exactly how much Saur was to know. Siegner had been careful to let the rest of the team know the contents of the order; Strasser would no doubt be watching for slips.

"Well. We have got a nuclear fission pile running, to start off with." He went on to describe the results they had obtained, and the goals they sought, without actually revealing the methods they had used. Kruger had been extremely insistent on this point. When he had finished, Saur's eyes had become large circles.

"But the rumors said we were far away from anything like this. What—?"

"The rumors are correct," interrupted Roth wearily. "As far as the civilian teams working elsewhere are concerned. Those projects form a cover for this one, although I don't suppose they were intended to do so to begin with."

"That's why all the SS?" observed Saur tentatively.

"That's right."

They tramped on in silence for a few meters.

"When do we start?"

"As soon as possible. Have you had breakfast?"

"I ate on the journey. Will you show me the, what do you call it?"

"Pile. Yes, we'll take a short tour while your equipment's

being unloaded. Then we'll have a look at what you've brought.''

Saur was virtually speechless when they had finished and he, Roth, Siegner, and Anna-Marie were gathered around the packing cases in the storage room.

"What do you think of it?" asked Roth as he attacked the largest case with a crowbar. Even Roth could not keep an edge of pride out of his voice.

Saur hunted for words for a moment. Then he said, "It's hard to believe. I had no idea. If only we'd started before the war. You've done an incredible job, given what you've had to work with."

"To the SS, few doors are closed," intoned Roth, levering the top off the crate. He gestured at Siegner. "There's the genius responsible."

Siegner looked uncomfortable. "What have we got here?" he asked, and peered into the crate. Inside it was a gleaming cylinder, rather like a compressed-air bottle, about four feet long.

"That's it?"

"Not entirely. The important parts are in the other box."

While Roth opened the other crate, Saur explained. "The large cylinder is for the active agent itself. The other device is attached to the nipple on the end of the large cylinder, which is pressurized through that inlet on top. The pressure forces the liquid agent through a metering valve into the aerosol generating chamber, where a jet of compressed air is driven over the liquid's surface. The jet sweeps up small particles of the liquid; these become electrically charged and so can't combine to form larger particles. Some larger particles do occur, of course, so there are droplet traps in the outlet ducting to catch them and funnel them back into the generating chamber."

"Very ingenious. What's the result?"

"A fine mist of the active agent which will remain a mist, even at very high concentration. So it won't coalesce and drop to the ground; it stays in the air for a considerable length of time."

"Has this device been tested?" asked Anna-Marie.

"Oh, yes. Or one very like it. At the Practical Research Institute in Military Science. At Natzweiler."

Anna-Marie could barely repress a shudder. She stared at the little engineer with sudden loathing. Natzweiler was a concentration camp.

Siegner was gazing expressionlessly into the small crate. Now will you do something, she begged him, silently.

In the strained pause that followed the gas expert's words, Siegner was wondering: did he say that by accident, or was he told to, to find out the limits of my tolerance? Was this thing, or one like it, used to murder captive human beings? Am I being tested? If this really is the last chance for victory, am I right to try to stop it? If it's to be used on military targets, that's one thing. But they're going to use it on cities. Or are they? Anyway, remember Hamburg. Tens of thousands burned to death by the Allied bombers. I'm confused. In any case, they'll kill us all if we refuse to go on. And then someone else will finish it, it's close enough now. If we remain, at least we'll have some control—.

He started, realizing they were all staring at him. Brusquely, he turned to Roth. "You'll have to work out the shielding requirements with Anna-Marie and Dr. Saur and get it fabricated." He eyed Saur neutrally. "How much weight have we got to play with?"

Saur giggled uncertainly. "Up to eight and a half thousand kilograms. That should be far more than enough. It also leaves a wide safety margin."

Roth gaped at him. "Eight and a half thousand kilos? We've got no aircraft that will lift that. What are you talking about?"

Saur gaped back, incredulous. "You mean you weren't informed? It isn't one of ours, it's British. It's a captured Lancaster."

Isn't that just like the bloody military, thought Siegner viciously, scratching out one set of calculations and beginning over again. Leave it till the last moment, then tell us what it's going to be carried in.

It was startling to realize that they had never really stopped to think about the aircraft in which the system would be transported. It had, of course, depended on the size and weight of the aerosol equipment, but that had turned out to be ridiculously light in relation to the shielding they believed would be needed.

Shielding. Was the shielding enough? Once again, Siegner cursed himself for not setting up a series of tests on mice or rabbits to judge the lethality against which they would have to protect. No one had intended to go into the pile room anyway, while it was in operation; but it had been sheer blindness to think of starting the extraction without some such tests. They had better do some rudimentary ones, anyway—at least they would know how immediately deadly the wastes could be. The long-term danger would have to be ignored; there was no way around that. Not for the first time, he was sharply aware of the gimcrack nature of the *Fenris* installation, for all the impression it made on an outsider like Saur. It worked, certainly; but it had been put together so quickly and with so many shortcuts that there were dozens of patched-over errors that might end the whole business in some unpleasant way. Either they should have taken far longer, or put far more resources into the project. Secrecy, again. Keep it small, keep it quiet.

And now the Lancaster. He didn't particularly care if Saur wanted to tie his system onto a kite, but being told about the bomber by an outsider had made him angry. In a curt exchange over the telephone, Weil had told him that the decision had been made at the last moment, that Saur had been informed because of the piping and controls that would be necessary, and that neglecting to inform Siegner had been an oversight. Siegner didn't know whether to believe him or not. It could have been a way of reminding him that he was no longer indispensable; if it had, he reflected gloomily, the maneuver had succeeded. He was less sure than ever of his ability to stop things, should he decide to try.

A wave of depression swept through him. He would have to go on, hoping that someone in Berlin would regain enough sanity to call the whole thing off. He was certain that Kruger was working on Himmler, but if Hitler were behind it . . .

A tapping on the door interrupted his thoughts.

"Come in."

It was Strasser. The captain's face was expressionless, but from his stance Siegner guessed that he was concealing profound excitement. "Dr. Siegner. Can you spare a moment? Something's happened."

"By all means. Sit down." This was the first time in some weeks that Strasser had *asked* to talk to him: nowadays it was usually a thinly veiled summons.

Strasser closed the door firmly, and sat down on one of the hard chairs. He shifted about on it excitedly. "The invasion. Colonel Kruger telephoned a few minutes ago. The Americans and British started fighting their way ashore in France this morning."

"Where?"

"Normandy."

"That's a long way from England, isn't it?"

"The Pas de Calais is closer. I suppose OKW has taken both into account."

"Will they be able to stay ashore?" Siegner felt excitement rise within him. If the Allies were pushed back into the sea, perhaps they would negotiate, and then *Fenris* could be used as it should, to build a bomb, not the other loathsome thing . . .

"Don't know yet. Kruger said the news from the beachhead area was vague. It might even be a feint. The more of them that get ashore, though, the more will be in the bag when they're defeated."

"Suppose—"

"They beat us? And stay ashore? Well, in that case, your toy becomes even more to the point, doesn't it? Kruger said you could call him, by the way, if you wanted to, but that his orders were simply to carry on."

"Not speed up at all?" This was a surprise. Or was it?

"No." Strasser appeared mystified. "He didn't say that, for some reason. I suppose he felt you'd assume it."

"Very well. Whom else have you told?"

"Nobody, so far. The camp staff will get the news in the ordinary way, as soon as it's cleared for public information."

"I presume that doesn't include my people."

"Not as far as I'm concerned. Just tell them to keep it to themselves until it's public. That shouldn't be more than a day, anyway. I have to go. Heil Hitler."

"Heil Hitler." Strasser didn't normally use that salute; he must be feeling unusually stirred up.

When the SS captain had gone, Siegner leaned back in his chair and tried to think out the implications of the news.

His initial optimism had begun to fade. There was one very good reason for that. If there were peace, if the Russians were stopped, there would still be places like Natzweiler. And men like Saur.

Siegner got up from his chair and went to tell the others about the invasion.

On the day of the accident, Siegner was in his office reviewing the notes of the telephone conversation he had had with Weil the day after the news of the Allied assault. With the attack a month earlier than expected, the hope of using the *Fenris* weapon had gone glimmering into the dark. Nobody was to blame for this, Weil indicated; the work had gone as quickly as could be expected, but it should not slow down just because the original target had materialized too early. There were a number of other options; Weil had not specified what they were. During the subsequent three weeks it had become obvious that the Allies were ashore for good, as long as normal weapons were used. Even the guided bomb attacks on London had fizzled; they might be making life unpleasant in the enemy capital, but the effect on the battlefront had been unnoticeable. By yesterday, June 28, the Allies had overrun most of the Cotentin peninsula and were well inland everywhere else except around Caen. Siegner, with his experience of the Russian front, realized that the enemy was now too dispersed for a rapid, lethal blow except where he was close to German troops, and that this very proximity made the use of the *Fenris* weapon impossible. That left built-up, civilian targets. Siegner felt himself being slowly gripped by a kind of mental paralysis; he could still make technical decisions easily enough, but was powerless to do anything more. He had noticed that the others were staying away from him; there had been little conversation recently about anything except the demands of work.

Worse, he had felt too listless to set up the tests with the mice or rabbits. The request to Boehme to provide a set of experimental animals remained on the corner of his desk. There was still time for that, he reminded himself. The preparation of the active wastes had only begun two days ago. They should really have introduced a cage of mice into the pile chamber when the reaction was shut down and the uranium cubes lifted out and moved into the extraction alley. That would have given them some idea of the dangers with which they had to deal. I would never have been this sloppy a few months ago, he brooded. What's happening to my mind?

It was too late for that experiment, in any case. Several dozen cubes had already been removed from the core and were already being reduced to a solution of uranium and wastes. The uranium would be separated from the rest, which would be concentrated to form the liquid for the aerosol. But they had better get some experimental animals into the alley before they started loading Saur's bottle with the fluid. He would attend to it now. He shuffled his papers together, locked them away, and headed for the extraction lab.

The first thing he noticed on reaching the lab door was the strong draft blowing from behind him, from the corridor. What the devil?

Then he saw.

The heavy door to the extraction alley was open. Sommer was standing well away from it, surrounded by a small group of technicians. They were all peering anxiously into the alley. The draft was caused by air drawn from the corridor and into the alley by the ventilating fans in the shafts above it.

"What's going on here?"

They turned to look at him. Sommer answered, his face white. "One of the tracks jammed. Anna-Marie's gone in to free it."

Siegner was too frightened to swear. "You." He grabbed one of the technicians by the arm. "Get Dr. Roth in here. Now."

The man scurried out.

Siegner ran to the thick viewing port and looked into the alley. Anna-Marie was standing under the container that transported the wastes, dissolved in acid, to the precipitators that removed them for redissolving in less corrosive solvents. He was relieved to see that she was wearing acid-protection gear, and a breathing mask and tank against the fumes. One gloved hand grasped a heavy wrench.

He could see what had happened. A securing bolt on the transporting rail had unthreaded itself far enough to jam the rollers of the waste container suspension. Anna-Marie was reaching up past the container and was tightening the bolt. She was only inches from the gleaming canister. Pray she didn't drop the wrench into its open mouth, into the liquid. Oh. She had secured the wrench handle to her wrist with a length of light chain.

She was having trouble keeping a grip on the wrench. He saw her shake her head in frustration; the bolt was not quite far enough in. She shrugged, took the wrench away from the bolt, let it dangle from its chain, and removed the protective glove. She reached back up and turned the bolt firmly into its seat.

Siegner began to let out his breath.

The wrench slipped from her grasp and clanged against

the lip of the container. She jerked her arm in surprise. The tool caught on the container opening and swung the canister on its pivots. A dollop of straw-colored liquid slopped over the edge and over her bare hand and wrist.

Siegner spun around and shouted, "Get the emergency shower on!" Then he turned back to the port.

The pain must have been intense, but she used the chain, carefully, to draw the wrench from the container. Then she took off the other glove, undid the chain from around her acid-drenched wrist, and let the wrench drop to the floor. Only then did she run for the alley door.

Sommer had turned on the emergency shower in the corner of the lab and had siezed a can of neutralizer. Anna-Marie stumbled through the door, her face inside the breathingmask greenish-white with shock and fear. A whimper slipped from between her teeth. One of the technicians slammed the alley door. Siegner grabbed Anna-Marie as she was about to fall, and rammed her arm under the cold water. The hand and wrist were already beginning to swell in red and white patches. Sommer had picked up the emergency telephone to the compound sick bay and was shouting into it for Unger, the camp doctor.

Unger and Roth arrived together. While Unger treated Anna-Marie—she had begun to cry softly—Siegner told Roth what had happened.

Roth went quite pale. "Acid burn. Bad enough. What about the other?"

Siegner, nearly speechless with guilt and worry for Anna-Marie, lashed out at him. "How in Christ's name should I know? We didn't do any tests on that, did we? We were in too much of a hurry, weren't we?" He trailed off into silence. Two of the technicians and Sommer were placing Anna-Marie on a stretcher. Unger had given her morphine and her eyes were glazed. She had stopped crying. They bundled her out of the door and disappeared.

Siegner collapsed into a chair. He felt weak and faint. He put his fists on his knees and got a grip on himself. Remember Kharkov. It was worse there, remember? A lot worse, at Kharkov.

At last he said to the others, "Pack up for the day. We'll see about carrying on in the morning."

They left. Roth waited a few moments and then followed them, without a word. He came back fifteen minutes later. Siegner was standing at the port, staring at the wrench on the alley floor.

"Peter?"

With an effort, he pulled himself away from the window.

Roth looked at him with consternation. The physicist's eyes were sunk far back in his head, so that they were almost in shadow. His face was gaunt. Roth wondered why he hadn't seen how the man had aged in the last few months. Too close to him, too preoccupied, what?

"Anna-Marie?" Siegner's voice croaked. He swallowed twice.

"She's unconscious. Shock from the pain. Her hand's deeply burned. There'll be muscle and nerve damage."

"As long as that's all."

"Yes. Pull yourself together, Peter. We may need specialists. From Berlin, anywhere."

Siegner's face took on a little life. Here was something he could deal with. He sat down and began to think. "Some of the wastes will be burned into the tissues by the acid. Perhaps in the bloodstream by now, I don't know. We'd better get someone who's good with heavy-metal poisonings. That's what some of it will be, likely. We don't know exactly what the substances are, though, only in theory.

We'll have to do some analyses." He realized that he had begun to ramble. "We'll need a good analytical chemist, as well."

"Will we continue without her?"

"We'll have to. They won't let us stop now."

For the first time, Roth thought of killing him.

Dr. Anna-Marie Lerner required three days to finish dying. She recovered consciousness toward the evening of the first day and complained of nausea. Roth went to see her; Siegner couldn't bear to. When Roth found him late that night in his office, the physicist was staring blankly into space, a half-empty brandy glass on the desk.

"How is she?"

"Sick. Unger can't understand it. The burn is serious, but she ought to be in better shape than she is. He's shot her full of morphine again."

"Kruger's sending somebody down from Berlin."

Next day, Sommer continued with the extraction, feeling his way very slowly and working from Anna-Marie's notes. The specialist arrived in mid-afternoon, examined her, and came out of the sick bay looking grave. Siegner, Boehme, and Roth were waiting for him. When questioned by Roth, he could only say, "I don't think it's entirely heavy-metal poisoning. From what you told me, she couldn't have received a big enough dose of any of the usual metals to cause the symptoms she's got. Did you know she was running a high temperature?"

"Yes."

"It looks like an infection, but the burn isn't suppurating more than is normal. You don't know exactly what was in the solution?"

Siegner gestured helplessly. Kruger hadn't been able to

find an analysis man on such short notice. "Uranium, certainly. Some other things. Not common ones."

"I don't think I can help her much. I've never come across anything like this, and I haven't much to go on. She might come around by herself."

Unger and an orderly carrying a tray of vials and a hypodermic came out of the sick bay. "She's in a lot of pain," Unger told them. "There's some lung trouble, too. She's having difficulty breathing. I've given her more painkiller. We'd better move her to a quiet room and let her sleep. Do you want to stay? She'll probably be unconscious or nearly so for the next twelve hours."

"No, I guess not."

The three scientists left the sick bay and dispersed, Boehme to his paperwork, Roth to the design of the aerosol shielding. Siegner retreated to his office and the brandy bottle, but gave up trying to get drunk after the second glass. He put his head down on his arms and went to sleep.

Someone was shaking him. He thought for a moment it was the lieutenant, jerking him as he had that morning when the Russians came at Kharkov.

It was Unger. The brandy bottle was nowhere to be seen. Roth likely put it away while I was asleep, thought Siegner. Protecting my reputation. He dragged himself fully awake and sat up.

"What is it? What time is it?"

"It's five A.M. Dr. Lerner's conscious; she wants to see you. I can't quiet her down."

"Where's Dr. Roth?"

"I don't know. Are you coming or not?"

In the false dawn they stumbled down the slope to the sick bay. It was just light enough to see the edges of the mountains against the sky. A few birds twittered on the slopes above them.

"How is she?" asked Siegner as they climbed the steps.

"Worse. I think she's going to die."

It was brutal, even from an SS doctor.

He was not prepared for her. Her eyes were as he had known them, but now sunk in dark hollows. Some of her hair had fallen out. She was muttering feverishly.

Unger left them alone. Anna-Marie turned her head on the pillow to look at Siegner; she had trouble focusing. When she tried to speak, her voice was a rasping whisper. "I told him not to give me any more morphine till I'd seen you. I'm going to die, aren't I?"

He looked at her, helplessly.

She coughed, a deep racking convulsion. "I think I knew it as soon as the wastes hit me." Her eyes closed, then opened. "It only seems just. What are you going to do, Peter?"

He leaned closer. "I don't know. I'm trapped. We all are."

She made a slight motion with her bandaged hand. He put his ear inches from her lips. He could scarcely hear her as she breathed, "You must get away. Go to the British, the Americans. You've got to stop it. Roth will help."

"Roth?"

"Yes." Her voice was the merest thread of sound in his ear. "We were both Abwehr agents. To watch the SS. When the SD took over the Abwehr we were isolated. Roth still has some contacts. Go to him. Say yes. Say yes."

"All right. Yes."

"Find Unger. It's getting bad again. Good-bye."

She closed her eyes. He started to say something, he didn't know what, and changed it to "Good-bye." He stumbled out of the room to find Unger, and the morphine.

Anna-Marie Lerner died at four o'clock that afternoon. She did not regain consciousness.

Siegner and Roth sat on the grassy slope above the entrance bunker and watched the sun decline behind the shoulder of the mountains. They had been there for an hour, hardly speaking. At last Siegner managed:

"So you were working for the Abwehr all along."

"She told you. I thought likely she would."

"Why?"

"Why we were with the Abwehr? Well, Canaris, Oster, some of the others—they were concerned about this kind of thing being done. Originally the worry was gas. Now it's this."

"Canaris was sacked last February. Kaltenbrunner and the SD took over, Strasser told me. Who are you working for now?"

"There are parts of the system intact. Originally there would have been plans to head this kind of thing off by political means. That's what I was here for, to provide on-the-spot information. Anna-Marie too. But we were supposed to keep our outside contacts to a minimum until we got instructions to do otherwise. The instructions never came. I don't suppose there's anybody left in the Abwehr shambles to do more than leak the odd bit of information wherever it will do the most good. But I haven't any hope of a political end to the thing. It's gone too far. There's only one solution left that I can think of."

There was a long silence while the sun sank lower and redder.

Siegner took a deep breath. "Can you get me out? To Switzerland?"

Roth grimaced. "Anna-Marie and I talked about that, months ago. Would you have gone, then?"

"No. But I will now."

"What's different?"

"Anna-Marie. We can't use that . . . thing on civilians."

"Burning Hamburg was preferable?"

"No. Of course not. But we've lost the war, anyone can tell that. Using the *Fenris* weapon won't help us now. Even if it could, I don't think I could agree with using it, seeing what it does. It's so slow . . ."

Roth shrugged. "I agree it's got to be stopped, but we can't do that here. Not now. I wish you'd felt this way months ago. Anyway, I'll try to get you out. I'll need to photograph a copy of your identity photo. Preparations will take four or five days after I make contact. Also, we'll have to slow down the extraction process somehow, otherwise there'll be no time to do anything even if you do get away."

"If?"

"If. I didn't say it was a sure thing. We may each end up with our heads in a loop of chicken wire, or worse."

They buried Anna-Marie the next day. The coffin was closed. Siegner wrote a letter to her parents which Strasser read before allowing it to be sent. The area of authority the scientists had enjoyed was being constricted, day by day.

Roth decided to risk going into Innsbrück that afternoon, almost certain that he would be followed. He wheedled the keys of the Tatra out of Boehme, and then tried to find Strasser. The SS captain was unlocatable. Roth plucked up his nerve, told Bergmann, the adjutant, that he was leaving for an hour or two, and logged out of the compound. He watched the rearview mirror all the way into the city, but it remained empty.

He parked the Tatra near the Westbahnhof and idled around the streets until he was sure he had not been followed. Then he made his way quickly to the bookstore in the Maximilianstrasse.

There were no other customers in the tiny shop but he asked to see a copy of Junger's *Storm of Steel,* just in case. As he leafed through it, he said to the bookseller, "A man needs to go to Switzerland. Within four days. Abwehr business. Can it be arranged?"

The bell over the door jingled. The old man said, "As .you can see, it's a fine edition. Leather bound, properly cased, with good stitching. Prewar. Can I help you?" This to the dumpy woman standing impatiently by the till.

He sold her the ink she wanted and returned to Roth. "It could be done. I take it it's not for our new, ah, masters in Berlin."

"They're not my masters. No, it isn't."

The bookseller thought, and then said, "He can be put on a train, with false papers, by Saturday. After that it's up to him. There's still a stock of identities up the line, apparently. The best ones have been used, but . . . does he know anything about engineering?"

"Enough."

"Good. The papers will be at the old drop. He shouldn't come here, for his sake and mine."

Roth eyed the bent figure speculatively. "None of this has bothered you before."

"You haven't been here very often. Besides, I know about you. Him I don't know. Go. Tell him to come to the drop at ten A.M. on Saturday the eighth. There's a train to Buchs in Switzerland at ten-thirty. The Gestapo will check papers at Feldkirch, it's the last stop before the border. The journey takes at least five hours, barring unusual delays.

172

Do you have a photograph of him?''

Roth handed over the print he had made the night before.

"This will do, I suppose. How soon will he be missed?''

"I'll worry about that.''

"As you wish. Do you want the book?''

"I suppose I'd better. You've done this before, haven't you?''

The old man shrugged. "You had better tell me your authority. These identities aren't passed out on demand.''

"Mannheim.''

The bookseller's eyes widened briefly. "That's not what you used last time.''

"This is different. How much for the book?''

"Why don't you come as well?''

"I've told you before. There has to be someone here to delay things if necessary. Besides, both of us leaving the compound at once would be far too suspicious. Neither of us would get away. I can't understand why I wasn't followed last time. I did look for Strasser, as he 'suggested'.''

Siegner laughed, without mirth. "I can tell you why. Strasser didn't know you'd been out until you logged back in with the gate sentry. Bergmann must have forgotten to tell him you'd left. Our SS captain was up here in my office, reminiscing about Russia. I expect he was furious when he found out you'd been gone. Suppose you had been followed. What would you have done?''

"There's a drop I could have used. But it would have been much slower. This was just lucky. I didn't know Strasser went in for chats about old times, by the way.''

"Boehme told him about the French brandy we had.''

"Christ. What excuse are you going to use for being in Innsbrück for five hours?'' Roth went on. "They'll close

173

the border as soon as you've been gone longer than that, even if they don't believe you've defected. Also, we have to find a way to keep you from being followed."

"I don't know about the excuse, yet. If I'm followed, I'll have to kill the tail. Or knock him unconscious for a long time, at least."

"Can you manage that?"

"I didn't do all my fighting in Russia from a tank turret. It was hand-to-hand occasionally, during the retreat in '41. Killing the tail is safer than giving him the slip, anyway. If he finds I've got away from him he'll simply raise the alarm."

"D'you think you'll be able to spot a shadower?"

"I'm sure of it. Strasser likely has men stationed in Aldrans, to follow anyone heading into Innsbrück. All he'd have to do would be to telephone whenever someone left the compound. If I see a car behind me after going through Aldrans, I'll know I'm being followed. You were very lucky to get away so easily."

"He'll make sure it doesn't happen again."

"He will." Siegner got the brandy bottle out of his desk. "Help me think of a good reason to go to Innsbrück."

They decided to keep it simple. Siegner was in Strasser's office at nine on Saturday morning, following the captain's "suggestion" that the scientists inform him before leaving the compound.

"What do you need in the city?" Strasser asked. "I'll send down for it."

"Clothes," Siegner told him. The length of pipe inside his jacket weighed on his chest like a stone. "I've been wearing the same two pairs of trousers for the past year. They're practically falling to pieces from the messes I've got on them up on the hill. Can you get me a lift? Boehme says the Tatra's out of order."

Strasser's interest in the jaunt had apparently disappeared. "All right. Tell Bergmann to get Peikert to take you down in the Kübelwagen. I hope you don't mind a little dust." He picked up a sheaf of orders and started to sign them. "How long will you be gone? Peikert can pick you up, if you telephone."

"I was going to stop for lunch and a beer, maybe a walk along the river. I'll ask Peikert to be in front of the Hauptbahnhof at four. It'll save me waiting for him to drive back down."

"Whatever you like."

Siegner left. Strasser went on signing orders. When he heard the buzz of the open, jeep-like Kübelwagen receding beyond the main gate, he picked up the telephone.

He would have been unpleasantly surprised to know that Siegner was laying bets with himself as to how long it would take him to call ahead to the surveillance post in Aldrans. Siegner glanced behind as they left the village; sure enough, there was a nondescript gray Citroën well back in their wake. As far as he could tell, there was only one person in the car. Clumsy bastards, he thought.

"Where do you want me to drop you, sir?"

"Same place you'll pick me up. In front of the Hauptbahnhof."

As Peikert halted the Kübelwagen, Siegner gazed longingly at the facade of the train station. Please be on time today, he prayed. He got out; the little vehicle rattled away. The Citroën had turned down a side street. He waited a moment to give its driver time to park and walk back to the Südtingler-Platz, and then started off toward Heilig-Geist

175

Strasse. There were few people about, but enough to make disposal of his follower a possible problem.

The drop was in a bombed-out row of buildings on the Templestrasse. Second alley on the right, Roth had said. There's a section of wall still standing, at the end. Tenth course of bricks up, third brick from the left side of the broken windowframe. Lift the brick out. The papers will be behind it. In God's name don't get caught, he had added unnecessarily.

Siegner glanced at his watch. It was ten past ten. He stopped to peer in a shop window. In the reflection he could see a man on the other side tying a shoelace.

If he's no better than that, thought Siegner, this shouldn't be too difficult. If I can just get him alone.

The alley was coming up. As he came abreast of it, Siegner faltered, bent almost double, and reached out his right arm to steady himself against the masonry. He missed the wall and staggered sideways into the alley, traveling perhaps six meters down before he sank to his knees. The sound of hurrying footsteps grew louder behind him. His hand slipped inside his jacket, gripping the pipe. He half turned.

His follower hurried around the corner into the alley. He was a small, spare man, trotting with quick, jerky steps. No one was in sight beyond the alley mouth.

"Hey! What's the matter?"

Hit him hard, then tumble him behind that rubble pile. Cover him up. God, I haven't much time.

Siegner choked, grimacing, his right hand inside his jacket, "Chest. Wounded. Got worse suddenly. Doctor."

The man rushed up and siezed his left arm. Siegner clutched at the follower's elbow and bent over, drawing the pipe from his jacket under the cover of his body and swinging it down and back. When he came up the pipe came up too. He hit the man under the left ear, almost as hard as he could.

It was hard enough. The man's eyeballs turned up and his knees folded. Siegner dropped the pipe, oblivious of the clang, and caught the man under the armpits. He looked over the other's shoulder toward the street.

A man stood there, watching him calmly.

My God, I'm done.

The man looked irritated. He glanced up and down the street and made jabbing motions with his thumb toward the rubble. Siegner regained control of himself and dropped his shadower into the chaos of bricks and beams. He checked the pulse. It was weak. The man would be out for hours at least; he might not die. There was a buckled sheet of lath and plaster a foot away. Siegner dragged it over the body.

Tenth course up, third brick from the frame. It was ten-fourteen. He was sweating in the July heat. Rail pass, ticket, identity papers, they were the most important. Yes. There. Check the rest in the train. He walked hurriedly back down the alley, pretending to adjust his fly buttons. The man—no longer blurry with adrenalin, Siegner realized that he was quite an old man—was still there. As Siegner passed him, he muttered, "That was the only one," and tramped away.

Ten-sixteen. Just time enough.

He was still perspiring heavily when he reached the station. My God, the train was there, it was on time, so was he.

The guard barely glanced at the pass and identity papers, and waved him on board. The train was nearly empty. Siegner found a seat on the side of the carriage away from the station and stared out at the reaches of the rail yards, still bomb-scarred from the April raids. He willed the train

177

to move. He was trembling from the aftereffects of adrenalin.

Slowly he calmed down. Well, Anna-Marie, he thought, I'm on my way. Can't go back now, it'd be the chicken-wire noose for sure. Although still tense, he felt the first stealings of relief. For the first time in months, he was committed.

To treason, he thought. Well, it can't be helped now.

The old man heard the train's whistle as it pulled out for Switzerland.

Siegner waited for an hour before going to the lavatory. There were only a few other passengers in the carriage; Swiss, by their well-fed, prosperous look. When he was sure from the speed of the train that they were unlikely to stop for a while, he got up and slipped back to the cubicle. Sitting on the rocking toilet seat, he pulled out the sheaf of papers and gave them a closer inspection.

Rail pass. He had checked that. It was good for two weeks. Next, the identity papers, at which he had only been able to glance during the hurried walk to the station. He was Heinz Büchler, a design engineer. He worked for Bayerische Motoren Werken and had been employed there since April 1942. He lived in Munich, was a member of the National Socialist Party, and had been exempted from military service because of his technical skills. There was also a letter of introduction from the production head of the Munich branch of BMW to the sales department of the Züricher Maschinen Fabric in Zurich. It stated that Heinz Büchler was interested in acquiring surplus machine tools, particularly milling equipment, to replace those lost in the bombings. Prices could be discussed in terms of a two-month delivery date, with penalties for late delivery. Other documents confirmed the purpose of his journey. Finally, there was a Swiss railway schedule, and a wad of several score Reichsmarks.

The major problem was the time he had before the alarm was raised. If his shadower were found too soon, he would be caught for certain; if not, he might just get away with it. Not only did he have to get out of the Reich, however; he also had to get into Switzerland. Siegner mentally crossed his fingers, stood up, carefully flushed the toilet, and returned to his seat.

The train stopped and started for another five hours. The Alps slid by, in varying heights. Once there was a tunnel.

The last stop before the border was Feldkirch. The train rolled in at fifteen minutes to four. Peikert will be waiting for me by now, thought Siegner. He wouldn't like me to tell Strasser he was late.

Two Kriminalpolizei stamped into the carriage, followed by a pair of nondescript men in light jackets. Gestapo. They started down the aisle. Siegner stared out the window at the mountains. The Kripo halted by his seat.

"Papers. You're German?"

"Yes." Siegner looked up. "First time I've ever been over the border. What do you want to see?"

"Everything. Why are you going to Switzerland?"

He felt remarkably calm.

"It's here in the letter."

The Kripo read it. The Gestapo hovered.

"All right. You can go on."

They blundered away down the carriage. Now, only the Swiss, thought Siegner.

The time edged onward, and still the train didn't move. Surely by now Peikert was telephoning Strasser, Strasser was calling Weil, and the whole dense net of the SS and

SD was about to drop over his head. He crossed and uncrosssed his legs.

The train jerked, and began to move. It rumbled slowly across Lichtenstein, over the Rhine bridge, and stopped at the Swiss checkpoint at Buchs. Siegner watched the Bundespolizei man walk down the platform to the carriage door. He looked bored. Here's another one I have to convince, Siegner thought. Ironic. He's not even German.

The policeman appeared at the end of the carriage and began to check papers. He took his time. After centuries he came to Siegner.

"You're not Swiss."

"No. German."

"Why are you coming to Switzerland?"

It was almost identical to the question the Kripo had asked.

"I'm on my way to Zurich to negotiate for machinery."

"The picture doesn't look much like you."

He knew he was on safer ground here, and said, without thinking, trying to make a joke of it, "Neither would yours, if you'd been through what I have."

It was a mistake. The Bupo turned red and opened his mouth. Then an authoritative voice said from the front of the carriage, "Leave the German alone. You're making us all late for supper."

The Bupo half-turned to look for the speaker, and then shoveled the documents back into Siegner's lap. "You can go," he said angrily, "but keep a civil tongue in your head in future. Borders are not places to try to be funny." He stamped irritably to the front of the carriage and disappeared out the door. Siegner caught a glimpse of him stalking away down the platform.

I'd buy that gentleman at the front of the carriage a drink

180

if I could, he thought. I'd forgotten what a country at peace was like. You can talk back to the police and get away with it.

The rest of the journey was uneventful. At nine o'clock that evening, he presented himself at the British Consulate in Zurich.

V

England

"There's something there all right," said the WAAF at the stereoscopic viewer, "but it doesn't look like very much."

"It wasn't very much even from close up," said Patterson. "Brian may have seen more than I did, though." He glanced at his navigator. "I was rather busy dodging Germans at the time."

Mackenzie shrugged. "The structure on the mountainside just looked like a big concrete block. There were some men about, guards, I suppose. There was a bunkerlike affair backed up against the slope a lot lower down, in the barracks area."

"May I have a look?" The WAAF stepped back from the viewer and Pierce took her place. He peered into the lenses, jigged the focus, and said, "There's another structure lower down than the concrete block, let me see, northwest of it. Any ideas on that?"

"I'm sorry, sir," said the WAAF. "I've never seen anything like it before. There is another bunker that might be a second entrance, though, down below it. It's not even camouflaged."

"Might be emergency exit or access. No telling how

many camouflaged entrances there are. Have a look, Alan, Gordon.''

They took turns inspecting the photograph. Mackenzie stood up from the viewer and suggested, thoughtfully, ''That odd structure below the concrete block. Air intake?''

''Maybe.'' Devereaux was staring into the viewer. ''Damn. The lenses are misting. I thought I saw something else.''

Pierce handed him a handkerchief. Devereaux wiped the lenses and looked again. ''There appears to be dead foliage on the trees around the highest block. As though it were a chimney, and whatever's coming out is killing off the vegetation. Anybody else want to look?''

They looked. There were indeed signs of bare tree branches near the chimney.

''How many men could you house in those barracks, do you think?'' said Gilford.

''About a hundred,'' the WAAF told him. ''You can see where there were other buildings, too. They've taken them down, now. There must have been upward of five hundred people on the site, earlier on. There're traces of a light rail line going up to that bunker affair at the edge of the compound, as well.''

''What've we got, then?'' asked Gilford.

Pierce glanced significantly at the WAAF, who was peering into the viewer again.

''Oh, of course. Could you excuse us, please, Sergeant Jennings, Colin, Brian? You had better leave the pictures and the viewer.''

The young woman and the two airmen filed out, looking disappointed. Gilford shut the office door. ''You can hardly blame the aircrew for feeling left out.'' he said as he resumed his chair. ''They got shot at getting the ruddy pictures and now they don't know what it was they photographed."

"They shouldn't," said Pierce.

"Mn. Well, to rephrase my question, what do you think it is?"

"Gordon?"

Mclennand ticked the ideas off on his fingers. "One, there's a fenced camp, capable of holding a hundred people or so. Two, there's something backed up against the mountain that looks like an entrance to a tunnel, and there's evidence that a rail line led to it at one time. Three, there's a—a chimney of some sort a few hundred feet farther up. Four, something from the chimney appears to have killed off vegetation around it. Five, evidence of another entrance. Six, one odd structure that might be the entrance to an air intake. For ventilation or cooling."

Gilford interposed, "I take it the whole thing is something unpleasant."

"Could be," said Pierce. "Very. I can't tell you everything, Patrick, I haven't the authorization. But what Gordon has said makes me believe even more strongly than I did that we're dealing with an exceedingly dangerous German attempt to bring the war to a screeching halt. In their favor."

Gilford puffed out his cheeks and then exhaled. "Doesn't seem like much to go on. The photograph, I mean. What's causing the dead vegetation?"

Mclennand answered. "There are two possible causes. One is that the operation of the place results in corrosive fumes."

"And the other?"

Mclennand looked at Pierce.

"Sorry, Patrick."

"Well, you can't have everything. That's all you want from me at the moment?"

"At the moment. We'd like to take the photographs with us."

"By all means. Try to keep me out of the way of most of the fuss you'll cause with them. My authority for that flight was a bit, shall we say, dodgy. Can you stay for lunch?"

"Like to. But we ought to get back to London."

"Call me if I can help you again."

As they got into the staff car a pale blue Mosquito thundered over, very low. When they could hear each other again, Pierce asked, "Still hard at it in France?"

"That's an understatement. We can't keep up with the demands for more reconnaissance. Two Group's even busier, if possible. It can't be long till the invasion now."

Pierce started the car. "Any guesses as to when?"

"June. Put a fiver on it?"

"That's my guess, too. No bet."

"Too bad. Good-bye, then."

As they rolled out the gate Devereaux asked, "What's the next step?"

"Take the whole works to the Joint Intelligence Committee and see if they think we should lay on a raid."

"I thought we agreed an air raid wasn't sure enough."

"Not an air raid. A ground raid. A sabotage team."

Darlington had managed to assemble an impressive array of officers, together with two high-level civilian scientists. They all sat around a polished oval table in a conference room in the War Office. There were pads of paper and sharpened pencils in front of each chair. A subdued June sun struggled past the heavy curtains.

Darlington chaired the meeting. He glanced around the table as if to take attendance, and tapped lightly on the polished wood with his pencil. "I suggest we begin, gentlemen. I'd like to ask Commander Pierce to review what has so far been discovered about *Fenris*. Most of you will be unfamiliar with what lies behind that code name; accordingly, I've asked Commander Pierce to go into some detail."

As Pierce's dry, precise voice recounted the events leading to the overflight and the evaluation of the photographs, Devereaux covertly surveyed the reaction of the others around the table. The scientists appeared politely interested; one or two of the military looked merely bored. When Pierce mentioned the reconnaissance flight, a spasm of irritation crossed the face of the ranking RAF officer there, an Air Vice-Marshal.

There was a short silence when Pierce finished, as though his audience were expecting something more. Then a major from Army Intelligence spoke up. "Apart from the four radio intercepts, and the photographs, do you have any further evidence? I have to say that I find the material so far not, um, unconvincing, but insufficient for the purposes of a valid decision in the matter."

What he means, thought Devereaux, is that we don't know enough to be able to do the right thing.

"That's all we have," admitted Pierce. Under the unsympathetic eyes, Devereaux was beginning to feel a bit of a fool. Looked at objectively, the evidence was rather thin and unconvincing. Had they blown a piece of minor intelligence into something out of all proportion?

Darlington appeared unabashed. "I believe the potential danger of the situation warrants more than the evidence would suggest," he told them smoothly. "Assuming, for the moment, that this place near Innsbrück is what Commander Pierce and his staff"—here he nodded toward

186

Mclennand and Devereaux—"fear it to be, what options do we have for dealing with it?"

The Air Vice-Marshal broke in irritably. "Was the overflight for these pictures authorized properly? We have enough to do in Western Europe at the moment, without side trips to the Alps."

"I'm sure the authority will be forthcoming, if it has not already been given," said Darlington, rather sharply. The Air Vice-Marshal glowered at him for a moment, and then subsided. "We're open to suggestions," said Darlington.

"Our resources for operations other than invasion preliminaries are very limited," said the Army staff officer at the end of the table. "I'd hesitate to ask the RAF for an air raid that deep inside Germany at the present time. I gather," he said, turning to the RAF intelligence officer beside him, "that the German nightfighters are still very active over their home soil."

"Very, I'm afraid to say. They've not slowed down much, if at all."

"We'd lose a lot of aircraft on that deep a penetration," grunted the Air Vice-Marshal. "To flatten a few lumps of concrete and a barracks wouldn't be worth it. Very hard to hit, anyhow. There's not much in the way of aiming points for the target markers to work with."

"We could use Innsbrück's center as the initial point," suggested the RAF intelligence officer, and immediately succumbed under the Vice-Marshal's scowl.

The latter said, "Quite true. But the mass of the aircraft tends to bomb on the fires lit by the first incendiaries. There's not much on the mountain to burn, at this time of year. A few fires would inevitably be started in Innsbrück, and you'd have the main force plastering that. Hardly a dent on the real target."

Devereaux stared at his hands while the wrangle went

on. The problem, he realized, was that the authorities at the meeting—or those for whom they spoke—had already formed their priorities around the invasion. There were never enough planes, resources, or men to do everything. The Vice-Marshal might or might not have been entirely candid in his reasons for discouraging an air raid; whether he had been or not, his attitude was representative of that of the other men around the table. Pierce and Darlington had been unable to convince them so far, and it was unlikely that they would be able to do so during the remainder of the meeting. Devereaux could hardly condemn people like the Vice-Marshal. He himself found the thought of a city-destroying weapon rather unbelievable. The scientists, cautious men, were not much help. They would prefer not to act until all the evidence was in.

Eventually Darlington tapped on the table for silence. "It's nearly five o'clock. Can we come to some conclusion by five, or at least agree to come to none?"

A mutter of consent went around the table. One of the scientists said, "Commander Pierce hasn't offered his opinion of what we ought to do. Surely he should indicate his preference in the matter?"

Pierce glanced at Darlington, who nodded. "By all means. Go ahead, Ian."

Pierce took a deep breath. "I needn't go over again how important I believe this is. The fact of this meeting is sufficient evidence that others feel similarly, to some degree, at least.

"I have to agree with the Air Vice-Marshal that bombing is not the way to deal with this installation, even if it is what we fear it to be. It is certainly true that it is difficult to hit, and hard to damage because of the protection given by the mountain shielding it. The American Fortresses could certainly hit it in daylight, but the opinion here is that they are fully committed elsewhere, as well as carrying a rather small bomb load. The bombs themselves are too small to penetrate into such a deeply buried installation. Naturally there is also the question of aircraft losses, which would be considerable for a penetration of that distance.

"I hope I have summarized the Air Force's position correctly." He looked around the table, and went on. "There is also the question of the commitment of our bomber forces to France, both until the invasion and for a period of time after it. We certainly have no aircraft to spare, and I agree that from your vantage point it would be a waste to bomb on the slim evidence I have presented, even assuming we could do much damage.

"Can we at least agree that there is potential for a serious danger here?" He looked around the table again, received no disagreement, and went on once again.

"I would like to propose that, pending further information about *Ferris,* I be given authority to plan a sabotage operation against the installation, in conjunction with the Special Operations Executive. This attack would be carried out if the German project became a clear and present danger. If the attack failed, it would be backed up by bombing."

Several mouths had dropped open. A confused hubbub began. Darlington rapped his pencil again. "Gentlemen. Commander Pierce is asking authorization to plan, not to execute. That authorization would have to come from the SOE itself."

And there's nobody here from the SOE, realized Devereaux. Darlington and Pierce set this up very carefully. To get a free hand. So no one can say later they weren't informed. I'd bet a year's pay they've already approached SOE. It's just the kind of thing Churchill had Special Op-

189

erations organized for. He'd love it; no trouble with authorization there. Devereaux shot a look at Pierce, who responded with the faintest of smiles.

They argued about it until half past five, but, in the end, Pierce got his way. When the room had emptied of all but Devereaux, Pierce, Mclennand, and Darlington, the latter said, "Well, there you are, Ian. What are you going to do now?"

"Start planning. And quickly. Something's going to happen, I'm sure of it. We'll have to be ready to move when it does."

"You're off to see Cleve, then? When?"

"Tomorrow morning."

Major Robert Cleve was a tall, emaciated-looking soldier with a penchant and a talent for the more devious forms of warfare. Slightly wounded at Dunkirk, he had recovered in time to help develop the resistance network that would have opposed the Germans had they succeeded in occupying England; from there it was a natural step for him to carry the same kind of activity to Europe, as a planner for the Special Operations Executive. Pierce had known him slightly before the war.

Cleve inhabited a dingy office in Baker Street, in a warren that housed a good many others of his profession. Several dusty filing cabinets lined his office walls; a stained teacup sat on the windowsill next to an expiring geranium and a jar lid full of burned matches and pipe dottle. When Pierce knocked and opened the door, Cleve was walloping a rolled-up newspaper against the windowpane, trying to despatch a frantically buzzing bluebottle.

"Come in. Just a minute."

The newspaper connected. Cleve turned around and

knocked the remains of the fly off the newspaper into the wastebasket. "Ah. Ian. Haven't seen you for ages." He sat down without waiting for a reply. "The powers that be said you were going to drop by sooner or later. What's on your mind?"

Pierce looked carefully outside the door, and then closed it firmly. "I hope you haven't been too troubled with spies of late."

"The only ones here are tame."

"I'd just as soon they didn't hear me, even if they are. This is one case where I can't be too careful." He fished out his pipe and Cleve flipped him a box of matches. He took his time about lighting it, while Cleve contemplated the dying geranium.

"How would you like," said Pierce when the pipe was well alight, "to blow up a German atomic pile?"

Cleve removed his attention from the geranium and focused it on Pierce. "I beg your pardon?"

"It's the kind of thing the Americans are said to be working on. Superbombs and all that kind of rumor."

"Are you sure you ought to be telling me this?"

"I have Darlington's approval. Have to tell you some of it, in any case. Otherwise you'll say no to sending a sabotage team."

"Why no?"

"The team would have a very slim chance of getting out afterward. They might possibly make it to Switzerland. Have to be lucky, though."

"Switzerland? Where is this . . . pile? mound? hill?"

"Pile. Under a mountain a little south of Innsbrück. Almost on top of the road to the Brenner Pass."

Cleve whistled through his teeth. He had a habit of smoothing back the hair on both sides of his head when he was thinking, and he did so now. "That's farther than we usually go. Unless the team is made up of natives. I don't suppose you have a crew of Germans itching to blow the thing up."

"No." admitted Pierce.

"We don't either, I'm sorry to say. You're talking about a military operation rather than a partisan one, though?"

"That was my intention."

"The Germans would likely shoot anyone they caught, anyway, even if they were wearing British battledress. They've been getting quite savage lately, even for them."

Pierce, who knew a little about SOE's own brand of savagery, didn't respond. Instead he asked, "Did they tell you what I wanted to talk about?"

"No. They said you'd fill me in as far as necessary."

Pierce sighed. He was becoming weary of going through the explanation time and again. He decided to condense it. "If the Germans are operating a pile they might be able to produce a weapon that could flatten London. One of my staff says that even if they can't, the substances produced by the pile would be deadly enough to make a large area uninhabitable for a very long time. Nobody knows for sure. They might use it on the invasion. No telling the consequences."

"What do the scientists and the regular military think?"

"The scientists want more proof. They don't think the Germans are far enough advanced to do it. It's taken the Americans three years to get even close, apparently, with all their resources. The military are up to their necks in invasion planning and won't divert forces on the basis of the information we now have."

Cleve cracked his knuckles and studied the geranium. "There were a few odd rumors floating about a few months ago," he told Pierce. "One of our people was talking to a blasting expert in a bar in LeMans. This chappie said he had been knocking holes in a mountain in southern Germany, a couple of years back. Then he got frightened and shut up completely. There's been a few other hints of heavy construction in that area. But none recently."

"Jesus bloody hell," exploded Pierce. "Why didn't this get to me? Or Darlington?"

"It was very low-grade information. After all, they've been putting up large things all over Germany for years."

"That's true, but, dammit." Pierce sucked angrily on his pipe, which had gone out. He relit it. "In any case, what I want to do is plan a hypothetical raid on the place. In case it turns out to be necessary. A detailed plan."

"What about personnel?"

"If the men are fit, how long to get them ready?"

"Do you have information on the installation and area?"

"Photographs, aerial photographs. No interior details."

"Hm." Cleve retrieved his matches and lit his own pipe, flicking the spent match at the jar lid on the windowsill. It struck the windowsill and fell on the floor. "We should make a model of the area, simulate the operation, select weapons, lay on a plane. That could be a problem, these days. Select the men. Ask for volunteers, actually. Can't order if there's so little chance of getting out. I'm worried about the lack of information as to what this thing is like inside, though. Finding out when we get there could make life, um, interesting. We'd have to simply jam the place as full of explosives as we could, and hope for the best. No finesse. Well, anyway. Once the model is made, say ten days to two weeks training. We're restricted by the moon, too. We'd have to have a moonless night to drop that near such a densely populated area. The navigation could be tricky."

"We've got a Mosquito photoreconnaissance crew who've been there already."

"Good. I hope they're still alive when they're needed, if they are." He smiled slightly. "I don't suppose you'll be going?"

Pierce looked wistful. "Hardly. The Joint Intelligence people get nervous if I so much as leave London. I can't say I'd be that eager to go anyway. Although I'd like to see what the damned pile looks like. It's cost me a good deal of sleep."

"Any of your staff included in the assault plans?"

"Not at the moment."

"I ask because anyone who goes should be involved in the training." His face clouded. "We're rather in need of good German speakers at the moment. I don't suppose—." He looked hopeful.

"Alan Devereaux speaks fluent German. But he's not going unless it's absolutely essential."

"As you wish. When do you want to start work?"

"No time like the present," said Pierce, and opened his briefcase.

Devereaux and Pierce watched from the office window as the V-1 flying bomb droned over the skyline south of the Thames. It had got through the fighters and the anti-aircraft belts south of the city, buzzing steadily onward toward London from its launching site in Northern France. Now it lumbered unscathed through the flak with a sort of malevolent mindlessness that reminded Pierce of a shark. When its engine stopped—it made a noise rather like that of a distant motorcycle—it would plunge earthward with its ton of high explosive. They had started falling on London

194

a week after the invasion of Normandy, and had been coming more or less steadily for the last three weeks.

"Damned things. Good thing they didn't have them to use on the beachhead when we went ashore."

"They're killing a lot of civilians. What is it people are calling them?"

"Doodlebugs," said Devereaux.

The sound of the V-1 continued to reach them for a couple of seconds after the engine had stopped. The craft nosed over into a steep dive and plunged behind the rooftops. A cloud of smoke welled up, shot through with flame. After a short delay the boom of the explosion reached them across the Thames. The window rattled slightly.

"I hope they were all in shelters."

"So do I." Pierce turned away from the window and resumed his seat at the desk. Devereaux continued to gaze out at the slowly dispersing cloud. There didn't seem to be any fire.

"Alan?"

"Oh. Sorry." Devereaux sat down and Pierce handed him a slip of paper.

"That's the name of the officer in charge of the prisoner compound near the invasion beaches. While they were interrogating a batch they came across someone who might interest us. They can't bring him over here, because they haven't enough men to escort single prisoners back to England, and I don't want to wait until the whole lot is shipped back here. I can't get away at the moment, so I'd like you to go and talk to the German in question. That's his name at the bottom of the slip."

"How do I get there?"

"There's a Lysander going over from Croydon this afternoon. Come back tomorrow evening; earlier, if you can

195

manage it. I gather that getting around over there can still be a problem, though—you may not get to the POW compound before dusk."

"What's special about the German?"

"I was coming to that. He's a construction engineer. Apparently he worked on a large installation in the area we're interested in, a year or two back. Bring me his brains in your pocket, if you have to."

"D'you want me to escort him back?"

"No. We've got nowhere to put him. The information will do." Pierce looked at his watch. "It's one o'clock. You'd better be off. Sorry about the short notice."

"I keep some kit in the office."

"Good. See you tomorrow at the latest."

The stubby, single-engined Lysander droned across the Channel toward Normandy. Devereaux watched the masses of shipping scurrying back and forth below, and hoped that the wide white stripes on the Lysander's wings would identify the aircraft as Allied to the quickfingered gunners beneath. Eventually he grew tired of craning his neck at the window and slumped back in his seat to think about Catherine. They had spent as much time as possible together since their liaison had been consummated—was that the way to put it?—but it still wasn't nearly enough. He had been unable to find any time to go to Sevenoaks, and Catherine's responsibilities on the farm kept her there most of the time. At first he had feared that the enforced separation would start them drifting away from each other, but so far that had not happened. In unspoken consent, they had not talked about the future; the present would have to do. He supposed that they were as content as they could be, under the circumstances.

The pilot had turned in his seat and was shouting something over the roar of the engine.

"What?"

"Up ahead. The invasion beaches. Have a look. You won't ever see anything like it again."

Devereaux scrambled up to stand behind the pilot. Ahead was the coast of Normandy. Along the shoreline, as far as he could see, were masses of ships, enormous artificial piers, floating harbors; on the beaches, men, guns, trucks, tanks, vast mounds of supplies, piles of wreckage, shell craters, rubble, all the detritus of a great invasion.

"They've got it pretty well cleaned up now," the pilot shouted. "You should have seen it a couple of weeks ago. That's Sword Beach. The Yanks went in farther west. Had a tough time about it, too."

"Where are we landing?"

The aircraft was already in a slow descent. The pilot gestured ahead to where a tiny airstrip had been laid out, just inland. "Ahead, there. I'd appreciate it if you'd get out as fast as you can. The Jerries are still dumping the odd shell on it. Don't know why, it's too small for fighters."

"All right."

The pilot brought the Lysander in low and fast. Dust whirled up from the undercarriage; the pilot let the plane roll to the end of the strip and then gestured for Devereaux to get out. He jumped to the ground with his kit as the Lysander turned in a cloud of grit and noise and lunged off down the strip again, gaining speed until it lifted into the hazy blue of the sky.

Devereaux remembered that he was in a shelled area, and started toward a distant knot of men clustered around the front of a bell tent. A harassed captain asked what he wanted and gave him directions to the interrogation center. There

197

was no transport available, but he could likely thumb a lift along the way.

A dusty corporal in a dented jeep picked him up after he had walked a quarter mile and delivered him to the POW compound. It was a makeshift place, nothing but a wire stockade with tents inside it. The Germans behind the wire looked dirty, unkempt, and exhausted.

The July sun was westering by the time he was able to see Rice, the captain in charge of the initial processing of the captives. Rice was obviously hot, sweaty, tired, and irritable, and less than happy to be confronted with a reasonably neat intelligence officer fresh from London.

"What d'you want?"

"I've come from Commander Pierce. You have a prisoner, Otto Klemp, I'd like to see him."

"Pierce? Never heard of him. Who are you?"

"His superior is Commodore Darlington," explained Devereaux patiently.

"Oh. You're the chap the brigadier said would be coming. Sorry. It's a madhouse here, as you can see. Wait in that tent over there. I'll have Klemp brought to you. You can talk to him in the tent; I'll put a guard on the entrance. Turn him over to the guard when you're done."

Sergeant Klemp was a short, square German with wide hands and thick fingers. He looked reasonably cheerful. Devereaux told him so, after introducing himself.

"Why not, Flight Lieutenant? I'm out of the war now. And I wasn't captured by the Russians. I count my blessings."

"You're a Bavarian?"

"You can tell by the accent? Yes, I am. Your German is very good, by the way."

"Thank you. I want to ask you some questions. Will you answer them?"

198

"For a packet of cigarettes I'll tell you Hitler's underwear size."

"That's hardly something I'm eager to find out."

"He won't be needing underwear much longer, anyway," said Klemp. "Yes, I'll tell the truth. There's no point in being heroic these days."

"All right. Cigarettes after the questions. You're an engineer?"

"Yes. Before the war, and during it. I was a civilian until 1944, I think it was December I went in. They were canceling all sorts of exemptions."

"Who were you with? The Todt organization? Working on the Atlantic Wall?"

Klemp grimaced. "I hope I would have made a better job of it than they did. No, up until the Army got me I was with a small construction and engineering firm. Very specialized. That was how I stayed out of the Army so long. We did a lot of contract work for the SS."

"Oh? Where?"

"All over."

"Anything in the south? Around Innsbrück, say?"

"Some." Klemp's eyes had become wary. "How about those cigarettes?"

Devereaux ignored him. "Innsbrück?"

"There was a project there, yes. Very secret. I've never seen security that tight. You could hardly pick your nose without somebody wanting to see what you'd got. When we left we were told that if anything got out about what we'd been doing, we'd disappear in short order, along with our families. I don't think anybody talked."

Too right they didn't, thought Devereaux. "Tell me about the place. How long were you there?"

"About three months. Let me see. October, November, December, 'forty-two. We came in to clean up some work

199

the SS engineers had buggered. Blasting, mostly. Some concrete pouring.''

"Describe the place.''

"Well, it was dug into the side of a mountain called the Patscherkofel. There were a few large chambers, one with a pit sunk in the floor at one end. Several smaller caverns, like offices, storerooms, what-have-you. We also put in a light railway, leading to the largest chamber, the one with the pit. The damnedest thing was the shaft going straight up from the big chamber to the slope way up above. There were two other shafts that went out lower down. One was likely an access tunnel, the other was too steep. Then there was the main tunnel that went in from the barracks compound.''

"Any unusual machinery around?''

"I didn't see any.''

"Who was in charge?''

"There was an SS major named Weil. We didn't see much of him, though. The man who gave the orders on the construction was named Siegner. There was a technical man, a really good engineer. I can't remember his name. Oh. Roth. And there was a girl. Good-looking. Didn't see enough of her.'' Klemp looked wistful. "A few other civilians, scientists, I suppose. We weren't allowed to have much to do with them. There were separate eating and sleeping quarters.''

"Can you draw me a plan of the installation, as far as you knew it?''

"I suppose so. A cigarette would help me think, though.''

Devereaux tossed a packet of Players and a box of matches onto the rough table. He got pencil and paper from his kitbag and waited while Klemp drew. When he had finished, Devereaux asked, "Did you ever hear anything about the installation afterward?"

"Not a peep. If I had, I would have forgotten it on purpose. I had a wife and two children at the time."

"Had?"

"Railway accident."

"I'm sorry."

"Yes. You wouldn't have another packet of cigarettes, would you? I have some friends behind the wire."

Devereaux questioned him until he was satisfied that he had got everything of importance out of the man. Then he gave him the other packet of Players and waited while the guard led him away. He looked at Klemp's plan.

The place was real. They were doing it. He had to get back to London.

He hurried out of the tent and began looking for Rice. The captain might be able to get him a plane to England before morning.

"What was it like, in Normandy?" asked Jean. She, Catherine, and Devereaux were waiting in the Mclennands' flat for Mclennand to return from an expedition concerning whiskey.

"Busy. There was a lot of equipment being moved inland. The place was a madhouse, actually. Or at least it looked like one. I suppose it was better organized than it looked."

"Did you get what you went for?" asked Catherine. "Whatever it was?"

Devereaux smiled at her. She had taken to teasing him a little, lately. "Yes, precisely what I wanted." Klemp's original offer came back to him. "Hitler's size in underwear."

"I—what? You can't be serious."

"Why not? There's a conviction in Intelligence circles that Hitler started the war because tight underwear made him irritable. The idea is that we substitute some a size larger in his wardrobe, and he'll be immediately sorry for what he's done and stop the fighting."

"If that's what passes for Intelligence we had better surrender now," said Jean. "I think that's Gordon on the stairs. Let him in, would you, Alan?"

Mclennand was looking cheerful and was carrying a longish cylindrical parcel. He passed it to Jean and fished in his pocket. "I've managed to get four tickets for this evening's performance at the Windmill. Practically everywhere else is closed because of the flying bombs. We've just time for a drink, then we'll have to go."

They toasted Mclennand's resourcefulness, Devereaux in particular contented by the prospect of Saturday and Sunday with Catherine. Her mother and father had left the city temporarily, because of the V-1s, and they would have the weekend to themselves.

They rinsed their glasses in the kitchen, argued briefly as to whether Catherine would need a sweater for the journey back from the Windmill, and trooped downstairs to the street. There was a faint buzz somewhere in the pale, cloud-flecked sky.

"Wonder where that one is?" said Mclennand, craning his neck. "It's getting a bit louder, isn't it?"

They gazed nervously upward. The buzz faded.

"It must have sounded louder because of the wind," suggested Devereaux. "Most of them have been falling on the East End, anyway. We ought to go or we'll be late."

"Oh, damn," said Catherine. "I think I'll take my sweater after all. "Can I have your key, Jean? I won't be a minute."

"Here. D'you want me to come up?"

"No. I can manage. Back in a moment."

She disappeared up the steps into the building. Mclennand had opened his mouth to speak when the wind that had been carrying the sound of the V-1 away from them suddenly dropped. The buzz was very loud. They looked upward, startled. The buzz stopped.

"Where the devil is it," asked Devereaux. "I can't—"

A horrendous roar blotted out the rest of his words. A hot wind, reeking of explosives, blew them to their knees. Slates rained down, glass popped out of the windows of the building and sleeted around them. A sliver struck Jean on the scalp, slashing it open. She fell forward onto her arms. From behind the block of flats rose a dense cloud of smoke and dust streaked with flame. The building swayed, and then decided to remain upright.

"Cat!" shouted Devereaux, and leaped up the steps to the door. It was jammed by the blast. He looked back desperately to where Mclennand was bending over his wife. No help there. He stepped back from the door and kicked. It shot open. He flew upstairs in a murk of dust and—Oh, God—smoke. Something was burning in the rear of the building. Fallen lath and plaster had partly blocked the stairs at the first landing; he shoveled the wreckage aside and scrambled on upward. The stairs creaked uncertainly.

He found her at the top of the staircase, a few feet from the Mclennands' open door. A chunk of the roof had come down; she was lying partly under a mess of beams and plaster. Her eyes were closed. The sweater was clutched tightly in one hand; she had obviously heard the approach of the bomb and made a run for it.

He found the beam pinning her across the waist and tried to move it. It shifted slightly. Her eyelids flickered.

"Catherine?"

She opened her eyes and muttered dazedly.

"What? Are you all right?" What a stupid bloody question, he thought furiously. Of course she's not all right.

"The sweater. Did I—? Something hit me on the head." She closed her eyes and then opened them again. They were pleading. "Can you get me out?"

"Yes. Can you feel your feet?"

She was getting her bearings. "I think so. Yes. But my stomach hurts."

The odor of smoke was stronger. Devereaux could hear crackling and there was a reddish light that was not the setting sun, falling through the hole in the roof. He tried the beam again. It was almost immovable. He began to clear some of the wreckage to reduce the weight on it and Catherine. This lightened it enough for him to lift it a few inches.

"Can you crawl out? While I lift?"

"I'll try." She strained. "It's tight, and I can't get anything to push on. I can't move."

There was a thumping on the staircase below. Mclennand's head appeared in the stairwell. "Gordon," said Devereaux desperately, "this beam. Shove something under it while I lift."

He strained it upward and Mclennand slid a half-dozen fallen bricks under it. Together they took Catherine under the arms and slid her out of the debris. She was white from head to foot with mortar and plaster dust, except for a trickle of blood from her forehead where some masonry had struck her. Her eyes took in the blood on Mclennand's jacket. "Jean?"

"She's cut on the scalp. She's all right. She sent me up. In no uncertain terms. What about you?"

"I'm not sure. It feels as though there's something not right inside." Her voice was apprehensive.

They made a four-handed lift and got her downstairs into the street. An ambulance bell was clanging in the distance, coming nearer. Jean had torn a strip from her skirt and was holding the wad of bloody cloth to her head. "Catherine?"

"Is that ambulance coming here?" asked Mclennand urgently, of no one in particular.

As if in answer, the vehicle careered around the corner of Great Russell Street and clanged to a halt beside them. Two young women jumped out, looked at the women slumped on the curb, and hurriedly unloaded a pair of stretchers. "Anybody else in there?" one of them asked.

"I don't know."

"Have a look, would you, while we get the ladies into the ambulance. You're not hurt?"

"We're all right." Devereaux and Mclennand searched the building quickly. There was no one else in it.

"That's a bit of luck, then," said the driver when they told her. "We're taking the ladies to Middlesex Hospital. It's not far. I'm sorry, we haven't room to take you. D'you know where it is?"

"My wife works there," Mclennand told hear.

"Right. You come along as quick as you can, then." The vehicle clanged away.

They started walking. The evening rang with the racket of ambulance bells and fire vehicles on the other side of the block.

"She'll be all right, Alan."

"God, I hope so. A few more feet of altitude and that thing would have landed smack on top of us." They were both quivery with delayed shock.

By the time they reached the hospital, Jean had been stitched up and was waiting for them at the entrance. Her face was pale under the bandages. "They've got Catherine in the operating theater. Internal bleeding."

"How bad?"

"They didn't know for sure. We'd better wait."

"I should get you somehwere to rest," said Mclennand.

"No. I want to be sure Cat's going to make it. I can ask Matron for a cot somewhere if I need it."

They waited. Somewhere a clock struck eight, then nine. At twenty-five minutes to ten a tired doctor entered the waiting room.

"Mrs. Mclennand?"

"Over here. How is she?"

The doctor said gently, "Your friend is going to be fine. She was very lucky that you were able to get her out so quickly. We'll be able to release her in four weeks or less. She's sleeping now; you should go and do the same." He hurried away.

"Where are you going to go?" asked Devereaux outside. "You can't possibly go home."

"Cat gave me the keys to her parents' flat," said Jean. "We can stop there until ours is either cleaned up or we can find another. Do you want to come with us?"

"Yes," said Devereaux. "I would. Very much."

"I gather the Germans dropped a brick on you Friday evening," Pierce said as he poked his head in their office door.

"How did you know?" asked Mclennand in surprise.

"Oh, I pick up information here and there," said Pierce vaguely. "I phoned around to see if either you or your wife had been admitted to any of the central hospitals when I heard your block had been hit. How is she?"

"Feeling better. She went back to work this morning."

"That's good. By the way, Alan," he went on, "your German's map has aroused considerable interest among the

206

powers that be. They've given us authorization to select a team and start preliminary training immediately. I'm having Klemp kept track of, incidentally, in case we want to ask him anything else. He won't be packed off to the Canadian camps until we give the word."

"He was very cooperative."

"As well he might be. Good morning."

After he had gone, Mclennand said. "The old devil doesn't miss much, does he?"

"No, he doesn't. Nice of him to ask after Jean."

They worked steadily for an hour, in silence. About ten o'clock the internal telephone rang. Devereaux picked it up and listened. His face took on a look of surprise. Mclennand glanced up as he replaced the receiver.

"What's up?"

"Pierce wants us in his office right away. He actually sounds excited about something."

"But he wanted this report by noon—"

"He said right away."

When they arrived, Pierce was pacing up and down in front of his office window. His face showed a mixture of equal parts exhilaration and worry. When he saw them he said, "You had better sit down for this one."

They did so and waited expectantly. Pierce loaded his pipe, obviously enjoying their curiosity. At last he said:

"We've got the chief scientist of the *Fenris* project."

There was a stunned silence.

Devereaux found his voice first. "I beg your pardon?"

"His name's Siegner. Peter Siegner, the same man that Klemp mentioned. They're looking for references to him in prewar scientific intelligence records right now. He turned up at our consulate in Zurich on Saturday evening. They didn't know what to do with him at first. He just kept

207

telling them his name and that he was a scientist who knew about fission piles. Somebody finally got in touch with the Joint Committee and they practically blew their collective gasket. He's being flown here this afternoon—he'll be in London by this evening. He'll be packed off to Wandsworth Prison till we decide what we want to ask him. Darlington and I are to handle the debriefing; Alan, you're to translate. Gordon, I want you as an observer. There will be a very few of the top scientists allowed in on it; we want to keep this whole business as dark as possible until it's resolved.

"How the dickens did he manage to get out of Austria?"

"I don't suppose they ever imagined he'd go over to the enemy. We'll sort that out at the debriefing. The scientists will be able to tell whether or not he's a plant. But I don't think he is, myself."

"Well, I'm damned," said Devereaux.

"My sentiments exactly. You two had better start a list of questions for him to answer. The interrogation starts at eight this evening; he'll be brought here. He'll be tired, so he'll be easier to catch out if he's hiding things. It's going to be a long night, I'm afraid."

"How did you get out of Germany?" Darlington asked, through Devereaux.

The debriefing team was seated in comfortable chairs around the long conference table. Siegner had been placed at the end, where everyone could see him easily. He did not look well. He was exhausted from the long flight from Switzerland, and the interrogation had barely started. All they had done so far was to establish his identity and his professional background.

"Dr. Siegner?"

"I had help. The chief technical officer was an Abwehr

208

agent. He supplied false papers. I would never have gotten out, otherwise."

"So you just got on a train and went to Switzerland."

"I did. It sounds improbable, I know, but that is what happened."

They worked on that for a while, trying to make him contradict himself. He didn't. Eventually Darlington turned the questioning over to Pierce.

"What is the purpose of the fission pile?"

"To produce enough element-94 to build a fission bomb."

"When did it begin operation?"

"April fifth of this year."

"Will such a weapon be possible?"

"No. There is not enough time to produce the required quantity of the metal."

"How long would that take?"

"Years."

A sigh of relief circled the table.

"Why did you come over, then, if there is no danger of the weapon being built? You indicated in Zurich that there was extreme danger for the Allies."

Siegner heaved a sigh. Here it went again. "The fission byproducts—"

"Are very deadly and that is the weapon," Devereaux finished for him. "That's what's going on, isn't it?"

"What did you say?" asked Darlington.

Devereaux repeated the exchange in English. Darlington said, "Do you want to pursue that line with him, Flight Lieutenant?"

Devereaux turned back to Siegner, who was looking astonished. "How did you know?" asked the German.

"Inspired guess. Did you come here because of that?"

"Yes. I had no desire to see the substance used on humans. Not after I saw what they did to a person."

"Explain, please."

"One of our scientists, a young woman, was exposed to the byproducts. She died, very horribly, in three days."

Devereaux translated what he had learned so far. There was an uneasy stirring around the table.

"Ask him where they got enough heavy water to do it," Pierce instructed.

"From Norway. The drums that you sank with the ferry were dummies."

Pierce looked sour, Darlington furious. "Ask him if, and when, this stuff is to be used in combat," said Pierce.

"I don't know, exactly. The original target was the second week in July. But it was delayed by Anna-Marie's death. She's the one who was exposed to the wastes. She was Abwehr too, by the way."

"She and the technical officer were working together? They felt the same way about the weapon that you do now?"

"Yes."

"Can you estimate the earliest possible date for the use of the weapon?"

Siegner thought. Today was Monday, the tenth of July. Roth had said he would slow it down if he could. "As early as four days from now. Far more likely ten days to two weeks."

"What target?"

"Originally the invasion beaches. That's not possible now. Likely a city. I would guess London. Although it wasn't mentioned in any of the meetings I attended."

"What would be the result of such an attack?"

"Judging from what I saw of the lethality of the wastes, you would have to write it off completely, for a long time."

"Translation, please?" asked one of the scientists. Devereaux complied. When he had finished, Pierce asked, "Is that an accurate assessment?"

The scientist nodded glumly.

"How does he propose to get an aircraft all the way to London, given our air superiority?" Darlington wanted to know.

"I haven't seen it, but apparently there is a captured Lancaster available."

That shook them. There were mutters of disbelief from several of those present. Darlington wanted to know where the bomber was kept, and who was to fly it. Siegner didn't know.

"Ask him," instructed Darlington, "whether this is a final decision or whether there are some remnants of sanity in the German leadership."

To this, Siegner answered, "I don't think the SS officers I've been in contact with are very fond of the idea. The more senior ones, at least. I wouldn't be surprised if they're trying to get Himmler to abort the project somehow."

"The decision to go ahead with this alternative wasn't Himmler's?"

"No. Hitler's."

"Good God. How do you know?"

"I was there." Siegner's voice was subdued.

"What do you think of all this?"

"I wish I had tried to stop it earlier."

Darlington whispered to Pierce a moment, and then told Devereaux, "Show him the map Klemp made. Ask him if it's accurate."

Devereaux laid the sheet of paper in front of the German physicist. Siegner's eyes widened and he looked up at them.

211

"You know," he whispered. "Why haven't you done something?"

"Do I answer him?" Devereaux asked after translating. Darlington nodded.

"We've only known for a few days. Is the map accurate?"

Siegner studied it. "Yes. Very close. Except that the rail line and the huts on the south perimeter are gone now. Where did you get this?"

Darlington wouldn't permit an answer to that. "What is the code name of the project?"

Devereaux translated, knowing ahead of time what the answer would be.

"Fenris."

There was no need to put it into English.

Darlington leaned back in his chair and closed his eyes. He looked old. After a moment he turned to Pierce and said, "Turn the scientists loose on him."

The interrogation grew extremely technical. Devereaux didn't know many of the German equivalents for the English, and often had no idea what the English meant, either. There was extensive resort to sign language and drawing of diagrams. Around four in the morning fatigue put an end to the debriefing.

"You'd better call Cleve immediately and tell him we have to go," Darlington told Pierce. "I'll contact the other interested parties as soon as possible. We'll continue with this . . . discussion at eleven tomorrow morning, I mean this morning. I'm sorry, gentlemen," he said to the civilians at the table, "but I'm afraid this has to be the extent of your participation until the military discussions are over. After that you can drain him dry at your leisure."

The scientists nodded and began to shuffle papers into

212

their briefcases. They looked worried. Darlington rubbed his eyes. "That's all for tonight. Have the prisoner returned to Wandsworth."

Prisoner. He knew enough English to understand that word. It shamed him. He had hoped to be better treated, as a scientist who knew at least as much as the best Allied scientists. Objectively, he knew that that was ridiculous. These men were fighting a bitter war against his country, and a scientist, however repentant, who had done his best to defeat them was hardly an object of sympathy.

The worst of it was that he badly wanted to go back and help Roth destroy the frightfulness they had created. Would the British let him help?

Not very likely. His exhausted mind tried to sort out the options they had. He tossed on the hard cell bunk, running the possibilities through his imagination. Bombing would be ineffectual; he and Roth had seen to that with their deep caverns and reinforced tunnels and shafts. It would have to be an armed raid. They would need a guide to the complex. But they had the map. How much did they really know? And how the devil had they found out?

Boehme. Had they intercepted Boheme's rash messages about the heavy water and deciphered them? How ironic that the convinced National Socialist would assist, however unwittingly, in *Fenris'*s discovery. Strasser would shoot the man on the spot, if he knew. Siegner felt an urge to giggle, and stifled it. He realized that he was near hysterical with exhaustion.

I'll have to work on it when I've had some rest, he thought. I'll make mistakes if I try to plan when I'm this worn-out. I haven't been so tired since Russia. Anna-Marie, please don't come into my dreams again tonight.

He let himself fall into the abyss, and if he had dreams, he did not remember what they were.

The military debriefing went on for the next three days. On the third evening they were convinced enough of Siegner's good faith to let Devereaux take him for a short walk on the Embankment. An armed guard strolled unobtrusively behind.

"I don't know what your people think I'm going to do," growled Siegner. "I'm hardly likely to sprout wings and fly back to Germany."

"There was some doubt at first as to how well you would cooperate. We weren't really sure whether you were here for the reasons you gave, or simply to save your skin. You have to remember you're the enemy. Or one of them."

"Still?"

"I don't think they've decided on that yet."

Siegner let out a sigh. "I'm still a German, if that's what you mean. I don't want to see my country destroyed because of Hitler. He doesn't speak for all of us, you know."

"I'd hate to think he did. D'you believe, personally, that the attack on London will be tried?"

"I don't know." Siegner stopped to watch a pair of gulls scudding the surface of the Thames. "If it's ordered, Kruger will probably go through with it. His worry about the consequences for Germany doesn't extend to putting his head in a noose."

They reached Cleopatra's Needle and turned back toward the War Office. "You're going to raid the place, aren't you?" the German said. "All the questions you've asked me about the layout of the place point that way. What kind of defenses, guard rotation, all that?"

"I'm afraid I can't tell you."

"Loyalties become confusing, don't they?" Siegner went on irrelevantly. "By most standards, I'm a traitor, although I don't feel like one."

"I've never had that problem. I admit I have difficulty seeing you as a traitor . . . one can't talk as much as we have for three days and not find out something about the other person. I confess I didn't like the look of you much when you arrived, though. Picturing the arrogant Nazi trying to cut his losses, I suppose."

"If I had any of that, it got knocked out of me in Russia. Not many Party members in the front line, except maybe in the SS. Just soldiers."

"Believing in Hitler, though."

"Most of us did, yes."

They were nearing the War Office. "I would like to go on the raid," said the physicist.

Devereaux stopped short. "You're joking, surely."

"Not about this. There will be a raid; you don't have to tell me for me to know."

"They'd never let you go. You're too valuable. Besides, if you were taken prisoner, you'd be killed. Very unpleasantly."

"I feel I have to pay somehow for what I have done."

They walked on a little. "You've done nothing yet."

"Not for what might be done. For Anna-Marie."

"Were you involved with her?"

"No. Although I almost certainly would have been if she had lived. I didn't realize that until afterward, when it was too late."

Devereaux shrugged. "I'll pass your request on to Pierce. But they won't let you go."

Siegner gazed up at the delicate pink of the evening sky. "Perhaps not," he said. "Although if I tell your scientists everything I know, it might make a difference. There would be nothing left to learn from me.''

"It's still very unlikely."

"I suppose that's true," agreed Siegner.

He was glad he had failed to tell them about the demolition preparations in the tunnels.

"Absolutely not!" exploded Darlington. "The man must have lost his wits."

"He'd be useful in the raid," Pierce reminded him. "we're very short of training time. A model, no matter how good, can't replace a competent guide. Also," he mused, "I'd be willing to bet a month's pay he's holding something back, to blackmail us into letting him go. He's also pointed out that the pile will be difficult to destroy completely with the explosives the team can carry, unless we know its vulnerable spots. Which he *has* been good enough to tell us. Or so he said. The extraction apparatus is apparently no problem."

Pierce's grudging support for Siegner's request had surprised Devereaux. He had expected him to be as adamant as Darlington. "If we tell him now that he can't go, he may refuse to provide any more information," he pointed out.

Darlington thought about that. "Very well, then. Tell him that we'll consider his proposal, if he goes on cooperating as he has done. I suppose there's no way of finding out what he's keeping back?"

"Not unless we want to use German methods. He was in Russia, remember? He's a tough bugger, not like one's usual picture of the woolly minded scientist."

"I suppose, if pressed to the wall to ensure the raid's success, we might let him go," admitted Darlington. "But that's a very large if. There would also have to be somebody

216

along on the combat team to keep an eye on him. Also to kill him if he were in danger of capture. It wouldn't do for them to get him back. They might decide to go on using him instead of executing him."

"The training is going well, given the time limitations," Pierce said, diplomatically changing the subject. "Cleve says they'll be ready to go in six days."

"How many men has he got?"

"Seven, including himself. All very experienced. No gung-ho lieutenants just out of Sandhurst. Sorry, you two."

" 'An old soldier is a cautious soldier,' " quoted Darlington. " 'That's why he is an old soldier.' I hope they aren't *too* experienced."

"Cleve says not."

"He's going, then?"

"He says he's going to. How he got permission, I don't know. They must want this raid to be a success very badly, or SOE wouldn't have allowed it."

"Let's get Siegner in here, then."

The German physicist sat in the leather chair and waited, his hands folded. "The flight lieutenant gave us your request," Darlington told him through Devereaux. "We will consider it, provided you continue your cooperation."

Siegner's face, blank until now, brightened considerably at the words. He really does want to go back, thought Devereaux.

The debriefing continued until noon. When Siegner had been taken away for lunch, Darlington said, "I think we've got everything of significance to the raid out of him. Any disagreements?"

There were none.

"Fine. I suppose we can let the scientists at him now. Ian, you'd better get all this information over to Cleve and work with him until the planning is completed in detail. Alan, would you be so good as to continue to interpret this afternoon?"

"Yes, sir."

"I'd like to move the date of the raid up," fumed Pierce as he tapped out his pipe. "But we've carved the training to the bone as it is."

"We'll simply have to cross our fingers and hope that Siegner's longest estimate was the correct one," answered Darlington calmly. "Would you care for some wine with lunch?"

The scientific debriefing began that afternoon. It was tiring work. Again Devereaux did not know the precise English equivalents for many of the terms, and the group had to resort once more to diagrams, the smattering of German the scientists knew, and a dictionary of English-German technical words. Security prevented adding a fluent German-speaking specialist to the group. As time went on, the British scientists became progressively gloomier. Eventually one of them said to Devereaux, "I hope you chaps are planning to do something about this. The Germans have a much narrower knowledge than we do, but they're not nearly as far behind in this specific area as we had hoped."

Devereaux made a noncomittal answer.

In the middle of the third afternoon the scientists declared themselves satisfied "for now," and decamped. Siegner was taken away by two plainclothes guards. Devereaux went to his office, which he had barely seen for the past seventy-two hours, and collapsed behind his desk. Mclennand looked up in surprise. "Well, hullo! I thought you were trapped for the rest of the day, at least."

"They've finished with him, for the moment." He told

Mclennand about the debriefing. When he had finished, the other sat staring out the window. At last he said, "I wish to hell we had picked up on it earlier."

"So do I. How's Jean?"

"Healing nicely. I expect you're going over to see Catherine?"

"Yes. Visiting hours start shortly. Has Pierce been in?"

"No. I believe he's off somewhere with the assault team. D'you know when they're due to go?"

"The twentieth or twenty-first. Good God. That's tomorrow or the next day. I didn't realize how close the target date was."

"Better them going than us. Have they much chance of getting out?"

"Not much, although Pierce didn't say so in so many words." Devereaux checked his watch. "I'd better be off."

"Will you be coming back?" We can nip out for a drink if you do."

"Should be all right."

"See you later, then."

Catherine was sitting up in bed, reading, when he arrived in the ward. She dropped the book in delight. "Alan. You got away."

He took her hands and sat on the edge of the bed. "We finished early this afternoon. Bit of luck. You're looking well, much better than yesterday."

She shivered. "I dreamed about the bomb again last night. It was horrible." She mused for a few seconds. "It's the oddest sensation, to lie here and realize that one mightn't have been here, or anywhere, any more at all. Does that make sense?"

"I think so."

By mutual consent they turned to more pleasant things.

Toward the end of visiting hours she said, feelingly, "I can hardly wait to get out of this *bloody* hospital and go somewhere with you. I'm so *bored*. And I keep worrying about the farm. Jacob's coping well enough, but. . . ."

"Have they said when you can leave?"

"About ten days. Have I mentioned lately that I love you?"

"Not lately enough." He leaned over and kissed her gently.

A nurse bustled through the ward, announcing the end of visiting hours. Catherine instantly turned serious. "Alan, I know we agreed not to discuss the future. But this . . . accident has made me want to reconsider that. Could we talk about it, anyway? After I'm out of this place?"

"I've been feeling the same way. I wasn't certain I should mention it yet. There's one small thing, though. There's just the ghost of a chance I might have to be out of the country for a few days. I'm not sure of it, it probably won't happen, but it's possible. I wouldn't be able to tell you that I was going."

She stared at him, the fear plain on her face. "That's a small thing?"

"Well, no, not really," he admitted. "But I may not have any choice."

"This is what I was afraid of when we started," she told him sadly. "The war getting in the way."

"Yes. I know."

With an effort, she pulled herself together and smiled at him. "Go and do what you have to do, then. I'll be waiting when you get back."

He kissed her and made his way between the rows of beds to the end of the ward. At the door hr turned and waved to her, and then disappeared.

She didn't begin to cry until she was sure that he was gone.

Mclennand handed Devereaux a slip of paper as soon as he entered the office after lunch the next day. "Pierce wants you to call him. That's the number. He said it was important."

"When isn't it?" grumbled Devereaux, and dialed. "Sir? It's Alan."

The voice on the other end of the line sounded tired. "I'm sorry, Alan, but I'll have to ask you to get out here as soon as you can. Our—guest—is being difficult. Apparently there's something he didn't tell us. As we suspected there would be. He was brought out here this morning to look at the training ground and the mockups, to check them for accuracy, and he's decided he's going to go."

"Where's here?"

"Oh, I'm sorry. The SOE school at Beaulieu. I'll give you directions; you'd better write them down."

When Pierce rang off Devereaux slowly replaced the receiver and sat staring dully at the telephone. Mclennand looked up.

"What's the matter? You don't look happy."

"I'm not," said Devereaux. "I have a terrible suspicion that I'm going to Germany."

It was nearly dark by the time Devereaux reached the old estate outside Beaulieu. The home of the barons Montagu, it had been in use since early in the war as a training school for SOE agents before they were dropped into Europe. Now it was, as well as that, a temporary training ground for the team that would attack *Fenris*.

Devereaux left the car in the drive, showed his pass to the sentry, and went up the steps into the house. Pierce was waiting for him and took him along a corridor to a conference room. Darlington was already there.

"What's happened?" asked Devereaux as he slumped into a chair.

"Our German friend started asking for you late this morning. We had Cleve find out what he wanted. He says he has something very important to tell us, but won't go into detail until we've agreed to let him go on the raid. I believe he wants you here because he trusts you. We're bringing him in here now."

Siegner was escorted into the room, looking pale and tired. The questions began.

"What's the trouble, Dr. Siegner?"

"I've already told you. I want to go on the raid."

"We never actually promised you that. Why should we do so now?"

"There's something I haven't told you. Not to do with the pile, on that I've been totally open. Something else."

"We suspected as much. Would you care to elaborate?"

"There's no doubt that the pile can be disabled by the explosives your men can carry. This will take time, however. You'll almost certainly not have any more than that time if the defenses are alerted by mischance, or otherwise. At best, if you go in through the emergency tunnel, you will have fifteen minutes in the pile control room before the SS discovers that the tunnel has been penetrated. This reduces the chance of escape for your men to zero, assuming they take the time to lay the charges required. Do you agree or not?"

"Go on," said Darlington.

"There's a possible solution to the problem. Long before I left, chambers were cut in the access tunnels and the main complex. These were to be packed with explosives and

222

wired to a central firing unit which can be controlled from two separate locations. The trigger at either position can blow the mines. The idea was to deny the complex to the Russians or yourselves, should we be defeated.

"When I escaped, the explosives hadn't been placed. They may have been by now, although I admit I hadn't heard anything about it by the time I left. If they *are* in position, the solution to the time problem is a simple one. When the switch to trigger the mines is thrown, there is a timer which delays the explosion for five minutes. It is a safety measure. It gives time enough to leave by the emergency tunnel, and a chance for your men to get up into the mountains."

"Where are the control positions?" asked Devereaux, after translating.

"That is what I will not tell you. Furthermore, one needs the combination of a lock to get at the switches. I know the combination."

"The lock could be blown."

"More time lost. Plus the danger of damaging the circuit and having to bypass the wiring."

"The bastard has us over a barrel," snarled Darlington, "if we want to give the attack team any kind of chance at all."

"Unless he's lying," suggested Pierce.

"I don't think he is."

Pierce ordered, "Ask him what happens if the charges haven't been laid after all."

Devereaux complied, and then told Pierce, "He says we're no worse off than we were before. Plus we have him as a guide."

"What d'you think, Ian?"

Pierce studied the German scientist. Siegner's face was

calm, neutral. "We've got most of the important information out of him. I say we let him go."

"What do you think, Flight Lieutenant Devereaux? You're aware of what letting him go means for you, I suppose."

"Yes." Devereaux licked his lips. He was rather pale. "I go too. To keep an eye on him because the rest of the assault team has its own business to take care of. And I kill him if he's going to be captured." His throat was dry. "I still say let him go."

Darlington capitulated, "I'll have to get permission," he glowered, and stamped out of the room. There was no conversation during the considerable time he was gone.

He didn't look any happier on his return. "The old man said all right. But we'll answer with our heads if he's captured." He looked squarely at Devereaux. "You'd better do a thorough job preventing that, if you have to." Turning to Pierce he went on, "You'd better get these two over to the training ground first thing in the morning. There's not much time."

This is madness, thought Devereaux as he raced between the white stripes that represented the emergency tunnel leading to the pile chamber. He was stifling in the heavy battledress; the unfamiliar weight of the silenced Sten gun tugged naggingly at his shoulder. I'm a Lancaster pilot, not a bloody commando. And in a few hours I'm going to be parachuted into Germany to protect a crazy German scientist until it's necessary to kill him. Mad.

The legs of the soldier in front of him rose and fell like pistons, leading him toward the tapes outlining the center of the *Fenris* mockup. He could hear Siegner panting behind him. Siegner was at least free of the weight of the gun; they

224

had refused to give him one. He had protested bitterly at first, and then given an odd half-smile and shrugged. Devereaux didn't know what to make of that smile.

Tow of the assault team had been left behind at the tunnel entrance, to secure the escape route. One more would guard the way in from the main tunnel and hold any prisoners. The other three soldiers of the team, together with Cleve, Devereaux, and Siegner, would head for the extraction lab and the pile control room, or for the demolition switch, if the mines were in place. Cleve had slipped into German to ask Siegner, "How will you know whether the explosives have been laid?"

"We'll know as soon as we're in the tunnel. The chambers were open when I left. If the charges are ready, the chambers will be sealed, with the ignition cables running along the walls. If that's the case, I'll lead you directly to the demolition switch."

Cleve had accepted the last-minute change in plan with reasonable grace. They were, however, to continue to rehearse as though the explosives would be absent. If they had been laid, the assault team would guard Siegner while he opened the switch vault, or blow its door if the combination had been changed.

Panting for breath, Devereaux followed the pounding heels toward the outline of the extraction lab. Siegner accelerated past him and darted through the door, behind the first and second soldiers. He had dredged enough English out of his schooldays to be able to give understandable directions on the placement of the explosives.

Devereaux's job was to stand and watch Siegner, while keeping one eye cocked down the passageway. Six minutes were required to simulate laying the explosives in the mock extraction lab. Cleve and the others were busy inside the outlines of the adjoining pile control room for almost as long. Then, as one man, they raced for the emergency tunnel.

"Time?" Cleve asked one of the men watching as they halted outside the tapes.

"Ten minutes, twenty-seven seconds."

Cleve stared accusingly at Devereaux. "You're slowing us down. There's only a five-minute delay on those fuses. We've got to have a few minutes at least, to get into the woods."

"I'm sorry. But I didn't realize I was going on this jaunt until yesterday."

"It'll have to do. Are you sure you've a good idea of the layout of the place?"

Devereaux nodded. He was wondering how good his chances were of reaching Switzerland. Unlike the rest of the assault team, he and Siegner had been given false papers to enable them to use their German to get over the border, once clear of the *Fenris* installation. Devereaux would be wearing civilian clothes under his battledress. Siegner had refused the British uniform, pointing out that he would be executed anyway if caught, battledress or none. They both had a low estimate of the combat team's chance of a getaway, especially if the Germans had not laid the mines. Devereaux had tried to work out why anyone would volunteer for what amounted to a suicide mission, but was yet to think of an answer.

They sat on the grass in the hot July sun while Cleve talked with a civilian who had trotted into the training area. Devereaux studied the others covertly. They were lean, hard-faced men who looked as though they would have knives hidden in various places about them. Only two of them were British; the other four spoke English with varying thicknesses of accent. Maybe that's why they don't give

226

a damn, he thought. He went over their names again: Mrosek, he would be carrying the radio; Carpenter and Jameson, the two Anglo-Saxons; Lindgaard and DeVries were Norwegian and Dutch, respectively; Placzek, he couldn't place.

Cleve sauntered back to them, his face split in a broad grin. Now what the hell, wondered Devereaux. Would he look that happy if we weren't going? Not bloody likely. Probably the reverse.

The tall major sat on the grass and told them, without preamble, "Somebody tried to blow Hitler up with a bomb yesterday. Unfortunately, the bastard wasn't killed, so we still have to go. But it was apparently some of his own army staff officers, so the Germans are going to be running about like wet hens for the next few days, looking for conspirators among their own people. This place we're going to is guarded by the SS, so they'll probably be watching out for the army. They'll fire at shadows, so we'll have to be doubly careful."

"What's he smiling about?" whispered Siegner.

"God knows," Devereaux muttered, and translated.

"That's bad," Siegner whispered back. "I know Strasser. He'll put everyone on full alert and double the guards."

"All right," Cleve was saying. "We'll have lunch now and then go over the operational details again, with the models. After that I want everyone to sleep. We'll eat a meal here at six o'clock and be at the airfield at a quarter to nine. Takeoff is at nine. We'll be over the target at midnight."

The briefing hut was stifling. On a long table in its center was a model of the north face of the Patscherkofel and the area surrounding it. Next to that model was a smaller one, a cutaway of the *Fenris* complex itself.

Cleve picked up a pointer. "The drop will be in an alpine

meadow well above the village of Tulfes, here. Fifteen minutes are allowed to collect the explosive and weapons canisters and make sure we're all present. The dropping aircraft will fly as slowly as possible, to keep us together. Anyone not in the group when we leave for the tunnel will try to catch up, if possible.

"We'll then go down the shallow valley, here"—again the pointer—"to the wooded area short of the tunnel entrance. There are two guards posted there. They'll be disposed of, along with any others who come along while we're inside."

"What about prisoners we take inside?" asked Devereaux. "Do we take them with us on the way out?"

Cleve favored him with a cold look. Jameson shifted uncomfortably. "We haven't any time for prisoners, Flight Lieutenant," said Cleve. "Any German who surrenders will be held under guard by Mrosek at the main tunnel. Any others will be killed. On no account can we let anyone go before we're out. There should be time for prisoners to escape before the explosions begin, after we leave. Just."

"Oh," Devereaux mumbled.

"Any other questions?"

"Ask him about Roth," whispered Siegner. Devereaux did so.

"It's been decided that Dr. Roth's best chance of remaining unsuspected will be to treat him exactly as one of the others. Any special attention might be fatal to him. Good enough?"

It would have to be. It was far too late to think of taking him with them.

The briefing went on. And on. Devereaux, despite his tension, began to feel drowsy in the heat. He had to force himself to listen to the drone of Cleve's voice. As the briefing drew to a close he fought an urge to yawn.

"One last thing," Cleve ended. "Carpenter will connect the radio to the lighting cable at the emergency tunnel entrance. That'll give us enough range to contact the relay station in Normandy. If there's trouble laying the explosives, or if we don't report at all, they're going to take other measures. Expensive ones. So let's not have any slips." He looked squarely at Devereaux and Siegner.

They're going to bomb it if we fail, realized Devereaux.

"Go and get some sleep. We'll meet at the mess hall at ten to six. No shop talk in front of anybody but other team members."

How Cleve expected anyone to sleep with the prospects before them, Devereaux could not imagine. Added to this, it was roasting in the barracks hut. He had stripped to his undershorts but was still slick with perspiration. The others seemed to have dropped off with no trouble.

"Alan?"

The whisper came from the next bunk. He turned his head on the hot pillow. Siegner was still awake.

"What is it?"

"I'm sorry to have made it necessary for you to come. Do you understand why I have to go back?"

Devereaux thought for a moment and then whispered, "Yes. I think so." He paused. "Don't worry about it. I wouldn't miss this for the world."

Siegner gave a silent laugh. "That is the famous British stiff upper lip, isn't it? There is one thing you could try to do for me, though."

"What's that?"

"I'd like to have a weapon. Would you be able to persuade Major Cleve?"

Devereaux considered it. The German had been a soldier, after all, on that most ferocious of all battlefields, the Rus-

229

sian front. Another Sten could make all the difference, if the raid went awry.

"I'll do what I can."

"Thank you. We'd better sleep now."

Despite the heat, Devereaux sank into a restless, dream-filled slumber. He was roused by a hand shaking his arm.

"Wake up, Flight Lieutenant. It's twenty to six."

He rolled stiffly out of the bunk and yawned. Around him the others were already dressing. With a lurch he remembered why he was here.

They ate a solid meal despite the heat: beefsteak, potatoes, peas, a sweet rich dessert. When Devereaux had finished, his stomach contained a hard cannonball of food to fuel him through the raid. He went back to the hut, washed, and put on the civilian clothes with the oversized battle-dress over them. He was, he noticed with very slight amusement, a private. Would the battledress protect him from treatment as a saboteur if he were caught? He rather doubted it. He would simply have to avoid capture.

The rest of the team was at the armory when he arrived. Each of them, except for Siegner, was issued with a silenced Sten submachine gun and a pistol. While the others were checking their gear, Devereaux drew Cleve aside.

"Is there any reason Siegner has to go unarmed? He could be a good deal of help; remember, he's experienced."

Cleve studied the German physicist and came to a decision. "Very well. He's as dead as the rest of us if we're caught. Thorpe," he called to the armorer, "give the German a pistol and a Sten. Jameson. Take him down to the range and show him how to use them."

Siegner shot Devereaux a grateful look.

They returned, Siegner looking satisfied. To Devereaux he said, as they were getting into the truck that would take them to the airfield, "Thank you. It's not as accurate as our Schmeisser but I feel less naked with it. You also?"

"It's the first time I've ever handled one. It's remarkably quiet."

"That's just as well."

The light was fading when they reached the airfield. A blackish-green Lancaster squatted at the end of the taxiway. The truck pulled up to it.

The assault team clambered up the ladder, through the entrance door just forward of the tail, and into the belly of the huge aircraft. Metal benches ran along each side of the fuselage. There were nine parachute packs in the space between them. An exit hatch had been cut in the Lancaster's underside, near the entrance door.

"Flight Lieutenant," said Cleve. "You and Siegner will jump fifth and sixth, so that the more experienced parachutists will land behind and ahead of you. That way, if you're unable to steer the chute, you'll have a better chance of landing near the rest of us. After we're in the air, please show Siegner how to clip the chute on. We're going out on a static line, so you won't have to worry about pulling the ripcord. That'll be done automatically."

The Lancaster's engines began to rumble as the pilot started the warmup. The tail gunner came out of his turret, made certain the entrance door was secure, and disappeared again behind the folding turret doors. The single lamp in the roof of the fuselage cast a dim glow.

As the Lancaster began to move, Devereaux was assaulted by memories. The fatigue, the backache after six hours in the air, the smell of varnish, oil, hot metal, coolant, petrol . . . he wished he were flying the aircraft. Being someone else's passenger had always made him nervous.

The Lancaster lifted from the dim flarepath, into the gathering night.

VI

The Reich

July 8–13, 1944

Roth kept his movements obvious after Siegner left the compound on his way to Innsbrück. Part of the afternoon he spent with Saur, supervising the preliminary assembly of the aerosol container shielding. After that he went to the extraction lab where Sommer was painfully following the worknotes that Anna-Marie had left. Roth couldn't look at her graceful, meticulous handwriting without a pang of loss.

"When will we be ready to load the canister, do you think?"

Sommer wrinkled his forehead. "I'm having to go very slowly. None of us wants another accident. July eleventh would be a safe estimate, I think."

Christ, only three days. Siegner would never get action from the British in that time, even if he weren't caught. If he *is* caught, Roth reflected gloomily, I won't need to worry about the damned stuff. I'll have enough to do to save my own skin.

Some of the worry must have shown on his face. "What's the matter?"

"Thinking about Anna-Marie."

Sommer winced. "A great pity. She was a brilliant sci-

232

entist. Much better than I am," he admitted, looking around at the cluttered lab and the busy technicians. "I'm only following the notes she made. I'd never be able to do it otherwise."

"It isn't your specialty," Roth said, to cheer him up. "But I'm still concerned about the possibility of another accident. If we had a bad spill in there"—he gestured toward the extraction alley—"I don't know how we'd get it cleaned up. Not without using some of Saur's friends' methods, anyway."

Sommer lowered his voice. "Do you think that sort of thing happens? It's hard to believe."

"I believe it."

Sommer began to say something, but changed his mind as Strasser entered the lab. "Excuse me. Have any of you seen Dr. Siegner? The orderly was supposed to meet him at Innsbrück at four but he didn't show up. I was wondering if he came back another way."

"Haven't seen him myself."

"Neither have I."

Strasser's green eyes flicked around the lab as though Roth and Sommer were as likely as not to lie, with Siegner in plain sight. The technicians became utterly absorbed in their work. Then he fixed his gaze on Roth. "Are you sure you haven't seen him since he left, Dr. Roth?"

Roth felt his bowels contract, but he answered evenly. "No. Last time I saw him was at breakfast. Is there a problem?"

"He wasn't where he said he would be when he was supposed to be there, if you follow me. That could be a problem. Let me know as soon as you see him. Better yet, tell him to come and see me himself."

When Strasser had gone, Sommer let out a slow breath.

"He's been getting nastier by the day. A few months ago it would have been please, and thank you."

"We're not as indispensable as we used to be," Roth reminded him. "We'd better not forget that. He's determined that we won't, anyway."

"Where d'you think Peter's got to?"

Roth motioned indifferently. "He'll turn up. Did the machine shop finally get the right dimensions for the aerosol filler pipe?"

Sommer went off into an involved explanation to which Roth half-listened. He was worried about the speed with which the aerosol was being prepared. He would have to find a way to slow it down, somehow. When Sommer finished, Roth made a vague excuse about work elsewhere, and departed. It was six o'clock; if Peter were going to escape he would have done so by now.

Roth walked down toward the mess building. Boehme came out of one of the storage huts and called to him. He waited while the pudgy administrative officer caught up to him.

"Going to supper? So was I."

They had achieved a sort of truce since Siegner had asked Roth to stop irritating the little man. The technical officer was in fact grateful for the distraction that Boehme offered at the moment.

"Is Sommer coming down?"

"He's still working."

"The project's going well, isn't it? Perhaps the war will be over in a few months."

"I certainly hope so."

"I never stopped believing in final victory even when the Allies landed," Boehme went on conversationally. "Even when they managed to stay ashore. It'll just make their defeat all the greater, when it comes."

Now why the hell is he pushing that National Socialist claptrap at me? Roth asked himself. He knows I don't pay any attention to it. "There's no doubt about final victory, that's true," he said dryly. Boehme glanced at him suspiciously, not sure of the tone.

Across the compound Strasser let the curtain fall back across his office window. Boehme's detestation of the technical chief would keep him watching Roth carefully, as Strasser had intended. If there were anything subversive about Roth, it would be uncovered sooner or later. Now where the devil was Siegner?

Strasser sighed. He had better report the apparent disappearance to Weil, immediately after asking the Gestapo and the Kriminalpolizei to start checking through the city.

An awful thought struck him. Should he have them check with the railway station guards as well? Was it possible that Siegner had fled the project?

No. Impossible. The man was a loyal German.

But he'd better have the station surveillance contacted, just the same.

He rang his opposite numbers at Gestapo and Kripo headquarters in Innsbrück and requested their assistance. They promised, grudgingly, to do what they could. Strasser would have liked to be able to issue direct orders to them, but he had no immediate authority off the *Fenris* installation, except over the watchers stationed in Aldrans. He cursed the bureaucracy and picked up the telephone. It rang several times before Weil answered.

"Captain Strasser here, sir. There's been a development I wanted you to know about."

"Oh? What?"

"Dr. Siegner went to Innsbrück late this morning. Our driver was supposed to collect him at four. Siegner didn't turn up. It's nearly half past six, and no sign of him."

There was a silence. Then Weil answered. "I assume you have protective surveillance on him?"

"Yes. The man hasn't reported in. I've contacted Gestapo and Kripo headquarters and asked them to start looking. But I'm afraid they may drag their heels."

"I'll have someone contact them. What are the names?"

Strasser gave them, and then ventured, "I'd like to believe it's not serious, but I daren't. Kidnapping's a possibility; it'd explain the loss of the tail."

"There's another possibility I'm sure has occurred to you."

"Yes. I'm having the railway station checked to see if anyone remembers him getting a train out of here."

There was a silence, which Strasser dared not break, on the other end of the line. Eventually Weil told him, "I'll see Colonel Kruger about this, directly; it may be necessary to close the Swiss border for a time, until we're sure that he hasn't ah, lost his head. Have there been any signs of anyone else acting strangely? I'm thinking particularly of Dr. Roth."

"Nothing unusual. But it's hard to tell, at the moment. The scientists are soft enough for Lerner's death to still be upsetting them."

"Could her accident have anything to do with Dr. Siegner's absence, do you suppose?"

"I can't see how it could. He must have got used to that sort of thing in Russia."

"He and the girl weren't close, were they?"

"I don't think so. Not even Boehme, that snoop, ever said anything about that sort of thing."

"How's that going, by the way?"

"I appealed to Boehme's National Socialist convictions. He's watching Roth for me. Also the others, but mainly Roth."

236

"Good. You did well to call. Call me back immediately if anything happens. I'll attend to the border situation and arrange for lookouts in railway stations outside your area. Good-bye."

Strasser put the telephone down. He was sweating. If the unthinkable had happened he was in serious trouble. Posting to a penal combat unit was a real possibility. Kruger would be looking for a scapegoat, he was certain. And if Himmler were in on it . . . Strasser shivered. For the first time since Kursk, he was frightened. And what in God's name had happened to the tail he had put on Siegner?

He found out at ten minutes past nine that evening. He had the telephone off the hook before it had completed its first ring. "Strasser here."

It was the Gestapo head. "We've found somebody that might belong to you," he said. "The identity papers don't fit for anyone else in the area."

"What's his name?"

"Lippmann."

Strasser's heart sank. They had found the tail, but not Siegner. "He's ours, all right. Let me talk to him."

"I would, but he's in a coma. He's under guard in the hospital. Somebody hit him with a pipe. It's chancy whether he'll live or not."

"Where did you find him?"

"Whoever bashed him covered him up with some rubble in a bombsite on the Templestrasse. We found him by luck, actually. Some children playing where they shouldn't have."

"D'you have the pipe?"

"Yes. I presume you want it."

"I'll send somebody down for it, also a guard for Lippmann to relieve your man. This is military business, by the way."

"So I understand from a phone call I got from Berlin."
The policeman's tone was sardonic. "You're welcome to take over."

"Nothing on the other man?"

"That's what I was going to tell you next. Somebody answering to that description boarded a train at the Hauptbahnhof at ten-thirty this morning. The one that goes to Switzerland. We checked the other stops. He didn't get off."

Strasser barely kept himself from exploding. The Gestapo man noticed the silence. "Your fish got away, did it?"

"That's my business," snapped Strasser.

The policeman sounded amused. "All right, all right. D'you want us to keep checking the railway people? Something might turn up."

"Yes, please."

"Fine. I'll call you back if we get anything."

Strasser put down the telephone and then, his face pale with fury, picked it up again to call Weil.

"The pipe's definitely from here," said Roth. "It's scrap left over from building the precipitation gear in the extraction alley. There's a fair amount of it still in one of the storage areas."

It was the evening of the day after Siegner's disappearance. Weil, Kruger, Strasser, and the remaining senior scientists were grouped around the table in the mess hut. There hadn't been any supper, and it was beginning to look as though there wouldn't be, either. The two SS officers had been questioning the scientific staff ever since their arrival, in mid-afternoon.

"Who besides Dr. Siegner would have access to this scrap?" asked Weil.

"Anybody. It's not valuable."

Kruger pushed his chair back and put his hands flat on the table in front of him. "This isn't getting us anywhere. I think we have to assume that Siegner is a traitor, and went to Switzerland to inform the Allies about *Fenris*."

No one had wanted to put it in such blunt terms, but it was what they had all been thinking.

"Now," continued Kruger, "I can't imagine what reasoning led him to do that, but I'm not interested in pursuing that matter now. If we ever catch him we can explore the question at our leisure."

This, as intended, sent a chill down the spines of all present.

"We are left with two major decisions," Kruger stated. "First, how much time do we have to execute the attack before the Allies try to do something about *Fenris*? Second, how do we ensure that whoever helped Siegner—if he had help, which seems likely—is neutralized or caught?

"For the first, our attack date is to be set for July twelfth, three days from now. This is subject to approval from higher up, but I'm sure the approval will be forthcoming. I would remind you that you've assured me that everything will be ready by the eleventh, and I expect that to be the case." He looked pointedly around the table. "The second decision is mine. An armed guard will be placed in each of *Fenris*'s vulnerable areas. Captain Strasser, you will see to this. These gentlemen will help you identify the danger points. In the meantime, all staff will be questioned to see if anyone had an opportunity to help Siegner. We'll begin with the junior technicians and work up."

Roth noticed that Kruger was no longer refering to Peter as Dr. Siegner. He must be convinced of defection, then.

"I have to return to Berlin," ended Kruger. "Major Weil will remain to assist with the investigation in any way he can. No one is to leave the compound without his written permission. That will be all."

The scientists and Strasser slunk out. When he was certain no one was in earshot, Kruger asked Weil, "What do you think of the situation?"

"Strasser was unlucky. Who would have thought Siegner would defect?"

"You're convinced he has, then."

"Aren't you?"

"I am. I wonder who got him the papers to slide him over the border?"

"Could have been Roth."

"Quite likely. That's convenient. He may assist us by slowing the attack preparations down without our being directly involved."

"We're still responsible, though."

"I know. That's why I had some guards put into the complex. Himmler will skin us both alive—not to mention Strasser—if we're obviously careless."

"Suppose Roth, if it is Roth, doesn't try to do anything?"

Kruger shrugged. "Then we'll have to go through with it. I don't love the British enough to risk my neck by trying to stop the attack myself. All I want is to prevent us from going too far, so that the Allies may not treat us too badly after final victory is won."

"Final victory?" Weil asked incredulously.

"Not ours," answered Kruger. "Theirs, of course."

"Himmler's going to be very unhappy over Siegner's disappearance."

"I know. Strasser may suffer for it. I'll try to protect him, though; he's efficient and will be very useful here, because there's no doubt about his loyalty. We mustn't all look like subversives, remember.''

"I'll remember," muttered Weil. Feelingly.

Roth spent most of the night thinking. He realized that he would have to slow the aerosol preparation so that Peter would have time to convince the British to act. But he also wanted to remain unsuspected, or if that were impossible, to have at least a chance of getting away. This conflict kept him awake until nearly dawn.

With the guards in place, it would be next to impossible to sabotage any critical part of the installation and *not* be suspected. They would note his presence even if he were able to cause the required damage in a delayed or unobtrusive manner. With a delay in the appearance of the damage, though, he might get enough of a head start to make contact with the underground and go into hiding. If there were any underground still operating. He thought it likely that there was but had no idea of how to reach it. His avenue to help would have to be the bookseller's contacts.

He thought some more. There was little chance of a successful assault on the pile room, or on the extraction alley or lab. The technicians or one of the other scientists would notice if he did something out of the ordinary, and they would alert the guards if only to save their own skins. The point of attack that was both vulnerable and private was the aerosol assembly room and the equipment it contained. The sprayer itself was machined to very close tolerances, and could be rendered useless by a solution of hydrofluoric acid poured into it. It would have to be that, then, tomorrow evening. He could then try to get down the mountain in the dark and into Innsbrück before he was missed. The compound fence . . . there were wirecutters

241

in the toolroom. Fortunately the entire perimeter wasn't lit at night, only the gate area.

He rolled over on the cot and tried to go to sleep. I wonder what my chances of escape are, he thought. Not very good. But I'm damned if I'll sit here and wait to be collected by Strasser, after I've done the dirty work. Not a chance.

Eventually he slept.

He spent most of the following day in the extraction lab, helping Sommer prepare the last concentration of the aerosol. He felt a perverse satsifaction in doing so. The SS trooper by the door didn't pay any more attention to him than to anyone else.

It would be easy to go along with it, he mused, and felt himself tempted. But that would make Anna-Marie's death useless. Not to mention the catastrophe the attack would be for Germany. At the end of the day, he went and took a shower, intending to have supper when the others had finished. He didn't much want to see any of them. Boehme was leaving the mess hut as he entered. "Late supper, eh?" the little administrator asked him. "Are you going back to work afterwards?"

"I've got a few things to clear up. Then I'm going to bed."

"See you tomorrow, then."

The food, despite Boehme's best efforts, was becoming worse. There's not much left for anybody now, reflected Roth, unless you're high up in the Party. The sooner the war's over, the better for everyone. Even if we lose.

He ate some of the unidentifiable stew and ignored the ersatz coffee. "It's been getting worse all the time, hasn't it, sir?" sympathized the orderly who removed the tray.

"Everyone's been grumbling about it. D'you think it'll ever get better again?"

"I haven't any idea," muttered Roth, and got up from the table. The orderly looked after him with a hurt expression as he went out.

Once in his quarters, Roth carefully locked his door, got down on his hands and knees, and crawled under the cot. He scrabbled around in the grit until he found the outlines of the flap he had cut in the paneling when he had had to move into the cubicle. A slight pressure on one end flipped it open. He removed the leather bag containing the Walther automatic and the spare ammunition clip and closed the flap. Except for a small spot of rust on the barrel the weapon was as clean as when he had hidden it.

Next step. Papers. They would have to come from the old man; the ones hidden in the lining of his suitcase were so out of date as to be worthless. He extracted them and burned them, grinding the ashes to powder beneath his shoe and kicking them beneath the cot. No point in giving them leads to his Abwehr connections.

The jacket was a little heavy for this weather but he needed somewhere unobtrusive to carry the gun. He checked the pistol's action and slid it into the inside pocket.

Now for the waiting. He didn't want to act until it was thoroughly dark outside. About an hour to go.

More than once, he thought his watch had stopped. He checked and rechecked the pistol until he was certain beyond any doubt that it would fire if he needed it. It would be best if he reviewed his plan of escape—if you could call it that—but he found himself unable to concentrate on anything past getting out of the compound. The emergency tunnel would have been a better escape route, as it led out to the wooded area, but Strasser's guards had orders to let no one pass except in a real emergency. Roth wished for the hundredth time that the explosives had been laid in the tunnels. It would have made it easy to put an end to *Fenris* for good.

At last, unbelievably, it was time to go. Ironically, he found himself wishing that there were a few minutes left before he had to commit himself.

The tunnel was deserted; the lights had been dimmed for the night. First the toolroom for the cutters, then the chemical stores for the acid.

No guard had been placed on the toolroom. He was able to select a pair of sharp cutters without difficulty. One of Strasser's men would be in the chemical stores, though; there were too many dangerous substances there for it to be left unguarded.

The soldier was actually outside the door to the room. He looked up sleepily as Roth came around the corner, but snapped awake as soon as he saw the technical head.

"Oh. Dr. Roth. Did you want something in here?"

Roth nodded. "I need some things for a test in the extraction lab. It won't take a minute." He was surprised at how calm he felt.

"Go ahead. I'll have to come in with you, though."

"That's all right. Orders are orders."

The guard watched him, nervously fingering his Schmeisser machine pistol, as he selected a number of bottles, put some back, muttered under his breath as if dissatisfied, and ended with three, only one of which he needed. It was half full of hydrofluoric acid. He handled it carefully.

"That's all I need, thanks."

"Yes, sir. Good night."

Roth went off down the passage without answering. The next part was harder.

The young sentry at the entrance to the aerosol equipment assembly room was more awake than the other had been. Roth hadn't seen him before. The sentry eyed him and his bottles suspiciously.

"Good evening. I'm Dr. Roth. You're new here, aren't you?"

"Yes, sir. Do you have your identity card with you?"

"What? Oh, yes, certainly." He set the bottles on the concrete floor and fumbled until he found the card. "Good enough?"

"Yes, sir. You're going in?"

He had an inspiration. "Yes. Isn't Dr. Saur here yet?"

"No, sir."

"Damn. We have to do a treatment on the aerosol container, to prevent corrosion from the active load." He hoped the boy would be blinded by science. "It's one of the last steps before it goes operational."

The young sentry looked mystified. "All right, sir. I'll have to watch what you're doing, though."

Roth shrugged indifferently. "Orders are orders," he said again, and went into the room.

The canister lay on its cradle by the heavy shielding which would surround it while the fission products were poured in. The filler connection jutted out of its upper surface. He unscrewed the dust stopper carefully and set the two bottles he didn't need behind some tools on the workbench. As he opened the third bottle and began to pour the acid carefully through the filler opening, he explained what he was doing. "This will start a reaction with the metal which will coat it with a layer of fluorides," he said, not caring if he made sense or not. "This layer will make the metal impervious to the corrosive action of the chemicals to be used later." The devil it will, he thought. The acid

245

fumes—which would etch unprotected glass—would play havoc with the delicate valves and filters of the sprayer head. He would have liked to get the acid itself into the filters and the aerosol generating chamber, but he would have had to dismantle the business end of the canister and there wasn't enough time. The fumes would have to do.

He restoppered the bottle, replaced the dust plug, and turned the feed valve control so that the aerosol chamber was open to the acid in the canister. The fumes generated by the acid would force their way out through the sprayer head; in two or three hours the sprayer would be unusable.

Roth put the acid bottle in an unobstrusive spot away from the other two and glanced at his watch. "I'm going to try to find Dr. Saur," he told the sentry. "We should be back shortly to continue the treatment. Heil Hitler."

"Heil Hitler," the other responded unenthusiastically, and followed him out the door. The man had already lost interest in the proceedings. You'll be interested once they find out what you've let happen, Roth thought. But how Kruger expects an uneducated SS private to avert sabotage when carried out by an expert . . . come to think of it, he reflected as he walked unhurriedly down the tunnel to the entrance, it would have made more sense to require that at least two of us work together at all times, one to watch the other. A disturbing thought occurred to him. Did Kruger foresee this action on someone's part, and decide to allow it so that the attack might be delayed, or even canceled? Peter had said that neither Weil nor Kruger was very keen on the use of the *Fenris* wastes.

He abandoned this line of thought as irrelevant to his predicament. He had gone too far to reconsider now. The acid was already in the canister; the gun and the wirecutters were heavy in his pockets.

He said good evening to the sentry at the entrance bunker and strolled down the dark path toward the barracks area. He had, over the weeks, managed to get a fair idea of the pattern with which the guards patrolled the fence. Once among the huts, he would be able to work his way unseen to a spot he had selected the previous morning, where the fence jutted close to a small stand of trees above the Aldrans-Innsbrück road. After cutting the wire, he would go cross-country the few kilometers to the city outskirts. Any police checks in Innsbrück itself he would have to avoid by bluff or good fortune.

At the fence he was able to cut a slit for himself in under a minute. The nearest guard was well away from him, barely visible in the glow from the dimmed light over the compound gates. He pulled the wire together behind himself to camouflage the gap and raced silently for the trees. Once among them, he stopped to look back and catch his breath. No alarms. With luck, they might not realize his absence until morning.

With a slightly lighter heart, he set off into the darkness.

The sentry at the door of the aerosol room was having a difficult time staying awake. He had to keep reminding himself of what Strasser would do if he found him dozing at his post. This worked, but only just. Another two hours until his relief.

A footstep down the corridor jerked him awake and erect. After a moment of listening he relaxed slightly; the sound wasn't from Strasser's jackboots. A pudgy civilian came around the corner, eyed him morosely, and began to pass by. Then the sentry remembered.

"Excuse, me, sir. Are you Dr. Saur?"

"Eh?" The pudgy man stopped. "No. I'm Dr. Boehme.

What d'you want with Saur?''

The sentry was thrown a little off balance. "I didn't want anything with him, sir. But Dr. Roth was looking for him a couple of hours ago. He said he was coming back here with Dr. Saur. They were going to do a, a treatment, he said, of the machinery in there." The sentry by now was cursing himself for having opened his mouth. He was making a fool of himself, interfering in things that weren't his concern.

"Where are they now?" The little scientist was oddly intent.

"I don't know, Dr. Boehme. Neither of them came back after Dr. Roth left the room here."

"Roth was in there?" Boehme looked excited. "Alone?"

"No, sir. I was there, as ordered. He did something with a bottle and then said he was going to come back with Dr. Saur. But he didn't."

"Oh, my God," exploded Boehme. "Get out of the way." He pushed by the guard, who by now was too upset to think of asking for identification, and opened the door. Acid fumes stung his eyeballs. He closed the door hurriedly. "Get Captain Strasser here immediately. The machine's been sabotaged. Tell him Roth did it. He may still be here. Hurry!"

The guard shot him one stricken look and raced away down the tunnel.

"Now I've got the bastard," Boehme muttered to himself, and jogged toward Saur's quarters. The gas expert was still awake.

"What's the matter?"

"Roth's sabotaged the aerosol equipment. The room's full of acid fumes. Hydrofluoric, from the bite."

"God damn." Saur pulled on his shoes and tied them

248

hurriedly. "The whole thing may have to be replaced. How did he manage it?"

Boehme told him as they hurried to the aerosol room. Saur took a quick sniff inside and slammed the door. "Hydrofluoric, all right. We'll have to use the acid protection gear from the lab and drag the whole thing outside. Where's Strasser?"

"I sent the guard for him. He should be here any time."

Strasser arrived four minutes later, red-faced and out of breath. Six SS troopers were hard on his heels.

"Tell me exactly what he's done."

Boehme and Saur told him.

"All right. You four. Search the complex. If you find Roth, don't kill him. Assume he's armed. Take him to the detention cells if you catch him, and don't take your eyes off him. Let me know as soon as you find him, if you do."

They clattered off into the dim tunnels. "Now. You. How did he get in?"

Miserably, the sentry recounted what had happened. When he finished, Strasser told him in a cold, dry voice, "You're under arrest. Dereliction of duty, until I can think of something worse. Braun, lock him up. Take his belt and tie."

When they had gone, Strasser turned back to the two scientists. "Roth's had a couple of hours' start. Come to the headquarters block with me immediately; I have to phone Weil. He may want to talk to you. Wait a minute. Boehme, before you come, wake up Sommer and Pickert. Bring them too. Also have the duty technicians relieved by technicians who were off duty when the sabotage happened. Have them assemble in the mess hall. I want everyone who was inside this mountain two hours ago in the mess hall in fifteen minutes. Get going."

Boehme scuttled away. As Strasser and Saur hurried for the entrance bunker, the latter ventured diffidently, "Do you think you'll catch him?"

"We'll catch him." Again the cold, dry voice. "Maybe not right away. I'll put patrols out in the surrounding areas, but if he's got two hours' start he's already in Innsbrück. But we'll catch him eventually. I give him a day."

"Suppose he has help?"

"If he has help, he has a day. No help, a few hours."

He rang the bell a third time, feeling the desperation well up in him like nausea. He was exhausted by the breakneck flight over the lower slopes of the Patscherkofel to the Paschberg; only once had he risked guiding himself by the road, and that was at the steep point near Aldrans where he could not risk a fractured leg or twisted ankle in the darkness. Even so, he had fallen a dozen times, and knew he was lucky not to have broken his neck. In daylight, being able to see where he was going, he probably wouldn't have dared travel so fast. And luck had attended him through the blacked-out streets of Innsbrück. No one had demanded his papers; if he had been seen close up by the police he would certainly have been detained, for his clothes were torn and his left hand was badly scraped from one of his falls. He was drenched with the sweat of fear and exertion.

He was about to give the bell a last despairing ring when there was a faint shuffle on the other side of the door and a muttered "Who's there?"

"Mannheim."

A bolt scraped and the door swung open. The bookseller pulled him inside with a strength unusual in one so old. The door closed. In the darkness, Roth could hear the man's ragged breath.

"Are you trying to kill both of us?" came a furious whisper. "Why are you here at this time of the night?" A pause. "Trouble. You can't go back."

"That's right. I need papers. Then I'll leave."

"Where to?"

"Switzerland?"

A dry laugh, like the crackle of dead leaves, then a cough. "Come to the back of the shop. Be quiet. There are people living upstairs."

In the apartment at the shop rear the bookseller turned on a single light. "You've had a time of it, haven't you? Falling down mountains in the dark?"

Roth was regaining his composure along with his breath. "I can do without jokes. Switzerland is out, of course."

The old man shrugged. "They'll close the border by dawn, if you're as important as you seem to be. You couldn't possibly get over; they'll have your description. They'll also be checking at the station here and on all the roads leading out of the city."

"What, then?"

"I can't hide you here past tomorrow morning. They'll be doing house-to-house searches by noon. Let me see." He thought for several minutes. Roth fidgeted but held his tongue. He was in far over his head, and knew it. Why hadn't he tried the mountains, tried for Switzerland across country? He finally said as much.

"Don't be ridiculous," the bookseller told him sharply. "You're not in shape, for one thing. And they'd use air searches and dogs."

Roth subsided. Finally his host asked, "Do they have photographs of you on file up at that place?"

"Yes. Of course."

"It'll take time to have those reproduced and put into the

251

appropriate hands, won't it?''

"By tomorrow afternoon, I'd guess."

"We have until tomorrow morning, then. Just a moment." He disappeared into the darkness of the shop and returned carrying a pile of nondescript books.

"Wonderful places to hide things, books." He took a penknife and slit the first binding carefully. Inside was a document. There were others in the other books. "I acquired these as spares when I set your friend up, just in case something like this happened. You know where they come from?"

"I'd rather not. Some of the Abwehr network, of course."

"Yes. You have a few friends left, even if you don't know about them."

"It was a good outfit to work for."

"It was before Kaltenbrunner and that slagheap the SD took it over. I'm surprised Canaris hasn't been shot by now."

"He's still alive?"

"So they say. In retirement. House arrest, more likely. I'll have to take your photograph; I hope the film isn't too old. First, though, wax pads for your cheeks, and glasses. I have an old pair somewhere, they're too weak for me now but you should be able to wear them for short periods. I'd dye your hair if it were paler but you're too dark to bleach. It always looks false, anyway."

Roth was surprised by the difference the fuller cheeks and the glasses made to his appearance. It might get him through a check if the police only had a verbal description to go on, but it wouldn't help much once photographs were in their hands. The two of them sat in the dark while the print developed in the lavatory washbasin.

"Do they know what you were wearing when you left?"

"The guard would have told them."

The old man sighed. "There's a suit you can have. My son was about the same build as you. You'll have to keep the shirt you're wearing. Mine won't fit you."

"Your son?"

The sigh again. "Yes. Killed in France in 1940. I'm not as old as I look. I was gassed and wounded in the last war, it put a lot of years on me."

"How did you start working for the Abwehr?"

"I was with Austrian Intelligence before Germany annexed us in 1938. I'd had some contacts with the Abwehr right along. They asked me to work for them in 1939. It was better than working for the SD, so I accepted. My health got bad a year later so they retired me here. Then when this business on the mountain got started a couple of years ago, they asked me to go back to work." He turned on the light and started rinsing the picture. "It'll do. You'd better get some sleep; it's well after midnight. There ought to be a train to Munich at seven. Go to 80, Friedrichstrasse. There'll be a man there named Hauser. Ask him if he remembers who won the most money from him the night before the battle of Caporetto. That's where I was wounded, incidentally. We beat the daylights out of the Italians, that time." He finished drying the photograph. "Pardon me. I ramble when I'm tired. Hauser will know who sent you and may be able to arrange your disappearance until the war ends. It can't be too much longer now, can it?"

"I hope not."

"You can sleep on the couch. I'll finish putting the documents together. I'll wake you at six."

The wax pads were uncomfortable in his cheeks and the

253

glasses made his eyes water. Nevertheless he was thankful for the sense of anonymity even this slight disguise gave him. The suit would help, too; it was of better quality than was common at this stage of the war and would make him look too prosperous to have run down a mountainside in the dark.

It was ten to seven. He had already walked by the station once but had been unable to tell whether the train was there or not. He couldn't afford to delay any longer. The more he hung about the station, the greater the chance of being stopped.

There was a short line at the checkpoint, with a knot of police at the barrier. People were getting through one at a time; the check was clearly a thorough one. Nothing else for it now; he had doubtless been seen entering the station and to leave would invite suspicion. He joined the line, his palms damp.

The soldier ahead of him was passed through. He handed his forged papers to the plainclothesman and waited. The man studied him closely, read the documents, and asked, "Where are you going?"

"Munich."

"What for?"

"I have business at the BMW plant there."

The policeman looked at the quality of his suit. "When are you returning?"

"Tomorrow evening."

"Go ahead."

He had almost reached the platform when a man came around a corner and nearly ran into him. They each backed up, stuttering apologies.

It was Boehme.

For an instant Roth thought the man wouldn't recognize

him. Then the pale blue eyes behind the spectacles widened and the mouth opened for a yell.

Roth hit him hard in the stomach and ran for the end of the train. A shout went up behind him. As he ran, he cursed himself and the old man for overlooking the obvious. Why bother with issuing photographs at the railway station when you could put an informer there? He would have to try to get out onto the rail lines and slip back into the city to some kind of hiding place. What then? He didn't know.

He still had the gun, though.

He jumped over a switch, nearly fell, and raced for a line of gondola cars a dozen meters away. The cars had begun to move. A glance behind showed three men stumbling over the tracks after him. He grabbed the ladder at the end of one of the slowly moving cars, clambered up it, and threw himself into the car as a bullet cracked over his head.

How fast was the train picking up speed? He risked a look over the side. A slow run. If it kept going he might have a free ride out of the station. He moved along a meter and risked another look. The three men were gaining, but slowly. One of them fired but the shot was so wide he didn't even hear the bullet pass. He pulled out the Walther and flipped off the safety catch.

The brakes of the train shrieked, and couplings crashed up ahead. God damn. The thing was slowing down. Either it was only switching or the engineer had been signaled to stop.

He hurled himself over the side of the car away from his pursuers, and raced along beside the train. There was a stationary line of cars a few meters away. If he could get in among them he had a chance of dodging the thugs behind him.

He made it to the last car of the other train just as a burst from a Schmeisser machine pistol ripped over his head. The shots were followed by angry shouting. They want me alive, he realized with a sick feeling. That's unpleasant. He was a poor target, though, in the alternating shadows cast between the freight cars by the slanting rays of the morning sun. It would be difficult to hit him with a pistol shot.

Someone yelled ahead of him. There must be railway police up there, attracted by the shooting. He was trapped between them and his original pursuers. Leaping over another set of tracks, he scuttled under a stationary tank car and ran for the other side of the yards, doubling back a little. No good. Two figures had cut wide across the tracks and were disappearing into the last line of carriages at the yard's edge.

There were scattered bomb craters and piles of rubble here and there in this area, left after the bombings in April. Roth squatted in the shadow of a smashed flatcar and gasped for breath. He couldn't go on much longer. How in hell was he going to get out now?

Three tracks away, the plainclothesman who had let him through the checkpoint edged out from between two carriages and looked around. Roth jumped involuntarily. The man saw the motion and raised his pistol.

"Come on out. You can't get away now."

Roth shot him through the chest. The man collapsed backward between the cars. They'll be more careful now, Roth thought. Not doing too badly for an out-of-condition engineer. There's one more man over there. If I can dispose of him, I might make it out of the rail yards. He was about to make a dash for the line of cars hiding the fallen policeman when he heard the chugging. A switching engine appeared around the bend, moving fairly quickly, oblivious to the commotion ahead of it. Roth ducked back under his flatcar. He might be able to jump aboard the engine as it passed, and force the engineer to speed up and get him well down the line before any switches could be thrown. He waited, tense. The engine kept up a steady pace.

As it came level with him he leaped from his hiding place and raced for the cab ladder. At the same instant a Gestapo man appeared around the corner of the pile of weckage, raised his pistol, and fired. The bullet caught Roth in the back of the thigh, just under the left buttock. It knocked the leg out from under him as he reached for the steel ladder to the engine cab. He fell forward, turning.

His last images were the astonished face of the engineer staring down at him from the footplate, and then the underside of the coal tender as it blotted out the sky.

"He's dead, then," stated Himmler.

"Yes, Herr Reichsführer. He fell under the train. It cut him in two."

Kruger and Weil were in Himmler's office in the Prinz Albrechtstrasse. The air was thick with the SS-Reichsführer's rage. The two junior men sat pale and upright, speaking only when spoken to.

"This business has gone from bad to worse for too long," Himmler informed them. Pedantically, he ticked off the items on the pad before him, glowering between each one. "First, the project is delayed because it is impossible to make enough of the explosive. Then, when an alternative is found, one of the scientists is killed in an accident, causing further delay. Next the team head disappears, probably going over to the British. Finally, the saboteur is killed instead of being retained for questioning." The prim voice became shrill. "Is *this* what you swore to do when you took the SS oath?"

Neither Kruger nor Weil ventured an answer.

The head of the SS continued in a softer voice. "I have it on high authority that the project—all of it—is to be completed without delay. Completed not later than ten days from now. That gives you until July twenty-second. Failure will result in serious consequences for both of you, as well as for Captain Strasser. Go back to *Fenris* and find out the earliest possible date for the attack. Be here to report the day after tomorrow. Now get out."

They didn't speak until they were back in their own office, with the door closed. Both men were perspiring freely.

"I wish to Christ I hadn't accepted this post when you offered it to me," Weil said fervently, mopping his forehead. "It's harder on the nerves than Russia."

"I wish I'd had a *chance* to refuse. Our whole idea's backfired, dammit."

"There's no hope of delaying the thing any more. It'll be the camps for sure if we try tinkering with the situation now."

"You're right," Kruger responded morosely. "I didn't think Himmler was so keen on going through with it. He must be under pressure from higher up. Hitler. Maybe Bormann through Hitler."

"I always thought the Führer refused to permit the use of poison or gas."

"He does. Or did. Maybe he doesn't consider this a gas. Maybe he's just desperate. We'd better head for Innsbrück. If this thing isn't ready in ten days we'll be cleaning latrines on the Russian front. At the very best."

"Can the aerosol gear be repaired by the twenty-first, then?"

Saur fiddled with a pencil. "Yes. Fortunately, the acid didn't have enough time to cause really extensive damage. Everything can be ready by then. The aerosol liquid is available now, in fact."

"What time on the twenty-first?"

"It's hard to be that accurate, there are tests—"

"What time?" Kruger repeated remorselessly.

Saur glanced from one to the other, a little desperately. Strasser sat with a motionless face. He had been told what depended on the answer.

Saur licked his lips. "Mid-afternoon. I guarantee it."

"Good." Kruger looked around the table at the rest of the scientists. Boehme quailed slightly. "The canister will be sent to the airfield as soon as you've finished." Kruger went on. "Captain Strasser, make security arrangements for the shipment but don't overdo it. A small motorcycle escort should be enough. Takeoff is at dawn on the twenty-second; the crew we have isn't trained for night operations on the Lancaster."

"Who did you get to fly it?" ventured Strasser, curious despite himself.

"Two ex-Luftwaffe bomber crewmen we got out of jail. They were put away a year ago for a swindle operation they were running in France. Pilot and navigator. Which brings me to another thing. Strasser, you'll have to detail two men to go along on the flight to make sure the plane goes where it's supposed to. The crew's been promised freedom on a successful return but I don't want them to get into their heads to defect to the British. Dr. Saur, by the way, is going as well, to operate the spray equipment over the target."

Saur looked unhappy, but held his tongue.

"What is the target, anyway?" asked Boehme.

"London."

There was a silence which went on and on. Then Kruger said, in a moment of unaccustomed self-revelation, "I can't do anything about it. It's orders."

VII

The Reich

July 22, 1944

It became colder in the Lancaster as they gained height.
After the aircraft had leveled off, Devereaux asked Cleve
if he could go forward for a chat with the crew. He hadn't
flown in a Lancaster for a long time and was surprised at
how he had missed the feel of the huge bomber.

"It won't bother me if it doesn't bother them. Go ahead."

He made his way up the fuselage and over the rear and
front spars onto the flight deck. He noticed again how tricky
the aircraft was to get out of in an emergency. The approved
exit was in the underside of the nose; the roof escape hatches
were safe to leave by only if the bomber were already down,
and if you jumped by the main entrance door while in flight,
you risked being killed by the tailplane.

He passed the radio operator at his position just ahead
of the front spar, and went on toward the nose. The navigator looked up as he went by, waved, and then grabbed
his sleeve. It was Mackenzie. He slipped his flying helmet
back to release his ears from the intercom headset, and
yelled over the racket of the four engines, "What are you
doing here? I thought you had a cushy job up in London."

"Didn't want to miss anything," Devereaux yelled back
with a jauntiness he did not feel. "What about you? Not

roaring around in Mosquitos with Patterson any more?''

"They asked me along on this one because I'd been there before. Colin was right browned off.''

"I can imagine.'' The shouting was beginning to hurt his throat. "Are they giving us any cover?''

Mackenzie gave him the thumbs-up. "Mosquito night-fighters to keep the Germans' heads down along the way. A few more Mosquitos to chuck bombs on Innsbrück.'' That's supposed to make us look like another bomber so they won't expect a parachute drop. No moon, either. Piece of cake.''

"Won't they see we're a lot slower than a Mossie? On radar?''

"They're some radar-jamming aircraft about and we'll be jamming ourselves. Should slow them down.''

"I hope so. See you later.''

I should have realized something like that would be laid on, he reflected as he went on forward. I came in on the briefings so late I never thought to ask. The precautions, now that he knew them, made him feel a good deal better. A lot of people were at work tonight to put him and eight other men into the Reich.

As to getting out again, that of course was something else. The civilian clothes felt suddenly itchy under the battledress.

The instruments cast a very dim glow in the cockpit. Devereaux felt the vibration of the airframe hammer the soles of his feet through his jump boots. He squinted at the dancing blur of the altimeter. Ten thousand feet. He realized he was a little short of breath. The crew was all on oxygen; it wasn't good to have the senses even slightly dulled by anoxia if you were flying.

The flight engineer saw him and passed him a spare

headset and microphone. Devereaux plugged into a spare jack. The pilot glanced up. "Evening. Nice black night, isn't it?"

"Not a bomber's moon in sight."

"No nightfighters out here, either." This was the engineer.

"That's fine with me," crackled an unidentified voice over Devereaux's earphones. Probably the mid-upper or tail gunner.

"Ever been up before?" asked the pilot.

"I did a tour with 207 Squadron earlier on. Pilot."

There was noticeable respect in the pilot's voice when he answered. "That's handy. If I feel like a nap I'll have you take over."

"Which route are you taking?"

"Down the Channel to near Bayeux. Then we turn inland and head for the Swiss border. We'll parallel that till we approach the drop zone, then start losing height."

"Shouldn't be much flak about for a while, then."

"Could be some light-to-medium stuff; we're low enough. But we're on a route to avoid most of the known concentrations. It might get warm around Innsbrück, though."

"Maybe the Mosquitos and jamming will keep them occupied."

"Hope so. We'll be dropping 'window' when we get close. It'll confuse the flak aiming radar a bit, anyway."

"Window" was aluminum foil strips that showed as a cloud of interference on a radar screen, hiding the aircraft dropping it.

They chatted until it was time to make the turn inland. Then Devereaux returned to his seat in the icy fuselage. Mackenzie gave him the thumbs up again as he passed.

Probably glad it's me and not him, Devereaux thought. I'll bet he hates flying in a Lancaster, after Mosquitos.

The other members of the assault team, except for Siegner, were dozing, their Stens across their laps or lying at their feet. The German physicist was staring at the stack of parachutes, his face immobile. Devereaux decided not to break in on his thoughts. Eventually he began to doze as well. Only Siegner remained fully awake, gazing into the gloom.

The Lancaster churned steadily across Occupied France toward the Swiss border. Occasional antiaircraft tracers reached desultory fingers after it, but the fire was weak and ill aimed. Pockets in the air caused more jolts and bumps than the distant explosion of the shells. Time passed.

Up at the navigator's station, Mackenzie drew another line on his chart and told the pilot, "You'd better let them know we're thirty minutes from drop zone. I'll be picking up Lake Geneva on the H2S any time now."

The flight engineer left his seat and made his way past the armored doors and the rear spar to the center fuselage. Waking Cleve, he yelled into his ear, "Half an hour to the drop zone. We may get some flak, so keep yourself braced for evasion."

Cleve straightened up from his slump and yawned. Jameson, next to him, felt the motion and woke up too. Moments later they were all open-eyed and stretching.

"Check your weapons, make sure they're on safety, and start getting your chutes on," Cleve shouted. "We'll be dropping from eight hundred feet, so you'll only be in the air for a few seconds. Siegner, Devereaux, remember to keep your knees flexed when you hit. Otherwise you'll break an ankle and we'll have to leave you. We'll clip onto the static line ten minutes from the drop zone."

While the others followed his instructions, Cleve went forward and leaned over Mackenzie. "What sort of wind on the zone?"

"From the west-northwest at about ten miles an hour, near as I can tell. There may be some rain on the way."

"Any word on the Mosquito attacks or cloud on the zone?"

"No. But we were only to be contacted if there was a problem."

Satisfied, Cleve returned to the assault team. He checked Siegner's parachute and then those of the other men. Twenty-five minutes to the drop. They were all cold and stiff, and dull from too little oxygen.

At twenty minutes out, the pilot started the Lancaster into a shallow dive to pick up speed. A few minutes later some faint reddish spots appeared well ahead of them. Fires.

"Mosquitos over Innsbrück," commented the pilot with satisfaction. "Probably Jerry nightfighters about too. Better start chucking out 'window.' "

Ahead of him, in the nose, the flight engineer began throwing the packets of foil into the slipstream, where they unravelled. The aluminum strips began their slow descent to earth. A shadow passed over them, a nightfighter, but whether German or British the engineer couldn't tell. Pity to get the chop from a Mosquito at this point, he thought. He threw the packets a little more quickly.

"Ten minutes," Mackenzie said over the intercom. He got up and came forward to the flight engineer's position, where he could see out through the windscreen. The pilot had already turned on the red light in the ceiling of the center fuselage. When it turned green, the men would start jumping.

Mackenzie found the visibility over the nose to be poor.

"I've got to get a better view of the terrain. D'you think I can squeeze down into the nose too?"

"Go ahead. Jimmy," the pilot said to the engineer, "you'll have to give up your intercom connection for a while."

The two of them hunkered down in the nose. The engineer continued windowing. At thirty-five miles from the drop zone the pilot increased the rate of descent and slid below 4000 feet. The fires ahead were clearer; it was obvious from the flashes that bombs were still going off. Mackenzie studied the ground intently, trying to pick out some recognizable features. They'd be at less than a thousand feet by the time they were near the drop zone and that would help him spot whatever landmarks there were.

They dropped lower. The air was rough at this height, heated by the ground below. The Lancaster bumped and juddered like a cart running over stones. Mackenzie picked out the line of the river Inn running along the edge of the city as they slowed to dropping speed.

"We're on course. Starboard a little, though. Keep her at this height; the ground rises. Two minutes."

They felt vulnerable in the lumbering aircraft, at this speed a perfect target. There were no more bomb flashes off to the left; the Mosquitos must have gone. It looked as though there were fires in the railway yards. A tendril of tracer reached out toward them; shell fragments rattled on the fuselage and then were gone.

The approach was perfect, the foothills rising to meet them until they were eight hundred feet up. "Go!" shouted Mackenzie. The pilot pressed the jump button.

The assault team was standing ready at the open belly hatch when the green jump light went on. Jameson let himself fall into the night. Cleve slapped the next man on the shoulder. They tumbled out of the bomber until there was a line of nine closely spaced men and their equipment canisters floating through the dark.

The Lancaster's engines roared under full throttle as the aircraft climbed away into the night, leaving the men to drift like seeds toward the land below.

Strasser stood behind Weil and Kruger as the technicians worked half-in, half-out, of the bomb bay of the captured Lancaster. The dilapidated hangar was only now, at one o'clock in the morning, cooling down from the heat of the day.

The SS captain had never seen such an enormous aircraft; it only just fit into the hangar. How they were going to fly it out of this tiny airstrip defeated him. He supposed that it wouldn't be fully loaded, but even so . . . . One of the technicians dropped a wrench with a clatter. Saur, standing on the scaffolding that supported the shielded bulk of the aerosol container, cursed.

Kruger turned away. "Not much to look at for the moment. We might as well go back to the operations hut." He looked at his watch. "Four hours till we go. They'd better be finished in time."

The three men strolled across the dewy grass of the airfield toward the hut. A few drops of rain spattered around them.

"I hope this weather doesn't get worse," muttered Weil. "If the ground gets soaked they may have a hard time getting the plane into the air."

"Don't even think about it," snapped Kruger. They were all jittery, not least because of the attempt on Hitler's life two days before. Kruger and Weil had been in Berlin at the time; for several hours they had expected to be arrested by the Army. But the attempt at revolt had failed and it was plain that Hitler was firmly in control once again. The reprisals, it was being whispered, were savage.

Strasser, when Weil had telephoned him about the coup, had doubled the guards and prepared to repel all boarders. But nothing had happened. When they left the *Fenris* installation that afternoon for the wretched airstrip at Weilheim, he had allowed the guard to relax slightly, but only slightly. He had had the mines laid in the tunnels after that first phone call, on Kruger's instructions—for none of them wanted *Fenris*'s existence known to anyone but the SS—but he had become nervous about it after the first alarm had died away. Twice he had attempted to get Kruger's permission to remove them.

As Weil opened the door to the operations hut he tried again. "Colonel," he said formally, "may I have permission to call my adjutant and order the dismantling of the explosives?"

"What?" Kruger seemed preoccupied, unsurprisingly. "Oh. I suppose so. There's no rush. It's going well here."

Strasser snatched up the telephone and managed, after several minutes, to contact the adjutant. "Bergmann? Strasser. I want the mines disconnected from the firing circuits immediately. The charges will be removed in the morning." He listened to the other end of the line for a moment, annoyance spreading over his face. "I know they've just gone to bed. Get them up again." Another pause. "All right, if you're that worried, let them sleep for two hours. Then get them at it."

He replaced the receiver. Weil looked at him questioningly. "My adjutant," apologized Strasser. "The engineers have been on duty with no break, for two days. Bergmann doesn't want them fooling about with explosives until they've had some sleep."

Kruger waved a hand. "It will keep for two hours." he said, and sat down in a chair to wait.

The ground seemed far away at first. Devereaux had been unprepared for the jolt as the static line pulled the bag away from his parachute and the dark green canopy bloomed in the sky above him. He swayed under it and studied the terrain below. They had dropped over a ravine cut from solid rock millenia ago by the glaciers roaming down from the Alps. The valley floor was narrow, smooth, and curved. Rocky slopes bordered it.

He had no idea of how to steer the parachute. He seemed to be drifting toward the lower slopes; a few vague blots in the night around him were the others. The wind must be different, he worried. The landing ground wasn't supposed to be this narrow.

The earth came up with a rush. At the last instant he remembered to flex his knees. The landing shock was harder than he had expected and he rolled over twice before coming to rest on his back. His right arm was tangled in the parachute shroud lines; the canopy began to tug at him as the wind tried to blow it farther down the slopes. With his left hand he released the harness, struggled to his knees, and fought the chute until it collapsed.

A faint hiss came from the darkness downslope. Very quietly, he called back. There was an answering mutter from above him. That's three of us anyway, he thought. I hope one of them's Siegner.

A form appeared out of the darkness. "Devereaux?"

It was Jameson. Little by little the group enlarged. Last to arrive was Cleve. "You can talk out loud if you keep

269

it low," he told them quietly. "The wind's strong enough to cover it. Where's Siegner?"

"Here."

"Where are we? We're too low down, that's all I'm sure of."

"I'm not certain. There's a narrow valley leading down the mountain; it comes out half a kilometer above Tulfes. I think that's where we are. But we drifted so quickly we're likely almost at the valley bottom."

"Damn. Much farther away than we planned to be?"

"About half again. A little more, a little less."

"We'd better get a move on, then. We're about ten minutes ahead of schedule, fortunately. The supply containers are a few yards farther down. Let's get cracking."

They located the canisters and distributed the packs and explosives, along with the grenades. Siegner and Devereaux were burdened only by their pistols, a Sten each, and extra ammunition clips. To Devereaux, sweaty inside his double layer of clothing, it seemed quite enough.

"Better to go up to the original zone and then to the target, or downhill and then on?" asked Cleve.

"Down, I think," answered Siegner. "We can skirt the bottom of the slope parallel to the Tulfes-Rinn-Sistrans road, after we get out of this valley. There'll be some rough terrain to cross for the last quarter of the way but we're so far down here now that this will be faster. And not so tiring as going back uphill."

"Good enough." Cleve translated the plan to the others and they set off, Jameson and DeVries in the lead. The going was reasonably easy. Half a kilometer on, the valley opened and the ground leveled out. They halted while Siegner took over the lead and turned to his left. Somewhere below, a dog barked. There were still fires in Innsbrück, reflecting pinkishly from the low cloud cover that had begun to crawl across the sky. They felt the odd drop of rain on their faces.

It was half-past two before Siegner halted them. "From here we have to cross a spur of the mountain," he told Cleve. "I'll try to bring us out just across from the emergency exit bunker, on the far side of the ravine. It'll take about forty minutes. Will that keep us on schedule?"

"We're about fifteen minutes behind. It'll start getting light a little after five. We don't have a lot of time. Go as fast as you can."

The ground was much rougher now. The reflected light of the fires in Innsbrück, which had given them an orientation point, was obscured by trees. Siegner worked out an approximate course and led them using Cleve's compass. Devereaux was surprised by the way Cleve turned the navigation over to the German, without question. He was obviously intent on using Siegner's knowledge of the terrain to the fullest extent.

They were all nearly blown after half an hour of scrambling over stones and fallen branches, being slapped in the face by pine needles, and skinning their knees on rocky outcrops. At last Siegner halted. Devereaux nearly ran into Lindgaard before he realized that they had stopped. He sank down thankfully, and began to recover his breath.

"We're there," Cleve whispered. "Bang on. The ravine's on the other side of those trees and the exit bunker's dead across from us. We'll wait until the next patrol goes by and then Carpenter and Placzek will deal with the bunker guards. The rest of us will follow right after that. We'll have twenty minutes to get in and get out. Let's move up to the tree line. No talking."

They were lucky with their timing. Four minutes later

two figures tramped up the ravine, chatting quietly. In peacetime they might have been two hunters, out for an early start. A shadow detached itself from the bunker wall and came out to meet them. After a muttered conversation, the shadow withdrew and the two patrolling soldiers trudged on up the ravine.

As they went out of sight, Devereaux heard the slightest of rustles as Carpenter and Placzek slipped away. The assault team waited. A boot scraped near the bunker, and a splashing sound carried to them on the night breeze. The sentry was urinating against the bunker wall. The splashing stopped and the man appeared, a darker blot in the dark. He walked up and down, a bored soldier trying to stay awake.

A shadow rose from the ground behind him. There was the faintest of thumps. Devereaux found that his teeth were aching, and forced his jaw to unclench. A band of yellow light splashed across the ground and was instantly extinguished. Devereaux thought he heard a muffled exclamation from inside the bunker, muffled by the concrete walls. The bar of light reappeared and Carpenter was motioning to them from the open doorway, the blackout curtain pushed slightly back. The light went out again.

They scrambled across the ravine and into the darkened bunker. The first thing Devereaux saw was a terrified young SS trooper sitting on the floor with his hands clasped behind his head. Carpenter was busy cutting the telephone wires. At the back of the bunker was a large steel double door.

"Open it," ordered Cleve.

Placzek drew down the steel handle. The doors swung silently outward on greased hinges. Beyond them, the emergency tunnel was swallowed up in blackness. Siegner darted into it with a flashlight; the yellow beam skittered about and came to rest on a heavy wiring harness.

"They're laid." The relief in his voice was unmistakable. "The charges are laid."

Cleve turned to the apprehensive soldier. "How frequent are the patrols outside?"

The man had regained some of his composure, but was still shaky.

"Every half hour."

"What about inside? How many men there?"

"Three."

Siegner was astonished. "Only three? Wasn't security tightened after they tried to kill Hitler?"

"Yes. But it was relaxed tonight. It's said there's no danger now." The guard eyed Siegner's civilian clothes with disbelief.

"Where are the guards stationed inside?"

"I don't know. I was posted here only a few days ago."

"Is he telling the truth?" asked Cleve.

Siegner inspected the guard closely. "I think so. I don't remember ever seeing him in the compound."

"Tie him up. Carpenter, Placzek, start running the leads from the lighting cables to the radio. We'll switch the power on when we get to the bottom of the tunnel. Siegner, where's the safe with the explosives trigger?"

"In the pile control room. The other's in Strasser's office."

"What about the other guard?" Devereaux asked.

"He's dead," said Carpenter. "I'll drag him inside, though. No use alarming the natives unnecessarily."

That's a callous bastard and no doubt about it, thought Devereaux fleetingly, as they trotted into the maw of the tunnel. I wonder how he got that way?

At the blast doors separating the tunnel from the main

section of the complex, Siegner found the knife switch for the emergency lighting and pushed it over. A dim yellow glow sprang up. They huddled against the door. Cleve asked Siegner, "D'you still think the guards will be where you predicted? Pile control, aerosol room, extraction lab?"

"Yes. Only, I expected two in each position. Strasser's made it easy for us."

"Easier," corrected Devereaux, and was silenced by a cold look from Cleve.

"I'll go first," said the major. "Jameson, you're next. Siegner, if nobody shoots us, follow. Then the rest of you. We're following the alternate plan. We'll use the German mines to blow the place."

Lindgaard slowly pulled back the right-hand leaf of the door while Cleve knelt at the widening crack, his Sten ready. When the door was open half an inch, Lindgaard stopped. Cleve waited a moment, then whispered, "Open it," and went through as soon as the gap was wide enough. The others followed into the short passage leading to the main tunnel. Cleve inched forward and peered around the corner toward the main entrance.

An SS trooper was staring straight at him.

Cleve stepped unhurriedly around the corner and raised his Sten. The guard opened his mouth to shout; saw the submachine gun pointed straight at his belly, and closed his mouth, hard. He raised his hands.

"Clever lad," muttered Cleve. "Put the handcuffs on him, Mrosek." The Czech did so while Jameson and DeVries closed the blast doors behind them.

"Where are the others?" hissed Siegner. The guard closed his mouth tighter and looked grim. Cleve put the muzzle of the Sten under the man's nose and pushed upward, staring into his eyes.

274

The guard swallowed and said, "One in the control room. One where, where the woman was hurt."

"Extraction lab," explained Siegner. The guard had recognized him. His jaw dropped. Siegner took advantage of his surprise to ask, "No one in the aerosol room?"

The guard looked blank. Siegner's face clouded. "That's odd. There ought to be one there." He looked up and down the tunnel. "How many of the scientific and technical staff are on duty?"

The guard shook his head. "None," he whispered.

"*None*? Why not?"

"I don't know. Everything's been mixed up since they tried to kill the Führer."

Siegner turned to Cleve. "This is very peculiar. I don't like it at all."

Cleve looked at his watch. "We're behind. Mrosek, guard him. Jameson'll bring you any others we find."

They stole along the dim passageway toward the pile control room. The complex seemed deserted. Siegner looked more and more worried.

The main corridor ended in a T-junction, with the control room entrance down the left branch on the far side, and the extraction lab similarly placed on the right-hand corridor. The offices and sleeping quarters were also left, and the storerooms and the aerosol assembly room to the right. At the junction, Cleve peeped around the corner. No one to be seen. He and Jameson slipped toward the pile control room. Lindgaard and DeVries went the other way, to the extraction lab and the aerosol chamber. Siegner and Devereaux waited where they were. Far off down the main tunnel, Mrosek watched them and the captive alternately.

Cleve raised his arm and jerked it down. The men hurled themselves into the entrances before them and disappeared.

A muffled yelp emanated from the extraction lab, followed by a soft stuttering and a tinkle of broken glass. No sound came from the pile control room for a moment, and then there was the clank of a weapon striking the floor. DeVries came out of the aerosol room and shook his head. No one there.

Cleve's arm appeared from the control room entrance and gestured Siegner and Devereaux forward. Lindgaard joined them from the extraction lab. He smelled of gunfire.

"What happened?" This from Cleve.

"The guard tried to shoot. He's dead."

"Any sign of the civilian staff?"

"No."

"Wasn't there a guard in the aerosol room?" asked Devereaux.

"No. It was empty. There was a kind of cradle affair but it was empty, too."

Devereaux told Siegner.

"*No canister*?"

"Just a cradle."

"Oh, my God. Where the devil is it?"

"First things first," said Cleve. "Siegner. Get in here and blow this place up."

Jameson took the surviving guard to Mrosek. Lindgaard took up a position in the cross-corridor outside the control room entrance. Siegner located the switch vault behind a blank panel in one of the instrument racks and began to work on the combination. After a minute he gave up.

"They've changed it. It'll have to be blown."

They had been inside for five minutes.

DeVries extracted a wad of plastic explosives from his pack and began to shape a charge. The only sound in the room, other than that of the ventilation fans, was the men's breathing.

A creak broke the quiet. Only Siegner knew what it was; the office door hinge that he had never bothered to oil. He sprinted for the control room entrance, followed by Cleve.

Down the corridor, a lone figure was bent over the door handle, obviously locking it. Whoever it was had over-looked Lindgaard standing not fifteen yards away, or had assumed that he was the control room guard. The figure straightened, started toward them, and stopped in shock, swaying a little.

"Dr. Boehme," called Siegner gently, "you've been drinking my brandy."

Boehme stood transfixed. The half-empty brandy bottle slid from his fingers and smashed on the concrete. He made no move to run, even when Lindgaard and Siegner started toward him. When they reached him, he said weakly:

"You. Peter. You've come back."

"Bring him into the control room," ordered Cleve. "He may know more than the guards."

Boehme was slightly drunk, and staggered a little as they dragged him into the control room and dumped him into a chair. Already pale, he went paler as he stared from one member of the assault team to another.

"You'd better find out what's going on here," Cleve told Siegner.

"Hans," said the physicist, "where's the night staff?"

Boehme mumbled something. Cleve fiddled obtrusively with his Sten. The administrative officer flinched and said, "Strasser's had us living outside since the attack on the Führer. To keep a closer eye on us. There's no work being done tonight."

"Why not? Is the canister ready to go?" asked Siegner, knowing already what the answer would be.

Boehme's eyes flicked desperately from one hard face to another. "Yes. They finished loading it this afternoon. It would have been ready sooner but—"

"But what?"

Boehme shifted in the chair. His face showed an odd mixture of shame and triumph. "Sabotage. It was delayed several days. Roth did it."

"Roth," murmured Siegner. "Where is he?" he asked, without hope.

"He tried to get away. He fell under a train. It killed him."

"Did you help catch him?" asked Siegner, sadly. Boehme looked at the floor.

"Where's the canister now?" Cleve was becoming impatient. Boehme stared sullenly in front of him.

"Hans," Siegner told him gently, "these men will kill you if you don't answer."

"They've taken it to the Weilheim airstrip."

"What then?"

"They're installing it in the Lancaster. Saur's doing it. Strasser, Weil, Kruger, they all went. They're afraid of failing."

"The attack's soon, then?"

The look of triumph returned. "The plane flies at dawn. You'll never stop it."

"Holy Christ," Cleve breathed. Devereaux felt his lips go numb.

Siegner turned to Cleve. "It will all be for nothing, even if we do destroy this place, if the canister's used."

Cleve was impassive again. "How far to the airstrip? No. If we had transport, how long to get there?"

"Driving as fast as possible, an hour."

"You've been there?"

"Yes. I flew to Berlin from there. I could find it at night, if that's what you're thinking."

Without answering, Cleve grabbed a chair, reversed it, and sat with his arms cradling the Sten along its back. "Dr. Boehme," he said tonelessly, "please answer my questions as fast as you can. If you don't I'll shoot your fingers and toes off, one joint at a time. This gun is silenced; no one will hear. Will you answer?"

Boehme nodded, his eyes enormous with fright. Siegner turned away.

"How many guards went with the canister?"

"Ten. Plus Saur, Strasser, Weil, Kruger. And the driver of the truck and the staff car."

"Have any of them returned?"

"No."

"How many men still here?"

"About forty. The adjutant's in charge while Strasser's away. You know of Strasser?"

Cleve nodded. "You're the admin officer, I gather. How much transport is here?"

Boehme scrabbled in his memory. "The Kübelwagen. Two trucks. An armored car. It's broken down. The Tatra, that's an automobile."

"I know what it is. How many guards at the main gate?"

"Two. There's also one outside the bunker entrance, where you come in."

"Are they very alert?"

"Yes. Strasser's been very strict since the assassination attempt."

"He relaxed security tonight, though, didn't he?"

279

"The men were very tired. He worked them night and day since the attempt."

"Laying the explosives?"

Boehme nodded. "Also doubled patrols. Until the canister left."

"Where's the radio?"

"In the headquarters block. Next to Strasser's office. The adjutant's office is next to that."

Cleve turned to DeVries. "Tell Lindgaard to go up the tunnel and get Carpenter and Placzek down here with the radio. Have him take Morsek's two prisoners up there with him; they should be gagged and hidden in the woods, away from the bunker. Hide the dead one, too. We'll take Boehme with us—he might be useful. Now, we have about eleven minutes before the next patrol finds the bunker empty. Siegner, how long will it take the patrol to get back down to the compound and raise the alarm?"

"Fifteen minutes."

"Where are the keys to the vehicles kept?"

"In a cupboard in the adjutant's office."

Cleve studied Boehme, and asked, "Is the other mine trigger still in Strasser's office?"

Boehme licked his lips. "Yes."

"Is there a guard at the HQ block?"

"One at the front door. There isn't a back door."

"Dr. Siegner, is he giving us the truth?"

"As far as I can tell."

"Good. DeVries," he said to the Dutchman, who had returned from giving Lindgaard his instructions, "Handcuff Boehme to that pipe. We've got to do some planning out of his hearing."

With Boehme secured, the assault team assembled in the corridor. Devereaux translated Cleve's staccato orders as he gave them. Siegner took them in somberly. At the end, Cleve said, "There's no doubt that this is a lashup, but it's the best we can do under the circumstances. Anyone separated from the rest of us can try to make it over the border on his own. This goes especially for you lot in the rearguard. If you can't follow the airstrip assault section within three minutes, head for Switzerland. Without Siegner to lead you to the airstrip, you'll get lost and be captured. Everyone has his map?"

Everyone did. Jameson unshackled Boehme from the pipe and prodded him down the tunnel behind them. Cleve had had him gagged, which made it difficult for him to breathe; his breath came in quick snorting spasms. Siegner kept well away from him. At the main blast doors, Siegner paused to look back along the dim tunnel. Two years, a first-order scientific achievement back there in the yellowish gloom. I almost wish I had stayed in Russia, he thought. Would they have found someone else to do it?

Devereaux caught his eye and he turned away.

Mrosek was already pushing the doors slightly open. He peered through the crack, down the five yards of tunnel to the interior of the entrance bunker. It was deserted. He and Cleve stole noiselessly down to the half-open steel door set into the bunker wall.

"Können Sie mich helfen, Schütze?" said Cleve, mumbling.

Boots scraped outside. "Ja. Ich komme, Herr Professor." The private walked unsuspectingly through the door and was instantly bludgeoned on the back of the neck by Mrosek. He crumpled soundlessly. Cleve knelt beside him. "He's still alive. Cuff his wrists and ankles and gag him. Put him in the corner."

"He'll be killed when the mines go," whispered Siegner as the rest of them came up.

"We can't leave him outside. This is risky enough. Would you rather I shoot him now? This way he has a chance, at least."

Siegner didn't answer. *I saw worse in Russia,* he reminded himself. *But it still makes me feel sick.*

The compound outside was dark and deserted, except for the pale light over the main gate and the figures of the two sentries by the tiny guardhouse. Cleve looked over the situation and then hissed, "Let's go. Mrosek and Jameson to secure the Kübelwagen and one truck, Carpenter and DeVries to disable the other vehicles. The rest of you, follow me."

The transport party—which would also form the rearguard in the truck—curved away toward the vehicle park behind the barracks. Cleve and Placzek, followed by Devereaux and Siegner, stole down the slope toward the headquarters block. Lindgaard lagged a few yards behind with the terrified Boehme and the radio.

In the dark, the sentry at the HQ block door could see only four indistinct figures walking slowly toward him. The other two were invisible in the night. It was only at the last instant that he remembered that there should be only three sentries coming from the installation, not four. He raised his Schmeisser and took a breath to challenge the intruders.

A stream of bullets from Placzek's silenced Sten knocked him back against the door. The thump of his fall on the wooden porch was certain to be heard inside. Instantly, Cleve was up the steps and waiting beside the door. It opened, and a man's head emerged. He had barely opened his mouth when a vise closed around his throat and rammed

282

him back inside. There was a confused thumping of boots on the steps, and the door closed firmly.

Cleve placed the muzzle of his Sten over the man's navel and released the grip on his throat. "Placzek, do we have any more cuffs?"

"No. I can use some of the wiring flex from the explosive packs. I'll gag him with his tie."

"Put him at the end of the corridor when you're finished, and watch the door. Keep Boehme here, too. And get the dead man in here. I presume you're the duty officer?" he said in German to the petrified soldier. White-faced, the man nodded. He kept glancing in disbelief at Siegner, who ignored him.

"Anyone else in the building?"

A shake of the head.

"Lindgaard, get the radio into the radio room and connect it to the Germans' aerial. That'll give us a lot more range. Set demolition charges on both our radio and theirs, then rig another charge on the telephone switchboard. We'll set them all to go at the same time as the mines. Siegner, get all the vehicle keys from the adjutant's office and then meet me and Devereaux in Strasser's room. I'll put a charge on the switch vault while you're busy."

This is the first, and I hope the only, time I'm ever in an SS officer's territory, thought Devereaux as they entered Strasser's cubicle. Cleve checked the blackout curtains and turned on the light. Except for the picture of Hitler above Strasser's chair, and the absence of maps, it could have been Gilford's office in England: the same rough furniture and unfinished floorboards, the same yellowing paint.

The switch vault was behind a panel in the wall. Cleve pried it open with his assault knife and began to arrange plastic explosive around the safe's door hinges. "I hope the thing doesn't have a cutout to disable the firing circuit if the door's forced," grumbled Cleve as he worked. "It'd be just like the bloody Germans."

"There isn't one as far as I know," Siegner told him as he entered and dumped the keys on the desk. "There they are, all I could find."

"Are they identified?"

"Yes."

"We'll want one truck and the Kübelwagen. Cut the shanks off all the others. There's a pair of cutters in the pack. You hang onto the Kübelwagen key; you'll be driving."

Devereaux waited while Siegner destroyed the keys and Cleve finished setting the charge. Then all three of them went to the radio room. Lindgaard had finished connecting the transmitter. Lumps of explosive stuck on the casing like warts.

"Everything ready?"

"Yes. All charges laid. Fuses are ready."

"Try to raise the link station."

Lindgaard put on the headset and fiddled with dials. "Calling Grenadier One. This is Grenadier Two. Do you read me?" Nothing. He adjusted the squelch and tried again. "Grenadier One. This is Grenadier Two. Do you read?"

Devereaus's palms were damp. Lindgaard tried twice more.

"Atmospherics or jamming?" asked Cleve.

Lindgaard scowled. "No. They don't seem to be—" His face brightened. "Got them. Grenadier One, this is Two. We have information for you. Hang on." He passed the microphone to Cleve.

"Grenadier One," said Cleve. "Yes, I know we're sending in clear. A new situation's come up. We're about to

284

blow the complex, so you can scrub the raid. But the canister's been taken to an airstrip nearby where it's being put on the Lancaster. We're going to try to destroy it before it leaves the ground, but we haven't much time so there's a chance it'll get away.'' He paused and listened. ''No, we don't know the route it'll take. But you'd better make arrangements to intercept any unidentified Lancaster on a heading from this area, in case we fail. Understood? Over.'' Another pause. ''Good. We won't be in contact again. The radio's too bulky to take, so we're destroying it. Over.'' He listened and grimaced. ''Thank you. Two closing down. Out.''

He pulled off the headset. ''They wish us good luck. Let's get it over with. Set the fuses here and on the switchboard for seven minutes from now. Siegner, come with me. Wait a minute. Are you willing to wear the guard's uniform? It might help at the airstrip.''

The physicist shrugged. ''I'm dead however they catch me. I can put it on over the civilian clothes.''

''Devereaux, help him strip the guard.''

They waited nervously while Siegner struggled into the uniform. Then Devereaux pointed out, ''Boehme probably knows we're going to the airstrip. He'll tell them after we've gone.''

Cleve frowned. ''Kill him?''

Siegner stopped with one arm in the tunic. ''What did he say?''

Devereaux translated. Siegner made no move to continue dressing. ''I will not permit that,'' he said flatly. ''Why can't we take him with us and put him out along the road on the way there?''

Cleve appeared indifferent. ''As you like. But if he tries to slow us down, we'll have to kill him. Put him in the

285

truck with the rearguard; there won't be room in the Kübelwagen.''

Siegner put his other arm into the tunic and fastened it silently.

''It's three twenty-two,'' Cleve informed them. ''Set the fuses in here for six minutes. I'll deal with the switch vault. Come along, Dr. Siegner.''

Back in Strasser's office, Cleve cut two thirty-second lengths of fuse, crimped them to the detonators, and inserted the detonators into the explosive. He lit the fuses.

''Outside.''

They waited in the corridor, while the fuses burned. Finally, a muffled bang. Cleve tore the door open and they shot into the office. The safe door was askew, hanging from one partially severed hinge. Inside the compartment was a large red knife switch, and a timer dial. They both stared at the switch. Finally, Siegner reached out and grasped the handle. He looked at Cleve.

''Go ahead. It was yours, after all.''

Siegner pulled the switch firmly down. The timer hand began to move. ''It's running,'' he said simply. ''We'd better all get out of here.''

Two hundred yards away, at the compound gate, the two guards had looked around in surprise at the muffled thump of the safe door being blown. Behind them, the HQ block was invisible in the darkness.

''Did you hear that? What was it?''

The other sentry had been in Russia and the sound was familiar. He looked puzzled. ''It sounded like a demolition charge. They've been piddling around with explosives ever since we got the order to mine the tunnels. Maybe somebody had an accident." He sighed. "I'd better call the duty officer. Who is it tonight?"

"Kellermann."

The sentry went into the guard house and picked up the telephone. He could get no answer from the duty officer. He jiggled the cradle and frowned. Still nothing. He put his head out the door and told the other sentry. "The phone's not working. You'd better go up to the HQ block and find Kellerman. Tell him about the noise, if he didn't hear it."

The other trotted obediently up the lane toward the headquarters hut. As he climbed the steps he noticed that they were slippery. That's odd, he thought. It hasn't rained that much tonight. And where's the guard?

The lights inside were off. He fumbled nervously for the switch and found it.

Above the gag, Kellermann's furious eyes met his.

Bergmann groaned as the alarm clock went off. He had had all of ninety minutes sleep and his eyeballs felt gritty. He turned on the lamp beside his cot and looked at the clock. Three twenty-seven.

He began to put his boots on. There hadn't been any point in undressing for an hour and a half in bed, and his uniform was wrinkled. I'd better do something about that before Strasser gets back, he grumbled to himself. Why the devil couldn't we have waited till morning to pull the firing circuits?

He left his quarters and stumbled across the worn grass to the engineering squad's barracks. He snapped on the lights. A few groans and carefully muffled curses floated among the bunks.

"That's enough of that," he said sharply. "Up you get. We have to start dismantling the mine firing circuits, starting now." He watched the twelve yawning men with respect. They were all Russia veterans, and tough as old boot leather. Bergmann, who hadn't been in combat since 1940, was slightly in awe of them.

There was a faint shouting outside, muffled, as though it were coming from the interior of a building. The adjutant, startled, cocked his head. It seemed to be coming from the HQ block. The others heard it too, and out of long experience reached for their Schmeissers.

The charge on the switchboard was a large one. The guard, ordered by the shouting Kellermann, had tried to reach it before it went off, but had barely started to open the door when it went off. The blast knocked him and the door across the corridor and deposited both in a motionless heap. Kellermann, still tied though no longer gagged, lay dazed by the concussion. An instant later the charges in the radio room went off.

At the double bang, Cleve, jammed with Siegner, Devereaux, Placzek, and Lindgaard into the Kübelwagen, peered at the luminous dial of his watch. "Ten seconds till the tunnel mines go. We'll start up as soon as they do. It should take the SS a couple of minutes to react properly."

Had Strasser not ordered the removal of the mines, or had the adjutant's clock run a minute or two slow, Cleve would have been right. But the reverberations of the twin explosions had barely died away before the SS engineers were scrambling out the barracks door. Their sergeant was already shouting commands as they deployed into skirmish order.

"God damn," Cleve snarled as the harsh voice drifted over the roofs into the vehicle park. "That's blown it." He walloped Siegner on the shoulder. "Let's go. Hurry!"

The German stabbed the ignition button. The motor

ground and fired. Behind them, the truck's engine roared as Jameson switched on and gunned the throttle.

The timer in Strasser's office reached zero.

At first the explosion was no more than a shudder in the ground. Then a subterranean rumble grew at the roots of the mountain. The SS engineers stopped and looked around, dismayed. Inside the *Fenris* complex thousands of tons of rock cascaded into the pile room, the storage chambers, the sleeping quarters, the extraction lab. The force of the explosion, roaring up the main tunnel, fired the blast doors like cannonballs out through the walls of the entrance bunker, taking the unfortunate sentry with them. Chunks of concrete and rock thudded into the compound. A gout of flame flooded out of the wrecked tunnel and disappeared. As the shock waves died away, everyone in the compound seemed gripped by paralysis.

"Holy Christ," breathed Devereaux:

Cleve recovered himself first. "Drive, God damn it!" he screamed at Siegner. "Go! Go! Go!" The Kübelwagen, followed by the truck, plunged down the lane toward the main gate. The SS engineers collected their wits and ran for the sound of the engines. Other troopers, still half-asleep, some with weapons, were pouring out of the barracks. There was a series of bangs as the demolition charges on the Tatra, the other truck, and the armored car went off.

The remaining sentry had begun to run toward the tumult in the compound. He stopped dead as the Kübelwagen and the truck roared around the corner of the HQ block, and got off one wild burst from his Schmeisser before Cleve's bullets knocked him into the dirt. The two vehicles smashed through the gates and roared down the road, into the dark.

"They're too close behind," gasped Cleve. "Stop."

Siegner obediently pulled up. Cleve shouted at the truck,

"You'll have to hold them for three minutes while we get far enough down the road to cut the telephone wires. Otherwise they'll rig a field telephone and call ahead of us. If you're more than three minutes, head for Switzerland."

"Right," Jameson shouted back over the idling engines. He backed the truck up a few yards, and stopped it with its rear facing the installation. The Kübelwagen vanished in the direction of Sistrans. Jameson, DeVries, Carpenter, and Mrosek leaped out of the truck, dragging the unfortunate Boehme with them, and melted into the roadside undergrowth.

Boehme was nearly witless with fright. As the SS engineers stormed down the road toward the rearguard, he wrenched his arm from DeVries' grasp and rolled away into the dark. DeVries, cursing, tried to follow him without losing sight of the advancing Germans, who were now clearly silhouetted by the fires in the vehicle park. Boehme wriggled farther away and DeVries didn't dare shoot at him for fear of giving away their position. He gave up and crawled back to his original spot.

All Boehme saw in the oncoming line of SS troops was salvation. Although thrown off balance by his handcuffed wrists, he stumbled to his feet and began a shambling run toward the indistinct forms. Jameson fired after him, but missed.

The only thing the SS sergeant could tell in the darkness was that a man was running toward him. He looked for upraised arms but saw none. Boehme had just time to see the Schmeisser's muzzle flash before the bullets took him in the chest and tossed him, face down, into the ditch beside the road. He thought of calling out to Siegner but the idea contracted into a pinpoint of consciousness, and then went out.

The assault team waited until the Germans were twenty yards away, and then opened fire. Three figures collapsed into the road and the rest flung themselves into the ditch and the roadside shrubbery. Jameson peered at his watch. Two minutes and they could try to fight their way out. Damn it. Reinforcements were running down from the compound; he could see them up the road in the fireglow.

A fusillade of bullets sleeted overhead and thudded into the tailgate of the truck. DeVries and Morsek fired back. One minute to go.

There was a thud by Jameson's elbow. Startled, he looked down. It was a grenade. He tried to roll away but had only raised one arm when it went off and killed him. Several Germans tried to follow up the explosion but were cut down or forced to ground by the surviving members of the assault team. There was a lull in the shooting. Carpenter slithered over to DeVries and whispered, ''Jameson's dead. The three minutes must be up. D'you think we can get out?''

''They're pressing us too closely. We'll have to put them off. Give me a couple of grenades. Throw when I do.''

Another shower of bullets spattered around them.

''Now.''

Four grenades arched in the direction of the enemy. The explosions were followed by silence, which was punctuated by groans.

''You and Mrosek get in the truck cab,'' DeVries whispered. ''Bang on the door when you're both in. I'll give them three more grenades and climb over the tailgate as you start to move.''

''All right. D'you think we can catch up with the others?''

DeVries grimaced in the dark. ''No. We'll never be able to by the time we get away, even if they stop. I think we'll have to try for the border.''

"I'll get Mrosek. Listen for my bang on the door."

DeVries nodded and slipped a new clip into the Sten as Carpenter crawled away. He laid three grenades on the turf in front of him.

A fist hammered on metal. Instantly DeVries rose to his knees, threw the first grenade, and followed with the other two. For good measure he flooded the road with a full clip of bullets. The hot silencer casing seared his hand.

The truck was beginning to move; there was no shooting from the Germans. DeVries sprinted for the tailgate and began to haul himself over it.

The SS sergeant raised his head from the ditch just in time to see a shadow flicker in the blackness. He sighted and fired quickly. The shadow sank to the ground while the truck vanished.

"That's another of the bastards, anyway," muttered the sergeant. The truck's engine noise was receding down the road. The sergeant rose to his knees and shouted, "They've got away. Somebody run back and get a field telephone. Hurry!"

They were approaching Sistrans when Cleve decided they had gone far enough. Siegner stopped the vehicle and Placzek shinned up the nearest telephone pole. Moments later the wires whispered down to the grass. As they roared off again, Siegner told them, "If we cut the wires below Sistrans they'll have to go all the way to Innsbrück to contact the airfield. With luck we'll be there before they can do it." Cleve nodded.

It was an exhausting drive. Siegner pushed the little vehicle to its limit, bucketing along the potholed roads until it seemed that the axles must break. They shot through Sistrans without being challenged, stopped to cut the telephone wires again, and careened on toward Innsbrück. There were still fires here and there in the city.

"We'll have to go round the west edge of the city," yelled Siegner over the racket of the engine. "They'll be too busy cleaning up from the air raid to worry about the mess we left on the mountain, but we can't go through Innsbrück or they'll spot your battledress."

By the time they were clear of the city and on the Weilheim road, Cleve was getting worried. "It's not long till dawn. How much farther?"

"A few kilometers. Ten or twelve minutes."

"Slow down a few hundred meters from the gates. Lindgaard, try to rig a pair of satchel charges with five-second fuses, without blowing us all up. Everybody else, get your weapons ready."

It took eleven minutes to reach the airstrip approach road. Siegner slowed the Kübelwagen to a walking pace. There was a very faint pale streak in the eastern sky.

"How much longer to takeoff?"

"Fifteen minutes," the meteorological officer told Kruger. "It'll be light enough then. They should have good weather all the way to England. They'll be keeping low, to avoid the Allied radar."

"I wish we'd been able to get Luftwaffe cooperation to give us a clear flight path all the way to the Channel," grumbled Weil. "It would be too God-awful if the plane were shot down by our own fighters."

"Be glad they agreed to have the flak batteries along the route hold their fire for three hours," Kruger told him. "Although it's no skin off the Luftwaffe's nose about the fighters. Most of them have been pulled back to Germany, anyway."

"They're rolling it out now," said the weather officer.

Across the airstrip a small tractor was towing the Lancaster out of the camouflaged hangar. Its fuselage melted into the trees in the three-quarters dark.

"What do our Luftwaffe hosts think of all this?" asked Strasser.

"Who cares?" Kruger shrugged. "It's only an emergency airstrip anyway. It was convenient for us, and not much use to them, so Goering cooperated. He'll expect something for it, eventually. You know how it works."

"Here comes Saur."

The gas expert, looking apprehensive, bustled into the operations hut. "It's ready to go. We can fly as soon as it's a bit lighter. They were about to start warming up the engines when I left."

As if to agree, the four Merlins burst into life, one after another. The windowpanes rattled slightly. "Good," said Kruger. "You'd better get on board. Remember, radio silence all the way there, one code group after the attack, and radio silence all the way home. If you have to you can divert to one of the French airfields. But try to make it back here. Was there any trouble replacing the British radio?"

"No. Everything went perfectly." The replacement transmitter was fixed to the airstrip frequency, to prevent an inadvertent security breach. Also, Kruger reminded himself, to prevent Saur or the flight crew from contacting the British, if they managed to deal with the SS guards somehow.

"You should get back to the plane," the meteorological officer said. "It'll be light enough in five minutes."

Saur left, dragging his feet.

"Have they the slightest chance of surviving?" asked Weil.

"Not the slightest. The British will shoot them out of the air on the way back. But it'll be too late for London, then. For us, too," he added, before he remembered Strasser's presence. But the SS captain was looking puzzled. "D'you hear something? Not the Lancaster, another engine. Up the road."

They were still a quarter-mile from the airstrip gate when they heard the Lancaster begin its warm-up. "Faster," said Cleve briefly. Siegner accelerated. It was still too dark to tell their uniforms apart easily; with luck, Siegner's SS tunic might deceive the guard long enough to prevent an immediate alarm. Devereaux, Lindgaard, and Placzek made themselves as inconspicuous as possible in the rear seat.

There were two sentries at the traffic barrier. One of them advanced to the Kübelwagen as Siegner slowed it to a crawl. Since the guard was approaching from the vehicle's left, Cleve was obscured by the bug-spattered windscreen and the three in the back were partly hidden by Siegner.

When the Kübelwagen was close enough, Morsek opened up with his silenced Sten and knocked both guards into the road. Cleve leaped out, threw the barrier up as Siegner accelerated under it, and scrambled back into the seat.

"Head for the Lancaster. We'll try to get the satchel charges under it."

Devereaux was trembling with excitement. The idea that had been unfolding in his mind ever since they left the compound was so preposterous he barely dared express it. Nevertheless, he leaned forward.

"Why don't we steal the damned thing and fly it to England? We'll never get away otherwise."

Cleve looked back over his shoulder in disbelief. "What?

295

We'd never make it. If the Luftwaffe doesn't shoot us down, the RAF will.''

"It's more of a chance than we've got here. We'll never escape in daylight this far from Switzerland. We can use the Lancaster's radio to tell them we're coming.''

Cleve calculated briefly, then nodded. "All right, we've got nothing to lose. We'll have to blow their radio and telephone. Siegner, where are they?''

"There. In the operations hut. Or were when I last flew to Berlin.''

"Head for it. Placzek, chuck one of the satchel charges in through the window as we go by. Siegner, don't slow down. It's a lot of explosive.''

Strasser had left the operations hut and was standing before its door, staring suspiciously at the small vehicle as it bounced toward him. The corner of the hut blocked his view of the now unmanned gate. It must be the Kübelwagen from the installation. But what was it doing here? An emergency? Why hadn't he been telephoned?

There was something wrong with the uniforms. The driver was SS, but . . . He swore and fumbled for his pistol. "Colonel Kruger! It's—''

The left fender of the Kübelwagen caught him below the waist and threw him against the hut wall. Stunned, he had just time to snap a shot at Placzek as Lindgaard shot out the hut window and the charge arched from Placzek's fist into the building. Placzek, a hole in the center of his forehead, collapsed over Devereaux.

Strasser was trying to roll over and fire after the rapidly receding Kübelwagen when the satchel charge went off. Powerful enough to cut the Lancaster in two, it blew the hut and everyone in it to fragments. Strasser was flung, unconscious, twenty meters across the grass. A hot wind followed the assault team as they raced for the aircraft.

"Placzek's dead," Devereaux shouted into Cleve's ear.

"Damn. Damn. Look sharp, there're SS by the hangar." The Lancaster was beginning to taxi. It was at the wrong angle for the crew to see behind it to the devastated operations hut. The technicians by the hangar had dropped to the ground. Two SS men were frantically unslinging their weapons. Lindgaard fired a burst in their direction; they dropped and lay still.

Siegner wrenched the Kübelwagen around the Lancaster's rear turret and accelerated past the tailplane. The bomber was moving at a slow running pace. Its propeller wash battered at them.

"Drive alongside the entrance door," Devereaux screamed in Siegner's ear. "I'll try to get it open."

One of the fallen guards struggled to his knees and fired after them. Bullets punched holes in the Kübelwagen's bodywork; two struck Lindgaard in the throat and he collapsed over the side of the vehicle. Devereaux, standing on the lurching rear seat, yanked at the entrance door handle and shoved inward. The door opened. He threw himself over the lip of the opening and levered himself into the aircraft. Cleve had scrambled into the rear of the Kübelwagen and was reaching upward. Using the limits of his strength, Devereaux grabbed him by the back of his battledress and threw him into the fuselage. Siegner looked up desperately from behind his steering wheel. The Lancaster's engine noise was shattering.

"Jump! Jump!"

As soon as Siegner's foot left the accelerator the Kübelwagen began to slow. He launched himself despairingly upward. Cleve and Devereaux grabbed his forearms and dragged him inside. The Lancaster's tailplane skimmed over the top of the Kübelwagen and sliced off its windshield, then cleared the battered vehicle.

Gasping for breath, Devereaux slammed the door. With the engines at full takeoff power, there was no chance that their entry had been heard. Nevertheless, Cleve was lying full length on the aircraft's floor, his Sten sighted on the crew compartment beyond the rear wing spar and the armored doors.

Siegner was lying on his back, staring at the fuselage roof. Devereaux's stomach knotted suddenly. "Are you all right?" he screamed above the din of the engines.

To his relief, Siegner nodded and sat up. Cleve put his mouth to Devereaux's ear and shouted, "What now? I don't know anything about these damned things."

The Lancaster was gaining speed. "We'll have to wait till we're up and have some height. If we try to take over now, we'll crash."

"There wasn't anyone in the tail turret, was there?"

"No."

The bomber began to crab sideways as the wings took some of the weight from the wheels. I hope that German has had lots of practice, Devereaux worried. Otherwise we're going to end in the trees. He could feel the pilot fighting the aircraft, the determination of the thirty-ton machine to swing right. The starboard engines roared louder, correcting. The wheels bumped once or twice, and the vibration from the undercarriage stopped. They were in the air. Still no one had looked through the armored doors into the rear fuselage.

"They can't know we're aboard."

Cleve nodded. "I don't think they could see us behind them, or the operations hut, either. Likely they're on radio silence, so they won't realize their base is gone."

Devereaux staggered to his feet and peered out of one of the small windows cut in the Lancaster's side. They were at about 1500 feet. He squatted down next to Cleve. "We're not climbing any more. They must be planning to stay low to avoid radar. They'll have to be lower than this, though. I think this is all the height we're going to get."

"We'd better move, then."

Siegner had had to leave his Sten in the Kübelwagen. "Give him yours," Cleve shouted. "You may have to take over in a hurry, if the pilot's hit. How much gunfire can this thing take inside?"

"Quite a lot, if the control cables aren't damaged. We need the radio and compass, though."

"Which way do those doors open?"

"Toward us."

"You pull the right-hand leaf open. I'll go through, then Siegner. Be ready to go for the controls if you have to."

They clambered over the rear spar and stopped at the armored doors. Cleve and Siegner checked their ammunition clips. I never did fire the damned thing, Devereaux realized suddenly. But it's just as well I didn't leave it behind.

Cleve nodded. Devereaux reached out and yanked back the leaf of the door. The front wing spar was a few feet ahead of them. Beyond it, a German in a flying suit was sitting at the navigator's table. He caught the movement out of the corner of his eye and looked around in astonishment. An SS trooper, squatting on the floor behind him, followed the glance.

It was Cleve's misfortune that the man was alert, and that his machine pistol was cradled across his knees, pointing aft. The German squeezed the trigger an instant before Cleve's bullets hit him, and fired three rounds before he died. One bullet went through the fuselage roof. The second struck Cleve just above the right nipple, bounced off a rib and exited underneath the shoulder blade. The last hit him a glancing blow above the right eye and went on out through the skin of the aircraft.

Even over the rasp of the engines, the three-round burst was unmistakable. The other soldier, who had been wedged behind the pilot's seat, spun around and began to fire. But Siegner had dropped behind the thigh-height wing spar and presented a difficult target as he shot back. The guard, hit fatally, collapsed backward over Saur, who had been sitting in the flight engineer's seat on the pilot's right. Unfortunately, the last bullet to leave Siegner's gun hit the pilot in the back of the neck and threw him forward over the control column. The Lancaster nosed downward. Siegner slipped and fell to the floor plating.

Devereaux lunged over him, across the wing spar, and raced for the pilot. There was blood everywhere. He pulled the limp body off the control column and eased the bomber's nose up carefully. At a thousand feet they leveled off.

"Siegner! Help me get him out of the seat!"

Saur, struggling out from under the guard's body, was transfixed. The body slipped off him and fell partly into the bomb aimer's position down in the nose. Saur stared at the physicist, trying to make some sense out of Siegner's materialization.

Siegner shocked him out of it. "Saur! Help the Englishman! Hurry!" The muzzle of the Sten was centered between Saur's eyes.

Together he and Devereaux got the dead pilot out of the seat, losing only another two hundred feet of altitude in the process. Devereaux slipped thankfully behind the control column. Siegner gestured to Saur. "Sit down. Back to the

300

fuselage. Hands on top of the head." He had to shout it twice before the man understood. Even then he looked dazed.

"Where's the navigator?" yelled Devereaux over the racket of the engines. Siegner backed swiftly to the navigation position. The man was slumped over his table but a check of the pulse in his neck showed that he was alive.

Siegner leaned over Devereaux, keeping one eye on Saur all the time. "He's unconscious, but there's no blood. A bullet must have bounced. I tied his hands to a fuselage rib with his belt. But he'll be out for a long time."

Devereaux nodded. "I'll hold this course till you tie this one up. Then see if Cleve's alive."

As Siegner was binding him, Saur found his voice. "You went over to them," he screamed. "You're no German! Traitor! Traitor!"

Siegner flushed red but went on tying him. Saur shouted at him again, nearly incoherent with rage and fright. At last the physicist grabbed him by the collar. "You're the traitor!" he screamed back. All the tension and fury of the past weeks poured into his shout. "We all should have stopped this long ago. People like you, concentration camp experimenters, you're the traitors to Germany. You—"

"For Christ's sake!" Devereaux bellowed. "Save the political discussions for later. Cleve may be bleeding to death. There's a first-aid kit aft of the entrance door. Put on the navigator's headset when you check him and let me know how he is."

Siegner collected himself, gave Saur's collar one last shake, and went aft to tend to Cleve. The tall major was face down, one small pool of blood by his head, another under his outstretched arm. He was breathing. Siegner re-

301

moved the clip from Cleve's Sten and put it into his own pocket. He slipped on the headset.

"How is he?" said Devereaux's voice in his ears.

"The head wound isn't bad. I saw worse in Russia and they lived. The chest, I don't know. If the bullet missed the lung, he'll likely be all right. Otherwise he'll bleed to death internally. I'm going for the first-aid gear now."

"All right. On the way back here, bring all the maps you can find."

Siegner laid pressure bandages over the exit and entry holes in Cleve's chest, as he had seen the field surgeons do in Russia. He bound the head wound, laid Cleve on his back, struggled out of the SS uniform and spread it over the wounded man. Even at this low altitude it was cool so early in the morning. He collected all the maps and documents from the navigator's position and made his way to the cockpit.

Saur watched in poisonous silence as he took the flight engineer's seat. Siegner didn't bother to look at him. Devereaux gestured back at the gas expert. "Is he tied good and tight?"

Siegner checked the knots, ignoring the curse that Saur spat at him. "They're tight."

"Nasty piece of work, he is. Did you spend much time with him, back there?"

"No more than I had to. He worked in a concentration camp, once. His name's Saur."

"Oh." Devereaux gestured at the sheaf of maps. "Try to find a likely looking one in that mess."

The second map from the bottom was obviously the right one. A penciled line ran from Weilheim, passed south of Nancy in France, and turned northwest just short of Paris to travel midway between Rouen and Amiens toward the

Channel. The landfall in England was Beachy Head. From there the line went almost straight north to London.

Devereaux whistled into his microphone. "I don't know how they expected to get past the south coast radar unless they were right down on the wavetops. That must be how they planned it. There's no return route marked, either."

"Maybe they were going to use the same one."

"That makes sense if their flak was told not to fire at anything on the route for a few hours. We'll use their track, anyway. You'd better get on the radio and try the Grenadier One frequency; they might still be listening. If you can't raise them, come back and I'll give you another list of frequencies to try. Oh, Christ, I forgot. You don't speak English."

"Tell me what I say and I'll memorize it."

"It's worth a try. Say, 'Grenadier One from Grenadier Two. We have the bomber and are bringing it to England. Don't shoot us down.' "

Siegner repeated it until Devereaux was satisfied. Then he gave the German instructions for using the transmitter. Siegner went aft.

He returned moments later. Devereaux looked up. Furiously, Siegner rammed his headset on and said, "It's a German radio. I've never seen one like it before. There's no frequency selector."

"Damnation. Just what we need. Find out if Saur knows anything about it."

Siegner's Sten was still over his shoulder. He unslung it and put the muzzle under Saur's nose. "Tell me about the radio."

The gas expert sneered at him. Siegner gently nudged Saur's upper lip with the gun barrel. Saur capitulated and said, "It's turned to one frequency. It can only contact the

Weilheim base." He grinned malicioiusly. "It looks as though your own people will shoot you down, doesn't it?"

"You're on this thing, too," Siegner reminded him. The other spat on the floor plating and turned away.

"Well? What?" Devereaux's voice was anxious in his ears.

Siegner told him. Devereaux thought hard. Then he said, with finality, "We can't be shot down over land. If the canister burst, it might not do much damage, but we can't take the risk. I'll try to get us to England, but if we're intercepted and shot up by either your lot or mine over the Channel I'll have to put her down in the water. We'll try to get Cleve out the hatch over the rear wing spar, and then follow him into the dinghy."

"Saur and the navigator?"

"Cut Saur loose after we're down. He'll have to take his chances. We might be able to get the navigator out, but it depends on how fast she's sinking."

Devereaux let the bomber descend to 800 feet and pushed the throttles forward. This aircraft was not in good condition; she wouldn't go over 230 miles an hour without tooth-rattling vibration. Devereaux backed the throttles off until she was just below the vibration point.

"How long d'you think we've been in the air?"

"About fifteen minutes."

Devereaux calculated rapidly. If they hadn't drifted too far off their heading during the takeover of the Lancaster, and if they had been doing 185 up until now, and if the winds weren't too strong. . . . "We've gone about fifty miles. Find some dividers and figure out how far to the coast on this track."

Siegner obeyed. "Five hundred miles, give or take a few."

Devereaux whistled gently through his teeth. Two and a quarter hours before they were over the Channel. Unless they got a headwind. Or tailwind. Their best chance lay in speed and low altitude. He gritted his teeth and settled down to fly the aircraft.

He felt better twenty-five uneventful minutes later when they passed a few miles north of a city that had to be Freiburg, since they hadn't yet crossed the Rhine. He corrected a degree north. Ninety-five minutes to the Channel. They were a bit ahead of his estimate, and were nearly on course. There wasn't any flak at Freiburg, either; that meant that their guess about the secure corridor was likely correct. At least I'll know if I wander out of it, he reflected. They'll start shooting at us.

By the time they turned northwest at Meaux, a few miles from Paris, Devereaux was near exhaustion from flying the heavy bomber at 500 to 800 feet above the earth. The air became rough as it warmed in the morning sun, and several bad pockets had come close to dragging them down in a cartwheel of flame. Less than a hundred miles to go, he told himself. I hope I have enough strength left to get out of the old bitch, if I have to ditch her.

"How's my navigation so far?" asked Siegner.

"Spot on," said Devereaux, in English.

"What?"

"Very good. Where do you think we are now?" The physicist had learned the rudiments in a hell of a hurry, even if it was only to spot prominent landmarks and calculate the course changes needed to bring them back on the track.

"Southeast of Beauvais. We ought to cross the Oise River any minute now."

Obediently, the river shot by 500 feet below. They flew

on in the early morning sun. It was a beautiful day.

I wish to Christ I'd got more sleep yesterday, Devereaux thought. My God, only yesterday. I feel as though I've been awake for a week.

"There's Beauvais, those steeples. Fifty-five miles to the coast."

"Fifteen minutes till we're over water. Strap Cleve into the rest bunk behind the armored doors and put Saur aft of the front spar, with his back against it. Make sure the navigator's strapped in too. Then open the emergency hatch above the rear spar. We'll be in a hurry after I put her down." If I put her down in one piece, he added to himself. I wonder how rough the Channel is today? "The dinghy will pop out of the wing automatically when we hit the water. If it doesn't, there's a release above the rear spar. The dinghy's tied to the plane with thirty feet of line, so we'll have to release it before she goes."

Siegner was gone for several minutes, and then returned, slumping tiredly into the flight engineer's seat. "All done," he shouted, and then remembering, put the headset back on. He looked thoughtfully out through the Perspex of the canopy, and then stiffened. In a tense voice he said, "I think there are fighters above and to the right, just ahead of us."

Devereaux looked. There were two specks there in the blue arch of the sky. The specks were getting larger and blacker.

"They've caught up with us. Somebody at Weilheim must have got to a telephone. They're not going to let us get to England if they can help it. Hang on, I'm going lower so they can't get underneath."

The Lancaster dropped until it was almost among the treetops. Devereaux turned slightly away from the oncoming fighters. German? Allied? Not that it mattered a lot.

"Should I try to man one of the turrets?"

"There wasn't any ammunition in the rear turret feed chutes, and I didn't see any belts for the mid-upper. I checked when we got in back there. We're going to have to take it till we reach the coast. If they're German, there might be some Allied patrols to peel them off us. On the other hand, they might all take it in turn to shoot us down."

Devereaux started to corkscrew the bomber, a useless defense in daylight against a flank attack, but the only thing he could think of. The black specks resolved themselves into aircraft.

"Ours," grimaced Siegner. "German, that is. Focke-Wulf 190s."

"Four cannon and two machine guns each," muttered Devereaux. "But why aren't there more of them? If word's got through from Weilheim the air should be thick with the buggers."

"Maybe two were all they could find at short notice. The Luftwaffe in France is short of planes, I've heard. If there were only a couple available at the forward airfields, they're all we'd see, especially if they only had a few minutes warning."

"Put your head into the astrodome and yell if you see their muzzle flashes, or if they try to get below us when I go up. Only five minutes to the coast."

Devereaux, sweating, flew the Lancaster while he waited for Siegner's warning. The Focke-Wulfs had curved around behind and were well out of his field of view. He went up to 400 feet.

"They're firing, from above!"

Devereaux chopped the throttles back viciously. The Lancaster slowed instantly, sagging toward stalling speed.

He shoved the nose down and rammed the throttles forward again, pulling her out just above the treetops. The two Folke-Wulfs screamed overhead, still firing. The bomber's unexpected slowing had thrown them completely off their aim. Devereaux watched them go, turning.

Ahead was a gray-blue line. The Channel.

"We're almost over the water," he shouted to Siegner. Christ, why won't they let us alone? We want to get rid of the damned thing too. Only we want to do it our way.

"Here they come again!"

This time the German pilots didn't make the same mistake: they judged their approach speed to a hair. Cannon shells exploded on the wings, the fuselage, the engines. The Lancaster staggered and dropped. Devereaux hauled her back up, but only just.

"Get back up here. We'll be able to ditch any moment."

Siegner's cheek was bleeding where a shell fragment had struck him. He looked shaken.

The shoreline flashed underneath.

"One of the engines is on fire," Siegner informed him, as though it were an occurrence he found normal. Devereaux looked past the physicist. The starboard outer engine was trailing gouts of flame that turned into black smoke at the tips. He stabbed the extinguisher button and held it in, then did the same with the feathering button. Cannon shells hammered on the Lancaster again, a shorter burst this time. The air stank with smoke and burning. The engine fire hesitated but didn't go out. The propeller hung uselessly in the slipstream.

Devereaux watched the blurred, vibrating instruments. The oil temperature gauge for the port inner engine was in the danger zone. He shoved the throttles for the remaining two good engines all the way forward, and backed off on the port inner. The airframe shook and the control column tried to twist itself out of his hands. They were no more than a hundred feet above the sea. It looked wrinkled, like a carelessly tossed blue sheet.

The instrument panel dissolved before his eyes and there was a numbing blow on his left arm. The control column nearly wrenched itself out of his grip. Siegner was shouting something, he couldn't tell what. The intercom must be wrecked.

The bomber was trying to sideslip into the sea. With his good arm he wrestled her level and looked out at the port inner engine, without hope. It was smoking. If he could hold her up through the next attack they might still get close enough to England to be picked up by Allied shipping. Otherwise it was a German prison camp. At the best. And death for Siegner.

Siegner yanked the earphones off Devereaux's head. "They've gone! Allied fighters! They're gone!"

Devereaux felt strange and lightheaded. There was a warm soaking feeling in his left sleeve. "Ours too?"

"Yes, way behind. I looked out the astrodome."

He pulled himself together. They still had about eighty feet. The oil gauges were shot away but he'd bet the port inner had only a couple of minutes left in it. He had to use all the strength of his right arm to keep the aircraft level. Just two more minutes and you can sit down in the nice cool ocean and stay there, with your bloody canister. Just 120 seconds.

They watched in fascination as the port inner seized and began to burn. Devereaux had Siegner hit the extinguisher and feather the propeller, but it didn't seem to help. The bomber kept trying to turn right as she sank lower and lower toward the water.

"I'm going to put her down. Hold on." Christ, the flaps. What was wrong with him? "Hold the control column right where it is. I'm going to let go a moment." Siegner, white-faced, grabbed the yoke and Devereaux put on 30 degrees of flap, praying that the hydraulics were still working. They were. He grabbed the controls again as the bomber slowed and went nose-up.

She brushed a wave top, then another, then another, tail down, knocking bursts of spray off the crests. Then her belly settled into the low swell and didn't bounce again. Thirty tons of bomber skidded into the cold waters of the English Channel, 44 miles southeast of Beachy Head.

As the Lancaster wallowed into the troughs the Perspex of the nose canopy cracked and cold salt water poured in. A cacaphony of clangs, smashes, and bangs hammered at the men's eardrums. The aircraft slued viciously and the left stabilizer, dragged by its fin, snapped off and sank. Water poured in through innumerable cannonshell and bullet holes.

Siegner was half-deafened and dazed by the time the bomber jolted to a stop. She already had a list to starboard. A sudden downward lurch shocked him back to his senses. Tearing off his straps, he grabbed Devereaux's arm and shouted, "Quick! We've got to get Cleve!"

Devereaux was motionless. In the last sideways jerk before stopping, his head had struck the canopy frame. He was unconscious.

Siegner cursed, released the harness, and levered him out of the seat. As he dragged him back to the emergency hatch, he saw that the navigator was dead. A cannon shell had taken the top of his head off. Cleve, though, slumped in the rest bunk, appeared to be still alive. Saur was face down in a pool of blood, very obviously dead.

Never mind Saur. Liferaft. Was the liferaft intact?

Blue sky glimmered through the escape hatch. The water in the rear fuselage was up to the bottom of the entrance door. He laid the unconscious Devereaux on the floor plating, poked his head out of the rectangular opening in the top of the fuselage, and looked for the raft.

Wonder above wonders, there it was, bobbing about at the end of its line a few meters away.

The water was rising along the starboard wing even as he scrambled out upon it. He dragged the dinghy onto the tilting surface and nestled it as high above the advancing water as he could. Back through the hatch, grab Devereaux around the waist, push him out. Don't let him slip off the wing and into the sea. The man's arm was broken. Siegner flopped him into the liferaft and looked at the water. It was halfway over the cowling of the starboard outer engine. Not much time. He thought for a moment, and released the clove knot securing the dinghy to the Lancaster.

When he dropped again into the dark fuselage there was a foot of water over the floor plates. He tried to unstrap Cleve, but the buckles had jammed. He tore at them, breaking his fingernails until the buckles came loose.

Cleve was a big man, and hard to lift. There were now no more than three feet between the water level and the top of the fuselage. Siegner heaved the unconscious form up through the hatch, so that Cleve was lying over on his chest, half in, half out of the aircraft, facing aft. Then he pushed him farther until only his legs were inside. There Cleve stuck. There was too much weight for Siegner to shift with the leverage he had below the narrow hatch.

The bomber lurched and was a foot deeper in the sea. It rose and fell gently with the waves. Siegner, up to his armpits in water, tried to haul Cleve back inside for another try. Cleve stuck.

A complete calm fell over Siegner. He knew he likely

had one last chance to get the major out of the hatch and into the dinghy, but the realization failed to trouble him. He studied the man's legs carefully, trying to select the best point of leverage.

A weak voice called:

"I've got his arm. I can pull him right into the raft if you push."

Now the Englishman wakes up, Siegner thought with amusement. Just in time. Aloud he said, "I'll push on the count of three. You pull at the same time."

Devereaux, half out of the liferaft, grasping Cleve's arm with his good hand, heard Siegner begin the count. At the same instant the nose of the Lancaster dug into a trough and failed to rise again. The starboard wing slid from underneath the dinghy and began to recede into the green depths. A three-foot wave boiled along the top of the fuselage as the bomber began to turn onto its side.

Cleve slid out of the hatch just as the wave reached it. The wave crest hesitated, seemed to fall back, and then poured into the hatch. Devereaux caught a glimpse of Siegner fighting the inrush, and then the water took him. The hatch slid beneath the surface, followed by the rest of the bomber. A foot above the waves, the port wingtip hesitated for an instant like a despairing hand, and then was gone.

When, one-armed, he had dragged Cleve aboard, Devereaux laid his face against the dinghy's yellow canvas and fainted.

Two hours later, an RAF rescue launch plucked them out of the Channel.

Epilogue

Both Gordon and Jean Mclennand survived the war, as did Catherine Gavin and Alan Devereaux. Mclennand stayed in the service after the war, and is now a very senior officer in Naval Intelligence. He and Jean had two daughters. Jean died of cancer in 1975.

Devereaux and Catherine married in December, 1944, and moved to Sevenoaks after Devereaux left the RAF. When his father died, they leased Sevenoaks to Jacob and went to the Devereaux farm near Bexhill. They had a daughter and two sons; the eldest son now works the Sevenoaks land.

Pierce retired from Intelligence work in 1962 and now lives quietly with his wife and several dogs near Battle, in Sussex. He discusses his activities between 1939 and 1945 with no one. Devereaux went to see him once, long after the war, but the old camaraderie was gone.

Carpenter and Mrosek managed to reach Switzerland, where they were interned until the fighting ended in Europe. Carpenter was killed in an automobile accident in London, in 1946. Mrosek returned to Czechoslovakia after the war and disappeared there during the Communist takeover.

Cleve lost the sight of his right eye as a result of the wound he suffered in the *Fenris* raid; he took to wearing a black patch over the eye, which made him look more piratical than ever. He died in an unexplained plane crash in Malaya, while involved in counterinsurgency operations there.

Strasser died of his wounds three days after the fight at the Weilheim airstrip. It saved him from being hanged at the express orders of Heinrich Himmler, this despite the fact that Strasser was the one who sounded the alarm about the hijacked Lancaster. Weil and Kruger, perhaps luckily for them, were killed in the explosion of the operations hut.

Neither the wreckage of the Lancaster, nor the body of Peter Siegner, was ever found.

NOW A BIG TV SPECIAL!

Murder In Amityville

Hans Holzer

PRICE: $2.50   T51408

MURDER IN AMITYVILLE
By Hans Holzer

This is the true story of Ronald DeFeo, Jr., now in prison for murdering 6 members of his immediate family in the house at Amityville, Long Island, where the next owners, the Lutz family, experienced the terrors depicted in "THE AMITYVILLE HORROR," the current best-selling book and movie.

Dr. Hans Holzer, renowned psychic investigator, who personally interviewed DeFeo in prison, reveals here for the first time the true story of DeFeo and others connected with this extraordinary case!

THE KESSLER ALLIANCE
By Thomas Horstman

PRICE: $2.25   BT51463
CATEGORY: Novel (original)

A devastatingly prophetic novel of what could happen to the world, if Nazi extremists remained unchecked and their forces overthrew the world. Munich, Germany is the focal point of events and the birthplace of Wilhelm Kessler, a youth who becomes fascinated with Adolph Hitler. Another youth, Leo Maeder, becomes a Catholic priest. The lives of these two men become entwined as a bizarre series of events shake the world, and nations convulse under tremendous economic, political and social pressures. Only one man knew of the diabolical plot, but no one would believe him!

The biography of Libby Holman, the torch singer accused of murdering her millionaire husband! Solved at last! The most sensational case of the 1930's

Libby

Milt Machlin

PRICE: $2.75   T51533

LIBBY
By Milt Machlin

She was Broadway. She was the 30's. Libby Holman possessed an allure irresistible to both men and women, and numbered among her lovers Tallulah Bankhead, Jeanne Eagels and Montgomery Clift. Though Libby was accused of murdering her millionaire husband, no conclusion was ever reached. That uncertainty shadowed the rest of her tragedy-haunted life. Award-winning author Milt Machlin has unearthed startling evidence that sheds new light on the most sensational murder case of the 1930's, and on this dazzling woman who still occupies center stage! ILLUSTRATED

DEATH OF A SCAVENGER
By Keith Spore

PRICE: $2.25   BT51465
CATEGORY: Mystery (Original)

Dr. Hugo Enclave takes on only the most clever and cunning crimes, and is intrigued by those considered unsolvable by the police. Enclave set out to unravel the tangled threads surrounding the death of Harland Rockmore, an investigator for a law firm, whose body was found near his boss's home after a scavenger hunt. Enclave moves through a torturous labyrinth of murder, mayhem and mystery to uncover a conspiracy aimed at the White House itself!

HITLER'S LAST GAMBLE
Jacques Nobecourt

PRICE: $2.25   T51474
CATEGORY: War

Here, in full detail, is the true account of the most
dangerous and dramatic battle of World War II—
the Battle of the Bulge.
In December 1944—when she seemed on the
verge of complete collapse, her armies driven
from Normandy almost to the Rhine—Germany
launched a sudden counter attack. The Battle of
the Bulge was the last gasp of the Third Reich's
great war machine and it proved to be the ulti-
mate challenge to the strength and bravery of the
U.S. Army.

SEND TO: **TOWER PUBLICATIONS**
P.O. BOX 270
NORWALK, CONN. 06852

PLEASE SEND ME THE FOLLOWING TITLES:

Quantity	Book Number	Price

IN THE EVENT THAT WE ARE OUT OF STOCK ON ANY OF YOUR SELECTIONS, PLEASE LIST ALTERNATE TITLES BELOW:

Postage/Handling ☐

I enclose... ☐

FOR U.S. ORDERS, add 50c for the first book and 10c for each additional book to cover cost of postage and handling. Buy five or more copies and we will pay for shipping. Sorry, no C.O.D.'s.

FOR ORDERS SENT OUTSIDE THE U.S.A., add $1.00 for the first book and 25c for each additional book. PAY BY foreign draft or money order drawn on a U.S. bank, payable in U.S. ($) dollars.

☐ **PLEASE SEND ME A FREE CATALOG.**

NAME_____
(Please print)

ADDRESS_____

CITY_____ **STATE**_____ **ZIP**_____

Allow Four Weeks for Delivery